ISAAC
BASHEVIS
SINGER

ISAAC BASHEVIS SINGER

A Day of Pleasure
and
Other Stories for Children

Photographs by
ROMAN VISHNIAC

Galahad Books • New York

First Galahad Books edition published in 1992.

Galahad Books
A division of Budget Book Service, Inc.
386 Park Avenue South
New York, NY 10016

Galahad Books is a registered trademark of Budget Book Service, Inc.
Published by arrangement with Farrar, Straus & Giroux, Inc.
Library of Congress Catalog Card Number: 92-72500

ISBN: 0-88365-798-8

Printed in the United States of America.

Contents

A Day of Pleasure

Contents

Photographs

Except for those of Isaac Bashevis Singer, his brother, and his grandfather, the photographs were taken by Roman Vishniac between the time the Nazis came to power and the invasion of Poland in 1939. Nearly all of them were taken in Warsaw, a few in nearby towns. The world portrayed in these photographs is essentially the same as the one in the stories, even though the stories take place a generation earlier.

Author's Note

The stories I tell in this book actually took place during the first fourteen years of my life. Only the last story, "Shosha," deals with a later time, but it too concerns my childhood. I have a good deal more to tell about myself, my family, and the Poland of days gone by. I hope to continue these memoirs and reveal a world that is little known to you but which is rich in comedy and tragedy; rich in its individuality, wisdom, foolishness, wildness, and goodness.

Fourteen of these stories previously appeared, in somewhat different form, in my book of memoirs entitled *In My Father's Court*. Five are collected here for the first time: "Who I Am," "The Trip from Radzymin to Warsaw," "Reb Itchele and Shprintza," "The Mysteries of the Cabala," and "Shosha."

The stories were translated from my original Yiddish by Channah Kleinerman-Goldstein, Elaine Gottlieb, Elizabeth Shub, Elizabeth Pollet, Rosanna Gerber, and my nephew Joseph Singer.

I. B. S.

A tutor and a young scholar on the way to cheder

Who I Am

I was born in the town of Radzymin, near Warsaw, the capital of Poland, on July 14, 1904. My father, Pinchos Menachem Singer, was a rabbi, a highly religious man. He had a red beard, long black sidelocks, and blue eyes. My mother, Bathsheba, was the daughter of the Rabbi of Bilgoray, which is not far from Lublin. She had red hair that she cut short and covered with a wig, as was the custom among pious married women.

Early in 1908, when I was three years old, my parents moved from Radzymin to Warsaw. There my father became a rabbi on a very poor street, Krochmalna. The tenement building where I grew up would be called a slum in America, but in those days we did not think it was so bad. At night a kerosene lamp lit our apartment. We were unfamiliar with such conveniences as hot running water or a bathroom. The outhouse was located in the courtyard.

Most of the people who lived on Krochmalna Street were poor storekeepers or laborers, but there were many scholars among them, as well as idle urchins, criminals, people from the underworld.

When I was about four years old, I began going to cheder to study. A tutor would come every morning to take me there. I carried a prayer book with me, and later a Bible or a volume of the Talmud. These were the only schoolbooks I knew. In cheder we were taught mostly religion: to pray, to read the Pentateuch. We also learned to write Yiddish. My first teacher was an old man with a white beard.

I had a younger brother, Moshe, who was an infant when we moved to Warsaw; a sister, Hinde Esther, who was thirteen years older than I; and a brother, Israel Joshua, who was eleven years older. All of us except Moshe became writers. My brother's novel *The Brothers Ashkenazi* has been translated into several languages, including English. He wrote in Yiddish, just as I do.

Our house was a house of learning. My father sat all day long and studied the Talmud. Whenever my mother had a free minute, she glanced into a holy book. Other children had toys, but I played with my father's books. I started to "write" even before I knew the alphabet. I would dip a pen in ink and scribble. I also liked to draw—horses, houses, dogs. The Sabbath was an ordeal for me, because it is forbidden to write on that day.

In our Warsaw apartment my father set up a rabbinical court. The people of Krochmalna Street came to our home to ask him for advice or to have him settle a dispute according to the law of the Torah. In a sense he was a combination of rabbi, judge, and spiritual leader. People also came to him to pour out their hearts. My father presided at weddings in our apartment and from time to time he granted a divorce. Among Jews of that time, a rabbi was a man of many trades and few blessings.

I was curious by nature. I observed the grownups, their behavior. I listened attentively to their talk, which I sometimes understood and sometimes did not.

At an early age I started to think all kinds of thoughts: What would happen if a bird flew in the same direction forever? What would happen if a ladder were built from the earth to the sky? What was there before the world was created? Did time have a beginning? But how can time begin? Has space an end? But how can empty space have an end?

Our apartment at 10 Krochmalna Street had a balcony and I would stand on it for many hours and muse. In the summertime all kinds of insects gathered there—flies, bees, butterflies. These creatures provoked extreme curiosity in me. What do they eat? Where do they sleep? Who gave them life? At night the moon and the stars appeared in the sky. I was told that some stars are larger than the earth. But if they are so big, how can they fit in the narrow strip of sky above the roofs of Krochmalna Street? I often asked my parents questions that even they were at a loss to answer. My father used to say that it is not good to indulge in such questions. My mother would say that when I grew up I would find the answers. But I soon learned that even adults do not know everything. People died on our street and the shock of death awakened fear and wonder in me. My mother comforted me by saying that the good souls go to paradise after death. But what do the souls *do* in paradise, I wanted to know. How does it look there? I brooded about the terrors of hell, where the souls of sinners are punished.

I was still young when I became aware of human suffering. Poland, torn and divided between Russia, Germany, and Austria, had lost its independence about one hundred years before. But we Jews had lost our land of Israel almost two thousand years before. My father assured me, however, that if the Jews conducted themselves piously, the Messiah would come and we would all return to the land of Israel. But two thousand years was too long to wait. Besides, how could you be sure that all the Jews would heed God's law? There were thieves on our street, all sorts of swindlers. Their kind could delay the coming of the Messiah forever . . .

The year I was born, a great Jewish leader died, Dr. Theodor Herzl. Dr. Herzl preached that the Jews must not wait for the coming of the Messiah but should start to build Palestine by themselves. But how could we do that when the land belonged to the Turks?

There were revolutionaries on our street who wanted to get rid of the Tsar of Russia. They dreamed about creating a state where all worked and there were no rich or poor. But how could anyone dethrone the Tsar when he had so many soldiers with swords and rifles? And how could there be no rich or poor? Some people would always have to live on Krochmalna Street and others would live on Marshalkovsky, a beautiful boulevard with trees and fancy stores. Some would live in big cities and others in distant villages. In our home these questions were often discussed by my family and visitors. I listened to every word.

My parents, my older brother, and my sister all liked to tell stories. My father would often tell of the miracles performed by various rabbis, also of ghosts, devils, imps. In this way he wanted to strengthen our belief in God and in the good and evil powers who reign in the world. My mother told us stories about Bilgoray, where her father was the rabbi and ran the community with a strong hand. My brother Joshua became worldly and started to read books that were not religious. He told me stories about Germany, France, America, about unfamiliar nations and races, about peculiar beliefs and customs. He described everything vividly, as if he had seen it for himself. My sister told romantic stories about counts who fell in love with servant girls. I had my own fantasies. At a very young age I began inventing all kinds of tales that I told the boys in cheder. Once I told them that my father was a king, and with such detail that they believed me. How they could have believed me is still a puzzle to me. I certainly was not dressed like a prince.

In 1914 the First World War began. In 1915, when I was eleven, the Germans occupied Warsaw. In 1917 I heard the extraordinary news that Tsar Nicholas II of Russia had been dethroned. The soldiers with the swords and rifles had not protected him; they themselves had backed the revolutionaries. If this could be so, was it also possible that soon there would be no rich or poor?

But apparently that time was still far away. In 1917 Warsaw was plagued by hunger and typhus. The Germans dragged people off the streets for forced labor. My family was starving, so it was decided that Mother and the younger children, Moshe and I, would go to our grandparents in Bilgoray, where the food shortage was not so severe. At that time I was thirteen, already a Bar Mitzvah boy, but I still had found no answers to any of my questions.

In the Jewish neighborhood of Warsaw

The Trip from Radzymin to Warsaw

The little train began moving. I was sitting at the window, looking out. People seemed to be walking backwards. Horse-drawn carts rode in reverse. Telegraph poles were running away. Beside me sat my mother and my sister, Hindele, who held the baby on her lap, my brother Moshe. We were on the way from Radzymin to Warsaw.

My big brother, Joshua, was making the trip in the horse-drawn wagon that carried our furniture and ragged belongings. My father was already in Warsaw. He had rented an apartment at 10 Krochmalna Street, where he was to establish his rabbinical court.

The move from the small town of Radzymin to the big city of Warsaw was a burden and a problem for the family. But for me it was a joy. Each moment new experiences were revealed to me. The tiny locomotive (it was jokingly called "the samovar") whistled gaily. From time to time it let off steam and smoke just like a big locomotive. We rode past villages, huts with straw roofs, pastures where cows and horses grazed. One horse leaned its neck on another horse's neck. Scarecrows stood in the fields, dressed in tatters, and birds circled them, cawing and screeching. I kept asking my mother questions. What is this? What is that? My mother and my sister answered me. Even strange women tried to explain things to me. But I still wasn't satisfied. I was possessed with curiosity and a thirst for explanation. Why do cows eat grass? Why does smoke come out of the chimney? Why does a bird have wings though a calf doesn't? Why do some people walk and others ride in wagons?

My mother shook her head. "The boy drives me crazy!"

The entire trip lasted barely two hours, but it left so many impressions that it seemed to me it was a long journey. The wonders increased as we neared Warsaw. Tall buildings with balconies emerged. We passed by a vast cemetery with thousands of tombstones. A red trolley car appeared. Factory buildings with high chimneys and barred windows loomed up. I realized that there was no longer any sense in asking questions and became silent. Then the little train stopped.

We took a droshky drawn by a gray horse. It rode over the Praga bridge and I was told the river beneath was the same Vistula that flowed in Radzymin. But how can the Vistula be so long, I asked myself. For the first time I saw boats and ships. One ship whistled and groaned so loudly that I had to cover my ears. On the deck of another, a band was playing. The brass instruments gleamed in the sun and dazzled me.

After we crossed the bridge, another wonder emerged,

the monument of King Zygmunt. Four stone creatures, half man and half fish, were drinking from huge stone goblets. I was about to ask what this was, but before I could open my mouth new marvels turned up. Streets lined with huge buildings. Store windows displaying dolls that looked strangely alive. Ladies on the sidewalks wearing hats trimmed with cherries, peaches, plums, grapes. Some had veils covering their faces. I saw men with top hats who carried silver-handled canes. There were many red trolley cars, some drawn by horses, others horseless. My sister said these moved by electricity. I saw mounted policemen, firemen with brass helmets, carriages rolling along on rubber wheels. The horses held their heads high and had short tails. The driver of our droshky, who wore a blue coat and a cap with a shiny visor, spoke Yiddish. He pointed out the sights of Warsaw to us provincials.

I was both delighted and humbled. What value has a small boy, compared to such a great, tumultuous world? And how could we find Father here? And how would we locate my brother Joshua and the wagon with our furniture? It seemed that the adults knew everything. Apparently they had built all of this, while I, a small boy, sat there helplessly, with my sister holding my hand so I wouldn't fall. Whenever the droshky made a turn, the sky turned with it and my brain rattled in my head like a kernel in a nut.

All of a sudden the coachman said, "Here is Krochmalna Street."

The buildings there seemed even taller. The gutter was filled with people. The throngs, the yelling, the pushing reminded me of the fire I had witnessed in Radzymin some weeks before and I was certain a fire had broken out here in Warsaw too. Boys shouted, jumped, whistled, and shoved one another. Girls laughed shrilly. Dusk was falling and a man who had a long stick with a flame on the end lit the street lamps. Women peddled all kinds of merchandise. Smoke curled from chimneys. The droshky drove up to the gate of a courtyard and I saw my brother Joshua. The wagon with the furniture had arrived before us.

My mother asked for Father, and Joshua answered, "He went to recite the evening prayer."

"Woe is me, this city is bedlam," she exclaimed.

"A gay street," my brother said.

"How come they're all outside?" my mother asked.

We entered the gate and went into our building. I was led up a stairway. I had never walked on steps before and climbing from one step to another seemed interesting and dangerous to me.

A woman met us on the staircase and said, "Are you the rabbi's wife? Woe, my God, you've been robbed from head to foot . . . A plague take the thieves, may a black fire consume their intestines. As soon as your things were unloaded, they dragged them away. Dear Father in heaven, may they be dragged to the cemetery!"

"Why didn't you watch?" my mother asked Joshua.

"You can't watch all of them. You start to argue with one and meanwhile ten others steal from you."

"Is any bedding left, at least?"

"They left something," he said.

"Jewish thieves?"

"There are few Gentiles here . . ."

A door opened and we entered a kitchen. The walls were painted pink. Then we walked into a large room with a window and a balcony. I went out on the balcony and I was both inside and outside at the same time. Downstairs the crowd milled. Up above, over the roofs, stretched a thin strip of sky. A moon hung in it, yellow as brass. Lamps glowed in all the windows, and when I narrowed my eyes to slits, fiery rays stretched out from them. Suddenly the din increased. A fireman came riding from somewhere, on a fast horse. His brass helmet glowed like fire. The boys started screaming: "The outrider, the outrider!"

Later on, I found out that the firemen were too often fooled on this street. They were frequently called when there was no fire, so a rider was sent to investigate. Yes, this time there really was a fire. Smoke billowed out of a window on a high floor and sparks flew. People filled the balconies. Wild horses harnessed to wagons arrived. Firemen ran into the building with hatchets, ladders, and rubber hoses. Policemen with swords chased the curious crowd.

In our apartment, my sister lit a kerosene lamp. My mother started to look through what was left of our belongings. "Yes, they stole," she said. What remained of our furniture was broken. Some of our Passover dishes were smashed.

Our new rooms smelled of paint and turpentine. Singing voices drifted in from neighboring apartments. My brother said they came from gramophones. A cantor sang, as in the synagogue; a girl laughed; women quarreled; but none of this was real. All these voices came through giant trumpets on gramophones. My brother already knew who discovered all this: Edison from America.

"How can trumpets sing and talk?" my mother asked.

"You talk into them and they repeat what you say,"

Joshua explained.

"But how?"

"With a magnet . . ."

"It's all electricity," said my sister.

"The children should be put to sleep," my mother decided after a while.

I was undressed and I didn't resist. I was too tired. I was put to bed and fell asleep immediately. I opened my eyes and the room was flooded with sunlight. The windows stood open. The floor looked new. I walked out on the balcony. The same street that yesterday had been wrapped in night was now radiant in the sun. Customers pushed about in the stores. Men went off to pray with prayer-shawl bags under their arms. Sidewalk peddlers sold loaves of bread, baskets of bagels and rolls, smoked herring, hot peas, brown beans, apples, pears, plums. A boy drove a bevy of turkeys down the middle of the street. They tried to scatter but he trickily ran alongside with a stick and forced them to stay together.

My father was already sitting at his table, bent over a volume of the Talmud. He noticed me and made me recite the prayer "I Thank Thee."

He said, "You will go to cheder here."

"I won't know the way."

"A tutor will take you there."

For breakfast my mother gave me food I had never tasted before; a bagel with cottage cheese and smoked herring. A neighbor came in and he started to tell us what had happened here during the 1905 revolution against the Tsar. The young revolutionaries shot off guns. All the stores had to be closed. Policemen struck the demonstrators with bare swords. Someone threw a bomb.

My mother shook her head sadly. My father tugged at his beard. A few years had already passed, but obviously the people of Krochmalna Street could not forget those days of terror. Many of the rebels were still imprisoned in the Citadel. Others had been sent off to Siberia. Many escaped to America.

My father asked, "What did they want?"

"To get rid of the Tsar."

My mother turned white. "I don't want the boy to hear of such goings-on."

"What can he understand?" the neighbor said.

But I listened anyway. My curiosity had no limits.

A busy street lined with droshkies

A Day of
Pleasure

When times were good, I would get a two-groschen piece, a kopeck, from Father or Mother every day, as every boy who went to cheder did. For me this coin represented all worldly pleasures. Across the street was Esther's candy store, where one could buy chocolates, jelly beans, ice cream, caramels, and all sorts of cookies. Since I had a weakness for drawing with colored pencils, which cost money, a kopeck proved not nearly so large a coin as Father and Mother made it out to be. There were times when I was forced to borrow money from a cheder classmate, a young usurer who demanded interest. For every four groschen, I paid a groschen a week.

Now imagine the indescribable joy I felt when I once earned a whole ruble—one hundred kopecks!

I no longer remember exactly how I came to earn that ruble, but I think it happened something like this: A man had ordered a pair of kidskin boots from a shoemaker, but upon delivery they proved to be either too tight or too loose. The man refused to accept them, and the shoemaker brought him to my father's rabbinical court. Father sent me to another shoemaker to ask him to appraise the value of the boots or perhaps even to buy them, since he also dealt in ready-made footwear. It so happened that the second shoemaker had a customer who wanted the boots and was prepared to pay a good price for them. I do not recall all the details, but I remember that I carried a pair of brand-new boots around, and that one of the litigants rewarded me with a ruble.

I knew that if I stayed home my parents would ruin that ruble. They would buy me something to wear, something I would have got anyway, or they would borrow the ruble from me and—though they'd never deny the debt—I would never see it again. I therefore took the ruble and decided to indulge myself for once in the pleasures of this world, to enjoy all those good things for which my heart yearned.

I quickly passed through Krochmalna Street. Here everyone knew me too well. Here I could not afford to act the profligate. But on Gnoyna Street I was unknown. I signaled to the driver of a droshky, and he stopped.

"What do you want?"

"To ride."

"Ride where?"

"To the other streets."

"What other streets?"

"To Nalewki Street."

"That costs forty groschen. Have you got the money to pay?"

I showed him the ruble.

"But you'll have to pay me in advance."

I gave the driver the ruble. He tried bending it to see if it was counterfeit. Then he gave me my change--four forty-groschen pieces. I got into the droshky. The driver cracked his whip and I almost fell off the bench. The seat under me bounced on its springs. Passers-by stared at the little boy riding alone in a droshky, without any bundles. The droshky made its way among trolley cars, other droshkies, wagons, delivery vans. I felt that I had suddenly assumed the importance of an adult. God in heaven, if I could only ride like this for a thousand years, by day and by night, without stop, to the ends of the earth . . .

But the driver turned out to be a dishonest man. When we had gone only halfway, he stopped and said, "Enough. Get down!"

"But this is not Nalewki Street!" I argued.

"Do you want a taste of my whip?" he answered.

Oh, if only I were Samson the Strong, I'd know how to take care of such a bandit, such a clod! I would pulverize him, chop him into little pieces! But I am only a small weak boy, and he is cracking his whip.

I got down, shamed and dejected. But how long can you mourn when you have four forty-groschen pieces in your pocket? I saw a candy store and went in to select my merchandise. I bought some of every kind. And as I bought, I tasted. The other customers looked at me with disdain; they probably suspected I had stolen the money. One girl exclaimed, "Just look at that little Hasid!"

"Hey, you ninny, may an evil spirit possess your father's son!" one boy called out to me.

I left, laden with candy. Then I reached Krasinski Park. I

was nearly run over while crossing the street. I entered the park and ate some of the delicacies. A boy passed by and I gave him a chocolate bar. Instead of saying thank you, he grabbed it and ran off. I walked over to the lake and fed the swans—with chocolate. Women pointed their fingers at me, laughed, made comments in Polish. Daintily dressed girls, with hoops and balls, came over to me and I chivalrously and prodigally distributed my candy among them. At that moment I felt like a rich nobleman distributing largess.

After a while I had no more candies, but I still had some money. I decided to take another droshky. When I sat in the second droshky and the driver asked where I wanted to go, I really wanted to say, "Krochmalna Street." But someone inside of me, an invisible glutton, answered instead, "To Marshalkovsky Boulevard."

"What number?"

I invented a number.

This coachman was honest. He took me to the address and did not ask for the money in advance. On the way another droshky rode alongside ours; inside sat a lady with an enormous bosom and a big hat decorated with an ostrich feather. My driver chatted with the other driver. Both spoke Yiddish, which the lady did not like at all. Even less did she like the little passenger with the black velvet hat and the red earlocks. She threw angry looks at me. From time to time both droshkies stopped to let a trolley car or a heavily laden wagon pass by. A policeman standing near the trolley tracks stared at me, at the lady, seemed for a minute about to come over and arrest me—and then began to laugh. I was terribly afraid. I was afraid of God, of my mother and father, and I was also afraid a hole had suddenly appeared in my pocket and my money had fallen through. And what if the driver was a robber carrying me off to some dark cave? Perhaps he was a magician. And perhaps all this was only a dream. But no, the driver was not a robber, and he did not carry me off to the twelve thieves in the desert. He took me exactly to the address I had given him, a big house with a gateway, and I paid him the forty groschen.

"Who are you going to see?" he asked me.

"A doctor," I answered without hesitation.

"What's the matter with you?"

"I cough."

"You're an orphan, eh?"

"Yes, an orphan."

"From out of town?"

"Yes."

"From where?"

I gave him the name of some town.

"Do you wear the fringed garment?"

This last question I did not answer. What concern of his were my ritual fringes? I wanted him to drive off, but he remained there with his droshky, and I could delay no longer—I had to enter the gateway. But behind the gate there lurked a gigantic dog. He looked at me with a pair of knowing eyes that seemed to say: "You may fool the coachman, but not me. I know you have no business here." And he opened a mouth full of sharp, pointed teeth.

Suddenly the janitor appeared. "And what do you want?"

I tried to stammer something, but he shouted at me, "Get away from here!"

And he began to chase me with a broom. I started to run, and the dog let out a savage howl. The droshky driver was probably a witness to my shame--but against a broom, a janitor, and a dog, a small boy cannot be a hero.

Things were not going well for me, but I still had some money left. And with money one can find pleasures anywhere. I saw a fruit store and went in. I order the first fruit I saw, and when it came to paying, my money was just barely enough. I parted with my last groschen.

I no longer remember what kind of fruit it was. It must have been a pomegranate or something equally exotic. I could not peel it, and when I ate it, it had a poisonous taste. Nevertheless I devoured it all. But then I was overcome by a horrible thirst. My throat was parched and burning. I had only one desire--to drink. Oh, if only I had money now! I could have emptied a gallon of soda water! But I had nothing and furthermore, I was far from home.

I started to walk home. I walked and suddenly I felt a nail in my boot. It pierced my flesh at every step. How did the nail happen to be there just then? I stepped into a gateway. Here there were no dogs and no janitors. I took off the boot. Inside, right through the inner sole, a pointy nail was sticking up. I stuffed some paper into the boot and set out again. Oh, how bitter it is to walk when an iron nail pricks you at every step! And how bitter it must be to lie on a bed of nails in Gehenna! This day I had committed many sins. I had said no blessing before eating the candy, I had not given even one groschen of all my money to the poor. I had only gorged myself.

The walk home took about two hours. All manner of frightening thoughts beset me as I walked. Perhaps something terrible had happened at home. Perhaps I had not been lying when I told the coachman I was an orphan, but at the very moment when I said it I was in truth orphaned. Perhaps I had no father, no mother, no home. Perhaps my face had changed, like that of the man in the storybook, and when I got home Father and Mother would not recognize me. Anything was possible!

A boy saw me and stopped me. "Where are you coming from? Your mother has been looking for you everywhere!"

"I was in Praga—I rode on a trolley," I said, telling lies now just for the sake of lying. Because once you have eaten without a blessing and committed other sins, then you can do anything—it no longer matters.

"Who did you visit in Praga?"

"My aunt."

"Since when do you have an aunt in Praga?"

"She just came to Warsaw."

"Go on, you're fibbing. Your mother is looking for you. Swear you were in Praga."

I swore falsely too. Then I went home, tired, sweating—a lost soul. I pounced upon the water faucet and began to drink, to drink. Thus must Esau have devoured the mess of pottage for which he sold his birthright.

Mother wrung her hands. "Just look at that child!"

Selling Geese

Why the
Geese Shrieked

In our home there was always talk about spirits of the dead that possess the bodies of the living, souls reincarnated as animals, houses inhabited by hobgoblins, cellars haunted by demons. My father spoke of these things, first of all because he was interested in them, and second because in a big city children so easily go astray. They go everywhere, see everything, read nonreligious books. It is necessary to remind them from time to time that there are still mysterious forces at work in the world.

One day, when I was about eight, he told us a story found in one of the holy books. If I am not mistaken, the author of that book is Rabbi Eliyahu Graidiker, or one of the other Graidiker sages. The story was about a girl possessed by four demons. It was said that they could actually be seen crawling around in her intestines, blowing up her belly, wandering from one part of her body to another, slithering into her legs.

The Rabbi of Graidik had exorcised the evil spirits with the blowing of the ram's horn, with incantations, and the incense of magic herbs.

When my brother Joshua questioned these things, my father became very excited. He argued: "Was then the great Rabbi of Graidik, God forbid, a liar? Are all the rabbis, saints, and sages deceivers, while only atheists speak the truth? Woe is us! How can one be so blind?"

Suddenly the door opened, and a woman entered. She was carrying a basket with two geese in it. The woman looked frightened. Her matron's wig was tilted to one side. She smiled nervously.

Father never looked at strange women, because it is forbidden by Jewish law, but Mother and we children saw immediately that something had greatly upset our unexpected visitor.

"What is it?" Father asked, at the same time turning his back so as not to look upon her.

"Rabbi, I have a very unusual problem."

"What is it?"

"It's about these geese."

"What's the matter with them?"

"Dear Rabbi, the geese were slaughtered properly. Then I cut off their heads. I took out the intestines, the livers, all the other organs, but the geese keep shrieking in such a sorrowful voice . . ."

Upon hearing these words, my father turned pale. A dreadful fear befell me, too. But my mother came from a family of rationalists and was by nature a skeptic.

"Slaughtered geese don't shriek," she said.

"You will hear for yourself," replied the woman.

40

She took one of the geese and placed it on the table. Then she took out the second goose. The geese were headless, disemboweled--in short, ordinary dead geese.

A smile appeared on my mother's lips. "And *these* geese shriek?"

"You will soon hear."

The woman took one goose and hurled it against the other. At once a shriek was heard. It is not easy to describe that sound. It was like the cackling of a goose, but in such a high, eerie pitch, with such groaning and quaking, that my limbs grew cold. I could actually feel the hairs of my earlocks pricking me. I wanted to run from the room. But where would I run? My throat constricted with fear. Then I, too, shrieked and clung to my mother's skirt, like a child of three.

Father forgot that one must avert one's eyes from a woman. He ran to the table. He was no less frightened than I was. His red beard trembled. In his blue eyes could be seen a mixture of fear and vindication. For my father this was a sign that not only to the Rabbi of Graidik, but to him too, omens were sent from heaven. But perhaps this was a sign from the Evil One, from Satan himself?

"What do you say now?" asked the woman.

My mother was no longer smiling. In her eyes there was something like sadness, and also anger.

"I cannot understand what is going on here," she said, with a certain resentment.

"Do you want to hear it again?"

Again the woman threw one goose against the other. And again the dead geese gave forth an uncanny shriek—the shriek of dumb creatures slain by the slaughterer's knife who yet retain a living force; who still have a reckoning to make with the living, an injustice to avenge. A chill crept over me. I felt as though someone had struck me with all his might.

My father's voice became hoarse. It was broken as though by sobs. "Well, can anyone still doubt that there *is* a Creator?" he asked.

"Rabbi, what shall I do and where shall I go?" The woman began to croon in a mournful singsong. "What has befallen me? Woe is me! What shall I do with them? Perhaps I should run to one of the Wonder Rabbis? Perhaps they were not slaughtered properly? I am afraid to take them home. I wanted to prepare them for the Sabbath meal, and now, such a calamity! Holy Rabbi, what shall I do? Must I throw them out? Someone said they must be wrapped in shrouds and buried in a grave. I am a poor woman. Two geese! They cost me a fortune!"

Father did not know what to answer. He glanced at his bookcase. If there was an answer anywhere, it must be there.

Suddenly he looked angrily at my mother. "And what do you say now, eh?"

Mother's face was growing sullen, smaller, sharper. In her eyes could be seen indignation and also something like shame.

"I want to hear it again." Her words were half pleading, half commanding.

The woman hurled the geese against each other for the third time, and for the third time the shrieks were heard. It occurred to me that such must have been the voice of the sacrificial heifer.

"Woe, woe, and still they blaspheme . . . It is written that the wicked do not repent even at the very gates of hell." Father had again begun to speak. "They behold the truth with their own eyes, and they continue to deny their Maker.

They are dragged into the bottomless pit and they maintain that all is nature, or accident. . . ."

He looked at Mother as if to say: You take after *them*.

For a long time there was silence. Then the woman asked, "Well, did I just imagine it?"

Suddenly my mother laughed. There was something in her laughter that made us all tremble. I knew, by some sixth sense, that Mother was preparing to end the mighty drama being enacted before our eyes.

"Did you remove the windpipes?" my mother asked.

"The windpipes? No . . ."

"Take them out," said my mother, "and the geese will stop shrieking."

My father became angry. "What are you babbling? What has this got to do with windpipes?"

Mother took hold of one of the geese, pushed her slender finger inside the body, and with all her might pulled out the thin tube that led from the neck to the lungs. Then she took the other goose and removed its windpipe also. I stood trembling, aghast at my mother's courage. Her hands had become bloodied. On her face could be seen the wrath of the rationalist whom someone has tried to frighten in broad daylight.

Father's face turned white, calm, a little disappointed. He knew what had happened here: logic, cold logic, was again tearing down faith, mocking it, holding it up to ridicule and scorn.

"Now, if you please, take one goose and hurl it against the other!" commanded my mother.

Everything hung in the balance. If the geese shrieked, Mother would have lost all: her rationalist's daring, her skepticism, which she had inherited from her intellectual father. And I? Although I was afraid, I prayed inwardly that the geese *would* shriek, shriek so loud that people in the street would hear and come running.

But, alas, the geese were silent, silent as only two dead geese without windpipes can be.

"Bring me a towel!" Mother turned to me.

I ran to get the towel. There were tears in my eyes. Mother wiped her hands on the towel like a surgeon after a difficult operation.

"That's all it was!" she announced victoriously.

"Rabbi, what do you say?" asked the woman.

Father began to cough, to mumble. He fanned himself with his skullcap.

"I have never before heard of such a thing," he said at last.

"Nor have I," echoed the woman.

"Nor have I," said my mother. "But there is always an explanation. Dead geese don't shriek."

"Can I go home now and cook them?" asked the woman.

"Go home and cook them for the Sabbath." Mother pronounced the decision. "Don't be afraid. They won't make a sound in your pot."

"What do you say, Rabbi?"

"Hmm . . . they are kosher," murmured Father. "They can be eaten." He was not really convinced, but now he could not pronounce the geese unclean.

Mother went back to the kitchen. I remained with my father. Suddenly he began to speak to me as though I were an adult. "Your mother takes after your grandfather, the Rabbi of Bilgoray. He is a great scholar, but a cold-blooded rationalist. People warned me before our betrothal . . ."

And then Father threw up his hands, as if to say: It is too late now to call off the wedding.

Jewish boys of Warsaw

Reb Asher the Dairyman

There are some people in this world who are simply born good. Such was Reb Asher the dairyman. God had endowed him with many, many gifts. He was tall, broad, strong, had a black beard, large black eyes, and the voice of a lion. On the New Year and the Day of Atonement he served as cantor of the main prayer for the congregation that met in our house, and it was his voice that attracted many of the worshippers. He did this without payment, although he could have commanded sizable fees from some of the larger synagogues. It was his way of helping my father earn a livelihood for the holidays. And as if this were not enough, Reb Asher was always doing something for us in one way or another. No one sent my father as generous a Purim gift as did Reb Asher the dairyman. When Father found himself in great straits and could not pay the rent, he sent me to Reb Asher to borrow the money. And Asher never said no, nor did he ever pull a wry face. He simply reached into his pants pocket and pulled out a handful of paper money and silver. Neither did he limit himself to helping out my father. He gave charity in all directions. This simple Jew, who with great difficulty plowed through a chapter of the Mishnah, lived his entire life on the highest ethical plane. What others preached, he practiced.

He was no millionaire, he was not even wealthy, but he had a "comfortable income," as my father would put it. I myself often bought milk, butter, cheese, clabber, and cream in his shop. His wife and their eldest daughter waited on customers all day long, from early in the morning till late at night. His wife was a stout woman, with a blond wig, puffy cheeks, and a neck covered with freckles. She was the daughter of a farm bailiff. Her enormous bosom seemed to be swollen with milk. I used to imagine that if someone were to cut her arm, milk would spurt out, not blood. One son, Yudl, was so fat that people came to stare at him as at a freak. He weighed nearly three hundred and fifty pounds. Another son, slight of build and something of a dandy, had become a tailor and gone off to Paris. A younger son was still studying at cheder, and a little girl attended a secular school.

Just as our house was always filled with problems, doubts, and unrest, so everything in Asher's house was whole, placid, healthy. Every day Asher went to bring the cans of milk from the train. He rose at dawn, went to the synagogue, and after breakfast drove to the railroad depot. He worked at least eighteen hours every day, yet on the Sabbath, instead of resting, he would go to listen to a preacher or come to my father to study a portion of the Pentateuch with the commentary of Rashi. Just as he loved his work, so he loved his Judaism. It seems to me that I never heard this man say no. His entire life was one great yes.

Asher owned a horse and wagon, and this horse and wagon aroused a fierce envy in me. How happy must be the boy whose father owned a wagon, a horse, a stable! Every day Asher went off to distant parts of the city, even to Praga! Often I would see him driving past our building. He never forgot to lift his head and greet whomever he saw at the window or on the balcony. Often he met me when I was running about the streets with a gang of boys or playing with those who were not "my kind," but he never threatened to tell my father, nor did he try to lecture me. He did not, like the other grown-ups, pull little boys by the ear, pinch their noses, or twist the brims of their caps. Asher seemed to have an innate respect for every one, big or small.

Once when I saw him driving by in his wagon I nodded to him and called out, "Reb Asher, take me along!"

Asher immediately stopped and told me to get on. We drove to a train depot. The trip took several hours and I was overjoyed. I rode amid trolley cars, droshkies, delivery vans. Soldiers marched; policemen stood guard; fire engines, ambulances, even some of the automobiles that were just beginning to appear on the streets of Warsaw rushed past us. Nothing could harm me. I was protected by a friend with a whip, and beneath my feet I could feel the throbbing of the wheels. It seemed to me that all Warsaw must envy me. And indeed people stared in wonderment at the little Hasid with the velvet cap and the red earlocks who was riding in a milk wagon and surveying the city. It was evident that I did not really belong to this wagon, that I was a strange kind of tourist . . .

From that day on, a silent pact existed between me and Reb Asher. Whenever he could, he would take me along as his passenger. Fraught with danger were those minutes when Reb Asher went off to fetch the milk cans from the train, or to attend to a bill, and I remained alone in the wagon. The horse would turn his head and stare at me in astonishment. Asher had given me the reins to hold, and the horse seemed to be saying silently, "Just look who is my driver now . . ." The fear that the horse might suddenly rear up and run off gave to these moments the extra fillip of peril. After all, a horse is not a child's plaything but a gigantic creature, silent, wild, with enormous strength. Occasionally a Gentile would pass by, look at me, laugh, and say something to me in Polish. I did not understand his language, and he cast the same sort of dread upon me as did the horse: he too was big, strong, and incomprehensible. He too might suddenly turn on me and strike me, or yank at my earlock—a pastime some Poles considered a great joke . . .

When I thought the end had come—any moment now the Gentile would strike me, or the horse would dash off and smash into a wall or a street lamp—then Reb Asher reappeared and all was well again. Asher carried the heavy milk cans with the ease of a Samson. He was stronger than the horse, stronger than the Gentile, yet he had mild eyes and spoke my language, and he was my father's friend. I had only one desire: to ride with this man for days and nights over fields and through forests, to Africa, to America, to the ends of the world, and always to watch, to observe all that was going on around me . . .

How different this same Asher seemed on the New Year and the Day of Atonement! Carpenters had put up benches in my father's study, and this was where the women prayed. The beds had been taken out of the bedroom, a Holy Ark brought in, and it had become a tiny prayer house. Asher was dressed in a white robe, against which his black beard appeared even blacker. On his head he wore a high cap embroidered with gold and silver. At the beginning of the Additional Service, Reb Asher would ascend to the cantor's desk and recite in a lion's roar: "Behold me, destitute of good works . . ."

Our bedroom was too small for the bass voice that thundered forth from this mighty breast. It was heard halfway down the street. Asher recited and chanted. He knew every melody, every movement. The twenty men who made up our congregation were all part of his choir. Asher's deep masculine voice aroused a tumult in the women's section. True, they all knew him well. Only yesterday they had bought from him or from his wife a saucepan of milk, a pot of clabber, a few ounces of butter, and had bargained with him for a little extra. But now Asher was the delegate who offered up the prayers of the People of Israel directly to the Almighty, before the Throne of Glory, amid fluttering angels and books that read themselves, in which are recorded the good deeds and the sins of every mortal soul . . .When he reached the prayer "We will express the might," and began to recite the destinies of men—who shall live and who shall die, who shall perish by fire and who by water—a sobbing broke out among the women. But when Asher called out triumphantly: But repentance, prayer, and charity can avert the evil decree!"—then a heavy stone was taken from every heart. Soon Asher began to sing of the smallness of man and the greatness of God, and joy and comfort enveloped everyone. Why need men—who are but passing shadows, wilting blossoms—expect malice from a God who is just, revered, merciful? Every word that Asher called out, every note he uttered, restored courage, revived hope. We indeed are nothing, but He is all. We are but as dust in our lifetime, and less than dust after death, but He is eternal and His days shall never end. In Him, only in Him, lies our hope . . .

One year, at the close of the Day of Atonement, this same Asher, our friend and benefactor, saved our very lives. It happened in this way. After the daylong fast, we had eaten a rich supper. Later a number of Jews gathered in our house to dance and rejoice. My father had already put up, in the courtyard, the first beam of the hut for the coming Feast of Tabernacles. Late that night the family had at last fallen asleep. Since benches and pews had been set up in the bedroom, and the entire house was in disorder, each of us slept wherever he could find a spot. But one thing we had forgotten—to extinguish the candles that were still burning on some of the pews.

Late that night Asher had to drive to the railroad station to pick up milk. He passed our building and noticed that our apartment was unusually bright. This was not the glow of candles or a lamp, but the glare of a fire. Asher realized that our house must be burning. He rang the bell at the gate but the janitor did not rush to open it. He too was asleep. Then Asher set to ringing the bell and beating on the door, making such a commotion that at last the janitor awoke and opened the gate. Asher raced up the stairs and banged on our door, but no one answered. Then Asher the Mighty hurled his broad shoulders against the door and forced it open. Bursting into the apartment, he found the entire family asleep, while all around benches, prayer stands, and prayer books were aflame. He began to shout in his booming cantorial voice and finally roused us, and then he tore off our quilts and set to smothering the conflagration.

I remember that moment as though it was yesterday. I opened my eyes and saw many flames, large and small, rolling about and dancing like imps. My brother Moshe's blanket had already caught fire. But I was young and was not frightened. On the contrary, I liked the dancing flames.

After some time the fire was put out. Here indeed something had happened that might well be called a miracle. A few minutes more, and we all would have been taken by the flames, for the wood of the benches was dry and they were saturated with the tallow of the dripping candles. Asher was the only human being awake at that hour, the only one who would ring the bell so persistently and risk his own life for us. Yes, it was fated that this faithful friend should save us from the fire.

We were not even able to thank him. It was as though we had all been struck dumb. Asher himself was in a hurry and left quickly. We wandered about amid the charred benches, tables, prayer books, and prayer shawls, and every few minutes we discovered more sparks and smoldering embers. We all might easily have been burned to cinders.

The friendship between my father and Reb Asher grew ever stronger, and during the war years, when we were close to starvation, Asher again helped us in every way he could.

After we had left Warsaw (during the First World War), we continued to hear news of him from time to time. One son died, a daughter fell in love with a young man of low origins and Asher was deeply grieved. I do not know whether he lived to see the Nazi occupation of Warsaw. He probably died before that. But such Jews as he were dragged off to the death camps. May these memoirs serve as a monument to him and his like, who lived in sanctity and died as martyrs.

At the market: a fruit and vegetable stall

To the Wild Cows

In all the years that we lived in Warsaw, I never left the city. Other boys used to talk about their vacations. People went out to Falenica, to Miedzeszyn, Michalin, Swider, Otwock—but for me these were only names. No trees grew on Krochmalna Street. Near No. 24, where I went to cheder, there was a tree, but No. 24 was far from our house.

Some of the neighbors had potted flowers, but my parents considered this a pagan custom. I, however, had an inborn love of nature. In the summertime I would sometimes find a leaf still attached to the stem of an apple, and such a leaf would arouse both joy and longing in me. I would sniff at it and carry it around with me until it withered. Mother brought home a bunch of carrots, parsley, red radishes, cucumbers—and every vegetable reminded me of the days in Radzymin, where I had been surrounded by fields and orchards. Once I found a whole ear of corn in my straw mattress. This ear of corn awakened many memories. Among other things it reminded me of the dream of Pharaoh, wherein the seven lean ears of corn devoured the seven fat ones.

Many different kinds of flies used to alight on the railing of our balcony: large, small, dark, green-gold. When a butterfly would stray there, I would not try to catch it, but would hold my breath and stare in wonder. The little fluttering creature was for me a greeting from the world of freedom.

But Mother Nature did her work even on Krochmalna Street. In the winter the snow fell, in the summer the rains came. High over the rooftops the clouds passed—dark ones, light ones, some like silver, some in the shapes of fish, snakes, sheep, brooms. Occasionally hail fell on our balcony, and once, after the rain, a rainbow stretched above the roofs. Father told me to recite the blessing "Who remembereth the Covenant." At night the moon shone and the stars appeared. It was all a great mystery.

My friend Boruch-Dovid was always talking about the fields and wastelands that lie beyond Warsaw, and about the wild cows that graze there. I began to demand that he take me there. He delayed as long as he could and put me off with various excuses. But finally it reached the point where he had to make good on his promises or our friendship would end.

One Friday in the summertime I arose very early, so early that the sky was still glowing from the sunrise. To my mother I made some pretext or other, put a few slices of bread and butter in a paper bag, took from its hiding place a kopeck I had somehow saved from my allowance, and went off to meet Boruch-Dovid. I had never been up so early in the morning, and everything looked cooler, fresher, and somehow like a fairy-tale landscape. Here and there a stone was damp and Boruch-Dovid said it was because of the dew. This meant, then, that there was dew even on Krochmalna Street. I had thought that dew fell only in the Land of Israel . . .

Not only the street, but the people too looked fresher. I discovered that early in the morning various farm wagons came to our street. Gentiles from the surrounding villages brought vegetables, chickens, geese, ducks, and freshly laid chicken eggs (not the lime-preserved eggs one could buy in Zelda's shop). On Mirowski Street, behind the market halls, was the wholesale fruit market. The abundance of all the orchards around Warsaw was brought here: apples, pears, cherries, sour cherries, gooseberries, currants. Here too were traded strange fruits and vegetables that most Jewish children had never tasted and thought forbidden: tomatoes, cauliflowers, green peppers. Inside the market halls proper, one could get pomegranates and bananas. These were bought only by grand ladies, whose shopping baskets were carried by servant girls.

Boruch-Dovid and I walked quickly. As we walked, he told many strange tales. His father, he said, had gone on foot from Warsaw to Skierniewice and on the way he had met a wild man. I was very curious about the appearance of the wild man and Boruch-Dovid gave me a detailed description: tall, with scales instead of skin, long hair reaching to the ground, and a horn growing in the middle of his forehead. For breakfast such a creature always ate a live child. I was panic-stricken and I asked, "Maybe a wild man will attack us?"

"No, they are far from Warsaw."

I should not have been so gullible. But I always believed everything Boruch-Dovid told me.

We passed through Nalewki and Muranow Streets, and from there the road led to the open country. I saw broad meadows covered with grass and all sorts of flowers, and mountains of a kind I had never known to exist. At the top they were indeed mountains, but at the bottom there were brick walls with small, sunken windows covered by iron grates.

"What is that?" I asked.

"The Citadel."

A feeling of dread came over me. I had heard of the Citadel. Here were imprisoned those who had tried to overthrow the Tsar.

I had not yet seen any wild cows, but what I had seen already was wonderful and strange. The sky here was not a narrow strip as on Krochmalna Street, but broad, spread out like the ocean, and it descended to the earth like a heavenly curtain. Birds flew overhead in swarms, with a twittering, a cawing, a whistling—large birds and small birds. Two storks were circling above one of the hills of the Citadel. Butterflies of all colors fluttered above the grass: white, yellow, brown, with all kinds of dots and patterns. The air smelled of earth, of grass, of the smoke of locomotives, and of something more that intoxicated me and made my head reel. There was a strange stillness here, and yet everything murmured, rustled, chirped. Blossoms fell from somewhere and settled on the lapels of my coat. I looked up at the sky, saw the sun, the clouds, and suddenly I understood more clearly the meaning of the words of Genesis. This, then, was the world God had created: the earth, the heavens, the waters above that are separated by the firmament from the waters below.

* * *

Boruch-Dovid and I climbed up a hill and below us we saw the Vistula. One half glittered like silver, the other half was green as gall. A white ship sailed past. The river itself did not stand still—it flowed, it was headed somewhere, with an eagerness that hinted at miracles and the coming of the Messiah.

"That's the Vistula," explained Boruch-Dovid. "It flows all the way to Danzig."

"And then?"

"Then it flows into the sea."

"And where is the Leviathan?"

"Far away, at the end of the earth."

Then the storybooks did not tell lies, after all. The world *is* filled with wonders. One need merely pass through Muranow Street and one street more, and already one was in the midst of marvels. The end of the earth? Was not *this* the end of the earth? . . .

Locomotives whistled, but no trains could be seen. Gentle breezes were blowing, and each brought with it a different fragrance—aromas long forgotten or never dreamed of. A honeybee came from somewhere, alit on a flower, smelled at it, hummed, and flew on to the next flower. Boruch-Dovid said, "She wants to collect honey."

"Can she bite?"

"Yes, and she has a special poison."

He, Boruch-Dovid, knows everything. If I were alone, I could not find my way home. Already I have forgotten even the direction toward Warsaw. But he is as much at home here as in his own courtyard. Suddenly he starts to run. He pretends to run away from me. He throws himself down and is hidden by the tall grass. Boruch-Dovid is gone! I am alone in the world—a lost child, just like in the storybooks.

"Boruch-Dovid!" I began to call. "Boruch-Dovid!"

I call, but my voice rebounds from somewhere. There is an echo here, as in a synagogue, but it is thrown back from a great distance and the voice is changed and terrifying.

"Boruch-Dovid! Boruch-Dovid! . . ."

I know that he is only playing a joke on me. He wants to frighten me. But though I know it, I am afraid. My voice is breaking with sobs.

"Bo-r-uch Do-v-id! . . ."

He reappears, his black eyes laughing like a gypsy's, and begins to run about in circles like a young colt. His coattails fly. His fringed vest billows in the wind. He too has become like a wild creature in the lap of nature.

"Come on, let's go to the Vistula!"

The path leads downhill, and we cannot walk—we run. Our feet seem to be running by themselves. I have to hold mine back so they won't run even faster and jump right into the water. But the water is farther away than I had thought. As I run, the river becomes broader, like an ocean. We come to dunes of pebbles and moist sand, long and marked with lines, like giant cakes made by children playing in the sand. Boruch-Dovid takes off his boots, rolls up his pants legs, and wades into the water up to his ankles.

"Ouch, it's cold!"

He tells me to take off my boots. But I am embarrassed. Walking barefoot is not in my nature. Only rowdies and Gentile boys go barefoot.

"Are there any fish here?"

"Yes, lots of fish."

"Do they bite?"

"Sometimes."

"What will you do if a fish bites you?"

"I'll grab it by the tail ..."

Compared to me, Boruch-Dovid is a country boy, a peasant. I sit down on a rock and everything inside me flows, gurgles like the waters of the Vistula. My mind sways with the motion of the waves and it seems to me that not only the Vistula, but everything around me--the hills, the sky, I myself—is swaying, flowing away into the distance, toward Danzig. Boruch-Dovid points to the other shore and says, "Over there is the Praga forest."

This means that near me there is a real forest, full of wild animals and robbers.

Suddenly something extraordinary happens. From the left, where the sky and the waters meet, something comes floating on the water, but it is not a ship. At first it seems small, enveloped in a haze. Soon it grows larger and more distinct. It is a group of rafts made of logs. Men lean against long poles and push them with all the weight of their bodies. On one of the rafts there is a little hut—a small house out on the water! Even Boruch-Dovid stares in open-mouthed wonder.

It takes a long, long time for the rafts to come close to us. The men yell something to us. I notice someone who looks like a Jew. He has a beard. I think I can even make out a Jewish skullcap. From my reading of the parables of the Preacher of Dubnow, I know that Jewish merchants make voyages to Danzig and Leipzig. I have even heard that timber is shipped by water. But now I see it with my own eyes—a tale of the Dubnow preacher brought to life! For a while the rafts are near us. A dog stands at the edge of one of them and barks directly at us. Woe to us, if he could jump across the water! He would tear us to shreds. After a while, the rafts move on. Time has passed, the sun has already reached the middle of the sky and is now moving into the West. Only after the rafts have disappeared beneath a bridge do we start to go back, not the way we came, but in a different direction.

I remember the wild cows and am about to ask Boruch-Dovid where they are, but I don't. I suddenly realize that the wild cows and the wild man are nothing but his imagination. We would never encounter any of them. As a matter of fact, when I had told my mother about the wild cows, she had asked, "If there are such cows, why don't they catch them and sell them to the dairies? And how is it possible that they have only been seen by your friend Boruch-Dovid?" She was just as skeptical about the wild cows as she had been about the shrieking geese.

The sun is reddening. At home Mother is surely beginning to worry—she is so nervous. Soon it will be time to take the Sabbath stew to the baker, and who will be there to carry it? We begin to walk quickly, each sunk in his own thoughts, while above our heads the birds play, and the windows of the Citadel glow red and gold in the sunset.

I think of those who lie inside in chains because they tried to overthrow the Tsar. I seem to see their eyes, and suddenly everything is filled with a Sabbath Eve sadness and eeriness.

A family of bagel peddlers

The
Washwoman

Our home had little contact with Gentiles. The only Gentile in the building was the janitor. Fridays he would come for a tip, his "Friday money." He remained standing at the door, took off his hat, and my mother gave him six groschen.

Besides the janitor there were also the Gentile washwomen who came to the house to fetch our laundry. My story is about one of these.

She was a small woman, old and wrinkled. When she started washing for us, she was already past seventy. Most Jewish women of her age were sickly, weak, broken in body. All the old women in our street had bent backs and leaned on sticks when they walked. But this washwoman, small and thin as she was, possessed a strength that came from generations of peasant forebears. Mother would count out to her a bundle of laundry that had accumulated over several weeks. She would lift the unwieldy pack, load it on her narrow shoulders, and carry it the long way home. She lived on Krochmalna Street too, but at the other end, near the Wola section. It must have been a walk of an hour and a half.

She would bring the laundry back about two weeks later. My mother had never been so pleased with any washwoman. Every piece of linen sparkled like polished silver. Every piece was neatly ironed. Yet she charged no more than the others. She was a real find. Mother always had her money ready, because it was too far for the old woman to come a second time.

Laundering was not easy in those days. The old woman had no faucet where she lived but had to bring in the water from a pump. For the linens to come out so clean, they had to be scrubbed thoroughly in a washtub, rinsed with washing soda, soaked, boiled in an enormous pot, starched, then ironed. Every piece was handled ten times or more. And the drying! It could not be done outside because thieves would steal the laundry. The wrung-out wash had to be carried up to the attic and hung on clotheslines. In the winter it would become as brittle as glass and almost break when touched. And there was always a to-do with other housewives and washwomen who wanted the attic clotheslines for their own use. Only God knows all the old woman had to endure each time she did a wash!

She could have begged at the church door or entered a home for the penniless and aged. But there was in her a certain pride and love of labor with which many Gentiles have been blessed. The old woman did not want to become a burden, so she bore her burden.

My mother spoke a little Polish, and the old woman would

talk with her about many things. She was especially fond of me and used to say I looked like Jesus. She repeated this every time she came, and Mother would frown and whisper to herself, her lips barely moving, "May her words be scattered in the wilderness."

The woman had a son who was rich. I no longer remember what sort of business he had. He was ashamed of his mother, the washwoman, and never came to see her. Nor did he ever give her a groschen. The old woman told this without rancor. One day the son was married. It seemed that he had made a good match. The wedding took place in a church. The son had not invited the old mother to his wedding, but she went to the church and waited at the steps to see her son lead the "young lady" to the altar.

The story of the faithless son left a deep impression on my mother. She talked about it for weeks and months. It was an affront not only to the old woman but to the entire institution of motherhood. Mother would argue, "Nu, does it pay to make sacrifices for children? The mother uses up her last strength, and he does not even know the meaning of loyalty."

And she would drop dark hints to the effect that she was not certain of her own children: Who knows what they would do some day? This, however, did not prevent her from dedicating her life to us. If there was any delicacy in the house, she would put it aside for the children and invent all sorts of excuses and reasons why she herself did not want to taste it. She knew charms that went back to ancient times, and she used expressions she had inherited from generations of devoted mothers and grandmothers. If one of the children complained of a pain, she would say, "May I be your ransom and may you outlive my bones!" Or she would say, "May

I be the atonement for the least of your fingernails." When we ate she used to say, "Health and marrow in your bones!" The day before the new moon she gave us a kind of candy that was said to prevent parasitic worms. If one of us had something in his eye, Mother would lick the eye clean with her tongue. She also fed us rock candy against coughs, and from time to time she would take us to be blessed against the evil eye. This did not prevent her from studying *The Duties of the Heart, The Book of the Covenant*, and other serious philosophic works.

But to return to the washwoman. That winter was a harsh one. The streets were in the grip of a bitter cold. No matter how much we heated our stove, the windows were covered with frostwork and decorated with icicles. The newspapers reported that people were dying of the cold. Coal became dear. The winter had become so severe that parents stopped sending children to cheder, and even the Polish schools were closed.

On one such day the washwoman, now nearly eighty years old, came to our house. A good deal of laundry had accumulated during the past weeks. Mother gave her a pot of tea to warm herself, as well as some bread. The old woman sat on a kitchen chair trembling and shaking, and warmed her hands against the teapot. Her fingers were gnarled from work, and perhaps from arthritis too. Her fingernails were strangely white. These hands spoke of the stubbornness of mankind, of the will to work not only as one's strength permits but beyond the limits of one's power. Mother counted and wrote down the list: men's undershirts, women's vests, long-legged drawers, bloomers, petticoats, shifts, featherbed covers, pillowcases, sheets, and the men's fringed garments. Yes, the Gentile woman washed these holy garments as well.

The bundle was big, bigger than usual. When the woman placed it on her shoulders, it covered her completely. At first she swayed, as though she were about to fall under the load. But an inner obstinacy seemed to call out: No, you may not fall. A donkey may permit himself to fall under his burden, but not a human being, the crown of creation.

It was fearful to watch the old woman staggering out with the enormous pack, out into the frost, where the snow was dry as salt and the air was filled with dusty white whirlwinds, like goblins dancing in the cold. Would the old woman ever reach Wola?

She disappeared, and Mother sighed and prayed for her.

Usually the woman brought back the wash after two or, at the most, three weeks. But three weeks passed, then four and five, and nothing was heard of the old woman. We remained without linens. The cold had become even more intense. The telephone wires were now as thick as ropes. The branches of the trees looked like glass. So much snow had fallen that the streets had become uneven, and sleds were able to glide down many streets as on the slopes of a hill. Kindhearted people lit fires in the streets for vagrants to warm themselves and roast potatoes in, if they had any to roast.

For us the washwoman's absence was a catastrophe. We needed the laundry. We did not even know the woman's address. It seemed certain that she had collapsed, died. Mother declared she had had a premonition, as the old woman left our house that last time, that we would never see our things again. She found some old torn shirts and washed and mended them. We mourned, both for the laundry and for the old, toil-worn woman who had grown close to us through the years she had served us so faithfully.

More than two months passed. The frost had subsided, and then a new frost had come, a new wave of cold. One evening, while Mother was sitting near the kerosene lamp mending a shirt, the door opened and a small puff of steam, followed by a gigantic bundle, entered. Under the bundle tottered the old woman, her face as white as a linen sheet. A few wisps of white hair straggled out from beneath her shawl. Mother uttered a half-choked cry. It was as though a corpse had entered the room. I ran toward the old woman and helped her unload her pack. She was even thinner now, more bent. Her face had become more gaunt, and her head shook from side to side as though she were saying no. She could not utter a clear word, but mumbled something with her sunken mouth and pale lips.

After the old woman had recovered somewhat, she told us that she had been ill, very ill. Just what her illness was, I cannot remember. She had been so sick that someone had called a doctor, and the doctor had sent for a priest. Someone had informed the son, and he had contributed money for a coffin and for the funeral. But the Almighty had not yet wanted to take this pain-racked soul to Himself. She began to feel better, she became well, and as soon as she was able to stand on her feet once more, she resumed her washing. Not just ours, but the wash of several other families too.

"I could not rest easy in my bed because of the wash," the old woman explained. "The wash would not let me die."

"With the help of God you will live to be a hundred and twenty," said my mother, as a benediction.

"God forbid! What good would such a long life be? The

work becomes harder and harder . . . my strength is leaving me . . .I do not want to be a burden on anyone!'' The old woman muttered and crossed herself, and raised her eyes toward heaven.

Fortunately there was some money in the house and Mother counted out what she owed. I had a strange feeling: the coins in the old woman's washed-out hands seemed to become as worn and clean and pious as she herself was. She blew on the coins and tied them in a kerchief. Then she left, promising to return in a few weeks for a new load of wash.

But she never came back. The wash she had returned was her last effort on this earth. She had been driven by an indomitable will to return the property to its rightful owners, to fulfill the task she had undertaken.

And now at last her body, which had long been no more than a shard supported only by the force of honesty and duty, had fallen. Her soul passed into those spheres where all holy souls meet, regardless of the roles they played on this earth, in whatever tongue, of whatever creed. I cannot imagine paradise without this Gentile washwoman. I cannot even conceive of a world where there is no recompense for such effort.

In the one-room apartment of a metal worker

I Become
a Collector

A rabbi like my father was supported by the people of his neighborhood. In need of his advice on matters of religious law, and knowing that he had to earn a living, they gave various sums each week to his collector. True, the collector made out receipts, but it was an easy matter for him to keep more than the 20 percent commission that was his due.

Our first collector was an honest man, but he later married and became a ritual slaughterer. Each of those who followed was more of a thief than the last, and by the time I was nine we had a collector who was taking most of the money for himself. Every week he would turn in less and less, with complaints: "I can't get them to pay!" or "There's a shortage, a crisis!" It was beneath my father's dignity to suspect another Jew.

Finally there wasn't a piece of bread in the house, and the

storekeepers refused us credit. I no longer received a daily two-groschen piece for candy or chocolate. We could not pay the rent and the landlord threatened to take us to court and auction our furniture. When Father recited grace— "And let us not partake of the gifts of flesh and blood"—he would look heavenward, sighing more deeply than usual. Was it possible to study the Torah and be a Jew if there was no Sabbath food?

One day when Father had been telling me his troubles, I said, "Let me collect!"

Stunned, Father looked at me. "But you're only a boy. You have to study."

"I'll study."

"What do you think Mother would say?"

"Why tell her?"

After deliberating awhile, he said, "Well, we'll try it."

I took the collection tickets to the necessary addresses, and in spite of the excuses made by my corrupt predecessor, donations were generous. Since we had discharged the collector several weeks before, many people were behind in their payments and within an hour my gaberdine pockets were full of copper and silver coins. In two hours, finding that both pockets were full, I began stuffing my breast pocket and my pants.

The shame I had felt diminished. Everyone was so gracious, the men pinching my cheeks, the women blessing me and treating me to cookies, fruit, and candy. My father, they told me, was a godly man, a saint. I kept climbing stairs, knocking at doors. Krochmalna Street, which I had thought I knew, was now turning itself inside out for me. I found tailors, cobblers, furriers, brushmakers, numerous artisans. In one apartment, girls were stringing coral, and colorful beads gleamed in piles on tables, chairs, and beds. It looked like an enchanted palace to me.

But when I opened the door of another apartment, I screamed. Dead animals were heaped on the floor. This tenant bought hares from a hunter and sold them to restaurants. In another apartment, girls were winding thread from spindles to bobbins, singing Yiddish songs while bits of thread flew into their disheveled hair.

In one place, people were playing cards, and in another an aged, white-bearded man planed a board while shavings and chips fell everywhere and a bonneted old woman prayed from a holy book. In a bookbinder's apartment I was horrified to find workers tramping over Pentateuchs and other holy books. Then in another apartment I found a female freak with a head that came almost to a point. She had huge calf's eyes and an extraordinarily broad body, and she grunted like a mute and made frightening sounds. Much to my surprise, I found that she had a husband.

Somewhere else I saw a sallow-faced, paralyzed man lying on a kind of shelf while a woman fed him and the food dribbled over his withered beard. His eyes seemed crossed. I shut that door almost as soon as I opened it. Up an incredibly filthy stairway I climbed to an attic, past barefoot, scurvy children playing with shards and mud. One boy's skull had been shaved. He was pale, his ears were swollen, and he had long, unkempt sidelocks. A girl spat at him and he cried out some kind of curse. Taking out a ticket, I asked, "Where does Yenta Flederbaum live?"

"In the *shtchonka* . . ."

In Warsaw this was the name for a dark hallway. I was inclined to be fearful, but that day I was somehow infused with great courage, as if I had been transformed. Stumbling along the dark corridor, bumping into baskets and crates, I heard a rustling noise, as if mice were about. Lighting a match, I discovered that there were no numbers or even latches on the doors. When I pushed one open, I was transfixed by what I saw. A corpse wrapped in a sheet lay on the floor, a pair of candles at its head and a woman beside it on a footstool, weeping, wringing her hands, and crying out. The mirror on the opposite wall had been draped. My ribs tingling with fright, I slammed the door and backed into the hallway, fiery spots before my eyes, my ears throbbing. I began to run but became entangled in a basket or crate. It was as if someone had clutched my coattail, drawing me backward; bony fingers dug into me, I heard a dreadful scream. In a cold sweat, I ran, tearing my gaberdine. There would be no more collecting for me. I threw up, and shivered. The coins burdened me as I walked. It seemed to me that I had grown old in that one day.

I had no appetite, even though I hadn't eaten since morning. My stomach felt swollen. I went into the Radzymin study house, where the men in our family prayed, and found it deserted because it was midday. Like an old man, I sat there resting, with aching feet and a pounding head. I looked at the sacred books and felt estranged from them; I seemed to have forgotten my studies.

Suddenly I realized that I had done something wrong, and felt contemptuous of myself. I made a resolution then to which I still adhere: never do anything for money that goes against the grain, and avoid favors and presents. I wanted to relieve myself as soon as possible of the miserable job.

When I arrived home, Mother happened to be out and

Father, in his study, looked at me anxiously, asking, "Where were you all day?" Then he blurted, "I'm sorry about the whole thing, You've got to continue studying . . ."

Emptying my pockets, I discovered that I had collected more in a day than the collector had given us in a month. Without counting the money, Father shoved it into a drawer. I felt relieved.

"I can't do it any more," I said.

"God forbid!"

But the new collector also stole. Finally Father put up a notice that no more money should be given the collector. He tried to get along on his fees from lawsuits, weddings, and divorces, but oursituation grew worse, and even though he took pupils they did not remain with him very long. Mother went on a trip to Bilgoray to get help from her father and stayed there for weeks.

At home there was chaos. We lived on dry food and there was no one to supervise me. My sister, Hinde Esther, had married the son of a Warsaw Hasid and they were living in Antwerp, Belgium. I suddenly felt a great urge to study. I began in some inexplicable way to "read" a page from the Talmud by myself and even to understand a commentary explaining it. I examined Maimonides's *The Strong Hand* and other books I had not understood until then. One day in my father's bookcase I found a volume of the Cabala, *The Pillar of Service* by Reb Baruch Kosower. Although I missed the meaning of most of it, I did understand a little. A part of my brain that had been sealed seemed to be opening. I now experienced the profound joy of learning . . .

At cheder

The
Strong Ones

Cheder, too often described as a place where innocent
children suffered at the hands of a sloppy, ill-tempered
teacher, was not quite that. What was wrong with society
was wrong with cheder.

There was one boy with constantly clenched fists who
kept looking for a chance to hit someone. Assistant bullies
and sycophants surrounded him.

Another boy, for whom it was not practical to use
violence, acted the little saint, smiling at everyone, doing
favors, and all with an expression that implied immeasurable
love. But in his quiet way he schemed to acquire things, to
taste something wonderful for nothing. Pious though he was,
he showed friendship for the bully while feigning sympathy
for his victims. When his friend the bully decided to give
someone a bloody nose, the little saint would run to the
victim with a handkerchief while gently admonishing the

bully, "You shouldn't have done that . . ."

There was another boy who was interested only in business, trading a button for a nail, a bit of putty for a pencil, a candy for a roll. He was always losing out on bargains, but in the end he got the best of everyone. Half the cheder was indebted to him, since he lent money on interest. He and the bully had an arrangement whereby anyone who reneged had his hat snatched off.

Then there was the liar who boasted that his family was rich and famous and that Warsaw's elite visited his home. Promising us dates, figs, St. John's bread, and oranges from theoretical weddings and circumcisions, and a projected summer vacation, he demanded advance presents from all of us.

Then there was the victim. One day the bully drew blood from him and the next day he gave the bully a present. Smiling with sly submissiveness, the victim indicated another boy who needed a beating.

From my seat in cheder I saw everything, and even though the bully had punched me, I presented him with neither smiles nor gifts. I called him an Esau and predicted that his hereafter would be spent on a bed of nails. He hit me again for that, but I didn't weaken. I would have nothing to do with the bully, the priggish saint, the moneylender, or the liar, nor would I pay them any compliments.

I wasn't making out too well. Most of the cheder boys had grown hostile, informing against me to the teacher and the tutor. If they caught me in the street, they said, they'd break my leg. I recognized the danger. After all, I was too small to take on the entire cheder.

The trip to cheder each morning was agonizing, but I

couldn't complain to my parents--they had their own troubles. Besides, they'd probably say, "That's what you get for being different from everyone else . . ."

There was nothing to do but wait it out. Even the devil had to weary. God, if He supported truth and justice, must inevitably side with me.

The day came when it seemed to me impossible to go on. Even the teacher, in that hellish atmosphere, opposed me, though I knew my Pentateuch. The rebbetzin made malicious remarks about me. It was as if I were excommunicated.

Then, one day, everything changed. The bully miscalculated the strength of a new boy, who just happened to hit back. Then the teacher hurled himself at the bully, who already had a lump on his head. He was dragged to the whipping bench, his pants were pulled down, and he was whipped before all of us. Like Haman, he was punished. When he tried to resume his reign of terror, he was repulsed in favor of the victor.

The moneylender also met his downfall. The father of one boy who had paid out too much interest appeared at cheder to complain. A search of the moneylender's pockets proved so fruitful that he too was whipped.

The saint's hypocrisy was recognized at last, despite his whispered secrets and his flatteries.

Then, as if in response to my prayers, the boys began speaking to me once more. The flatterers and the traders offered me good will and bargains—I don't know why. I might even have formed a group of my own, but I wasn't inclined that way. There was only one boy whose friendship I wanted, and he was the one I chose. Mendel was a fine, decent person without social ambitions. We studied from the same Pentateuch and walked with our arms about each other. Others, jealous, intrigued against us, but our friendship remained constant. We were like David and Jonathan . . .

Even after I left cheder, our friendship persisted. I had attended several cheders, and from each one I retained a friend. Occasionally, in the evenings, we would meet near the markets and walk along the sidewalk, talking, making plans. My friends' names were Mendel Besser, Mottel Horowitz, Abraham something-or-other, Borush-Dovid, and others. More or less their leader, I would tell them things my older brother had told my mother. There was a great feeling of trust among us, until one day I had the impression that they resented me. They grumbled about my bossiness; I had to be demoted a little. They were preparing a revolution and I saw it in their faces. And even though I asked how I had offended them, they behaved like Joseph's brothers and could not answer in a friendly way. They couldn't even look at me directly. What was it they envied? My dreams . . . I could actually hear them say as I approached them, "Behold this dreamer cometh . . .Let us slay him and cast him in some pit . . . Let us sell him to the Ishmaelites . . ."

It is painful to be among one's brothers when they are jealous. They had been good to me, they praised me, and then they were mean. All at once they grew angry. Turning away as I approached, they whispered . . .

Friendships with me are not casual; I cannot make new friends easily. I wondered if I had sinned against them, or deceived them. But, if so, why hadn't they told me what was wrong?

I could not recollect having harmed them in any way, nor had I said anything against them. And if someone had slandered me, why should my friends believe it? After all, they were devoted to me.

There was nothing to do but wait it out. My kind has to become accustomed to loneliness. And when one is alone there is nothing to do but study. I became a diligent scholar. I would spend whole days in the Radzymin study house and then pore over religious works at home. Purchasing and renting books from peddlers, I read constantly. It was summertime and the days were long. Reading a story of three brothers, I imagined that I could write too, and began to cover both sides of a sheet. "Once there was a king who had three sons. One was wise, one foolish, and one merry . . ." But somehow the story didn't jell.

On another paper I began to draw freakish humans and fantastic beasts. But this too wearied me, and going out to the balcony, I looked down at the street. Only I was alone. Other boys were running, playing, and talking together. I'll go mad, I thought—there was too much happening in my head all the time. Shouldn't I jump from the balcony? Or spit down on the janitor's cap?

That evening, at the Radzymin study house, a boy approached me, acting as a go-between. He spoke tactfully, suggesting that my friends were eager for an understanding but, since I was the minority, it was up to me to make the first move. In short, he suggested that I submit a plea for a truce.

I was infuriated. "It wasn't I who started this," I said. "Why should I be the one to make up?"

"You'll regret it," he warned.

"Leave!" I commanded.

He left angrily. His job as a trucemaker had been spoiled.

But he knew I meant what I said.

Now that they had sent an intermediary, I knew my friends were remorseful. But I would never give in to them.

I grew accustomed to being alone and the days no longer seemed interminable. I studied, wrote, read stories. My brother had brought home a two-volume book called *Crime and Punishment*. Although I didn't really understand it, it fascinated me. Secluded in the bedroom, I read for hours. A student who had killed a crone suffered, starved, and reasoned profoundly. Coming before the prosecutor, he was questioned . . . It was something like a storybook, but different. Strange and lofty, it reminded me of the Cabala. Who were the authors of books like this, and who could understand them? Now and then a passage was illuminated for me, I understood an episode and became enthralled by the beauty of a new insight.

I was in another world. I forgot about my friends.

At evening services in the Radzymin study house, I was unaware of the men among whom I stood. My mind was wandering, when suddenly the intermediary approached.

"Nothing you have to say can interest me," I said.

"Here's a note," he told me.

It was like a scene from a novel. My friends wrote that they missed me. "We wander about in a daze . . ." I still remember what they said. Despite this great triumph, I was so immersed in my book that it scarcely seemed important any more that they wanted to make amends. I went out to the courtyard, and there they were. It reminded me of Joseph and his brothers. They had come to Joseph to buy grain, but why had my friends come to me?

Nevertheless, they did come, ashamed and somehow

afraid—Simon, Levi, Judah. . . . Since I had not become Egypt's ruler, they were not required to bow down to the earth. I had nothing to sell but new dreams.

We talked together late and I spoke of my book. "This is no storybook, this is literature . . ." I said. I created for them a fantastic mélange of incidents and my own thoughts, and infected them with my excitement. Hours passed. They begged me to forgive them, confessed that they had been wrong and never would be angry with me again . . .

They kept their word.

Only time separated us. The rest was accomplished by the German murderers.

A Talmudic scholar

Reb Itchele
and Shprintza

How did a pious Jew get hot tea on the Sabbath, when cooking is forbidden? In small towns a basin of hot water was placed in the oven, along with the Sabbath meal, and in the city, teahouses kept hot water on the stove in a big kettle. The stoves were heated on Friday before sundown, so the water stayed hot all through the Sabbath.

As the young men and girls drank tea in the teahouses, they smiled at each other and conversed. Children would be arriving with teapots to buy hot water on credit, since it is forbidden to carry money on the Sabbath.

After the Sabbath midday meal, my father always sent me to buy our hot water at Itchele's grocery store. Itchele's combination store, home, and teahouse was located at 15 Krochmalna Street. His wife, Shprintza, a large, harassed, untidy woman who was in a constant state of excitement, was known for her good heart. Through hard work, this woman was able to support a large family. One of her sons, Noah, had gone to cheder with me.

Shprintza did everything: carried babies, bore them, worked in the grocery, stocked the store, pickled cucumbers, made sauerkraut, minded the Sabbath kettle, and even found time for charity.

She was always preoccupied. With one eye she would watch a customer who was sloshing her hand about in the brine, trying to pick out a herring from the bottom of the barrel, and with the other eye, boys who liked to play with the beans in the sacks.

Shprintza was forever being forced to chastise fussy customers who behaved as if the goods in her store belonged to them. She waddled about in a decrepit, stained apron and a pair of battered shoes. Her hands were as large and tough as a man's. Her matron's wig was always disheveled.

A foreign traveler, coming upon a store with such a proprietress, surely would have thought her a barbarian, but Shprintza was a civilized and virtuous woman. Her life was dedicated to the highest of all tasks, that of supporting her family and—to the extent she could—Jewishness and the study of the Torah.

Her husband, Reb Itchele, was supposedly a merchant, but his days were spent in praying, arranging banquets for Hasidim, discussing saints, and studying the Mishnah. He was as small as his wife was large. He was as busy with Hasidic affairs as she was with storekeeping. A man who aspired to do everything at once, Itchele recited the Zohar, listened to the stories of Reb Meir the Eunuch, and pondered the interpretation of a difficult verse while collecting a few gulden for some pauper.

Shprintza never got away from her pickle barrels, sacks of provisions, bundles of wood, and customers. Reb Itchele, red-haired in youth, already had a yellow-gray beard when I knew him. He walked with short, quick strides. When he prayed at the study house, he swallowed many of his words; others he kept repeating as he paced back and forth, clapping his hands and raising his ritual fringes swiftly to his brow. His keen ear detected when it was his turn to answer amen. In God's house, as well as in the grocery, he kept his eye on everything, so that he would not fail to take part in some pious act.

During the week this couple was so busy it was impossible to speak to either the man or the wife. But when I came with my teapot on the Sabbath, things were very different.

The family lived in a small apartment in back of the store. If I remember correctly, they had only a single room, where the stove stood with the kettle on it. But a mood of Sabbath repose hovered over this room and its covered table, its benediction cup, and its bread knife with a mother-of-pearl handle.

Shprintza would be wearing a neatly combed wig and a Sabbath dress decorated with arabesques. Reb Itchele would have on a satin capote and a fur-edged hat.

The couple had two daughters, pious girls, almost the same age. When I was still a very small boy, these girls would ask me the same question every Sabbath. "Which of us would you prefer as a bride?"

Embarrassed, I would point to the smaller of the two.

"Why her?" the taller would ask, and I would reply, "You're too big."

My answer always evoked laughter.

But as I grew older, the question was asked less frequently, until finally I was considered too old for such jokes. Nevertheless, the girls and I never forgot the little game we had played and we would feel both constrained and roguish whenever we were in one another's company.

In this household, as in mine, Jewishness and worldliness were forever at odds.

Reb Itchele's oldest son refused to study the Talmud, became an artisan, and shaved off his beard. On Friday evenings, after the Sabbath candles had been lit, I would see this young man sitting in the shop of Zeitag the barber, being lathered and shaved. He caused Reb Itchele and Shprintza unutterable grief.

Sabbath afternoons he sat at their table, wearing a modern cap on his pomaded hair, a modern jacket, a paper collar, and a paper dickey. He was in a rush to get done both with the meal and with the table chants so he could take his young lady to that new sensation, the moving pictures. Reb Itchele avoided looking at this young rebel but dared not drive him from the house, fearful that what he would do next would land his parents in Gehenna.

Nor did Itchele and Shprintza derive much satisfaction from their younger son, Noah, my former classmate in cheder. True, Noah was still only a boy, but he did not want to study either, and they had been forced to take him out of school. He also refused to wear sidelocks.

I remember one Sabbath afternoon in particular. Entering Reb Itchele's back room, I said, "Good Sabbath. May I have some hot water?"

"Why do you have to tell us you want hot water?" Reb Itchele chanted. "Don't you think we know already?"

Shprintza rushed to my defense. "What do you want him to say?"

"Good Sabbath is enough."

"All right, then, good Sabbath."

"Good Sabbath, good year," replied Reb Itchele. "It is written that when the Messiah comes, all the days of the week will be one continual Sabbath."

"When will the people cook?" one of the daughters inquired.

"Who'll want to cook? This world will be a paradise. The saints, seated at God's table, will partake of Leviathan as they listen to the angels divulge the secrets of the Torah."

"Eva, draw him some water," Shprintza commanded.

"What's the hurry?" Reb Itchele asked. "How is your father, eh?"

"So-so."

"A wonderful man. A sage. Do you intend to follow in his footsteps?"

"Yes."

"What are you doing after dinner?"

"Nothing."

"Why don't you and Noah study together? To study by oneself is good, but if one does it with another it is even nobler."

"Not today, Papa," Noah said.

"Why not?"

"I have to visit a friend."

"Who is he? Where are you supposed to meet? It is written that because God wanted to bestow his grace upon the Jews, he gave them the Torah and the Commandments. Why don't you accept His gift? If someone offered you a sackful of pearls and gold coins, would you tell him to keep them until you got back from visiting some boy? Gold and diamonds have value only in this world. When one dies, one takes nothing with him. But the Torah and the Commandments follow a person beyond the grave."

"Yes, Papa, but he expects me."

"What does he want? Who is he? What do you do together?"

I know very well what Noah did. He had a pocketful of buttons decorated with crowns and eagles and he played with these buttons the entire Sabbath through. He also hung around the fellows who took girls to moving pictures.

He boasted that he had hitched rides on the back of droshkies on the Sabbath. What transgressions hadn't Noah committed? And here sat Reb Itchele staring disapprovingly at him from under his yellow brows.

"Nu, what did you say?"

"Another time."

"Well, if you don't want to, so be it. Eva, give the boy his hot water."

Eva took my teapot and filled it.

"Tell your father that next Tuesday is the anniversary of our rabbi's death and, God willing, there'll be a memorial banquet," Reb Itchele said.

"I'll tell him."

"Do you still go to cheder?"

"No, I'm reading the Talmud by myself."

"Do you hear that, Noah? Which part of the Talmud are you studying?"

"The part that concerns an egg laid on a holiday."

"Do you understand what you're reading?"

"Yes, I understand. If I'm confused about something, I look it up in Rashi's commentary."

"And if you don't understand Rashi's commentary?"

"I ask my father."

"Of course. 'Ask thy father and he shall tell thee.' But a generation has grown up that refuses to ask the father. Nowadays the father knows nothing, only the loafers are smart. What becomes of a Jew when he abandons his religion? To the Gentiles he remains a stranger. He has neither this world nor the world to come. Well, hurry along—your water is getting cold."

"Regards to your mother," Shprintza called after me.

Through the half-draped door I could see into the store, where all week long customers swarmed under the gas lights, but which now was filled with Sabbath shadows and an eerie stillness. All the objects there appeared to have withdrawn into a Sabbathlike contemplation, particularly those it was forbidden to touch on this holy day. Everything emanated peace, the packages of chicory and yeast, the sacks of peas, the piles of kindling. God rested on the seventh day and so did they . . . Would a time really come when there would be only one eternal Sabbath?

Outside I saw Reb Meir the Eunuch. This man was a great enigma to me, a man who grew no beard. What could be odder than a beardless Jew? Moreover, he was out of his mind for two weeks out of every month. When deranged, he would mumble to himself, smile, and rub his hands. When he was in possession of himself, he poured forth wisdom, quotations from the Torah, Hasidic witticisms, tales of Wonder Rabbis.

Today was apparently one of his sane days. He passed

wearing a satin capote and a fur-trimmed cap. It was his custom to pray at the study house until late in the afternoon. Only then did he return home.

But where was home? Who did he go to? He had no wife and certainly no children. Who prepared the Sabbath meal for him? Who would take in a eunuch, and a crazy one besides? Someone was willing to have him, watch over him, do his laundry, make his bed at night. Somewhere some merciful woman had assumed this task.

"Good Sabbath, Reb Meir."

"Good Sabbath. You've finished eating already? Remind your father that next week is the anniversary of the rabbi's death, and there'll be a banquet."

And Reb Meir the Eunuch headed home to recite the benediction over the wine and to sing the Sabbath hymns. Eunuch or not, sane or insane, a Jew is a Jew.

Coal porters

The Mysteries
of the Cabala

Everyone knew us on Krochmalna Street. My friend
Mendel and I walked there every day for hours, my hand on
his shoulder, his on mine. We were so preoccupied telling
each other stories that we stumbled into baskets of fruits and
vegetables belonging to the market women, who shouted
after us, "Are you blind or something, you slobs?"

I was ten or so. Mendel was already eleven. I was lean,
white-skinned, with a scrawny neck, blue eyes, fiery red hair.
My sidelocks were always flying as if in a wind; my gaberdine
went unbuttoned, its pockets loaded with storybooks I rented
two for a penny. Not only could I read a page of the Talmud
by myself, I kept on trying my father's volumes of the Cabala,
still without understanding much. On the end pages of these
books I would draw, with colored pencils, six-winged angels,
animals with two heads and with eyes in their tails, demons
with horns, snouts, snakes' bodies, calf's feet. In the evening,

when I stood on our balcony, I stared up into the star-studded sky and brooded about what there was before the creation of the world. At home everybody said I was growing up to be a crazy philosopher, like that professor in Germany who pondered and philosophized for years, until he arrived at the conclusion that a man should walk with his head down and his feet up.

My friend Mendel was the son of a coal porter. Every few weeks his father brought a huge basket of coal for our stoves, and my mother gave him a kopeck. Mendel was taller than I, dark like a gypsy, his hair so black it had a bluish tinge. He had a short nose, a chin with a split in the middle, and slanting eyes like a Tartar's. He wore a tattered gaberdine and torn boots. His family lived in one room at 13 Krochmalna Street. His mother, blind in one eye, dealt in crockery in a stall behind the markets.

We both had the same passion: inventing stories. We never got tired of listening to each other's tales. That late afternoon in summer, as we passed Yanash's bazaar, Mendel halted. He had a secret to tell me: It was not true his father was a coal porter. That was only a disguise. Actually he was richer than any Rothschild. His family had a palace in the forest, and another castle on the sea, full of gold, silver, and diamonds. I asked Mendel how they had become so rich, and he said, "Swear by your fringed garment you will never tell anyone."

I swore.

"Let's split a straw."

We picked up a straw and, each taking an end, tore it between us as a bond. In Mendel's Tartar eyes a dreamy smile appeared and he opened a mouth of extremely white teeth, just like a gypsy's. He said, "My father is a robber."

A shiver ran down my back. "Who does he rob?"

"He digs tunnels into banks and drags out their gold. He hides in the forest, waiting to ambush merchants. He wears a gun and a sword. He is a sorcerer, too, and he can enter the trunks of trees, even though no one can see any opening."

"So why does he have to be a porter?" I asked.

"So the police won't find out . . ."

Mendel told me that his father did not operate singlehanded. He was the chief of twelve hundred thieves, whom he sent all over the world to rob people and bring back the booty. Some sailed the seas and attacked ships; others held up caravans in the desert. Mendel said that, besides his mother, his father had twelve concubines, captive princesses. And when he, Mendel, became Bar Mitzvah, he would also become a robber. He would marry a princess from the other side of the River Sambation. She was already waiting for Mendel to come to the palace and wed her. She had golden hair falling to her ankles and wore golden slippers on her feet. To keep her from running away, Mendel's father had bound her to a pillar with a chain.

"Why does she want to run away?" I asked.

"Because she is yearning for her mother."

I knew it was all lies and even realized which storybooks the different parts came from, but his story enchanted me all the same. We were standing near the fish market, where carp, pike, and chub swam in tubs of water. It was Thursday and women were buying fish for the Sabbath. A blind beggar wearing dark glasses, with a cottony gray beard, plucked chords on a mandolin as he sang a heartrending song about the sinking of the *Titanic*. On his shoulder stood a parrot picking at its feathers with its beak. The beggar's wife, young and as agile as a dancer, collected alms in a tambourine. Over the Wola section, the sun was setting, larger than usual, as yellow as gold. Farther out lay a huge, sulphur-yellow cloud blazing like a fiery river upon a bed of glowing coals. It made me think of the River of Fire in Gehenna, where the wicked are punished.

Mendel and I, even though we were best friends, were also silently engaged in a struggle. He was envious of me because my father was a rabbi and because we lived in an apartment with two rooms, a kitchen, and a balcony. He was always trying to prove that he was the stronger, cleverer, and more learned one. Now I was trying to invent a story as wonderful as Mendel's, or even more so. Abruptly I said, "I also have a secret I've never told you."

Mendel's Tartar eyes filled with mockery. "What's your secret?"

"Swear you won't tell anyone."

Mendel swore with a false smile and a look that almost seemed to be winking at someone unseen.

I said: "I know the Cabala!"

Mendel's eyes narrowed into slits. "You? How could you know it?"

"My father taught it to me."

"Is it allowed—to teach a boy the Cabala?"

"I'm different from other boys."

"Well . . .! So what did you learn?"

"I can create pigeons. I can make wine flow from the wall. I can recite a spell and fly up in the air."

"What else?"

"I can take seven-mile steps."

"What else?"

"I can turn invisible. And I can change pebbles into pearls."

Mendel began to twist one of his sidelocks. Just as mine were disheveled, his were twirled tightly like two little horns.

"If that's so, you could have more money than the richest man in the world."

"Yes. True."

"So why haven't you got it?"

"One is not allowed to make use of the Cabala. It's very dangerous. There is one spell that if you utter it the sky turns red like fire, the sea begins to churn, and the waves rise until they touch the clouds. All the animals drown; all the buildings collapse; an abyss opens and the whole world becomes black as midnight."

"How does that spell go?"

"Do you want me to destroy the world?"

"Nnn . . . no."

"When I'm older, I will get permission from the prophet Elijah to fly to the Holy Land. There I will live in a ruin and bring the Messiah."

Mendel bent his head. He picked up a piece of paper from the sidewalk and began to fold it into a bird. I expected him to ask many more questions, but he remained stubbornly silent. All at once I felt that in my ambition I had overdone it; it was Mendel's fault. He had driven me to try to make myself too great. My own words had frightened me. One is not allowed to play games with the Cabala. Terrible nightmares might invade my sleep. I said, "Mendel, I want to go home."

"Let's go."

We moved toward the gate that led to Mirowski Street,

no longer walking with our arms about each other's shoulders, but a little apart. Instead of drawing us closer, our talk had separated us. But why? I suddenly noticed how ragged Mendel's clothes were. The toe of his left boot had opened like a mouth and the nails stuck up like teeth. We came out on Mirowski Street, which was littered with horse dung, straw off farmers' carts, rotten fruit thrown out by the fruit merchants. Between the two city markets stood a building where ice was manufactured. Though it was still day outside, inside the electric lights were burning. Wheels turned rapidly; leather conveyor belts flowed; signals lit up and extinguished themselves. Not a single person was to be seen. Uncanny noises came from in there. Under our feet, through grates, we could see into cellars where tanks full of water were turning to ice. For quite a while Mendel and I stood there gawking; then we moved on. I asked suddenly, "Who feeds her?"

Mendel seemed to wake up. "What are you talking about?"

"I mean the girl with the golden slippers."

"There are maidservants there."

Not far from the second market, I saw two coins, two copper six-groschen pieces that lay side by side as if someone had placed them on the sidewalk. I bent down and picked them up. Mendel, seeing them too, cried out, "Partners!"

I gave him one immediately, though at the same time I thought that if it had been he who had picked them up, he would not have given me one. Mendel looked at the coin from every angle and then he said, "If you can turn pebbles into pearls, what do you want a six-groschen for?"

I would have liked to ask him: And if your father is such a rich robber, what do *you* want a six-groschen for? But something held me back. I was suddenly aware how yellowish his skin was and what high cheekbones he had. Something in that face spoke to me, but what it was saying I couldn't grasp. The lobes of his ears were attached to his cheeks; the wings of his nostrils rose and fell like a horse's. The corners of his mouth curled with envy and his black eyes scorned me. He asked, "What are you going to buy with your money? Candy?"

"I will give it to charity," I answered.

"Here—here's a poor man."

In the middle of the sidewalk, in a board with little wheels, sat half a man; he looked as if he had been sawed across the middle. Both hands gripped pieces of wood padded with cloth, on which he leaned. He wore his cap visor over his eyes, and a torn jacket. On his neck hung a cup to throw alms in. I knew very well what could be bought for six groschen—colored pencils, storybooks, halvah—but some pride ordered me not to hesitate. Stretching my arm out, I tossed the coin in the cup. The cripple, as if afraid I might change my mind and ask for it back, rolled away so quickly that he almost knocked somebody over.

Mendel's eyebrows came together. "When do you study the Cabala? At night?"

"After midnight."

"So what's going on in heaven?"

I lifted my eyes to the sky and it was red, with black and blue streaks across the middle, as if a storm were coming. Two birds flapped up, screeching, calling each other. The moon had come out. Only a minute ago it had been day. Now night had fallen. The women at the street stands were cleaning up their merchandise. A man with a long stick was walking from one lamppost to the next, lighting the gas flames. I wanted to answer Mendel but couldn't think what to say. I was ashamed of my pretending, as though I were suddenly a grown-up. I said, "Mendel, enough of these lies."

"What's the matter, huh?"

"I don't study the Cabala and your father is not a robber."

Mendel stopped. "Why are you so angry? Because you gave your six-groschen to the beggar?"

"I'm not angry. If you have a palace in the forest, you don't carry coals all day long for Haim Leib. And you haven't got a girl with golden slippers. It's all a fairy story."

"So you want to quarrel? Don't think just because your father is a rabbi I'm going to flatter you. Maybe I have lied, but you'll never know the truth."

"What is there to know? You made it all up."

"I'll become a bandit, a real one."

"They will roast you in Gehenna."

"Let them roast me. I'm in love!"

I looked at him, shocked. "You're lying again."

"No, it's the truth. If not, may God strike me dead on the spot."

I knew Mendel would not swear such an oath in vain. I felt cold, as if someone with icy fingers had touched my ribs. "With a girl?"

"What else? With a boy? She lives in our courtyard. We'll get engaged. We'll go to my brother's in America."

"Aren't you ashamed . . . ?"

"Jacob also was in love. He kissed Rachel. It is written in the Bible."

"Girl-chaser!"

And I began to run. Mendel screamed something after me and I even imagined that he was pursuing me. I ran until I reached the Radzymin study house. Near the door Mendel's father was praying, a tall, lean man with a sharp Adam's apple, a bent back, and a face that was coal black, like a chimney sweep's. His loins were girded with a rope. He shook, leaned forward, and beat his chest. I imagined he must be asking God's forgiveness for the blasphemies of his son.

At the east wall stood my father in a velvet gaberdine, wearing a broad-brimmed hat and a white sash about his waist. His head touched the wall as he swayed back and forth. A single candle burned in the menorah. No, I did not yet know the Cabala. But I knew that everything that was happening to me tonight was filled with its mysteries. I felt a deep sadness such as I had never felt before. When my father finished praying, I walked over to him and said, "Papa, I have to talk to you."

At my serious tone, my father looked at me out of his blue eyes. "What's the matter?"

"Papa, I want you to teach me the Cabala."

"So that's it? At your age it is forbidden to study the Cabala. It is written that these mysteries should not be divulged to a man before he is thirty."

"Papa, I want it now."

My father clutched his red beard. "What's your hurry? You can be a decent man without the Cabala."

"Papa, can one destroy the world with a holy spell?"

"The ancient saints could do everything. We can do nothing. Come, let's go home."

We moved toward the gate, where Rebecca, the baker's

daughter, stood with baskets full of fresh rolls, bread, bagels warm from the oven. Women were picking over the baked goods and their crusts crackled. My father and I walked out into the street, where the gas lamps cast a yellow glow. Between two chimneys spouting smoke and sparks hung a large, blood-red moon.

"Is it true that people live there?" I asked.

My father was silent for a while. "What makes you think so? Nothing is known. Cabala is only for strong brains. When weak little brains are immersed in the Cabala—one can easily fall into insanity."

My father's words frightened me. I felt myself close to madness.

He said, "You are still a boy. When, God willing, you grow up, get married, have more sense, then you will find out what you can do."

"I'm not going to get married."

"What else? Stay a bachelor? It is written: 'He created it not in vain. He formed it to be inhabited.' You will grow up, be matched with a girl, and get engaged."

"What girl?"

"Who can know in advance?"

At that moment I realized why I was so sad. The street was full of girls but I didn't know who was going to be my betrothed. She, the one destined for me, didn't know either. It could be that we both bought candy in the same store, that we passed each other, looked at each other, not knowing that we were going to be man and wife. I began to look among the crowd. The street was full of girls my age, some a little younger, some older. One walked and licked an ice-cream cone. Another one nibbled cheese cake at Esther's candy store, holding it between her thumb and middle finger, with her pinky lifted up elegantly. A girl carrying books and notebooks under her arm, with red ribbons in her braids, a pleated skirt and a black apron, had black-stockinged legs that looked like a doll's. The streets were full of the aroma of fresh bagels, of breezes coming from the Vistula and the Praga forest. Around the street lamps a myriad of winged creatures—moths, butterflies, gnats—whirled, deceived by the light into believing night was day. I looked at the upper floors, where girls stood on balconies, gazed out of windows. They were talking, singing, laughing. I listened to the noise of sewing machines, to a gramophone playing. Behind a window I saw the dark shadow of a girl. I imagined she was staring at me through the mesh of the curtain. I said to my father, "Papa, can you find out from the Cabala who you are going to get engaged to?"

My father stopped. "What do you have to know for? They know in heaven and that is enough."

For a while we walked in silence. Then my father asked, "Son, what has happened to you?"

All the lampposts became bent and all the lights foggy as my eyes filled with tears. "Papa, I don't know."

"You are growing up, my son. That is what is happening to you."

And my father suddenly did something he had never done before: he bent down and kissed my forehead.

Chanting in the synagogue

The Satin Coat

It was our clothes that made our poverty apparent. Food was cheap, nor were we big eaters. Mother prepared a soup with potatoes, browned flour, and fried onions. Only on Passover did we eat eggs. True, a pound of meat cost twenty kopecks, but it produced a lot of broth. Flour, buckwheat, chickpeas, beans were not expensive.

But clothes were dear.

My mother would wear a dress for years and take such good care of it that it still looked new. A pair of shoes lasted her three years. Father's satin capote was somewhat frayed, but so were the capotes and skullcaps of most of the congregation at the nearby Radzymin study house. It was worse for us children. My boots wore out every three months. Mother complained that other children were careful but I messed up everything.

At the Radzymin study house, on the Sabbath, boys wore

satin or silk gaberdines, velvet hats, polished boots, and sashes. I went in a gaberdine that was too small for me. Now and again I did get a new piece of clothing, but not until what I had was nothing but rags.

But there was one time just before Passover when suddenly we got lucky.

This was always a good period of the year for us, for Father would get commissions for selling to a Gentile—our janitor, to be exact—people's hametz; that is, all those items, such as unleavened bread, flour, kneading boards, and rolling pins, that are not permitted in a Jewish household during Passover. There was a certain element of the spurious in this transaction because immediately after Passover all this property reverted to its original owners.

From listening to those who came to sell their hametz, I learned how little we had, in comparison to them. They had to dispose of whisky, cherry brandy, preserves; we, nothing but a few pots and pans. Occasionally someone listed a stable with horses, although I am uncertain how a horse can possible be considered as hametz. But, it's true, horses do eat oats. There was one man whose son was traveling with a circus and who felt it necessary to declare as hametz the entire menagerie.

Why was this particular Passover a lucky one for us? To begin with, we had received many fine gifts on Purim, which precedes Passover by only four weeks. But best of all, Jonathan, a tailor from Leoncin, where my father had once been rabbi, had moved to Warsaw. Jonathan, a tall, slender man with a pockmarked face, a spare beard, and brilliant eyes, dressed like a Hasid, not like a tailor. On the Sabbath he wore a satin capote; he took snuff, went to visit the Radzymin rabbi on holidays, and was, in fact, a learned man. Now that he was in Warsaw, he visited my father to discuss erudite matters. Seeing the condition of my wardrobe, Jonathan offered to clothe me on credit. We could pay for the material at our convenience.

What a stroke of luck! As he measured me, he beamed proudly, treating me as though I were a member of his own family. He had, as a matter of fact, been present at my circumcision. Noting my various measurements in chalk, he remarked to my mother, "Oh Rebbetzin, how the years do fly."

Jonathan apparently had no other work at the moment, for almost immediately after taking my measurements he had me down to his house for a fitting, testing me on my Hebrew at the same time, appreciative of the opportunity to use a few Hebrew phrases of his own and discourse in a scholarly way. Although he was only a tailor, he had a great love for Judaism and savored every Hebrew word. At the time of his marriage he had been familiar with only the required prayers, but later he studied the Scriptures in Yiddish, learned the Mishnah with a teacher, and got help from students. Ridiculed in Leoncin for his aspirations, he proved despite this that it is never too late to learn. Father had been one of those who helped Jonathan transform himself into a scholar, and the tailor was eager to show his gratitude.

His house was alive with girls, noise, and the odors of cooking. His three daughters, who had known me since early childhood and now saw me being outfitted like a man for a satin capote, could not keep from making comments. With their mother, they argued about whether the capote was the right length. My mother, in a lavish gesture, had also ordered new boots for me from Michael the cobbler. I was to look completely done over when I entered the study house on Passover.

Although I had had no great passion for clothes, I soon acquired one, becoming more intrigued with each new addition to my wardrobe. New shirts were being sewn for me by a seamstress, and my new velvet hat already lay in a box in the closet. I had visions of entering the study house triumphantly on Passover night, and amazing all the boys there. Previously, my clothes had made me feel inferior to them, even though I was more informed than they, knew about Zionism, socialism, the weight of air, and the origin of coal—having learned it all from my brother Joshua and an almanac. But now they would see that I could also have a new outfit for the holiday. Most tailors did not keep their word about having things ready for a holiday, but Jonathan was different.

All the same, I felt a premonition of disaster, for how could things go as smoothly as I dreamed them? But, on the other hand, what could go wrong, and why was I so apprehensive? Yes, of course, Jonathan might burn the cloth while pressing it, or the capote could even be stolen. From *The Rod of Punishment*, as well as from my own experience, I knew that the material world was full of snares. I had become too enamored of its pleasures.

Even so, things kept going smoothly. True to his promise, Michael the cobbler delivered a pair of boots that gleamed as though lacquered. The satin capote already hung in our closet. Shortly before Passover, people began coming to our house to sell their hametz, and standing behind Father's chair, I watched the ceremony, which wasn't terribly complicated.

The person selling the articles was told to touch the tip of a handkerchief, signifying that he agreed to sell his things to a Gentile. The bill of sale was begun, as follows: "The hametz of Reb so-and-so . . ." and in a mixture of Yiddish and Hebrew all the items were listed. I was sure I could do the job myself, if I had the chance.

The men would chat, sign, and talk about other Passovers. My father asked a deaf man if he had any alcohol to declare.

"Yes. A little wheat flour."

The others shouted into his ear, "Alcohol! Brandy!"

"Oh. Why didn't you say so? Of course I have alcohol."

A widow who came to sell her hametz didn't know how to sign her name, and Father told her to touch the pen, but she couldn't understand what he meant. Father repeated, "Just the shank of the pen, for a second."

She didn't know what "shank of the pen" meant. Efficient though she was in her stall at the marketplace, she was bewildered by Father's study and all the men there. Mother came in and explained what had to be done, and the woman was greatly relieved, and said, "Rebbetzin, I have no trouble understanding *you* . . ."

And she touched the pen.

Then, unknotting a kerchief, she counted out several copper coins. "Have a good Passover," she said to Father.

"May you live to see the next," he replied.

Suddenly, over her wind- and sun-ravaged face, the tears gushed, and everyone grew silent. After she left, Father said, "Who knows who is best-loved by God? She may be a saint . . ."

Mother reentered the study looking flushed and grimy, as she had come from stoking the stove to remove all traces of hametz. In the bedroom, the ordinary matzoh was suspended in sheets from the ceiling. The two portions of matzoh baked with extra care, to be eaten only by the most devout, had been put aside for Father and Mother. Mother, a rabbi's daughter, was granted this privilege usually reserved for men.

Everything went according to ritual. The night preceding Passover, Father searched the house, in the traditional manner, for hametz to be burned the next day. One was allowed to eat hametz until nine the next morning—and after that until sundown, neither hametz nor matzoh. From mashed potatoes, eggs, and sugar, Mother then prepared for us children a pancake that was indescribably delicious.

At sunset Passover began. So far nothing had gone wrong. I washed, put on a new shirt, new trousers, the new boots, the new velvet hat, and the satin capote that glistened festively. I had become a boy from a wealthy family, and I walked downstairs with my father. Neighbors, opening their doors to look at me, spat to ward off the evil eye; and the girls who sat on thresholds grating the traditional bitter herb, horseradish, smiled as I went by, while their eyes teared from the horseradish. Girls my own age, who had so short a time before shared toys and pebbles with me, looked on with approval. Now that we were growing up, they were too shy to speak to me, but their glances were reminiscent.

My father and I went to the Radzymin study house, climbed the stairs, and tried the door. It was locked, and a notice hung there: "Gas out of order. Closed until after the holiday."

Closed on Passover night? The Radzymin study house? Incredible! We didn't know what to do, and remained there, confounded. *The Rod of Punishment* had been right. One should not depend on the comforts of the material world; there was nothing in it but disappointments. Only service to God mattered, and the study of the Torah. Everything else crumbled . . .

At the Minsk study house, where we went to pray, no one knew me or cared about my new outfit. There were a few boys I recognized, but, as strangers here, we all huddled near the exit.

It was a harsh blow and a lesson not to get involved in worldly vanities.

Israel Joshua Singer, in his twenties

A Boy
Philosopher

My brother Israel Joshua, because of his emancipated
views, found it difficult to speak to my father, whose only
response was, "Unbeliever! Enemy of Judaism!" On the
other hand, my brother would have long talks with my
mother, and often, in my presence, they would discuss me.

"What's to become of him?" my brother would argue.
"Must he marry and open a store or become a teacher in a
cheder? There are too many stores already and too many
teachers. If you glance out the window, Mother, you can see
what Jews look like—stooped, despondent, living in filth.
Watch them drag their feet as they walk . . .Listen to them
speak. It's no wonder everyone else thinks of them as
Asiatics. And how long do you think Europe will stand for
this clump of Asia in its midst?"

"Gentiles have always hated Jews," Mother said. "Even
if a Jew wore a top hat, he'd be hated, because he stands for

truth.''

"What truth? Does anyone know what the truth is? Every religion has its own prophets and holy books. Have you heard of Buddhism? Buddha was just like Moses and he performed miracles too.''

Mother made a face as if she had some bad-tasting thing in her mouth. "How can you dare to compare them--an idol worshipper and the saint Moses? Woe is me! What my own flesh and blood says!''

"Listen, Mother. Buddha was no idol worshipper, he was a very profound thinker. He agreed with our own prophets. As for Confucius . . .''

"No more! Don't speak of those heathens in the same breath as our saints. The Buddha came from India... I remember that from *The Paths of the World*. They burn widows there and kill aged parents while everyone celebrates.''

"You don't mean India.''

"Who cares? They're all idolaters. A cow, to them, is a god. The Chinese, on the other hand, throw away their extra daughters. We Jews alone believe in one God; all the others worship trees, snakes, crocodiles, everything you can think of . . . They're all wicked. Even while they say, 'Turn the other cheek,' they murder each other and go on sinning. You want to compare them to us?''

"If we had our own country, we'd be involved in wars also. King David wasn't such a compassionate man . . .''

"Shush! Watch what you say! May God have mercy on you! Don't touch our anointed. King David and Solomon were both prophets. The Talmud says it is wrong to consider David a sinner . . .''

"I know what it says. But what about Bathsheba?"

Since that was my mother's name, every time I heard about Bathsheba I felt that Mother was somehow implicated. Mother's face flushed.

"Sh! You read idiotic books and repeat everything! King David will live forever and those trashy books aren't worth the paper they're printed on. Who are the authors? Loafers."

These discussions intrigued me. I had already discussed the subjects with my brother. I had no inclination to be a storekeeper or a Talmud teacher or have a "slovenly wife and a bunch of brats," as my brother put it. Once he said, "He'd better become a worker."

"With God's help he'll be a rabbi, not a worker. He takes after his grandfather," Mother said.

"A rabbi? Where? Everywhere there are rabbis. Why do we need so many?"

"And why so many workers? A rabbi, no matter how poor he is, is still better off than a shoemaker."

"Just wait until the workers unite."

"They'll never unite. Each one wants to steal the other's bread. Why don't soldiers unite and refuse to go to war?"

"Oh, that will come too."

"When? There's so much unnecessary killing. Every Monday and Thursday there's a Turkish crisis. The world is full of evil, that's all there is to it. We'll never find peace here—only in the other world."

"You're a pessimist, Mother."

"Wait, my soup is burning!"

How often I listened to discussions of this sort, with each side effectively destroying the arguments of the other! But when it came to proving the case, what was relied on were easily disputed quotations. I remained silent, keeping my opinions to myself. The Gentiles were idol worshippers, true, but King David actually had sinned. And when Jews lived in their own country, they too had killed. And it was true that each religion had its own prophets, but who could say which ones had spoken to God? These were questions that Mother did not seem able to answer.

"What kind of trade appeals to you?" my brother asked. "How about becoming an engraver and carving letters on brass and copper?"

"Good."

"Or a watchmaker?"

"Too hard."

"You can learn it. How about a doctor?"

"Let him be. What do doctors know? They take money for nothing. Jews will always be Jews and they'll always need rabbis."

"In Germany, rabbis attend universities!" my brother announced proudly.

"I know those reform rabbis," my mother said. "They can find a way to permit eating meat with milk dishes, but how can they justify shaving, when it's contrary to Mosaic law? What kind of rabbi defies the Torah?"

"They use a kind of powder for shaving, not a razor."

"Are they ashamed of beards because they want to look like Gentiles? If their rabbis are like that, I can imagine what the rest of them are like."

Suddenly Father appeared from his study. "Let's end these discussions once and for all," he cried out. "Tell me—who created the world? All they see is the body and they think that's all there is. The body is nothing but a tool. Without the soul, the body is like a slab of wood. The souls of those who gorge themselves and swill are evil and wander about in the desert, tortured by devils and hobgoblins. They've learned the truth too late. Even Gehenna is closed to them. The world is full of transmigrant souls . . ." Father said. "When a soul leaves a body unclean, it is returned to earth to wander about again, as a worm or a reptile, and its grief is tremendous . . ."

"Then, according to you, Father, God is wicked."

"Enemy of Israel! God loves man, but when man defiles himself, he must be cleansed."

"How can you expect a Chinaman to know the Torah?"

"Why worry about a Chinaman? Just think about God and His wonders. When I open a holy book I sometimes see a mite smaller than a pinpoint walking about. It too is a wonder of God. Can all the professors in the world get together and create one mite?"

"Well, what does it all add up to?"

After Father left and Mother went out to buy something, I asked my brother, "Who did create the mite?"

"Nature."

"And who created nature?"

"And who created God?" my brother rejoined. "Something had to come from itself, and later everything developed out of this original matter. From the energy of the sun, the first bacteria were created at the edge of the sea. Conditions happened to be favorable. Creatures fought among themselves and the strongest survived. Bacteria formed into colonies and a division of the functions began."

"But where did it all come from in the first place?"

"It was always like this; no one knows. Every people has

made up its own rites. There was the rabbi, for example, who said you mustn't urinate in the snow on the Sabbath because it resembles plowing . . .''

Although later in my life I read a great deal of philosophy, I never found more compelling arguments than those that came up in my own kitchen. At home I even heard about strange facts that are in the province of psychic research. And after such discussions I would go outside to play; but as I went through the games of tag and hide-and-seek, my imagination was at work. What if I found the kind of water that made one wise and a party to all secrets, or if the prophet Elijah arrived to teach me all the Seven Wisdoms of the World? And what if I found a telescope that saw directly into heaven? My thoughts, which were not the thoughts of other boys, made me both proud and lonely. And always there were the ultimate questions: What is right? What must I do? Why does God remain silent in the Seventh Heaven? Once a man came up to me and asked, "What's the matter? Why do you think so hard? Are you afraid the sky will fall on you?"

Life in a Warsaw courtyard

The Shot
at Sarajevo

For a long time our family had discussed the possibility of moving from our apartment at 10 Krochmalna Street, where we used kerosene lamps because there was no gas and shared an outhouse in the courtyard with everyone else in the building. This outhouse was the bane of my childhood. It was dark there all the time, and filthy. Rats and mice were everywhere, overhead as well as on the floor. Many children, because of it, were stricken with constipation and developed nervous disorders.

The staircase was another plague, because certain children preferred it to the outhouse. To make things worse, there were women who used it as a garbage dump. The janitor, who was supposed to light lamps along the stairway, seldom did so, and when he did, we were deprived of them by 10:30. The tiny, smoke stained lamps gave so little light that the darkness seemed to thicken around them. When I used this murky stairway, I was pursued by all the devils, evil spirits, demons, and imps of whom my parents spoke to prove that there is a God and life after death. Cats raced along beside me. From behind closed doors, one often heard a wailing for the dead. At the courtyard gate a funeral procession might be waiting. I was breathless by the time I reached my door. Nightmares began to come to me, so horrifying that I would wake from sleep drenched in sweat.

We found it hard enough to pay the twenty-four rubles a month rent for a front apartment and balcony; then how could we afford to move to 12 Krochmalna Street, a new building with gas lights and toilets, where the rent would be twenty-seven? However, we decided that changing our place would change our luck . . .

It was the spring of 1914.

The newspapers had for years referred to the explosive situation in the Balkans and the rivalry between England and Germany. But there were no newspapers in my home any more. It was my brother Israel Joshua who brought them there, and he had moved out after an argument with my father.

Everyone told us to change apartments. The No. 12 landlord, Leizer Przepiorko, was an Orthodox millionaire. Reputedly stingy, he had all the same never evicted a Jew. The superintendent, Reb Isaiah, was an old Kotzk Hasid, a friend of my father's. Since No. 12 had a gate that led to Mirowski Street, to the markets, Father would be rabbi for both Krochmalna and Mirowski Streets. Also, many lawsuits, weddings, and divorces were scheduled at that time, which meant extra money for us. We decided to move.

The new, ground-floor apartment, freshly painted, faced

a bakery, and the kitchen window looked out on a wall. There were five or six stories over us.

No. 12 was like a city. It had three enormous courtyards. The dark entrance always smelled of freshly baked bread, rolls, and bagels, caraway seed, and smoke. Koppel the baker's yeasty breads were always out in his courtyard, rising on boards. In No. 12 there were also two Hasidic study houses, the Radzymin and the Minsk, as well as a synagogue for those who opposed Hasidism. There was also a stall where cows were kept chained to the wall all year round. In some cellars, fruit had been stored by dealers from Mirowski Street; in others, eggs were preserved in lime. Wagons arrived there from the provinces. No. 12 swarmed with Torah, prayer, commerce, and toil. Kerosene lamps were unheard of. Some apartments even had telephones.

But it had not been an easy move, even though Nos. 10 and 12 adjoined. We had to load our things in a wagon, and some of them broke. Our wardrobe was unbelievably heavy, a fortress with lion heads on oaken doors and a cornice covered with engravings that weighed a ton. How it had been dragged from Radzymin is beyond me.

I will never forget lighting the two-jet gas lamp for the first time. I was dazzled and intimidated by the strange radiance that filled the apartment and even seemed to penetrate my skull. Demons would have a hard time hiding here.

The toilet delighted me. So did the gas oven in the kitchen. It was not necessary any more to prepare kindling for tea or bring in coal. You only had to strike a match and watch the blue flame ignite. Nor would I have to drag jugs of kerosene from the store, since there was a gas meter where one inserted a forty-groschen piece to get gas. And I knew many people here because it was at the Radzymin study house in this courtyard that I had always prayed.

For a while, our predicted good luck came true. Father's lawsuits were numerous. Things went so well that year that he decided to enroll me in a cheder again. I was past cheder age, but at 22 Twarda Street there was a special cheder for older boys where the teacher lectured instead of studying with his pupils. Some of my friends from other cheders attended this one.

I was reading non-religious books at this time and had developed a taste for heresy; it was rather ridiculous, therefore, for me to be attending cheder again. My friends and I made fun of the teacher, who had a yellow beard and bulging eyes, spoke with a village accent, ate raw onions, and smoked stinking tobacco in a long pipe. He was divorced and matchmakers came to whisper secrets in his hairy ears . . .

Suddenly there were rumors of war. The Austrian Crown Prince had been shot, they said, in Serbia. Newspaper extras with huge headlines appeared, printed on only one side. In our discussions of politics, we boys decided that it would be preferable for Germany to win—what would be gained from Russian rule? German occupation would put all Jews into short jackets, and the *gymnasium* would be compulsory. What could be better than going to worldly schools in uniforms and decorated caps? At the same time we were convinced (much more than the German General Staff) that Germany's strength could never match the combined forces of Russia, France, and England. One boy speculated that because of their shared language it was only natural that America should step in to help England . . .

My father began to read newspapers. New words were

prevalent--mobilization, ultimatum, neutrality. The rival governments sent notes. The kings wrote letters one to the other and called themselves Nicky and Willy. The common people—workers, porters—met in groups on Krochmalna Street to discuss conditions.

Suddenly it was the Ninth Day of Ab, the Sunday that is the postponed fast day. It was also the beginning of the First World War.

Women were everywhere, buying up food. Small though they were, they carried huge baskets of flour, groats, beans, and whatever else they could find in the stores, which were closed half the time. First the storekeepers rejected worn-out bank notes, then they demanded silver and gold instead of paper. They began hoarding their stock in order to increase prices.

People were in a festive mood, as if it were Purim. Weeping women trailed their husbands, bearded Jews with tiny white pins in their lapels, indicating that they had been called up for military service. Both annoyed and amused, these men strutted along while behind them children carried sticks on their shoulders and called out military commands.

Running home from the Radzymin study house, my father announced that he had heard the war would be over in two weeks. "They have cannons that can kill a thousand Cossacks at one blow."

"Woe . . . .." cried my mother. "What is the world coming to?"

Father consoled her: "Well, there won't be any more rent to pay, now that the government has made a moratorium . . ."

My mother went on, "And who will want lawsuits?

Where will we get the money to eat?"

We were in trouble. There were no more letters from my sister, who had married and lived in Antwerp; and my twenty-one-year-old brother, Israel Joshua, was supposed to report to Tomaszow, my father's home town, for conscription in the Russian army. He decided to go into hiding instead. We had no money with which to stock up on food, as our neighbors were doing. Knowing how hungry I was going to become, I experienced an extraordinary gnawing appetite. I ate insatiably. Mother would come home flushed, moaning about the food shortage.

Now, for the first time, I began to hear unflattering bits of gossip about other Jews on the street. Jewish storekeepers, just like the Gentiles, were hiding goods, raising prices, trying to capitalize on the war. Moshe the paper dealer, who lived in our courtyard, boasted in the study house about his wife's purchase of five hundred rubles' worth of food. "Thank God," he said, "I have provisions for a year. How much longer can the war last?" And he smilingly stroked his silver beard.

There was considerable confusion. Young men with blue cards were able to study the Talmud, but pale and concerned, the green-carded ones tried to lose weight to avoid the draft. Men who sold flour and groats were lucky, but not so the now unemployed bookbinders, teachers, and scribes. The Germans captured Kalisz, Bedzin, and Czestochowa. I felt the burden of growing up and expected a mysterious catastrophe. It seemed to me that if only we had accepted the lack of toilets and gas in No. 10, we might have been spared all this . . .

This was the war between Gog and Magog, Father said.

And every day he discovered new omens proving that the Messiah was soon to come . . .

Studying at cheder

Hunger

It turned out that the German occupation of Warsaw did not result in the Jews wearing modern dress and all Jewish boys being sent to *gymnasiums*. Jews remained in their gaberdines and the boys continued to attend cheder. Only the German constables in blue capes were new, and Polish and Jewish militiamen carried rubber truncheons in the streets. But the shortage of goods increased, the stores became more depleted, the women peddling fruit and provisions in Yanash's bazaar and the markets had almost nothing left to sell, and hunger began to be felt everywhere. German marks now mingled with Russian money, and the editorial writer of the Yiddish paper *The Moment* left off praising the Allies and began to vilify them. He prophesied the German occupation of St. Petersburg.

People came to worship at our house for the High Holy Days, but most of the women were unable to pay for pews.

When Asher the dairyman rose to recite, both men and women began to wail. The words "Some will perish by the sword and some from starvation, some by fire and some by flood" had become grimly vivid. One felt that Providence was preparing something terrible. Our Rosh Hashanah meal was meager, even though one is supposed to eat well on a holy day and especially at the beginning of the New Year. Father had not been called in very often for lawsuits, weddings, or divorces, though he was often consulted on questions of dietary law, for which he received no payment.

Nevertheless, the Germans did bring us one bit of luck, in the form of my brother Joshua's freedom. He no longer had to hide from the Russians under an assumed name. He could visit us, but every time he did, there was a quarrel between him and my father.

My brother and his worldly books had sown the seeds of heresy in my mind. We Jews with our belief in a God whose existence cannot be proved had neither country nor land to work, nor had we devoted ourselves to the study of trades. Storekeepers with nothing to sell now roamed the streets.

At 10 Krochmalna Street we had shared a hut in the courtyard with poor neighbors during the Feast of Tabernacles, but at No. 12, with families better off than we, the contrast between our food and theirs was all too evident. I especially remember my mother serving me a soup in which there was nothing "under the broth," as the saying goes. Reb Isaiah the superintendent, noticing this, threw in a pretzel, much to my consternation. All the same, I was grateful that he had been so considerate.

The war demonstrated for me how unnecessary rabbis were, my father among them. From all the towns and villages,

rabbis and other ecclesiastics converged on Warsaw, deject-
edly walking the streets in their silk gaberdines, looking for
a piece of bread. Thousands of matchmakers, brokers, and
small businessmen had no way of earning a living. Starving
men dozed over their Talmud volumes in study houses and
houses of prayer. The winter was cold and there was no fuel
for the ovens.

In the house of prayer, some Jews explained that when
Esau is stuffing himself, Jacob can find a small bone
somewhere; but when Esau goes to war and suffers, it's the
end for Jacob. If only God would take pity on Israel and send
help! But apparently heaven was not thinking of Jews at that
time.

I would like to tell about Joseph Mattes, who devoted
himself to religious matters while his wife sold geese. Even
before the German occupation, the cost of a goose had risen
to twenty-five rubles. Who on Krochmalna Street could
afford such luxury? Joseph Mattes, his wife, daughters, and
their husbands were left penniless. While other goose dealers
had managed to put something aside, Joseph Mattes had
given his whole fortune to charity and the Radzymin rabbi.

The extent of his poverty was not known to those in the
study house, and besides, the war had intensified individual
selfishness. Men with full pantries worshipped alongside
those who had nothing, but seldom thought of helping them.
There wasn't actually that much food to share. Fear of the
future haunted everyone. No one thought any longer that the
war would end soon.

I became personally acquainted with hunger, and I noticed
that the skin hung loosely on Joseph Mattes's pale face. But
his son-in-law, another Israel Joshua, was even paler and more

emaciated. Tugging at a barely sprouting beard, he hovered over the holy books, sighing and stealing glances beyond them. This delicate young man suffered from shame as well. He yearned to serve the Almighty, but hunger tormented him. Sinking ever more deeply into the Hasidic books, he twisted his sidelocks incessantly. What could he do about it, I wondered, this son-in-law living on his father-in-law's bounty and starving? Timid and weak, prematurely round-shouldered, he could do nothing but study and pray, and look into the *Grace of Elimelech* or *The Holiness of Levi* . . .

One Friday evening, Joseph Mattes, who had given his fortune toward Hasid banquets and the support of the Radzymin rabbi, slammed his fist on the table, shouting, "Men, I don't have the bread to usher in the Sabbath!"

His words were an indication of the times. Bread had to be substituted for the Sabbath wine when making the benediction.

For a moment there was silence, and after that, tumult, confusion. Reb Joseph's sons retreated into corners, painfully ashamed of what their father had said. Israel Joshua became chalk-white. Despite the collection of bread, fish, and Sabbath loaves that was taken up that night, nothing really changed. Paupers remained paupers, and benefactors were few. I felt terribly afraid that the same thing might happen to my father.

Like most of the rabbis, the Radzymin rabbi had moved to Warsaw, where he owned property. He was reputedly wealthy, but this was dubious, since real estate had ceased to provide income. I do not know whether he helped the Hasidim or not. Nevertheless, we were so much in need that Father paid a visit to the Radzymin rabbi's wife, the so-called "young rebbetzin." Unable to lend Father anything, she begged him to accept her diamond ring and pawn it. Father protested, but the rebbetzin swore: "By my life and health, take it!" showing him, at the same time, a Talmudic passage that prohibits the wearing of jewelry while others starve.

When Father, in his shame, returned home carrying the ring in a box, Mother made a face, perhaps from jealousy. But when Father pawned the ring, we bought flour, bread, and groats. Meat was too expensive. We began to use cocoa butter, which could be eaten with both meat and milk dishes.

The most difficult thing to bear at that time was the cold, and we could not afford to heat the apartment. Our pipes froze and it was impossible to use the toilet. For weeks, frost patterns decorated our windows and icicles hung from the frames. When I was thirsty, I broke off an icicle and sucked it.

At night the cold was unendurable. No amount of covering was enough. The wind, rustling through our apartment, made me think of goblins. Huddled in bed, I had fantasies of treasures, black magic, incantations that would help my parents, Joseph Mattes, and everyone else who suffered. I imagined myself Elijah, the Messiah, and what-not... Like the biblical Joseph, I filled storehouses with food and threw them open in the seven years of famine. A word from me made whole armies tremble, as well as their generals and the emperors behind them. I gave the Radzymin rebbetzin a basketful of diamonds.

It was too cold to get out of bed. Mother, my brother Moshe, and I never got up until late in the day, but Father forced himself to dress. The water for his ablutions froze. He rubbed his hands on the windowpanes and placed a pan of ice on the stove. He had learned to use the gas jet. The meter still required a forty-groschen piece but tea was his one luxury, although it consisted of hot water with just a pinch of tea leaves. Sugar was unavailable and he detested saccharin. Wrapped in a padded gaberdine, he drank his tea and studied, writing with frozen fingers. In *The Face of Joshua* everything was as it had been, and *Roar of the Lion* asked the ancient questions: Is the reading of *Shema* based on Mosaic or rabbinic law? Is one obliged to repeat all of it, according to Mosaic law, or only the first verse? Or the first section? Only there did Father feel comforted.

Before the war I used to buy him several small packs of cigarettes a day, and he also used to smoke a pipe. But now that cigarettes cost so much, he would fill his pipe with a peasant type of tobacco called Majorka. Smoking, drinking weak tea, he studied endlessly. What else was there but the Torah?

My brother Israel Joshua was living at home again, sleeping on a table in my father's study, where the cold was worse than it was outside. My mother covered him with whatever she could find.

In spite of the terrible frosts, mice invaded our apartment, attacking books and clothes, leaping about at night with suicidal abandon. Mother obtained a cat, but this creature observed their activities indifferently, her yellow eyes implying, "Let them run. Who cares?"

Her mind seemed to be far away, she was always dozing, dreaming. "Who knows?" Father said. "She might be a reincarnation . . ."

Father took care of her respectfully. Wasn't it possible that she might have the soul of a saint? After all, a saint who sins is returned to earth for a while. The earth was full of

160

transmigrant souls sent back to correct a single transgression. When Father ate, he would call the cat to him, and with an air of majesty she would allow herself to be coaxed, eating slowly and discriminatingly. Then she would look up gravely, as if to say, "If you knew who I am, you would feel honored to have me here . . ."

How could she go after mice?

A problem

The
Journey

In 1917 our situation became so bad that we could not stay in Warsaw any more. We were hungry all the time. There was an epidemic of typhus. My brother Israel Joshua got a job at an educational organization, Hazamir, but his salary barely covered his own needs. Now he became a "German"; he stopped wearing Orthodox dress and instead put on a derby and a short jacket. My father, pious as he was, became furious with him.

As for my father, he got a job with the Radzymin rabbi as editor of his religious writings. But the rabbi did not like to pay much.

There was one hope for us, the town of Bilgoray, where my mother's father was the rabbi. But Bilgoray was under Austrian occupation and although Austria and Germany were allies, the mail was irregular. Even in normal times, letter-writing was not a favorite sport of our relatives in

Bilgoray. My mother dreamed that Grandfather was dead.

It was known that there was more food in the villages occupied by Austria than in German-occupied territory, so tens of thousands of people waited in front of the Austrian consulate in Warsaw, trying to get visas. The line of waiting people was longer than the block itself and members of a family took turns holding their place. Our family waited for days, sometimes me, sometimes my mother, sometimes my brother Israel Joshua. At last, in July 1917, we received our visas! My mother, my brother Moshe, and I were to travel to Bilgoray; my father would join us later. As for Israel Joshua, he had different plans altogether. He was going with a girl in Warsaw and often stayed with her family for days at a time. He had begun to publish articles and stories in the Yiddish press of Warsaw. Bilgoray, a far-off village surrounded by forests, was not for him.

Now things were going well for us. I said goodbye to my friends and was ready to leave, but my shoes were in bad condition and I went to the cobbler in our courtyard to get them resoled.

The day was bright but the steps leading to his cellar room were dark, the corridor damp and moldy; I entered a tiny room littered with rags and shoes. The ceiling was crooked and the window small, the dirty panes patched with cardboard. I had thought that conditions were bad enough at home, but at least we had a spacious apartment with furniture and books. Here there were two beds covered with soiled bedding and on one of them, in the midst of its own filth, lay a newborn baby, wrinkled, bald, and toothless, like a miniature hag. The mother fussed at a stove that kept smoking, and a young, red-bearded man with sunken cheeks and a high forehead—yellowed like some of the leather about him—worked at the cobbler's bench.

Waiting while he resoled my shoes, I coughed from the dust and foul odors, and remembered something my brother had said about those who wore themselves out while idlers thrived. I was overcome with a sense of the injustice in the world, of young men going off to die or be wounded, of people whose constant work would not earn them a piece of bread, a shirt, or a baby crib. The cobbler, I knew, could not continue to struggle indefinitely. Sooner or later he would come down with typhus or consumption. And how could the baby flourish amid the smoke, dust, and stench?

It was my brother's opinion that there should be no rulers at all—that not only Nicholas, but Wilhelm, Karol, the English king, and all the rest, should be ousted and replaced by republics; wars should be abolished in favor of popular rule. Why had this never been done until now, and why were monarchs despotic?

When my shoes were repaired and I was out in the sunlight again, I felt guilty. Why should I be going on a wonderful trip while the cobbler was confined to his cellar? Today he still represents, to my mind, the ills of society. Although I was only a boy, I sympathized with the Russian revolutionaries. Nevertheless, I still pitied the Tsar, who was then being forced to chop wood.

My brother Joshua accompanied us in a droshky to the Danzig Station, which at that time was called the Vistula Station. He bought tickets for us, and we walked to the platform to await the train. It seemed strange to be leaving all the familiar places and friends. But before long the huge locomotive, coughing and hissing steam, was ready for us, the awesome wheels dripping oil, a fire blazing within. Few people were traveling, and we found ourselves in an empty car. The German-Austrian border was only four hours away, at Ivangorod, or Deblin, as it was later called.

With a screeching of whistles, the train began to move. On the platform, my brother Joshua seemed to grow smaller.

It was thrilling to watch the world glide away, houses, trees, wagons, entire streets revolving and drifting backward as if the earth were a huge carousel. Buildings vibrated, chimneys rose out of the earth, wearing smoky bonnets. The towers of the Sobol, the famous Russian Orthodox church, loomed over everything, its crosses glittering like gold in the sun. Flocks of pigeons, alternately black and gold, soared above the spinning, whirling city. Like a king or a great wizard, I rode through the world, no longer fearing every soldier, policeman, Gentile boy, and bum.

As we went over a bridge I glimpsed tiny trolleys on another bridge, and people resembling locusts, the way the spies during Moses' time must have looked to the giants. Beneath us, on the Vistula, a ship sailed, and in the summer sky there were clouds resembling other ships, beasts, and piles of down. The train whistled again and again. Mother took cookies and a bottle of milk from a satchel.

"Say the benediction . . ."

Eating the cookies and drinking the milk, I forgot war, hunger, and illness. I was in a paradise on wheels. If only it would last forever!

Even my friend Boruch-Dovid would not know about the existence of the parts of Warsaw and its environs that I now saw. I was amazed to see a trolley. If trolleys went this far, I could have come here myself. But it was too late now. We passed a cemetery that seemed like a tombstone metropolis. I'd faint with fear, I thought, if I had to walk there at night . . . or even during the day. But why fear the dead when you are on a moving train?

In Warsaw everyone was hungry, but the world we traveled through was beautiful and green. Mother kept pointing out the wheat, barley, buckwheat, potatoes, an apple orchard, a pear orchard—still unripe. She had been raised in a small town. Farmers mowed hay; women and girls squatting among the furrows dug out weeds, whose roots, Mother said, spoiled the grain.

Suddenly I saw a phantom-like, faceless creature, with arms outstretched. "What's that?" I asked.

"A scarecrow to frighten the birds."

My brother Moshe wanted to know if he was alive. "No, silly." I saw that he wasn't alive, nevertheless he seemed to be laughing. In the midst of the field he stood like an idol, while birds circled him and screeched.

At dusk, a conductor appeared, punched our tickets, exchanged a few words with Mother, and observed with fascination what to him was our strange, un-Gentile appearance. He was still bewildered, it seemed, despite the generations before him that had lived alongside the Jews.

In the fading light, everything became more beautiful, blossoms seemed more distinct, everything was green, juice-filled, radiant with the light of the setting sun, and aromatic. I recollected the Pentateuch verse: "The odor of my son is like that of a field the Lord has blessed."

It seemed to me that these fields, pastures, and marshes must resemble the land of Israel. The sons of Jacob were herding sheep nearby. Before Joseph's stacks of grain, other stacks bowed down. The Ishmaelites would arrive soon, riding camels, their asses and mules loaded with almonds, cloves, figs, and dates. The Plains of Mamre were visible behind the trees. God was asking Abraham: "Wherefore did Sarah laugh? Is anything too hard for the Lord? I will return unto thee and Sarah shall have a son . . ."

Suddenly I saw something and asked Mother what it was. "A windmill."

Before we could get a good look, it vanished, as if by magic. But then it appeared again behind us, its blades spinning to grind flour . . .

We saw a river, but Mother said it was not the Vistula. Then there were cows, red, black, spotted, grazing. We saw sheep. The world seemed like an open Pentateuch. The moon and the eleven stars came out, bowing before Joseph, the future ruler of Egypt.

Evening came and the lights were on at the Ivangorod Station when we arrived. We were at the border, beside a kind of highway, and Mother said, "We're in Austria." The station was full of soldiers who were not as tall, erect, or stiff-backed as the Germans. Many were bearded and seemed Jewish; they wore shoes and puttees. The tumult reminded me of the second night of a holiday at the Radzymin study house, when—to give their wives time to cook the holiday dinner—the men talked, smoked, and gesticulated. I felt at home. "Let's play chess," I suggested to my brother. We did not know how long we would have to remain there.

As soon as we had unpacked the chess set and sat down at a table to play, we were surrounded by soldiers and noncommissioned officers. Jewish soldiers asked us, "Where are you from?"

"Warsaw."

"And where are you going?"

"To Bilgoray, Grandfather is the Bilgoray rabbi."

A bearded soldier said he had been to Bilgoray and knew the Bilgoray rabbi.

One soldier stood beside me and showed me where to move, while another soldier helped Moshe. Finally it was the soldiers who played and we moved the pieces. Mother watched us with anxious pride. The soldiers were Galician Jews who probably wore fur hats and mohair coats on the Sabbath. Their Yiddish had a somewhat flatter sound than what was spoken in Warsaw. One soldier let my brother hold his sword and try on his cap.

I do not remember how we spent that night, but the following day we rode to Rejowiec in another half-empty railroad car.

In Rejowiec, where there was a Russian prisoner-of-war camp, I saw unarmed Russians with unkempt hair and shabby uniforms digging under Austrian guard. Austrians and Russians crowded the depot commissary, which was kept by a Jew with a trimmed beard.

Twisting their tongues to speak German, the Russians sounded as if they were speaking broken Yiddish. Certain Jewish soldiers among them did speak Yiddish.

The Russian prisoners had built a new track from Rejowiec to Zwierzyniec, and continued working at it the next day, as we rode. While Nicholas chopped wood, Cossacks were learning Yiddish. For all anyone knew, the Messiah *was* on his way.

The Rabbi of Bilgoray,
Isaac Bashevis Singer's grandfather

Bilgoray

Wе rode past evidence of the Russian retreat—charred forests in which an occasional half-burned tree still sprouted green leaves and twigs. Despite three days' travel by train, I continued to watch everything with love and curiosity: fields, forests, gardens, orchards, and villages . . . One tree with uplifted branches seemed to be begging for a gift from heaven; another, bowing low, appeared to have abandoned all hope of good from anything but the earth itself. Still another, completely black, was a disaster victim, everything gone but its roots. Whether it hoped for anything or was merely involved in dying, I could not know. My thoughts sped on with the wheels, stimulated by every tree, shrub, and cloud. I saw hares and squirrels. The odor of pine needles mingled with other scents, both exotic and recognizable, although I did not know from where. I wished that like some hero in a storybook I might leap from the moving train and lose myself amid green things.

Recently a short track had been laid between the villages of Zwierzyniec and Bilgoray, and although it was not finished, it was in use. Our train was a small, toylike locomotive with tiny wheels, and in the low flatcars there were benches where Bilgoray passengers sat.

Everyone in the car looked sunburned, their clothes had a sun-faded appearance. Many of the men had red beards and were dressed in gaberdines, and I felt related to them all.

"Bathsheba . . ." someone called. "The rabbi's Bathsheba . . ."

Although I knew this was my mother's name, I had never heard her called anything but "Listen here"—which was my father's method of gaining her attention, since the Hasidim did not approve of addressing a woman by name. Bathsheba, for all I knew, was merely a biblical name that no one actually used.

Here they were calling her Bathsheba and the women were embracing and kissing her. Although a dream had convinced her of her father's death, no one had confirmed it; yet now she asked them, "When did it happen?"

After a silence they began to tell her not only about her father but about her mother and sister-in-law, Uncle Joseph's wife, Sarah. Grandfather had died in Lublin, Grandmother a few months later in Bilgoray. Sarah and a daughter, Ittele, had died of cholera, and two cousins, Ezekiel and Itta Deborah, the son of Uncle Itche and the daughter of Aunt Taube, had also died.

In this sun-drenched day, in the midst of pine woods, in this green paradise, the terrible news came to her, and Mother began to cry. I too tried to cry, feeling it appropriate, but the tears would not come. I cheated, wetting my eyes with saliva, though no one was looking at me, nor did they care whether I wept or not.

Suddenly everyone shouted; the rear cars had jumped the track. There was a long wait while the cars were set back on the track with poles. That Sabbath, everyone agreed, a prayer of thanks would have to be offered. Other passengers, less fortunate than we, had been known to perish on this makeshift railroad.

Between Zwierzyniec and Bilgoray, the scenery was beautiful. We rode through forests and meadows, and passed an occasional straw-roofed hut or a white-washed house with a shingle roof. The train kept halting, to permit one person a drink of water, to allow another an interlude in the bushes; or the engineer would deliver packages or chat with the various peasants who lived beside the tracks. The Jews treated the engineer as casually as if he were the Gentile who entered Jewish households on the Sabbath to light the ovens, and they asked him to make various stops for them. Once, during one of the prolonged halts, a barefoot Jewess in a kerchief came out of a shack with a gift of dewy blackberries for my mother. Having heard that the rabbi's Bathsheba was coming, she had brought the berries as a present. Mother had no appetite, but my brother Moshe and I ate them all, staining out lips, tongues, and hands. The years of starvation had left their mark on us.

Though Mother had praised Bilgoray, it was even prettier than her descriptions. From a distance the pinewoods surrounding it looked like a blue sash. The houses were interspersed with gardens and orchards, and before them stood massive chestnut trees such as I had never seen anywhere in Warsaw, including the Saxony Gardens. There was a sense of serenity in this town that I had not encountered before, a smell of fresh milk and warm dough. Wars and poverty seemed far away.

Grandfather's house, an old wooden loghouse painted white, with a mossy roof and a bench beneath the windows, was near the synagogue, the ritual bath, and the poorhouse. The family came out to welcome us, the first to run up being Uncle Joseph, who had inherited Grandfather's position. Uncle Joseph always ran, even though he was thin and bent. He had a milky beard, a beaked nose, and bright, birdlike eyes, and was dressed in rabbinical gaberdine, wide-brimmed hat, and low shoes with white stockings. Without kissing Mother, he cried out, "Bathsheba!"

A stout woman, Aunt Yentel, his third wife, waddled after him. His second wife, Aunt Sarah, had died a year and a half before, and his first had died when he was sixteen. Aunt Yentel was as stout and relaxed as Uncle Joseph was narrow and agile. She seemed more the rebbetzin than he the rabbi. A horde of red-haired children trailed behind them. I who had fiery red hair myself had never seen so many redheads at once. Until then my red hair had made me a novelty in cheder, the study house, and the courtyard; it had seemed exotic, like my mother's name, my father's occupation, and my brother's talent for writing. But here there was a whole flock of redheads, and the reddest among them was my uncle's daughter Brocha.

I was taken into Uncle's large kitchen, where everything seemed novel. The oven was as big as a bakery's, and Aunt Yentel was baking bread. Over the stove there was a hooded chimney, and on the stove there was a tripod on which a pot boiled. Flies crawled over a huge lump of sugar on the table. The scents of leavening and caraway filled the air. My aunt offered us some prune cake, which tasted like it was made in Paradise. My cousins Avromele and Samson took me into the courtyard, which was actually a garden with trees, tall nettles, weeds, and wild flowers of all colors. There was also a sleeping porch; I sat down on the straw-mattress bed, and it seemed to me I had never known such luxury. The sounds of birds, crickets, and other insects rang in my ears, chickens wandered about in the grass, and when I raised my head I could see the Bilgoray synagogue and beyond it fields that stretched to the forest's edge. The fields were all shapes and colors, squares and rectangles, dark green and yellow . . . I wished I could stay here forever.

A water carrier in a Jewish town

The New
Winds

Upheaval marked Bilgoray, for so long successfully obscured from the world by my grandfather. Now its immutability was being threatened from many sources. A few months after we arrived, a Zionist society was established by the young people of the town. Certain young men indicated Bolshevik sympathies. Youthful worshippers at the house of prayer separated into two factions: The Mizrachi and the Traditionalists. My friend Notte Shverdsharf formed a pioneer division, the Hachalutz or Hashomer, and was trailed by hordes of children who called themselves Zebim, wolves. Whether larger cities showed the same tendencies as Bilgoray, I did not know. In the streets, boys passing each other would straighten up, click their heels in the Austrian manner, and shout, "*Chazak*!--Be strong!"

All kinds of evening discussions and parties were now being held in this town, which a year before had been a sleepy

Jewish community. A Warsaw dramatic company performed *Shulamit* in the firehouse. The Austrians, who had started a school in Bilgoray, erected a theater in the marketplace. The Hasidim resented my uncles because they made no objection to this, did not drive out the heretics as their father would have done. But his sons lacked his personality and strength.

Jonah Ackerman, a third-rate lawyer, opened a library of worldly books in his house. He was the son of an enlightened man, a sharp-tongued opponent of Hasidism. When the Gorlitz rabbi had come to town to be greeted with music and bells, old man Ackerman, standing in his doorway, had hissed, "Idol worshippers!"

Jonah Ackerman was dedicated to nothing but compromise. A lawyer, he said, must not antagonize his clients. In three-quarter-length surtout, Hasidic hat, and with a pointed yellow beard, he spent his Sabbath in the same Gorlitz study house that his father had vilified. Raised on Russian literature—not on Tolstoy and Dostoevsky, but on those before them, like Lomonosov and the writers of moralistic works—he had a principle to apply to everything, and enjoyed moral discussions. A pedant with a calligraphic handwriting, he was especially attentive to grammar and syntax.

His personality seemed to have evolved from print. He had an amazing memory, was said to know certain codices by heart, and owned numerous dictionaries and lexicons. Finally he decided to open a library and ordered both Yiddish and Hebrew volumes. He was in general a pure-hearted old bachelor, old-fashioned and a bit eccentric.

By this time my knowledge of Yiddish writers included Mendele Mocher-Sforim, Sholem Aleichem, Peretz, Asch, and Bergelson, but I had not read them thoroughly. Now I read enthusiastically the poetry of Bialik, Chernichovsky, Jacob Cohen, and Schneyur, and had an insatiable desire for more. I had never forgotten the two volumes of *Crime and Punishment* that intrigued me so, even though I scarcely had understood what I was reading.

Now, under the apple tree in the garden, I would start a book one day and finish it the next. Often, sitting on an overturned bookcase in the attic, I would read among old pots, broken barrels, and stacks of pages torn from sacred books. Omnivorously, I read stories, novels, plays, essays, works written in Yiddish, and translations. As I read, I decided which was good, which mediocre, and where truth and falsity lay. At that time America was sending us sacks of white flour and Yiddish translations of European writers, and these books fascinated me. I read Reisen, Strindberg, Don Kaplanovitch, Turgenev, Tolstoy, Maupassant, and Chekhov. One day I devoured *The Problem of Good and Evil* by Hillel Zeitlin. In this book Zeitlin gives the history and summation of world philosophy and the philosophy of the Jews. Sometime later I discovered Stupnicki's book on Spinoza.

I remembered how Father used to say that Spinoza's name should be blotted out, and I knew Spinoza contended that God was the world and the world was God. My father, I recalled, said that Spinoza had contributed nothing. There was an interpretation by the famous Baal Shem that also identified the world with the Godhead. True, the Baal Shem had lived after Spinoza, but my father argues that Spinoza had drawn from ancient sources, which no Spinoza disciple would deny.

The Spinoza book created a turmoil in my brain. His

concept that God is a substance with infinite attributes, that divinity itself must be true to its laws, that there is no free will, no absolute morality and purpose—intrigued and bewildered me. As I read this book, I felt intoxicated, inspired as I never had before. It seemed to me that the truths I had been seeking since childhood had at last become apparent. Everything was God—Warsaw, Bilgoray, the spider in the attic, the water in the well, the clouds in the sky, and the book on my knees. Everything was divine, everything was thought and extension. A stone had its stony thoughts. The material being of a star and a star's thoughts were two aspects of the same thing. Besides physical and mental attributes, there were innumerable other characteristics through which divinity could be determined. God was eternal, transcending time. Time, or duration, controlled only the modi, the bubbles in the divine cauldron, that were forever forming and bursting. I too was a modus, which explained my indecision, my restlessness, my passionate nature, my doubts and fears. But the modi too were created from God's body, God's thought, and could be explained only through Him . . .

As I write these lines today, I am critical of them, being familiar with all the defects and lapses of Spinozism. But at that time I was under a spell which lasted many years.

I was exalted; everything seemed good. There was no difference between heaven and earth, the most distant star and my red hair. My tangled thoughts were divine. The fly alighting on my page had to be there, just as an ocean wave or a planet had to be where it was at a specific time. The most foolish fantasy in my mind had been thought for me by God . . . Heaven and earth became the same thing. The laws of nature were divine; the true sciences of God were mathematics, physics, and chemistry. My desire to learn intensified.

Other boys, Notte Shverdsharf and Meir Hadas, were not, to my astonishment, at all interested in my discoveries. My absorption amazed them, just as their indifference shocked me.

One day Notte approached me and asked if I would be willing to teach Hebrew.

"To whom?"

"Beginners. Boys and girls."

"But what about Mottel Shur?" I asked. "He is the Hebrew teacher."

"They don't want him."

I still don't know why they didn't want Mottel Shur, unless it was because he had quarreled with the founders of the night school that now sought to employ me. Mottel had a weakness for telling people what he thought of them; also, he boasted too much—and perhaps he asked too high a fee. I hardly dared accept the position, knowing it would embarrass my mother and cause consternation in the town. But something made me accept.

In the private home where the first class was held, I discovered that my pupils were not, as I had assumed, children, but young men and women, and somewhat more of the latter. The girls, my age and even older, came dressed in their best clothes. I faced them in a long gaberdine, a velvet hat, and with dangling sidelocks. How, since I am naturally shy, I had the nerve to accept this assignment I do not know, but it has been my experience that shy persons are sometimes unusually bold. I told them everything I knew about Hebrew. The class created a furor in Bilgoray—to think that the rabbi's grandson had lectured worldly boys and girls on the Hebrew language!

After the lesson, the girls surrounded me, asking questions, smiling. Suddenly I was dazzled by a particular narrow face, a dark girl with coal-black eyes and an indescribable smile. I became confused, and when she asked me a question I did not know what she was saying. Many novels and a lot of poetry had filled my mind by then; I was prepared for the turmoil that writers call "love" . . .

Isaac Bashevis Singer, age twenty-two;
at about this time, he began to write

Shosha

In the days when we used to live at 10 Krochmalna Street, I mostly stayed home at night. Our courtyard was dark and the small kerosene lamps in the hallway gave more smoke than light. The stories my parents told about devils, demons, and werewolves made me afraid to go out, so I would remain indoors and read.

In those days, we had a neighbor called Basha, who had three daughters: Shosha, who was nine; Ippa, five; and Teibele, two. Basha owned a store that stayed open until late in the evening.

In the summertime the nights are short, but in winter they are very long. The only place I could go at night was Shosha's apartment, but to get there I had to pass through a dark corridor. It took only a minute, yet that minute was filled with terror. Luckily, Shosha would almost always hear me coming, running and breathing heavily, and would quickly open the door. At the sight of her, I lost all fear. Shosha, though she was a year older than I, was more childish. She was fair, with blond braids and blue eyes. We were drawn to each other because we loved to tell each other stories, and we also loved to play together.

The moment I entered the apartment, Shosha took out "the things." Her toys consisted of articles discarded by grown-ups: buttons from old coats, a tea-kettle handle, a wooden spool with no thread left, tinfoil from a package of tea, and other such objects. With my colored pencils, I often drew people and animals for Shosha. Shosha and her sister Ippa admired my artwork.

There was a tile stove in Shosha's apartment behind which there lived a cricket. It chirped the nights through all winter long. I imagined that the cricket was telling a story that would never end. But who can understand the language of crickets? Shosha believed that a house imp also made its home behind the stove. A house imp never does anyone any harm. Sometimes it even helps the household. Just the same, one is afraid of it.

Shosha's house imp liked to play little tricks. When Shosha took off her shoes and stockings before she went to sleep and placed them near her bed, she'd find them on the table in the morning. The house imp had put them there. Several times when Shosha went to bed with her hair unbraided, the house imp braided it while she was asleep. Once when Shosha was playing at casting goat shadows on the wall with her fingers, the shadow goat jumped off the wall and butted her on the forehead. This, too, was a trick of the house imp. Another time Shosha's mother sent her to the baker to buy fresh rolls and gave her a silver gulden to pay for them. Shosha lost the gulden in the gutter and came home frightened and crying. Suddenly she felt a coin in her hand. The house imp tweaked her left braid and whispered into her ear: "Shlemiel."

I had heard these stories many times, but they never failed to make me shiver with excitement. I myself liked to invent things. I told the girls that my father had a treasure that was hidden in a cave in the forest. I boasted that my grandfather was the King of Bilgoray. I assured Shosha that I knew a magic word that could destroy the world if spoken. "Please, Itchele, please don't say it," she would beg me.

The trip home was even more frightening than getting to Shosha's. My fear grew with the stories we told each other. It seemed to me that the dark hall was full of evil spirits. I had once read a story about a boy who had been forced by the demons to marry one of their she-devils. I was afraid that it might happen to me. According to the story, the couple lived somewhere in the desert near Mount Seir. Their children were half human and half demon. As I ran through the dark corridor, I kept repeating words that would guard me against the creatures of the night:

"Thou shalt not permit a witch to live—
A witch to live thou shalt not permit."

When we moved to 12 Krochmalna Street, there was no question of visiting Shosha at night. Also, it was not fitting for a Hasidic boy, a student of the Talmud, to play with girls. I missed Shosha. I hoped we'd meet on the street sometime, but months and years passed and we did not see each other.

In time Shosha became for me an image of the past. I often thought about her during the day and dreamed about her at night. In my dreams Shosha was as beautiful as a princess. Several times I dreamed that she had married the house imp and lived with him in a dark cellar. He brought her food but never let her go out. I saw her sitting on a chair, to which she had been tied with rope, while the house imp fed her jam with a tiny spoon. He had the head of a dog and the wings of a bat.

After the First World War, I left my family in Bilgoray and returned to Warsaw. I began to write and my stories appeared in newspapers and magazines. I also wrote a novel called *Satan in Goray* in which I described the devils and demons of olden times. I was married and had a son. I applied for a passport and a visa to emigrate to the United States, and one day they arrived. I was about to leave Warsaw forever.

A few days before I left, my feet led me to Krochmalna Street. I hadn't been there for years and I wanted once again to see the street where I grew up.

Few changes had taken place, though the buildings were older and even shabbier. I peered into some courtyards: huge trash cans; barefoot, half-naked children. The boys played tag, hide-and-seek, cops-and-robbers, just as we had twenty-five years ago. The girls occupied themselves with hopscotch. Suddenly it occurred to me that I might be able to find Shosha. I made my way to the building where we used to live. God in heaven, everything was the same—the peeling walls, the refuse. I reached the corridor that led to Shosha's apartment, and it was just as dark as in the old days. I lit a match and found the door. As I did so, I realized how foolish I was being. Shosha would be over thirty now. It was most unlikely that the family would still be living in the same place.

And even if her parents were still alive and living there, Shosha would surely have married and moved away. But some power I cannot explain forced me to knock on the door.

There was no reply. I drew the latch (as I had sometimes done in the old days) and the door opened. I entered a kitchen that looked exactly like Basha's kitchen of twenty-five years before. I recognized the mortar and pestle, the table, the chairs. Was I dreaming? Could it be true?

Then I noticed a girl of about eight or nine. My God, it was Shosha! The same fair face, the same blond hair braided with red ribbons, the same longish neck. The girl stared at me in surprise, but she didn't seem alarmed.

"Who are you looking for?" she asked, and it was Shosha's voice.

"What is your name?" I said.

"Me? Basha."

"And your mother's name?"

"Shosha," the girl replied.

"Where is your mother?"

"In the store."

"I once lived here," I explained. "I used to play with your mother when she was a little girl."

Basha looked at me with large eyes and inquired, "Are you Itchele?"

"How do you know about Itchele?" I said. A lump stuck in my throat. I could barely speak.

"My mother told me about him."

"Yes, I am Itchele."

"My mother told me everything. Your father had a cave in the forest full of gold and diamonds. You knew a word that could set the whole world on fire. Do you still know it?"

"No, not any more."

"What happened to the gold in the cave?"

"Somebody stole it," I said.

"And is your grandfather still a king?"

"No, Basha, he is not a king any more."

For a while we were both silent. Then I asked, "Did your mother tell you about the house imp?"

"Yes, we used to have a house imp, but he's gone."

"What happened to him?"

"I don't know."

"And the cricket?"

"The cricket is still here, but it chirps mostly at night."

I went down to the candy store—the one where Shosha and I used to buy candy—and bought cookies, chocolate, and halvah. Then I went back upstairs and gave them to Basha.

"Would you like to hear a story?" I asked her.

"Yes, very much."

I told Basha a story about a beautiful blond girl whom a demon had carried away to the desert, to Mount Seir, and had forced to marry him, and about the children that were born of the marriage, who were half human, half demon.

Basha's eyes grew pensive. "And she stayed there?"

"No, Basha, a saintly man called Rabbi Leib learned about her misfortune. He traveled to the desert and rescued her."

"How?"

"An angel helped him."

"And what happened to her children?"

"The children became completely human and went with their mother. The angel carried them to safety on his wings."

"And the demon?"

"He remained in the desert."

"And he never married again?"

"Yes, Basha, he did. He married a she-demon, one of his own kind."

We were both silent again, and suddenly I heard the familiar chirping of a cricket. Could it be the cricket of my childhood? Certainly not. Perhaps her great-great-great-granddaughter. But she was telling the same story, as ancient as time, as puzzling as the world, and as long as the dark winter nights of Warsaw.

Stories for Children

Contents

Author's Note

I never believed that I could write for children. I always had
the false impression that those who write for children are not
real writers, and those who illustrate books are not real painters.
It is true that as a child I read the Brothers Grimm in German
and also translations of Hans Christian Andersen's stories and I
loved them. I will never forget the great joy I felt reading a
Yiddish edition of Sherlock Holmes stories by Conan Doyle.
Just the same, the idea of writing for children never entered my
mind. But editors often know more about writers than the
writers themselves. This particular editor, Miss Elizabeth Shub,
was convinced that I could write for children, and nothing I
could say to her changed her conviction. She was after me for a
long time, and I finally wrote the stories which are now to be
found in the collection *Zlateh the Goat and Other Stories* and
in a dozen other books for youngsters. Many of them were
translated into English by Miss Shub and myself.

This particular collection of my children's stories is especially important to me. Although I love illustrations to stories for children and in many cases they are a very propitious addition to the story, I still think that the power of the word is the best medium to inform and entertain the minds of our youngsters. Most of the stories I read as a young boy were not illustrated. Needless to say, the stories in the Bible, which I read and reread, had no illustrations. In this volume I'm happy to speak to my young readers just in words. I still believe that in the beginning was the Logos, the power of the word.

I.B.S.

The Elders of Chelm & Genendel's Key

It was known that the village of Chelm was ruled by the head of the community council and the elders, all fools. The name of the head was Gronam Ox. The elders were Dopey Lekisch, Zeinvel Ninny, Treitel Fool, Sender Donkey, Shmendrick Numskull, and Feivel Thickwit. Gronam Ox was the oldest. He had a curly white beard and a high, bulging forehead.

Since Gronam had a large house, the elders usually met there. Every now and then Gronam's first wife, Genendel, brought them refreshments—tea, cakes, and jam.

Gronam would have been a happy man except for the fact that each time the elders left, Genendel would reproach him for speaking nonsense. In her opinion her highly respected husband was a simpleton.

Once, after such a quarrel, Gronam said to his wife, "What is the sense in nagging me after the elders have gone? In the future, whenever you hear me saying something silly, come into the room and let me know. I will immediately change the subject."

"But how can I tell you you're talking nonsense in front of the elders? If they learn you're a fool, you'll lose your job as head of the council."

"If you're so clever, find a way," Gronam replied.

Genendel thought a moment and suddenly exclaimed, "I have it."

"Well?"

"When you say something silly, I will come in and hand you the key to our strongbox. Then you'll know you've been talking like a fool."

Gronam was so delighted with his wife's idea that he clapped his hands. "Near me, you too become clever."

A few days later the elders met in Gronam's house. The subject under discussion was the coming Pentecost, a holiday when a lot of sour cream is needed to eat with blintzes. That year there was a scarcity of sour cream. It had been a dry spring and the cows gave little milk.

The elders pulled at their beards and rubbed their foreheads, signs that their brains were hard at work. But none of them could figure out how to get enough sour cream for the holiday.

Suddenly Gronam pounded on the table with his fist and called out, "I have it!"

"What is it?"

"Let us make a law that water is to be called sour cream and sour cream is to be called water. Since there is plenty of water in the wells of Chelm, each housewife will have a full barrel of sour cream."

"What a wonderful idea," cried Sender Donkey.

"A stroke of genius," shrieked Zeinvel Ninny.

"Only Gronam Ox could think of something so brilliant," Dopey Lekisch proclaimed.

Treitel Fool, Shmendrick Numskull, and Feivel Thickwit all agreed. Feivel Thickwit, the community scribe, took out pen and parchment and set down the new law. From that day on, water was to be called sour cream and sour cream, water.

As usual, when they had finished with community business, the elders turned to more general subjects. Gronam said, "Last night I couldn't sleep a wink for thinking about why it is hot in the summertime. Finally the answer came to me."

"What is it?" the elders chorused.

"Because all winter long the stoves are heated and this heat stays in Chelm and makes the summer hot."

All the elders nodded their heads, excepting Dopey Lekisch, who asked, "Then why is it cold in the winter?"

"It's clear why," replied Gronam. "The stoves are not heated in the summer, so there is no heat left over for the winter."

The elders were enthusiastic about Gronam's great knowledge. After such mental effort, they began to look toward the kitchen, expecting Genendel to appear with the tea, cakes, and jam.

Genendel did come in, but instead of a tray she carried a key, which she gave to her husband, saying, "Gronam, here is the key to the strongbox."

Today of all days Gronam was confident that his

mouth had uttered only clever words. But there stood Genendel with the key in her hand, a sure sign that he had spoken like a fool. He grew so angry that he turned to the elders and said, "Tell me, what foolishness have I spoken that my wife brings me the key to our strongbox?"

The elders were perplexed at this question, and Gronam explained his agreement with Genendel, that she should give him the key when he talked like an idiot. "But today, didn't I speak words of high wisdom? You be the judges."

The elders were furious with Genendel. Feivel Thickwit spoke out: "We are the elders of Chelm, and we understand everything. No woman can tell us what is wise and what is silly."

They then discussed the matter and made a new law: Whenever Genendel believed that her husband was talking like a fool, she was to come in and give the key to the elders. If they agreed, they would tell Gronam Ox to change the subject. If they did not agree, she was to bring out a double portion of tea, cakes, and jam, and three blintzes for every sage.

Feivel Thickwit immediately recorded the new law on parchment and stamped it with the seal of Chelm, which was an ox with six horns.

From that day on, Gronam could talk freely at the meetings, since Genendel was very stingy. She did not want the elders of Chelm to gorge themselves with her beloved blintzes.

That Pentecost there was no lack of "sour cream" in Chelm, but some housewives complained that there was a lack of "water." But this was an entirely new problem, to be solved after the holiday.

Gronam Ox became famous all over the world as the sage who—by passing a law—gave Chelm a whole river and many wells full of sour cream.

Translated by the author and Elizabeth Shub

A Tale of Three Wishes

Frampol. This was the name of the town. It had all the things that a town should have: a synagogue, a studyhouse, a poorhouse, a rabbi, and a few hundred inhabitants. Each Thursday was market day in Frampol, when the peasants came from the hamlets to sell grain, potatoes, chickens, calves, honey, and to buy salt, kerosene, shoes, boots, and whatever else a peasant may need.

There were in Frampol three children who often played together: Shlomah, or Solomon, seven years old; his sister, Esther, six years old; and their friend Moshe, who was about Shlomah's age.

Shlomah and Moshe went to the same cheder and someone there told them that on Hoshanah Rabbah, which is the last day of the Feast of Tabernacles, the sky opens late at night. Those who see it happen have a minute's time to make a wish, and whatever they wish will come true.

Shlomah, Moshe, and Esther spoke of this often. Shlomah said that he would wish to be as wise and rich as King Solomon, his namesake. Moshe's wish was to be as learned in religion as was the famous Rabbi Moshe Maimonides. Esther desired to be as beautiful as Queen Esther. After long discussions, the three children decided to wait until Hoshanah Rabbah, to stay awake the whole night together and, when the sky opened, to utter their wishes.

Children must go to bed early, but the three stayed awake until their parents fell asleep. Then they sneaked out of the house and met in the synagogue yard to wait for the miraculous event.

It was quite an adventure. The night was moonless and cool. The children had heard that demons lurk outside, ready to attack those who dare to go out on a dark night. There was also talk of corpses who after midnight pray in the synagogue and read from the Holy Scroll. If someone passed by the synagogue at such a late hour, he might be called up to the reading table, a most frightening event. But Shlomah and Moshe had put on fringed garments, and Esther had dressed in two aprons, one in the front and one in the back, all meant to ward off the evil powers. Just the same, the children were afraid. An owl was hooting. Esther had been told that bats flew around at night and that if one of them got entangled in a girl's hair she would die within the year. Esther had covered her hair tightly with a kerchief.

An hour passed, two hours, three, and still the sky did not open. The children became tired and even hungry. Suddenly there was lightning and the sky opened. The children saw angels, seraphim, cherubim, fiery chariots, as well as the ladder which Jacob saw in his dream, with winged angels going up and down, just as it is written in the Bible. It all happened so quickly that the children forgot their wishes.

Esther spoke up first. "I'm hungry. I wish I had a blintz."

At once, a blintz appeared before the children's eyes.

When Shlomah saw that his sister had wasted her wish on such a petty thing as a blintz, he became enraged and cried out, "You silly girl, I wish you were a blintz yourself."

In an instant, Esther became a blintz. Only her face looked out from the dough, pale and frightened.

Moshe had loved Esther for as long as he could remember. When he saw that his beloved Esther had turned into a blintz, he fell into terrible despair. There was no time to lose. The minute was almost over, and he exclaimed, "I wish her to be as she was."

And so it happened.

Immediately the sky closed again.

When the children realized how foolishly they had squandered their wishes, they began to cry. The night had become pitch black and they could not find their way back home. They seemed to be lost in some strange place. There were no mountains in Frampol; still, the children were climbing up a mountain. They tried to walk down again, but their feet kept climbing by themselves. Then there appeared an old man with a white beard. In one hand he held a stick, in the other a lantern with a candle inside. His robe was girded with a white sash. A strong wind was blowing, but the candle did not flicker.

The old man asked, "Where are you going? And why are you crying?"

Shlomah told him the truth, how they stayed awake all night and how they wasted their wishes.

The old man shook his head. "No good wish is ever wasted."

"Perhaps the demons confused us and made us forget our wishes," Moshe suggested.

"No demons have any power in the holy night of Hoshanah Rabbah," the old man said.

"So why did the sky play such a trick on us?" Esther asked.

"Heaven does not play tricks," the old man answered. "You were the ones who tried to play tricks on heaven. No one can become wise without experience, no one can become a scholar without studying. As for you, little girl, you are pretty already, but beauty of the body must be paired with beauty of the soul. No young child can possess the love and the devotion of a queen who was ready to sacrifice her life for her people. Because you three wished too much, you received nothing."

"What shall we do now?" the children asked.

"Go home and try to deserve by effort what you wanted to get too easily."

"Who are you?" the children asked, and the old man replied, "On high, they call me the Watcher in the Night."

As soon as he said these words, the children found themselves back in the synagogue yard. They were so weary that the moment they came home and put their heads on their pillows, they fell asleep. They never told anybody what had happened to them. It remained their secret.

Years passed. Shlomah had become more and more eager for knowledge. He showed so much talent and studied so many books of history, trade, and finance that he became the adviser of the King of Poland. They called him the King without a Crown, and King Solomon of Poland. He married the daughter of an important man and became famous for his wisdom and charity.

Moshe had always been deeply interested in religion. He knew the Bible and the Talmud almost by heart. He wrote many religious books and he became known as the Maimonides of Our Time.

Esther grew up to be not only beautiful but a learned and highly virtuous young lady. Many young men from rich houses sent matchmakers to her parents to ask for her hand in marriage, but Esther loved only Moshe, as he loved only her.

When the old rabbi of Frampol died, Moshe was made rabbi of the town. A rabbi must have a wife, and Rabbi Moshe married his Esther.

All the people of Frampol attended the wedding. The bride's brother, Shlomah, came to his sister's wedding in a carriage drawn by six horses, with grooms riding in front and on the back of the carriage. There was music and dancing, and the young couple received many gifts. Late at night, the bridegroom was called to dance with the bride, and so were all the guests, the bride holding one edge of the handkerchief and her partner the other, according to custom. When someone asked if everyone had danced with the bride, the wedding jester said, "Yes, except for the night watchman." As he uttered these words, an old man emerged from nowhere with a stick in one hand, a lantern in the other hand, his loins girded with a white sash. The bride, her brother, and the bridegroom recognized the old man, but they kept silent. He approached the bride, placed the lantern and the stick on a bench nearby, and began to dance with her, all the people staring in amazement and awe. No one had ever seen this old man before. The band stopped playing. It became so quiet that one could hear the sputtering of the candles and the chirping of the grasshoppers outside. Then the old man lifted up his lantern and gave it to Rabbi Moshe, saying, "Let this light show you the way in the Torah." He offered the stick to Shlomah with the words: "Let this stick protect you from all your enemies." To Esther, who was holding the white sash, he said, "Let this sash bind you to your people and their needs forever."

After saying these words, the old man vanished.

In the years following, it happened quite often that the Jews came to ask Esther to intercede for them before the rulers of the land. She would fasten the white sash around her waist, and she never failed to help her people. Everyone called her Queen Esther.

Whenever Rabbi Moshe had difficulties in understanding some fine point of the law, he opened the ark where the lantern stood with its eternal light, and things became clear to him. When Shlomah was in trouble, he would take hold of the stick and his foes became powerless.

All three lived to a ripe old age. Only before his death

did Rabbi Moshe reveal to the people of Frampol what had happened that night of Hoshanah Rabbah. The rabbi said, "For those who are willing to make an effort, great miracles and wonderful treasures are in store. For them the gates of heaven are always open."

The Extinguished Lights

It was the custom to light the Hanukkah candles at home, rather than in a synagogue or studyhouse, but this particular studyhouse in Bilgoray was an exception. Old Reb Berish practically lived there. He prayed, studied the Mishnah, ate, and sometimes even slept on the bench near the stove. He was the oldest man in town. He admitted to being over ninety, but some maintained that he was already past one hundred. He remembered the war between Russia and Hungary. On holidays he used to visit Rabbi Chazkele from Kuzmir and other ancient rabbis.

That winter it snowed in Bilgoray almost every day. At night the houses on Bridge Street were snowed under and the people had to dig themselves out in the morning. Reb Berish had his own copper Hanukkah lamp, which the beadle kept in the reading table with other holy objects—a ram's horn, the Book of Esther written on a scroll, a braided Havdalah candle, a prayer shawl and phylacteries, as well as a wine goblet and an incense holder.

There is no moon on the first nights of Hanukkah, but that night the light from the stars made the snow sparkle as if it were full of diamonds. Reb Berish placed his Hanukkah lamp at the window according to the law, poured oil into the container, put a wick into it, and made the customary benedictions. Then he sat by the open clay stove. Even though most of the children stayed at home on Hanukkah evenings, a few boys came to the studyhouse especially to listen to Reb Berish's stories. He was known as a storyteller. While he told stories he roasted potatoes on the glowing coals. He was saying, "Nowadays when snow falls and there is a frost, people call it winter. In comparison to the winters of my times the winters of today are nothing. It used to be so cold that oak trees burst in the forests. The snow was up to the rooftops. Bevies of hungry wolves came into the village at night, and people shuddered in bed from their howling. The horses neighed in their stables and tried to break the doors open from fear. The dogs barked like mad. Bilgoray was still a tiny place then. There was a pasture where Bagno Street is today.

"The winter I'm going to tell you about was the worst of them all. The days were almost as dark as night. The clouds were black as lead. A woman would come out of her kitchen with the slop pail and the water turned to ice before she could empty it.

"Now hear something. That year the men blessed the Hanukkah lights on the first night as they did every year, but suddenly a wind came from nowhere and extinguished them. It happened in every house at the same time. The lights were kindled a second time, but again they were extinguished. In those times there was an abundance of wood to help keep the houses warm. To keep the wind out, cracks in the windows were plugged up with cotton or straw. So how could the wind get in? And why should it happen in every house at the same moment? Everybody was astonished. People went to the rabbi to ask his advice and the rabbi's decision was to continue rekindling the lights. Some pious men kept lighting the candles until the rooster crowed. This happened on the first night of Hanukkah, as well as on the second night and on the nights after. There were nonbelievers who contended that the whole thing was a natural occurrence. But most of the people believed that there was some mysterious power behind it all. But what was it—a demon, a mocker, an imp? And why just on Hanukkah?

"A fear came over the town. Old women said that it was an omen of war or an epidemic. Fathers and grandfathers were so disturbed that they forgot to give Hanukkah money to the children, who couldn't play games with the dreidel. The women did not fry pancakes as they had in former years.

"It went on like this until the seventh night. Then, after everyone was asleep and the rabbi was sitting in his chamber studying the Talmud, someone knocked on his door. It was the rabbi's custom to go to sleep early in the evening and to get up after midnight to study. Usually his wife served him tea, but in the middle of the night the rabbi poured water into the samovar himself, lit the coals, and prepared the tea. He would drink and study until daybreak.

"When the rabbi heard the knocking on the door, he got up and opened it. An old woman stood outside and the rabbi invited her to come into his house.

"She sat down and told the rabbi that last year before Hanukkah her little granddaughter Altele, an orphan, died. She had first gotten sick in the summer and no doctor could help her. After the High Holidays, when Altele realized that her end was near, she said, 'Grandmother, I know that I'm going to die, but I only wish to live until Hanukkah, when Grandpa gives me Hanukkah money and I can play dreidel with the girls.' Everybody in Bilgoray prayed for the girl's recovery, but it so happened that she died just a day before Hanukkah. For a whole year after her death her grandparents never saw her in their dreams. But this night the grandmother had seen Altele in her dreams three times in a row. Altele came to her and said that because the people of the town had not prayed ardently enough for her to see the first Hanukkah candle, she had died angry and it was she who extinguished the Hanukkah lights in every house. The old woman said that after the first dream she awakened her husband and told him, but he said that because she brooded so much about her grandchild, she had had this dream. The second time when Altele came to her in her dream, the grandmother asked Altele what the people of the town could do to bring peace to her soul. The girl began to answer, but the old woman woke up suddenly before she could understand what Altele was saying.

Only in the third dream did the girl speak clearly, saying it was her wish that on the last night of Hanukkah all the people of Bilgoray, together with the rabbi and the elders, should come to her grave and light the Hanukkah candles there. They should bring all the children with them, eat pancakes, and play dreidel on the frozen snow.

"When the rabbi heard these words, he began to tremble, and he said, 'It's all my fault. I didn't pray enough for that child.' He told the old woman to wait, poured some tea for her, and looked in the books to see if what the girl asked was in accordance with the law. Though he couldn't find a similar case in all the volumes of his library, the rabbi decided on his own that the wish of that grieved spirit should be granted. He told the old woman that on a cold and windy night there is very little chance for lights to burn outdoors. However, if the ghost of the girl could extinguish all the lights indoors, she might also have the power to do the opposite. The rabbi promised the old woman to pray with all his heart for success.

"Early in the morning, when the beadle came to the rabbi, he asked him to take his wooden hammer and go from house to house, knock on shutters, and tell the people what they must do. Even though Hanukkah is a holiday, the rabbi had ordered the older people to fast until noon and ask forgiveness of the girl's sacred soul—and also pray that there should be no wind in the evening.

"All day long a fierce wind blew. Chimneys were blown off some roofs. The sky was overcast with dark clouds. Not only the unbelievers, but even some of the God-fearing men, doubted lights could stay lit in a storm like this. There were those who suspected that the old woman invented the dream, or that a demon came to her disguised as her late grandchild in order to scoff at the faithful and lead them astray. The town's healer, Nissan, who trimmed his beard and came to the synagogue only on the Sabbath, called the old woman a liar and warned that the little ones might catch terrible colds at the graveyard and get inflammation of the lungs. The blizzard seemed to become wilder from minute to minute. But suddenly, while the people were reciting the evening prayer, a change took place. The sky cleared, the wind subsided, and warm breezes wafted from the surrounding fields and forests. It was already the beginning of the month of Teveth and a new moon was seen surrounded with myriads of stars.

"Some of the unbelievers were so stunned they couldn't utter a word. Nissan the healer promised the rabbi that scissors would never touch his beard again and that he would come to pray every day of the week. Not only older children, but even the younger ones, were taken to the graveyard. Lights were kindled, blessings were recited, the women served the pancakes with jam that they had prepared. The children played dreidel on the frozen snow, which was as smooth as ice. A golden light shone over the little girl's grave, a sign that her soul enjoyed the Hanukkah celebration. Never before or after did the graveyard seem so festive as on that eighth night of Hanukkah. All the unbelievers did penance. Even the Gentiles heard of the miracle and acknowledged that God had not forsaken the Jews.

"The next day Mendel the scribe wrote down the

whole event in the parchment Community Book, but the book was burned years later in the time of the First Fire."

"When did this happen?" one of the children asked.

Reb Berish clutched his beard, which had once been red, then turned white, and finally became yellowish from the snuff he used. He pondered for a while and said, "Not less than eighty years ago."

"And you remember it so clearly?"

"As if it took place yesterday."

The light in Reb Berish's Hanukkah lamp began to sputter and smoke. The studyhouse became full of shadows. With his bare fingers the old man pulled three potatoes out of the stove, broke off some pieces, and offered them to the children. He said, "The body dies, but the soul goes up to God and lives forever."

"What do all the souls do when they are with God?" one of the boys asked.

"They sit in Paradise on golden chairs with crowns on their heads and God teaches them the secrets of the Torah."

"God is a teacher?"

"Yes, God is a teacher, and all the good souls are His pupils," Reb Berish replied.

"How long will the souls go on learning?" a boy asked.

"Until the Messiah comes, and then there will be the resurrection of the dead," Reb Berish said. "But even then God will continue to teach in His eternal yeshiva, because the secrets of the Torah are deeper than the ocean, higher than heaven, and more delightful than all the pleasures the body could ever enjoy."

Mazel & Shlimazel

OR THE MILK OF A LIONESS

In a faraway land, on a sunny spring day, the sky was as blue as the sea, and the sea was as blue as the sky, and the earth was green and in love with them both. Two spirits were passing through a village. One was called Mazel, which means good luck, and the other, Shlimazel, bad luck.

Spirits are not seen by man, but they can see one another.

Mazel was young, tall, slim. His cheeks were pink and he had sand-colored hair. He was dressed in a green jacket, red riding breeches, and wore a hat with a feather in it. There were silver spurs on his high boots. Mazel seldom walked. Usually he rode his horse, which was also a spirit. On this particular day, he felt like strolling through the village on foot.

Shlimazel limped along beside him with the help of a

knotty-wood cane—an old man with a wan face and angry eyes under his bushy brows. His nose was crooked and red from drinking. His beard was as gray as spiderwebs. He was attired in a long black coat and on his head sat a peaked hat.

Mazel spoke and Shlimazel listened. Mazel was in a boasting mood. "Everybody wants me, everybody loves me," he said. "Wherever I go, I bring joy. Naturally the people cannot see me because I am a spirit, but they all long for me just the same: merchants and sailors, doctors and shoemakers, lovers and card players. All over the world they call, 'Mazel, come to me.' Nobody calls for you, Shlimazel. You'll have to admit that what I say is true."

Shlimazel pursed his lips and clutched his beard. "Yes, I must agree that you're a charmer," he said. "But the world is ruled by the strong and not by the charming. What can take you a year to accomplish, I can destroy in one second."

Shlimazel had made a point and now Mazel bit his lip in annoyance. "We all know you can destroy," he replied. "But you always do it in the same way—either you kill, or you burn, or you send sickness or famine, war or poverty. I, on the other hand, am always full of fresh ideas. I know millions of ways to make people happy."

"I have billions of ways of making them unhappy."

"That's not true. You always use the same old tricks," Mazel insisted. "I'll bet that you can't even find a single new way of spoiling something nice that I've done."

"Is that so? What will you wager?" Shlimazel countered.

"If you win," Mazel said, "I will give you a barrel of the precious wine of forgetfulness. If you lose, you keep your red nose out of my business for fifty years."

"Agreed," Shlimazel replied. "Well, what will you do that's so nice?"

"I will go to the poorest hut in this village and bring happiness to whoever lives there. I will remain with that person for an entire year. The moment the year is at an end, you may take over, but only on condition that you will neither kill him through a mishap nor make him sick nor impoverish him. And on no account are you to use any of your old and tired games. Now, how much time will you need to undo what I have done?"

"One second," Shlimazel replied.

"It's a bet."

Mazel stretched out his hand. The green gem of hope sparkled from a ring on his third finger. He grasped Shlimazel's gaunt and wrinkled hand, which had crooked fingers with horny nails. The day was warm, but Shlimazel's hand was as cold as ice.

Soon after they parted, Mazel came to a hut which he knew must be the poorest in the village. The logs from which it had been built were rotted and covered with moss. Its thatched roof had turned black with time. There was no chimney and the smoke from the stove escaped through a hole in the roof. The glass panes had long since disappeared from the windows, which were boarded over.

Mazel had to bend his head to get through the door. Inside, toadstools sprouted from the unplastered walls.

On a broken-down cot which was covered with straw

sat a young peasant lad. He was barefoot and half naked. Mazel asked him his name.

"Tam," he replied.

"Why are you so down and out?" Mazel inquired.

Tam could not see Mazel, but nevertheless he spoke to him, thinking that he was talking to himself. Tam said, "I once had parents, but they were unlucky. My father died of consumption. My mother went to the forest to gather mushrooms and was bitten by a poisonous snake. The small piece of land they left me is so full of rocks that I can hardly farm it. And last year there was a drought and a locust plague. This year I won't even have a harvest because I had nothing to sow."

"Still, one shouldn't lose hope," Mazel said.

"What can I hope for?" Tam asked. "If you don't sow, you don't reap. My clothes are in tatters and the girls of the village laugh at me. A man without luck is worse than dead."

"Something good may still happen," suggested Mazel.

"When?"

"Soon."

"How?"

Before Mazel could reply, there was a sound of trumpets and galloping hooves. Twenty-four royal guards on horseback preceded the king's carriage drawn by six white stallions. The horsemen were uniformed in red pantaloons, yellow tunics, and plumed white helmets. A company of courtiers, also mounted, followed the carriage.

All the villagers had come out to admire the royal travelers. Whoever was wearing a hat removed it. Some of the villagers kneeled. The girls curtsied.

At first it looked as if the carriage would pass through the village without stopping and the people would hardly be able to catch a glimpse of their king. But Mazel had already figured things out. As the carriage reached Tam's hut, one of its wheels rolled off and the vehicle almost turned over. The riders reined in their horses and the entire company came to a standstill.

The door of the carriage opened and the king came out, followed by the seventeen-year-old Crown Princess Nesika, his only child. Nesika was famous for her beauty both at home and abroad. The royal party was returning from a ball given in her honor by the king of a neighboring land. The princess's golden hair fell to her shoulders, her eyes were blue, her skin white, her neck long, and her waist narrow. She was gowned in a white dress reaching to the tips of her slippers. The king had always spoiled her because her mother had died when Nesika was small. But today he was angry at his lovely daughter.

The purpose of the ball had been to introduce Nesika to Crown Prince Typpish and a match was to be arranged between them. However, Nesika had not liked the prince, and he was the seventh prince in a row that she had rejected. Of the first, she had said that he laughed too loud and too often. The second spoke of nothing but his skill at hunting foxes. She had seen the third beating his dog. The fourth had the most irritating habit of beginning each sentence with "I." The fifth had been a practical joker. The sixth had the habit of telling the same stories over and over again. As for Typpish, Nesika had simply announced that she would not have him because his boots were foolish.

"How can boots be foolish?" her father asked.

"If the feet are foolish, the boots are foolish," Nesika replied.

"How can feet be foolish?" her father insisted.

"If the head is foolish, the feet are foolish," Nesika retorted.

Each time Nesika had found a reason not to be married. The king was beginning to be afraid she would turn into an old maid.

According to the law of the land, Nesika could become queen on her father's death only if she had a husband to help her rule. If she failed to marry, the prime minister, whose name was Kamstan, would ascend the throne in her place. Kamstan was well known for being an intriguer, a coward, and a miser. He was so extremely stingy that for their golden wedding anniversary, when it is customary to present an object of gold, he gave his beloved wife a tin thimble wrapped in gold paper.

When the wheel fell off his carriage, the already angry king flew into a rage. He rebuked his attendants for endangering his life and demanded to know which one of them could set the wheel back in place the fastest.

Tam knew little about fixing a wheel and nothing about fancy carriages. But since Mazel stood behind him, he was filled with courage and called out, "I can do it, Your Majesty."

The king looked with curiosity at the half-naked lad. After some hesitation, and a nudge from Mazel, he said, "If you can do it—do it—and quickly."

The villagers, who knew Tam as a ne'er-do-well and a

bungler, watched in fear. They were sure that he would fail and that the king would vent his anger on the entire village.

When Mazel stands behind a man, that man succeeds in everything, and so it was with Tam. As a young boy he had worked for a short time in a smithy, but he was sure that he remembered nothing of what he had learned there. However, no sooner had he picked up the wheel than everything came back to him. The king looked on in amazement at how deftly the young lad worked. When the job was finished, the king asked Tam how it happened that such an able young man was going around in tatters and lived in a ruin.

"Because I'm unlucky," Tam replied.

"Luck sometimes changes very quickly," the king said. "Come along to court, and we'll find something there for you to do."

It all happened so suddenly that the villagers could not believe their eyes. The king simply opened the door of his carriage and told Tam to get in. Then he gave the command to drive on.

Tam was in constant fear that the wheel would come off again, but even though the horses galloped along at full speed, the wheel remained in place.

The king and Nesika questioned Tam about his life in the village. The lad replied in a humble manner and his answers were brief and clever. Mazel was talking through him. The king turned to Nesika and spoke in a foreign language which Tam didn't understand but Mazel did: "See what bright young men there are among our peasants." And Nesika replied in the same language, "Many a prince could learn from him." After a while she added thoughtfully, "He is handsome, too. All he needs are some decent clothes."

Since Mazel had only a year's time to work in, things began to happen at once. That very day, as soon as they arrived at the palace, the king gave orders that a bath be prepared for Tam and he be given fresh linen and new clothes. He was put to work in the royal smithy.

Tam very soon began to show unusual skill. He could mend carriages that were considered beyond repair. He could shoe horses so wild that no one else dared go near them. He also turned out to be a great horseman. In less than a month he was appointed master of the king's stables.

Once each year the royal races were held at court. Tam was permitted to take part and he managed almost immediately to enchant the courtiers, visiting dignitaries, the king's wise men, and, as a matter of fact, the entire country.

Tam had chosen to ride an unknown horse, but with Mazel's help it became the fleetest horse in the history of the land. With Tam as rider it easily cleared the broadest ditches, the highest fences, and won all the purses. He cut such an elegant figure that all the ladies of the court fell in love with him.

Needless to say, Nesika had been in love with him from the very start. As always with those who are deeply in love, Nesika thought that her feelings for Tam were her secret. Actually, the entire court knew about it, even her father, the king. He also knew that lovers can be very stubborn. And since the proud king did not want to marry his daughter to the son of peasants, he decided to give Tam a task so challenging that he was bound to fail. He sent him with a small group of retainers into the depths of the kingdom to demand the allegiance of a wild and rebellious tribe that no lord of the king had been able to win over. With Mazel's help Tam not only succeeded but returned with magnificent gifts for the king and Princess Nesika.

Tam's fame continued to grow. Bards and minstrels sang of his deeds. High officials came to him for advice. He became the most admired and best-loved man in the kingdom. When the humble achieve success, they often become haughty and forget those among whom they grew up. Tam always found time to help the peasants and the poor.

It is known that the greater a man becomes, the more powerful are his enemies. Prime Minister Kamtsan, who wanted the throne, intrigued against Tam. He and his henchmen spread the word that Tam was a sorcerer. How else could a lowly peasant have managed to succeed where lords had failed? They said Tam had sold his soul to the Devil. When that year, night after night, a strange comet with a long tail was seen in the sky, Tam's enemies insisted it was an omen that Tam would bring misfortune on the king and lead the country to ruin.

Shlimazel had promised Mazel to leave Tam in peace for a full year, but this did not prevent him from quietly preparing to trap Tam the moment the time was up. Shlimazel could not wait to win his bet and get hold of the barrel of the wine of forgetfulness. It was known that one sip of this wine gave more enjoyment than all other pleasurable things on earth. Shlimazel had for ages been suffering from sleeplessness and nightmares. He knew that the wine of forgetfulness would at last bring him sleep and sweet dreams of silver seas, golden rivers, gardens of crystal trees, and women of heavenly beauty. He also wanted to show his followers, the demons, goblins, hobgoblins, imps, and other evil spirits, that he was more powerful than Mazel and could outwit him.

Suddenly the king became ill. There were great doctors in the court but they could not discover what was wrong with him. At last, after long consultation, they decided that the king suffered from a rare disease for which the only cure was the milk of a lioness. Where does one get the milk of a lioness? There was a zoo in the capital, but at that moment it had no lioness with nursing cubs. The king's faith in Tam was so great that he sent for him and asked him to fetch the milk of a lioness. Anyone else in Tam's place would have been frightened out of his wits on hearing such a request. Since Mazel stood behind him, Tam replied simply, "Yes, my king, I will find a lioness, milk her, and bring her milk to you."

The king was so touched by Tam's brave reply that he called out to his courtiers, "You are my witnesses. The day Tam returns with the milk of a lioness, I will give him the hand of my daughter in marriage."

Prime Minister Kamtsan, standing among the courtiers, could contain himself no longer. "Your Majesty," he said, "no man can milk a lioness and live. Tam has made a promise that he cannot keep."

"And if he does bring milk, what guarantee is there that it will really be a lioness's milk?" added one of Kamtsan's followers.

"Your Majesty, I will find a lioness and milk her," Tam repeated with confidence.

"Go, and success be with you," the king said. "But I warn you: do not fool me by bringing me the milk of any other animal."

"If I deceive Your Majesty, I will deserve to die," Tam replied.

Everybody expected that Tam would arm himself with weapons and a net with which to ensnare the beast, or perhaps take along herbs with which to put the lioness to sleep. They could not believe he would travel without servants to help him. But he left alone and unarmed, riding his horse and carrying only a stone jug for the milk.

When the courtiers saw this, even those who had had confidence in Tam began to doubt. He had departed in such haste that he had not even stopped to bid farewell to anxious Nesika. Kamtsan's friends immediately spread the rumor that Tam had been so frightened by the difficult mission given him by the king that he had simply run away. All the wise men agreed that no lioness would let herself be milked by a human.

Of course, what nobody knew was that Mazel cantered along beside Tam. Tam had hardly ridden an hour's time when on a low hill he saw a large lioness. Her two cubs were standing nearby.

With the courage of those who are protected by Mazel, Tam approached the lioness, knelt down, and began to milk her as if she were a cow. He filled the jug with the lioness's warm milk, sealed it carefully, rose, and patted her on the head. Only then did the lioness seem to realize what had happened. Her yellow eyes seemed to say, "What have I permitted! Have I forgotten that I am queen of all the beasts? Where is my pride? My dignity?" And suddenly she let out a terrible roar. Luckily, Tam had already mounted his horse, for it bolted in fear and raced away in the direction of the capital.

When Tam returned so soon, everyone was convinced that the milk he brought back could not be that of a lioness. Lions lived in the desert, in a part of the kingdom that lay weeks away from the capital. It was clear to all that Tam intended to deceive the sick king so that when the king died Tam would rule through Nesika.

The king himself was as suspicious as the rest. Nevertheless, he summoned Tam to appear before him. Tam entered the royal chamber carrying the jug of milk in both hands.

Kneeling before the king, he said, "Your Majesty, I have brought what you sent me for—the milk of a dog."

A dead silence followed his words. The king's eyes filled with anger.

"You dare laugh at my misfortune. Milk of a dog you have brought me. You will pay for this with your life."

Why had Tam said that he had brought the milk of a dog?

It so happened that the very second that Tam approached the king's sickbed Mazel's year had come to an end and Shlimazel had taken his place. It was Shlimazel who made Tam say "dog" instead of "lioness."

Shlimazel had indeed in one second destroyed what had taken Mazel a year to do. And, as had been agreed between them, Shlimazel had not used any of his old tricks.

Tam tried to correct his mistake, but his voice had gone with his luck and he stood there speechless. At the king's signal, Kamtsan ordered two guards to seize Tam and place him in chains. They brought him to the dungeon where those condemned to death were kept.

When Nesika heard what had happened, she fell into despair. She ran to her father's chambers to beg him to save Tam. For the first time, the sick king refused to permit her into his presence.

That night the palace, indeed the whole capital, was dark and quiet. Only Kamtsan and his henchmen secretly celebrated Tam's downfall. They knew the king would soon die, and since Nesika was unmarried, Kamtsan would inherit the kingdom. The prime minister offered his guests bread and beer. Miser that he was, it was his custom to make his guests pay for their food and drink. On this occasion, however, he charged them only for their beer.

And in the deepest cellar of the palace, which was known to be haunted, Mazel and Shlimazel held their meeting. Shlimazel had expected Mazel to look disappointed and angry, as do those who have lost a bet. But Mazel was not a sore loser. As usual, he was calm and composed.

"Shlimazel, you've won, and I congratulate you," he said.

"Do you realize that your lucky Tam will be hanged at dawn?" Shlimazel asked.

"Yes, I do."

"Have you forgotten my wine of forgetfulness?"

"No, I haven't."

Mazel went out and soon returned, rolling a barrel covered with dust and cobwebs. He set it upright, handed Shlimazel a goblet, and said, "Drink, Shlimazel, as much as your heart desires." Shlimazel placed his goblet under the spigot, filled it, and drank greedily. A broad smirk spread over his devilish face. "For one who is the master of the unlucky"—he grinned—"I sure am lucky."

He took another long drink, and beginning to sound tipsy, he said, "Listen to me, Mazel. Instead of fighting me, why don't you join me? Together we'd make a great team."

"You mean together we could ruin the world," Mazel said.

"Absolutely."

"And what then? After a while we'd have nothing left to do."

"As long as we can drink the wine of forgetfulness, why worry?"

"To get wine, someone has to plant the vineyard," Mazel reminded him. "Someone has to pick the grapes, press them, and prepare the wine. Nothing produces nothing—not even the wine of forgetfulness."

"If this wine works, I don't care about the future."

"It will work soon," Mazel said. "Drink and forget yourself."

"Have a drink too, Mazel, my friend."

"No, Shlimazel, forgetfulness is not for me."

Shlimazel drank one goblet after another. His wrinkled face half laughed, half cried, and he began to speak about himself in the way drunkards sometimes do.

"I wasn't born Shlimazel," he said. "My father was poor, but he was a good spirit. He was a water carrier in Paradise. My mother was a servant of a saint. My parents sent me to Reb Zeinvel's school. They wanted me to become a seraph, or at least an angel. But I hated my parents because they forced me to study. To spite them, I joined a gang of imps. We did all kinds of mischief. We stole manna. We stuffed ourselves with pilfered stardust, moon milk, and other forbidden delicacies. At night we descended to earth, got into stables, and frightened horses. We broke into larders and left devil's dung in the food. We disguised ourselves as wolves and chased sheep. What didn't we do? Once, I turned myself into a frog and hid in Reb Zeinvel's snuffbox. When he opened it to take a pinch, I jumped out and bit his nose. I rose slowly but steadily in the ranks of the evil host until I became what I am today—Shlimazel, Master of Bad Luck." Shlimazel filled another goblet and began to sing in a hoarse voice:

> *You may plot and you may scheme,*
> *Mazel is an empty dream.*
> *Now Shlimazel's taken over,*
> *Tam will never be in clover.*
> *Mazel talks, Shlimazel acts,*
> *turning curses into facts.*
> *Mazel wins a round or two,*
> *Shlimazel sees the battle through.*

On Mazel no one can depend,
Shlimazel's victor in the end.

Shlimazel uttered a snort and fell down like a log.

That was what Mazel had been waiting for. There was little time, because dawn was approaching and in the palace courtyard the dignitaries were already gathering for Tam's hanging. The guards appeared with Tam in chains. Kamtsan, surrounded by his flatterers, was conspicuous among the lords. He had already taken bribes and promised the highest positions to those who paid the most.

At a signal from Kamtsan, the drummers began their drumming. The masked executioner, dressed half in red and half in black, prepared to place the noose around Tam's neck. At that moment Mazel appeared. No one saw him but everybody felt his presence. The sun suddenly rose and covered everything with a purple light.

Now that Shlimazel lay in a drunken stupor and Mazel stood near the prisoner, Tam was again filled with courage. He called out in a clear voice, "My lords, it is the custom, before the condemned dies, to give him one last wish. My wish is to see the king."

The drummers, in confusion, interrupted their drumming. Though Kamtsan protested, the other lords overruled him and commanded that Tam be led to the king, who lay on his sickbed.

Tam knelt before the king and spoke: "Your Majesty, allow me to explain why I said that I had brought you the milk of a dog. It is known that the lion is the king of the animals, yet in comparison with you, my lord, a lion is no more than a dog. And so I called the lioness a dog as an expression of my respect and admiration for Your Majesty. I did bring you the milk of a lioness. I beg you, drink it and it will make you well. I swear on my love for Nesika that I am telling the truth."

Since Mazel again stood at Tam's side, the king believed Tam.

"But the milk has been poured out," Kamtsan interrupted.

Nesika, who had not slept all night, praying and hoping that Tam would somehow be saved, had heard what had taken place and had rushed to her father's room. When Kamtsan said that the milk had been thrown away, she cried out, "No, Kamtsan, I have kept it. I requested the servants to give it to me because I believed in Tam."

She herself ran to bring the milk to her father. The amazement of all present grew as they watched the king drink the milk to the last drop. It worked so quickly that he became well before their very eyes. His cheeks lost their pallor, his dim eyes regained their former brightness, and his strength returned. The entire court rejoiced, except, naturally, Kamtsan and those to whom he had sold high positions in the kingdom. Nesika was the happiest of all.

She fell at her father's feet and said, "Father, Tam saved your life. Every word he spoke was true. Now keep your promise and let us be married."

The king immediately ordered that a wedding fit for a future queen be prepared. Royalty and dignitaries were invited from all the surrounding countries. Kings, queens, princes, and princesses came to the wedding accompanied by their royal entourages. They brought the most precious gifts.

Nesika was a splendid sight in her wedding dress, which had a train ten yards long that was carried by twenty pages. On her head she wore a dazzling coronet set with the diamond image of a lioness. On his uniform Tam wore the Order of Selfless Devotion, the country's highest honor.

Tam and Nesika were the happiest couple in the land. Nesika bore her husband seven children—four princes and three princesses, all handsome, healthy, and courageous.

Nobody lives forever. A day came when the king died. Nesika became queen, and Tam her prince consort. Nesika never decided any matters of state without the advice of her husband, because whatever Tam concerned himself with turned out well.

As for Kamtsan, he felt so sorry for himself that he took to drinking. Since he remained stingy as ever, he spent his time hanging around taverns, waiting for someone to treat him. Those who had once flattered him were the first to turn away.

Even though after some time Shlimazel awoke from his sleep, he never went near Tam again. For such was the power of the wine of forgetfulness that Shlimazel didn't even remember that Tam existed. As Shlimazel had always been fond of drink and drunkards, he now attached himself to Kamtsan. Mazel, of course, continued to help Tam. Actually, Tam no longer needed Mazel, except once in a while. Tam had learned that good luck follows those who are diligent, honest, sincere, and helpful to others. The man who has these qualities is indeed lucky forever.

Translated by the author and Elizabeth Shub

Why Noah Chose the Dove

When the people sinned and God decided to punish them by sending the flood, all the animals gathered around Noah's ark. Noah was a righteous man, and God had told him how to save himself and his family by building an ark that would float and shelter them when the waters rose.

The animals had heard a rumor that Noah was to take with him on the ark only the best of all the living creatures. So the animals came and vied with one another, each boasting about its own virtues and whenever possible belittling the merits of others.

The lion roared: "I am the strongest of all the beasts, and I surely must be saved."

The elephant blared: "I am the largest. I have the longest trunk, the biggest ears, and the heaviest feet."

"To be big and heavy is not so important," yapped the fox. "I, the fox, am the cleverest of all."

"What about me?" brayed the donkey. "I thought I was the cleverest."

"It seems anyone can be clever," yipped the skunk. "I smell the best of all the animals. My perfume is famous."

"All of you scramble over the earth, but I'm the only one that can climb trees," shrieked the monkey.

"The only one!" growled the bear. "What do you think I do?"

"And how about me?" chattered the squirrel indignantly.

"I belong to the tiger family," purred the cat.

"I'm a cousin of the elephant," squeaked the mouse.

"I'm just as strong as the lion," snarled the tiger. "And I have the most beautiful fur."

"My spots are more admired then your stripes," the leopard spat back.

"I am man's closest friend," yelped the dog.

"You're no friend. You're just a fawning flatterer," bayed the wolf. "I am proud. I'm a lone wolf and flatter no one."

"Baa!" blatted the sheep. "That's why you're always hungry. Give nothing, get nothing. I give man my wool, and he takes care of me."

"You give man wool, but I give him sweet honey," droned the bee. "Besides, I have venom to protect me from my enemies."

"What is your venom compared with mine?" rattled the snake. "And I am closer to Mother Earth than any of you."

"Not as close as I am," protested the earthworm, sticking its head out of the ground.

"I lay eggs," clucked the hen.

"I give milk," mooed the cow.

"I help man plow the earth," bellowed the ox.

"I carry man," neighed the horse. "And I have the largest eyes of all of you."

"You have the largest eyes, but you have only two, while I have many," the housefly buzzed right into the horse's ear.

"Compared with me, you're all midgets." The giraffe's words came from a distance as he nibbled the leaves off the top of a tree.

"I'm almost as tall as you are," chortled the camel. "And I can travel in the desert for days without food or water."

"You two are tall, but I'm fat," snorted the hippopotamus. "And I'm pretty sure that my mouth is bigger than anybody's."

"Don't be so sure," snapped the crocodile, and yawned.

"I can speak like a human," squawked the parrot.

"You don't really speak—you just imitate," the rooster crowed. "I know only one word, 'cock-a-doodle-doo,' but it is my own."

"I see with my ears; I fly by hearing," piped the bat.

"I sing with my wing," chirped the cricket.

There were many more creatures who were eager to praise themselves. But Noah had noticed that the dove was perched alone on a branch and did not try to speak and compete with the other animals.

"Why are you silent?" Noah asked the dove. "Don't you have anything to boast about?"

"I don't think of myself as better or wiser or more attractive than the other animals," cooed the dove. "Each one of us has something the other doesn't have, given us by God who created us all."

"The dove is right," Noah said. "There is no need to boast and compete with one another. God has ordered me to take creatures of all kinds into the ark, cattle and beast, bird and insect."

The animals were overjoyed when they heard these words, and all their grudges were forgotten.

Before Noah opened the door of the ark, he said, "I love all of you, but because the dove remained modest and silent while the rest of you bragged and argued, I choose it to be my messenger."

Noah kept his word. When the rains stopped, he sent the dove to fly over the world and bring back news of how things were. At last she returned with an olive leaf in her beak, and Noah knew that the waters had receded. When the land finally became dry, Noah and his family and all the animals left the ark.

After the flood God promised that never again would he destroy the earth because of man's sins, and that seed time and harvest, cold and heat, summer and winter, day and night would never cease.

The truth is that there are in the world more doves than there are tigers, leopards, wolves, vultures, and other ferocious beasts. The dove lives happily without fighting. It is the bird of peace.

Translated by Elizabeth Shub

Zlateh the Goat

At Hanukkah time the road from the village to the town is usually covered with snow, but this year the winter had been a mild one. Hanukkah had almost come, yet little snow had fallen. The sun shone most of the time. The peasants complained that because of the dry weather there would be a poor harvest of winter grain. New grass sprouted, and the peasants sent their cattle out to pasture.

For Reuven the furrier it was a bad year, and after long hesitation he decided to sell Zlateh the goat. She was old and gave little milk. Feivel the town butcher had offered eight gulden for her. Such a sum would buy Hanukkah candles, potatoes and oil for pancakes, gifts for the children, and other holiday necessaries for the house. Reuven told his oldest boy Aaron to take the goat to town.

Aaron understood what taking the goat to Feivel

meant, but had to obey his father. Leah, his mother, wiped the tears from her eyes when she heard the news. Aaron's younger sisters, Anna and Miriam, cried loudly. Aaron put on his quilted jacket and a cap with earmuffs, bound a rope around Zlateh's neck, and took along two slices of bread with cheese to eat on the road. Aaron was supposed to deliver the goat by evening, spend the night at the butcher's, and return the next day with the money.

While the family said goodbye to the goat, and Aaron placed the rope around her neck, Zlateh stood as patiently and good-naturedly as ever. She licked Reuven's hand. She shook her small white beard. Zlateh trusted human beings. She knew that they always fed her and never did her any harm.

When Aaron brought her out on the road to town, she seemed somewhat astonished. She'd never been led in that direction before. She looked back at him questioningly, as if to say, "Where are you taking me?" But after a while she seemed to come to the conclusion that a goat shouldn't ask questions. Still, the road was different. They passed new fields, pastures, and huts with thatched roofs. Here and there a dog barked and came running after them, but Aaron chased it away with his stick.

The sun was shining when Aaron left the village. Suddenly the weather changed. A large black cloud with a bluish center appeared in the east and spread itself rapidly over the sky. A cold wind blew in with it. The crows flew low, croaking. At first it looked as if it would rain, but instead it began to hail as in summer. It was early in the day, but it became dark as dusk. After a while the hail turned to snow.

In his twelve years Aaron had seen all kinds of weather, but he had never experienced a snow like this one. It was so dense it shut out the light of the day. In a short time their path was completely covered. The wind became as cold as ice. The road to town was narrow and winding. Aaron no longer knew where he was. He could not see through the snow. The cold soon penetrated his quilted jacket.

At first Zlateh didn't seem to mind the change in weather. She, too, was twelve years old and knew what winter meant. But when her legs sank deeper and deeper into the snow, she began to turn her head and look at Aaron in wonderment. Her mild eyes seemed to ask, "Why are we out in such a storm?" Aaron hoped that a peasant would come along with his cart, but no one passed by.

The snow grew thicker, falling to the ground in large, whirling flakes. Beneath it Aaron's boots touched the softness of a plowed field. He realized that he was no longer on the road. He had gone astray. He could no longer figure out which was east or west, which way was the village, the town. The wind whistled, howled, whirled the snow about in eddies. It looked as if white imps were playing tag on the fields. A white dust rose above the ground. Zlateh stopped. She could walk no longer. Stubbornly she anchored her cleft hooves in the earth and bleated as if pleading to be taken home. Icicles hung from her white beard, and her horns were glazed with frost.

Aaron did not want to admit the danger, but he knew just the same that if they did not find shelter they would freeze to death. This was no ordinary storm. It was a mighty blizzard. The snowfall had reached his knees. His hands were numb, and he could no longer feel his toes. He choked when he breathed. His nose felt like wood, and he rubbed it with snow. Zlateh's bleating began to sound like crying. Those humans in whom she had so much confidence had dragged her into a trap. Aaron began to pray to God for himself and for the innocent animal.

Suddenly he made out the shape of a hill. He wondered what it could be. Who had piled snow into such a huge heap? He moved toward it, dragging Zlateh after him. When he came near it, he realized that it was a large haystack which the snow had blanketed.

Aaron realized immediately that they were saved. With great effort he dug his way through the snow. He was a village boy and knew what to do. When he reached the hay, he hollowed out a nest for himself and the goat. No matter how cold it may be outside, in the hay it is always warm. And hay was food for Zlateh. The moment she smelled it she became contented and began to eat. Outside, the snow continued to fall. It quickly covered the passageway Aaron had dug. But a boy and an animal need to breathe, and there was hardly any air in their hideout. Aaron bored a kind of a window through the hay and snow and carefully kept the passage clear.

Zlateh, having eaten her fill, sat down on her hind legs and seemed to have regained her confidence in man. Aaron ate his two slices of bread and cheese, but after the difficult journey he was still hungry. He looked at Zlateh and noticed her udders were full. He lay down next to her, placing himself so that when he milked her he could squirt the milk into his mouth. It was rich and sweet. Zlateh was not accustomed to being milked that way, but she did not resist. On the contrary, she seemed eager to reward Aaron for bringing her to a shelter whose very walls, floor, and ceiling were made of food.

Through the window Aaron could catch a glimpse of the chaos outside. The wind carried before it whole drifts of snow. It was completely dark, and he did not know whether night had already come or whether it was the darkness of the storm. Thank God that in the hay it was not cold. The dried hay, grass, and field flowers exuded the warmth of the summer sun. Zlateh ate frequently; she nibbled from above, below, from the left and right. Her body gave forth an animal warmth, and Aaron cuddled up to her. He had always loved Zlateh, but now she was like a sister. He was alone, cut off from his family, and wanted to talk. He began to talk to Zlateh. "Zlateh, what do you think about what has happened to us?" he asked.

"Maaaa," Zlateh answered.

"If we hadn't found this stack of hay, we would both be frozen stiff by now," Aaron said.

"Maaaa," was the goat's reply.

"If the snow keeps on falling like this, we may have to stay here for days," Aaron explained.

"Maaaa," Zlateh bleated.

"What does 'maaaa' mean?" Aaron asked. "You'd better speak up clearly."

"Maaaa, maaaa," Zlateh tried.

"Well, let it be 'maaaa' then," Aaron said patiently. "You can't speak, but I know you understand. I need you and you need me. Isn't that right?"

"Maaaa."

Aaron became sleepy. He made a pillow out of some hay, leaned his head on it, and dozed off. Zlateh, too, fell asleep.

When Aaron opened his eyes, he didn't know whether it was morning or night. The snow had blocked up his window. He tried to clear it, but when he had bored through to the length of his arm, he still hadn't reached the outside. Luckily he had his stick with him and was able to break through to the open air. It was still dark outside. The snow continued to fall and the wind wailed, first with one voice and then with many. Sometimes it had the sound of devilish laughter. Zlateh, too, awoke, and when Aaron greeted her, she answered, "Maaaa." Yes, Zlateh's language consisted of only one word, but it meant many things. Now she was saying, "We must accept all that God gives us—heat, cold, hunger, satisfaction, light, and darkness."

Aaron had awakened hungry. He had eaten up his food, but Zlateh had plenty of milk.

For three days Aaron and Zlateh stayed in the haystack. Aaron had always loved Zlateh, but in these three days he loved her more and more. She fed him with her milk and helped him keep warm. She comforted him with her patience. He told her many stories, and she always cocked her ears and listened. When he patted her, she licked his hand and his face. Then she said, "Maaaa," and he knew it meant, I love you, too.

The snow fell for three days, though after the first day it was not as thick and the wind quieted down. Sometimes Aaron felt that there could never have been a summer, that the snow had always fallen, ever since he could remember. He, Aaron, never had a father or mother or sisters. He was a snow child, born of the snow, and so was Zlateh. It was so quiet in the hay that his ears rang in the stillness. Aaron and Zlateh slept all night and a good part of the day. As for Aaron's dreams, they were all about warm weather. He dreamed of green fields, trees covered with blossoms, clear brooks, and singing birds. By the third night the snow had stopped, but Aaron did not dare to find his way home in the darkness. The sky became clear and the moon shone, casting silvery nets on the snow. Aaron dug his way out and looked at the world. It was all white, quiet, dreaming dreams of heavenly splendor. The stars were large and close. The moon swam in the sky as in a sea.

On the morning of the fourth day Aaron heard the ringing of sleigh bells. The haystack was not far from the road. The peasant who drove the sleigh pointed out the way to him—not to the town and Feivel the butcher, but home to the village. Aaron had decided in the haystack that he would never part with Zlateh.

Aaron's family and their neighbors had searched for the boy and the goat but had found no trace of them during the storm. They feared they were lost. Aaron's mother and sisters cried for him; his father remained silent and gloomy. Suddenly one of the neighbors came running to their house with the news that Aaron and Zlateh were coming up the road.

There was great joy in the family. Aaron told them how he had found the stack of hay and how Zlateh had fed him with her milk. Aaron's sisters kissed and hugged Zlateh and gave her a special treat of chopped carrots and potato peels, which Zlateh gobbled up hungrily.

Nobody ever again thought of selling Zlateh, and now that the cold weather had finally set in, the villagers needed the services of Reuven the furrier once more. When Hanukkah came, Aaron's mother was able to fry pancakes every evening, and Zlateh got her portion, too. Even though Zlateh had her own pen, she often came to the kitchen, knocking on the door with her horns to indicate that she was ready to visit, and she was always admitted. In the evening Aaron, Miriam, and Anna played dreidel. Zlateh sat near the stove watching the children and the flickering of the Hanukkah candles.

Once in a while Aaron would ask her, "Zlateh, do you remember the three days we spent together?"

And Zlateh would scratch her neck with a horn, shake her white bearded head, and come out with the single sound which expressed all her thoughts, and all her love.

Translated by the author and Elizabeth Shub

A Hanukkah Eve
in Warsaw

I

For two weeks now Warsaw—and perhaps all Poland—had lain in the grip of a cold spell the likes of
which hadn't been seen in years. But I, a child not yet
seven, kept going to cheder early each morning. We—my
parents, my older brother Joshua, my sister Hindele, my
younger brother Moshe, and I—lived at 10 Krochmalna
Street and the cheder was located at 5 Grzybowska
Street. In the mornings, an assistant to the teacher came
to take me to cheder, and he brought me home again in
the evenings. To keep me from freezing on the way,
Mother wrapped me in two woolen vests, two pairs of
socks, and gloves. She stuck a hood on my head which
covered my red hair and earlocks; when I looked in the
mirror I couldn't recognize myself and stuck my tongue
out at the stranger.

The long winter night passed full of dreams. Now I
dreamed I was an emperor, and now a beggar. An old

crone of a gypsy snatched me and locked me in a cellar. I also dreamed that it was summer and that I was strolling with Shosha, the daughter of our neighbor Bashele, in a garden full of blooming flowers and singing birds. I sailed a boat on the Vistula but soon pirates captured me and spirited me off to Madagascar to be sold into slavery. My dreams blended with my fantasies and with the tales I had heard from my mother or read in storybooks.

That winter morning was a cold but sunny one. The sky above the rooftops loomed a light blue. Although our oven was heated with wood and coal, frost patterns had formed on our windows overnight. They resembled trees, not those common to Poland, but rather the date palms and fig and carob trees the Bible said grew in the Land of Israel.

Normally, I stayed at the cheder until nightfall, but that day was the eve of Hanukkah and I was scheduled to come home earlier than usual. I liked Hanukkah—the only holiday that came in the winter. In the evening, right after services, Father would bless the Hanukkah candles, Mother would fry potato pancakes, I would get a tin dreidel and money for the holiday. I could hardly wait to get home.

Before I left the house, Mother gave me a paper bag containing bread and butter, cheese, and an apple. This was to be my second breakfast. The assistant teacher took my hand and led me down the stairs into the street. Mother warned him not to let go of me. In such a large city a child could easily get lost. The streets were filled with sleighs and I was liable to be run over, God forbid. I was ashamed that my mother was such a worrier. She came from a small town and provincial people imagined all kinds of dangers in the big city. I had come to Warsaw when I was three and I considered myself a city boy. I could have gone to cheder by myself; I didn't have to be escorted there. I envied the other children my age who went to cheder alone. It seemed to me they laughed at me for being escorted like a baby.

God in heaven, how different the street looked today, all covered by the fresh snow that had fallen overnight! The sleighs and pedestrians hadn't yet managed to trample it, and it glared beneath the sun, reflecting dazzling crystals of every color of the rainbow. One solitary tree grew on our street and its naked branches were covered with frost. They reminded me of the arms of a huge Hanukkah candelabrum. Sleighs rode by with bells on horses' collars jingling. The animals' nostrils exuded steam. Cushions of snow lay on roofs and balconies. The whole world had turned white, rich, and dreamlike.

2

Coming to cheder was for me a daily trial. The other pupils quickly made friends with one another. They conducted all kinds of secret business transactions among themselves. One boy gave another a silver button and got a gold button in exchange. Quietly, so that the teacher wouldn't see, they traded pencils, pens, and sometimes chocolates and cookies they brought from home. Most of the students were sons of storekeepers or factory owners and were already little businessmen themselves. Their parents lived in the wealthier streets. Some of the

students brought a different toy to cheder each day—
lead soldiers, whistles, trumpets. One boy had a pen with
a peephole. When you looked into it you saw Cracow.
Another boy had a music box. When you turned the key
it played a tune. One boy had a real watch. Most of them
had black hair, and some were blond, but no one in the
cheder besides me had hair as red as fire. Nor did anyone
else wear such long earlocks. I was a rabbi's son and my
parents dressed me in the old-fashioned style. I had been
raised in Warsaw, but I looked like a yokel. The boys
laughed at me and my small-town costumes. They even
mocked the way I pronounced some words in Yiddish.
Besides, they couldn't do any trading with me. I brought
nothing to cheder except my Pentateuch.

I always felt ashamed when I came to cheder, and I
often prayed to God to let me grow up faster so that I
could be through with being a child. But I had some
satisfaction, too. All children love to hear stories and I
had acquired the reputation of a storyteller. I was also
able to add my own fantasies to the stories we read in the
Pentateuch. At Hanukkah time the teacher studied with
us the section that dealt with Joseph and his brothers. I
retained the meaning of the Hebrew words better than
many of the other children, and I repeated the tale as if
I had been there in person. Joseph's dreams became my
dreams. The brothers envied me and sold me into slavery
to the Ishmaelites, who in turn sold me to the Egyptians.
Potiphar had me imprisoned, and later I became viceroy
to Pharaoh. Jacob, Joseph, the other tribes, Laban,
Rachel, Leah, Bilhah, Zilpah were all as close and familiar to me as my own mother and father, as our neigh-

bor Bashele and her daughter, Shosha, with whom I carried on an unspoken love affair. As I sat in cheder over the Pentateuch, I yearned for her and her childish words, which held a thousand delights for me . . .

By three o'clock we had concluded our portion and the teacher, Reb Moshe Yitzchok, a patriarch of eighty, put down the pointer and the hare's leg with the thong that he used to whip bad pupils, and told us to go home.

The assistant teacher came up to me and began, with hesitation, "You always say that you could find your way home by yourself. Is this true?"

"Yes, it's true."

"You wouldn't get lost?"

"Lost? I could get home in the middle of the night!"

"I've got something to do and I don't have the time to take you home. Can I trust you to get home by yourself?"

"Yes, yes . . ."

"You won't tell your parents?"

"Tell? No, never!"

"Is that a promise?"

"I swear it on my ritual fringes."

"You don't have to swear on your ritual fringes."

"I wouldn't say anything even if they should kill me."

"Well, all right. Go straight home and don't stop along the way. You'll tell them I took you to the gate of your house."

"Yes."

The assistant teacher helped me put on my overcoat, the hood, the gloves, the galoshes. The other boys laughed and made fun of me. They called me a sissy, a mama's boy, a little rabbi, a spoiled brat. One of them showed me his tongue, another made the sign of the fig. A third said, "He is Joseph from the Bible. His father will make him a coat of many colors . . ."

3

I wanted to boast to the boys that I was going home all by myself, but the assistant teacher apparently guessed my intentions, for he put his finger to his lips.

I went out into the street, and for the first time I felt like a grownup. How short the days were in winter! It was just a quarter past three but the sky was already a dusky blue. Several cheder boys were sliding on the frozen gutter, trying to make the figure called "little shoemaker." When they saw me walking alone, they began to yell and make faces as if about to chase me. One of them threw a snowball at me. I moved away from them quickly. They only waited for a chance to start a fight and show off their strength. On Gnoyna Street I stopped in front of a shop window. Although the store belonged to a Jew, it sold the globes, bells, lights, and spangles Gentiles drape on Christmas trees. A man holding a long pole lit the gas streetlights. Women sat in doorways, on boxes and on footstools, hawking their wares—potato cakes, hot chick-peas, hot lima beans, bagels, oil cakes. The smells these delicacies sent out were delicious. I began to fantasize what I would do if I had a million rubles. I would buy all these goodies and make a feast for Shosha. We would munch on chocolate, halvah, tangerines, and take a ride in a sleigh. I would stop going to cheder and have a rabbi tutor me at home.

I was so preoccupied with my reveries I didn't notice that it had started snowing. A dense snow began to fall, dry and grainy as salt. My eyes crusted over. The street gaslights became covered with snow and their shine turned orange, blue, green, violet. This wasn't merely snow but snow mixed with sleet. Chunks of ice fell from the sky and a strong wind began to blow. Maybe the world was coming to an end? It seemed to me that there was thunder and lightning.

I started to run and I fell several times. I picked myself up, and to my alarm I saw that I had strayed into some other street. Here, the streetlights weren't gas but electric. I saw a trolley that wasn't drawn by horses. The rod extending from its roof to the wires overhead sprayed bluish sparks. A fear came over me—I was lost! I stopped passersby and asked them directions, but they ignored me. One person did answer me, but in Polish, a language I had never learned. I could barely keep from crying. I wanted to turn back to where I had come from, but apparently I only strayed farther away. I passed brightly illuminated stores and a building with balconies and columns like some royal palace. Music was playing upstairs, and below, merchants were clearing away their goods from the stalls. The wind scattered kerchiefs, handkerchiefs, shirts, and blouses, and they whirled in the air like imps. That which I had always feared had apparently happened—the evil spirits had turned their wrath on me.

Now the wind thrust me forward, now it dragged me back. It blew up the skirt of my coat and tried to lift me in the air. I knew where the gale sought to carry me—to

Sodom, to beyond the Mountains of Darkness, to Asmodeus's castle, to Mt. Sair, where the ground is copper
and the sky is iron. I wanted to cry out to God, to utter
some prayer or incantation, but my mouth had gone
numb and my nose was stiff as wood. The cold penetrated through my coat, and through both vests. My eyelids became swollen and I could no longer see in the
white maelstrom.

Suddenly I heard a shrill clanging and shouts. Someone sprang and, seizing me from behind, half dragged,
half carried me off. Was this a demon, a wraith? A man
in a long coat and a black beard turned white from the
snow and frost shouted at me in rage, "Where are you
running? Where do you creep to? You just missed being
run over by the trolley car."

I wanted to thank him but I couldn't utter a word.

The man asked, "Who lets a child out in such a blizzard? You have no parents?"

I still don't know why, but I said, "No, I'm an orphan."

"An orphan, eh? Who do you live with?"

"My grandfather."

"Where does your grandfather live?"

I gave a false address—13 Krochmalna Street.

"What are you doing here if you live at 13 Krochmalna? Got lost, eh?"

"No."

"Where were you going?"

"I wanted to say the mourner's prayer," I replied,
astounded by my own lie.

"No synagogues or prayerhouses on Krochmalna? I see
that you're lost. Come, I'll take you back."

He took my hand and led me along.

He asked, "What does your grandfather do? How does he make a living?"

"A porter," I said. The words issued from my mouth as if on their own.

"An old man a porter? He's still got the strength to carry? You hungry?"

"No. Yes."

"Wait, I'll get you something."

We walked only a few minutes. I had assumed I had strayed far from Krochmalna, but suddenly I saw it again. I wanted to get away from the man and my lies, but he held me firmly by the hand. He said, "Don't try to run away, boy. Poverty is no disgrace."

He led me into a restaurant. I had passed this restaurant earlier that day. Summer and winter a cloud of steam hovered inside it, and it always smelled of fried onions, garlic, meat, soup, beer. At night music was played there. I once heard my mother say that they served food that wasn't strictly kosher and that it was patronized by gangsters, thieves, the rabble. One boor there had bet that he could eat a whole roast goose. He was about to swallow the last bite when he got sick and had to be taken to the hospital. Now I was there myself. The floor was tiled in white and black like a checkerboard. Burly men and fat women sat at tables covered in red. Some ate boiled beef, others drank beer from mugs. Many gaslights were flashing. Waiters in white aprons carried huge trays with dishes above the diners' heads. There were other rooms here; from one came the sounds of singing, an accordion, hands clapping.

The man with me couldn't find a table. He stood with me in the crush and spoke to everyone and to no one: "An orphan. Nearly got run over. Hungry, poor thing. Half frozen. Give him something to eat. It's a good deed!"

He begged in my behalf. Again I tried to slip away from him, but he held me fast. The walls here were covered with red tapestries and hung with mirrors, so that I saw myself many times over.

A stout woman came up and asked my benefactor, "Why are you holding this boy? Has he done something?"

"Done something? He's done nothing. A poor orphan and hungry."

"An orphan? He's our rabbi's son. His parents are living. I saw his mother this very day at the butcher's."

"Eh? But he told me he was an orphan and that his grandfather is a porter—"

"A porter? Has he gone mad?"

The man apparently grew so confused that he let go of my hand. I dashed off. In a moment I was outside again.

4

I barely recognized the street. My brother Joshua had often spoken of the North Pole and the fact that the nights there lasted six months. Krochmalna Street now appeared to me like the North Pole. Huge mounds of snow had fallen. Whole towers and mountains had formed on the gutter. The pedestrians sank into the snowy depths. Misty trails extended from the street lamps. The sky hung low, reflecting a violet tinge with no moon or stars showing. I tried to run, fearing the man would catch me and punish me for my lies. I had committed so many sins! My parents would soon discover that I had deceived the man and posed as an orphan. They would also learn that the assistant teacher had let me walk home alone and that I had gotten lost. The boys at the cheder would have something to mock at and would make up new nicknames for me. The assistant teacher would become my enemy.

Suddenly I recalled a story my brother Joshua had told me about a boy who had been sent on a Passover night to open the door for the prophet Elijah and had vanished. Years later he came home a grown man and a professor. He had walked from the town where his parents lived to Warsaw, and then on to Berlin. Rich people there had helped him obtain an education. That's what I would have to do, too—run away from home! I would read all the books about the sun, the moon, the stars. I would learn how mountains, rivers, oceans, and the North Pole had formed. My father had one answer for everything—God had created it all. He wanted me to study only religious books. But the worldly books obviously had many other explanations.

Joshua often spoke about science. He said that a cheder education left one ignorant. He spoke of a telescope through which you could see the mountains and craters of the moon. Since we lived in Warsaw, I could proceed straight to Berlin. I knew that a train left for Germany from the Vienna depot. I would simply follow the tracks till I came to Berlin. But what would my parents do if I didn't come home? And what about Shosha? I would miss her terribly. A strange notion came to me: maybe Shosha would run away with me. In storybooks I often read of boys and girls who left home together on account of love. True, these were grownups, but I loved Shosha. I thought of her during the day and I dreamed about her at night. We would study together in Berlin, and when I became a professor, we would marry and come back to Warsaw. Everyone on Krochmalna Street would come out to greet us. My mother and Shosha's mother would weep and embrace. By then, everyone would have forgotten the silly things I had done today. The cheder boys who now pushed me around and called me names would come to me to teach them science and philosophy . . .

I had reached the gate of 10 Krochmalna Street, but instead of going home I went to Shosha's. I had to talk to her! In my mind I prayed to God that she would be home alone. Her father worked in a store and her mother often went to shop at the bazaar or to gossip with her sister. This time luck was with me. I knocked and Shosha opened. She seemed frightened by me and she said, "Oh, just look at you! White as a snowman."

It was warm in Shosha's kitchen and I promptly began telling her of my plans. She sat down on a footstool. She was blond, blue-eyed, and wore her hair in braids. She was exceptionally pale. Although she was my age, she was like a child of five. She played with dolls and got poor grades at the Polish school she attended. She couldn't read or figure properly. I now suggested that she accompany me to Berlin. Shosha heard me out calmly, then asked, "What will we eat?"

I was dumbfounded. I had completely forgotten that a person had to eat.

After a while I said, "We'll take food from home."

"And where will we sleep?"

I didn't know what to say. The trip to Berlin would undoubtedly take weeks. In the summer you could sleep outdoors, but in the winter it would be too cold. For a moment I wondered at my own stupidity and at Shosha's wisdom. Suddenly the door opened and my mother came in with my sister, Hindele, close behind her.

Hindele exclaimed, "There he is, Mama! What did I tell you?"

Mother stared at me in confusion. "So there you are . . . We've been searching for you two hours. I thought, who knows *what* happened . . ." And all at once she erupted, "Unfaithful child!"

I knew full well the meaning of this expression—a faithless son and a rebellious one. According to the law of the Pentateuch, I should be turned over by my parents to the town elders, who would condemn me to be stoned. An interrogation was forthcoming and I had no excuses ready.

My sister said, "We were waiting for you for the blessing of the Hanukkah candles."

"Where were you all this time? Didn't the assistant teacher bring you?" Mother asked.

"Yes, he brought me."

"When? You've been sitting here two hours?"

"He just came in this second," Shosha said.

"Why were you running around in such a storm? Why did you come here instead of home?"

"He wants us to follow the train tracks . . ." Shosha said, not intending to inform, but simply because she didn't understand the significance of it all.

My sister began to laugh. "He wants to run away with little Shosha! He's carrying on a love affair with her!"

"Don't laugh, Hindele, don't laugh!" Mother said. "The boy is making me sick!"

"Look at him! White as chalk!" my sister observed.

"Come!" Mother said.

She grabbed me by the collar and led me away. I anticipated a severe punishment, but when Father saw me, he only smiled and said, "I'm waiting for you with Hanukkah candles. I have a gift for you, too."

"He's got no gifts coming," Mother exclaimed. "He was outside in the cold the whole time. You didn't even ask where I found him!" she reproached Father. "At our neighbor's, at Bashele's!"

"Who is this Bashele?" Father asked.

"Abraham Kaufman's wife."

"What was he doing there?"

"They have a girl, some little fool, and he wants to run away with her."

Father arched his brows. "Oh, so? Well, it's Hanukkah. I don't want to spoil the holiday."

In honor of the holiday Father had donned his velvet housecoat. Our ceiling lamp was lit. The Hanukkah candelabrum stood ready. A red candle—the so-called sexton—rested in its holder. Father poured in olive oil and fussed with the wick. He made the benediction and lit a candle with the "sexton." Father's red beard glowed like fire. He took a prayer book with wooden covers from his pocket. It had a carving of the Western Wall on the front cover and one of the Cave of Machpelah on the back.

He said, "This prayer book comes from the Land of Israel."

"From the Land of Israel?"

I took the prayer book with joy and trepidation. I had never before held an object that stemmed from this distant and sacred land. It seemed to me that this prayer book exuded the scent of figs, dates, carob beans, cloves, cedar. All the stories from the Scriptures suddenly came to mind: of Sodom, of the Dead Sea, of Rachel's Tomb, of Joseph's dreams, of the ladder the angels climbed up to and down from heaven, as well as of King David, King Solomon, the Queen of Sheba.

My sister, Hindele, said, "Why does he get a gift?" And she added, "The worst dog gets the best bone."

"You'll see that the boy will cause us shame and disgrace!" Mother complained. "I don't believe that the assistant teacher brought him here at all. He always brings him into the house."

"Well, it's a holiday, a holiday!" Father said half to us, half to himself.

"You'll spoil him so, he'll become completely wild," Mother warned.

"With the Almighty's help, he'll grow up a decent man," Father said. He turned to me. "Pray from this book. Everything that comes from the Land of Israel is holy. This Wall is a remnant of the Holy Temple, which the evildoers demolished. The Divine Presence reigns there forever. Jews sinned; that's why the Temple was destroyed. But the Almighty is all-merciful. He is our Father and we are His children. God willing, the Messiah will come and we'll all go back to our homeland. A fiery Temple will descend upon Jerusalem. The dead will be resurrected. Our grandfathers, grandmothers, great-grandfathers, and all the generations will live again. The light of the sun will be seven times brighter than now. The saints will sit with crowns upon their heads and study the secrets of the Torah."

"Mama, the potato pancakes are getting cold," Hindele said.

"Oh, yes!"

And my mother and sister went back to the kitchen.

"Where did you go?" Father asked. "It's freezing outside. You might have caught cold, God forbid. You'd be better off glancing into a holy book."

"Papa, I'd like to study science," I said, astounded at my own words.

"Science? What kind of science?"

"Why summer is warm and winter is cold. How high is the moon and what happens up on the stars. How deep is the earth and how tall is the sky. Everything . . . everything . . ."

"All knowledge is contained in the Torah," Father replied. "Every letter of the Torah conceals countless secrets and infinite depth. Those who study the cabala acquire more truth than all the philosophers."

"Papa, teach me the cabala."

"Cabala isn't for boys. You may not study the cabala until you're thirty."

"I want it now!"

"Wait. You're still a child. What do you do there at the neighbors'? Who is that little girl? Since she's a fool, what do you need with her?"

"She is *not* a fool."

"Eh? Then what is she?"

"She is good. The boys at cheder call me names, but she is nice to me. When we grow up, I want to marry her," I said, baffled by my own words. It was as if a dybbuk had spoken out of me and I was overcome with fear.

Father smiled, but he promptly grew earnest. "Everything comes from heaven. It's said that forty days before a person is born, an angel in heaven calls out: 'This one's daughter will marry that one's son.' What's this girl's name?"

"Shosha."

"Shosha? I had an Aunt Shosha. She was my aunt and your great-aunt."

"Where does she live?"

"Aunt Shosha? In heaven, in Paradise. She was a saint. She would go to the Belz rabbi and he would place her in a seat of honor. In her old age she went to the Land of Israel and there she died. Oh, I have another gift for you, a dreidel."

The door opened and Mother and Hindele brought in the potato pancakes. During the brief time Mother had been in the kitchen her face had relaxed. My sister was smiling. I showed Mother the shining new dreidel and she gave me a sharp glance.

"You got lost, eh?"

I wanted to deny it, but I could not speak from too

much happiness. Besides, she knew everything, just like a prophetess. She often read my mind. Her big gray eyes seemed to say, "I know all your antics but I love you anyhow."

Translated by Joseph Singer

The Fools of Chelm & the Stupid Carp

In Chelm, a city of fools, every housewife bought fish for the Sabbath. The rich bought large fish, the poor small ones. They were bought on Thursday, cut up, chopped, and made into gefilte fish on Friday, and eaten on the Sabbath.

One Thursday morning the door opened at the house of the community leader of Chelm, Gronam Ox, and Zeinvel Ninny entered, carrying a trough full of water. Inside was a large, live carp.

"What is this?" Gronam asked.

"A gift to you from the wise men of Chelm," Zeinvel said. "This is the largest carp ever caught in the Lake of Chelm, and we all decided to give it to you as a token of appreciation for your great wisdom."

"Thank you very much," Gronam Ox replied. "My wife, Yente Pesha, will be delighted. She and I both love carp. I read in a book that eating the brain of a carp increases wisdom, and even though we in Chelm are immensely clever, a little improvement never hurts. But let me have a close look at him. I was told that a carp's tail shows the size of his brain."

Gronam Ox was known to be nearsighted, and when he bent down to the trough to better observe the carp's tail, the carp did something that proved he was not as wise as Gronam thought. He lifted his tail and smacked Gronam across the face.

Gronam Ox was flabbergasted. "Something like this never happened to me before," he exclaimed. "I cannot believe this carp was caught in the Chelm lake. A Chelm carp would know better."

"He's the meanest fish I ever saw in my life," agreed Zeinvel Ninny.

Even though Chelm is a big city, news traveled quickly there. In no time at all the other wise men of Chelm arrived at the house of their leader, Gronam Ox. Treitel Fool came, and Sender Donkey, Shmendrick Numskull, and Dopey Lekisch. Gronam Ox was saying, "I'm not going to eat this fish on the Sabbath. This carp is a fool, and malicious to boot. If I eat him, I could become foolish instead of cleverer."

"Then what shall I do with him?" asked Zeinvel Ninny.

Gronam Ox put a finger to his head as a sign that he was thinking hard. After a while he cried out, "No man or animal in Chelm should slap Gronam Ox. This fish should be punished."

"What kind of punishment shall we give him?" asked

Treitel Fool. "All fish are killed anyhow, and one cannot kill a fish twice."

"He shouldn't be killed like other fish," Sender Donkey said. "He should die in a different way to show that no one can smack our beloved sage, Gronam Ox, and get away with it."

"What kind of death?" wondered Shmendrick Numskull. "Shall we perhaps just imprison him?"

"There is no prison in Chelm for fish," said Zeinvel Ninny. "And to build such a prison would take too long."

"Maybe he should be hanged," suggested Dopey Lekisch.

"How do you hang a carp?" Sender Donkey wanted to know. "A creature can be hanged only by its neck, but since a carp has no neck, how will you hang him?"

"My advice is that he should be thrown to the dogs alive," said Treitel Fool.

"It's no good," Gronam Ox answered. "Our Chelm dogs are both smart and modest, but if they eat this carp, they may become as stupid and mean as he is."

"So what should we do?" all the wise men asked.

"This case needs lengthy consideration," Gronam Ox decided. "Let's leave the carp in the trough and ponder the matter as long as is necessary. Being the wisest man in Chelm, I cannot afford to pass a sentence that will not be admired by all the Chelmites."

"If the carp stays in the trough a long time, he may die," Zeinvel Ninny, a former fish dealer, explained. "To keep him alive we must put him into a large tub, and the water has to be changed often. He must also be fed properly."

"You are right, Zeinvel," Gronam Ox told him. "Go and find the largest tub in Chelm and see to it that the carp is kept alive and healthy until the day of judgment. When I reach a decision, you will hear about it."

Of course Gronam's words were the law in Chelm. The five wise men went and found a large tub, filled it with fresh water, and put the criminal carp in it, together with some crumbs of bread, challah, and other tidbits a carp might like to eat. Shlemiel, Gronam's bodyguard, was stationed at the tub to make sure that no greedy Chelmite wife would use the imprisoned carp for gefilte fish.

It just so happened that Gronam Ox had many other decisions to make and he kept postponing the sentence. The carp seemed not to be impatient. He ate, swam in the tub, became even fatter than he had been, not realizing that a severe sentence hung over his head. Shlemiel changed the water frequently, because he was told that if the carp died, this would be an act of contempt for Gronam Ox and for the Chelm Court of Justice. Yukel the water carrier made a few extra pennies every day by bringing water for the carp. Some of the Chelmites who were in opposition to Gronam Ox spread the gossip that Gronam just couldn't find the right type of punishment for the carp and that he was waiting for the carp to die a natural death. But, as always, a great disappointment awaited them. One morning about half a year later, the sentence became known, and when it was known, Chelm was stunned. The carp had to be drowned.

Gronam Ox had thought up many clever sentences before, but never one as brilliant as this one. Even his enemies were amazed at this shrewd verdict. Drowning is just the kind of death suited to a spiteful carp with a large tail and a small brain.

That day the entire Chelm community gathered at the lake to see the sentence executed. The carp, which had become almost twice as big as he had been before, was brought to the lake in the wagon that carried the worst criminals to their death. The drummers drummed. Trumpets blared. The Chelmite executioner raised the heavy carp and threw it into the lake with a mighty splash.

A great cry rose from the Chelmites: "Down with the treacherous carp! Long live Gronam Ox! Hurrah!"

Gronam was lifted by his admirers and carried home with songs of praise. Some Chelmite girls showered him with flowers. Even Yente Pesha, his wife, who was often critical of Gronam and dared to call him fool, seemed impressed by Gronam's high intelligence.

In Chelm, as everywhere else, there were envious people who found fault with everyone, and they began to say that there was no proof whatsoever that the carp really drowned. Why should a carp drown in lake water? they asked. While hundreds of innocent fish were killed every Friday, they said, that stupid carp lived in comfort for months on the taxpayers' money and then was returned sound and healthy to the lake, where he is laughing at Chelm justice.

But only a few listened to these malicious words. They pointed out that months passed and the carp was never caught again, a sure sign that he was dead. It is true that the carp just might have decided to be careful and to avoid the fisherman's net. But how can a foolish carp who slaps Gronam Ox have such wisdom?

Just the same, to be on the safe side, the wise men of Chelm published a decree that if the nasty carp had refused to be drowned and was caught again, a special jail should be built for him, a pool where he would be kept prisoner for the rest of his life.

The decree was printed in capital letters in the official gazette of Chelm and signed by Gronam Ox and his five sages—Treitel Fool, Sender Donkey, Shmendrick Numskull, Zeinvel Ninny, and Dopey Lekisch.

Translated by the author and Ruth Schachner Finkel

The Wicked City

When God commanded Abraham to leave the land of Haran, his nephew Lot decided to go with him. Lot was a lawyer in Haran, well known for his defense of criminals. In such matters he was very shrewd, though he had little feeling for justice. He instructed his clients to lie, hired false witnesses, and bribed the judges.

Lot had grown rich and powerful. He had a large house, a pretty wife, and two lively daughters, Bechirah and Tsirah. Nevertheless, his wife was not content. She wanted more gold, more pearls, and more slaves. She had heard that Sodom was an immensely rich city where there were many criminals who would need a lawyer, and she persuaded Lot that they should move there.

Abraham was a holy man, a servant of God, who knew nothing about the way his nephew conducted his affairs. God told Abraham to leave his country and he obeyed. When Lot suggested to him that they travel together in the direction of Canaan, which was near Sodom, his uncle readily agreed.

Before he left Haran, Lot sold his house, his cows, his oxen, his horses, his donkeys, and his camels. He and his family rode on Abraham's donkeys, ate his bread, and at night covered themselves with his animal hides.

Sarah, Abraham's wife, said to him, "Why does Lot use your belongings? He is not a poor man."

"He is my brother's son," Abraham replied. "Besides, we have no children and after our death he will inherit all we have. Why shouldn't he use now what will one day be his?"

When they approached the land of Canaan, God told Abraham that he was to settle there. But Lot said, "Uncle, I do not wish to remain a burden on you. I will go on to Sodom. I was told that there is a great need for lawyers there, and I surely will be able to earn my bread."

"Go, and may God bless you," Abraham replied.

Lot left for Sodom with his wife and daughters. When they arrived at the gates of the city, however, they were stopped. Strangers were banned from Sodom by law. The people were even forbidden to sell food to travelers. In those rare cases where a foreigner was allowed inside, he was usually killed during the night. Such was the custom of this sinful city.

Lot was about to turn back, but his wife addressed the gatekeepers: "My husband is a lawyer and a famous defender of criminals. In Haran there was a man who had murdered both his parents, but my husband got him off scot-free."

"How did he manage that?" asked one of the gate-keepers.

"He pointed out to the judge that the killer was an orphan and an orphan deserves mercy. The murderer was not only freed but inherited his parents' fortune as well and is now one of the richest men in Haran."

When the gatekeepers heard this story, they sent a messenger to the elders of Sodom. The elders were so impressed to hear of Lot's defense of the orphan that they not only decided to allow Lot to enter the city but invited him to remain and become a citizen of Sodom.

Lot quickly got used to Sodom and its customs. True, he spoke the local language with an accent, but otherwise he behaved like a born Sodomite.

His wife accustomed herself to Sodom's way of life even more readily. Once, when a beggar came to ask for bread, she replied, "I give only stale bread."

"I'm so hungry," the beggar said, "that even stale bread will satisfy me."

"But, alas, we baked today and the bread is still fresh. Come back in a few days. The bread will then be stale and I will give you some," Lot's wife said, although she knew very well that the beggar would die of hunger if he had to wait so long for food.

On another occasion, a peddler came to her and said, "I have two sacks of apples for which the usual price is a silver shekel per sack. But I am in need of cash, and so you may have both sacks of apples and I will only charge you for one. That gives you one sack free."

Lot's wife took one sack of apples but did not pay the peddler a penny.

"Why don't you pay me?" the peddler asked.

"I took the free sack," she replied. When he tried to argue, she set her dogs on him and he barely escaped with his life.

The neighbors who heard about these incidents were filled with admiration for Lot's wife. It wasn't long before she forbade her daughters to speak either Hebrew or Aramaic, the language of Haran. "In Sodom, behave like a Sodomite," she instructed them. She also told them never to mention their Great-uncle Abraham and their Great-aunt Sarah. "It is below our dignity as honorable citizens of Sodom to have an old fool in our family who believes in God and obeys his word," she said.

One day Lot's wife hired a drummer to walk the streets of Sodom and sing the praises of Lot. The drummer stood in the marketplace and called out, "My lord Lot in his wisdom is able to save from prison or death thieves, murderers, vandals, swindlers, and robbers. There has not been so great a defender of criminals as my employer since the days of the flood."

The number of Lot's clients immediately increased. He became one of the most popular men in the city and was appointed Chief Justice of the Supreme Court of Sodom. His daughters, Bechirah and Tsirah, married two young Sodomites who were studying law under Lot.

One thing annoyed Lot. He could not rid himself of his foreign accent, and sometimes he forgot himself and used Hebrew and Aramaic expressions. His wife and daughters were embarrassed by the fact that Lot could not hide his Hebrew origin. This was especially true when he drank too much. In Sodom it was the custom to drink excessively. Lot often drank, and at such times he used whole phrases of Hebrew and shamed his family.

One day a messenger arrived with the news that Abraham of Canaan was coming to visit Lot.

Lot was beside himself. In Sodom all men shaved, but Abraham wore a long white beard. He spoke only Hebrew or Aramaic, and what was worse, he did not believe in idols. He served a God who was said to have created heaven and earth and whom none had ever seen. Lot knew in advance that the visit from his old-fashioned uncle could bring him only shame and disgrace.

His wife and daughters were even more upset. Bechirah and Tsirah announced that if that old Hebrew uncle came to the house, they would leave. But Lot argued, "How can I not receive him? He is my father's brother. Besides, I am his heir. His wife, Sarah, is old and will certainly never bear a child."

"You've been talking about that inheritance for years," Lot's wife said. "Abraham is almost a hundred years old. It's time for him to die."

"What do you want me to do—kill him?" Lot asked.

"Why not?" his wife replied. "If Sarah dies and he marries a young woman, he may still have an heir and we won't get a shekel of his money."

Lot could scarcely persuade his wife to let the old man come.

Before long, Abraham arrived in Sodom. As a relative of the illustrious Lot, he was allowed to enter the city. But Abraham brought his nephew even more embarrassment than Lot had feared. His beard seemed even longer than before, and he carried a staff and sack like a beggar. He was accompanied by two servants, Gabriel and Raphael, who were as outlandish in appearance as he.

The very first day Abraham did something that grieved Lot immensely. He stood in the marketplace and in a hoarse voice called out, "People of Sodom, repent. Stop your thieving, swindling, murdering; desist from abusing strangers, dishonoring your parents, and eating the flesh of animals while they still live. If you do not forsake your evil ways, God will destroy Sodom!"

The people who heard Abraham's words laughed at him and mocked him. "What god is that, you old fool?" one of them asked.

"The God who created heaven and earth," Abraham replied, "a God who hates bloodshed and falsehood, cruelty and injustice."

"Where is this god of yours? Of what is he made? Stone? Gold? Copper? Ivory?"

"Neither stone nor gold nor copper nor ivory. No one carved or cast Him," Abraham answered. "He cannot be seen, He has created the oceans, the mountains, the deserts, the people and animals. He is all-merciful and provides for all that lives."

"Why did Lot allow his crazy uncle to come here?" one of the bystanders asked. Others pelted Abraham and his two companions with the dung of asses.

"This is what happens when one admits strangers," said another. "Sooner or later they bring other foreigners with them."

"He should be deported," cried a man in the crowd.

"No need to deport me," Abraham replied. "I do not want to stay. But I warn you for the last time: Repent!"

But no one showed any sign of repentance.

That evening in Lot's house Abraham repeated his warning: "Sodom will be destroyed." He said to Lot, "If you want to remain alive, rise at dawn, take your family, and leave the city behind. Soon after the sunrise, there will be nothing left of Sodom but sulphur and ashes."

"The old man is insane," screamed Lot's wife, no longer able to contain her anger.

Lot had ordered his servants to prepare a feast for Abraham and his companions. They had roasted a suckling pig, stewed beef in blood, and boiled a baby goat in its mother's milk. These were the delicacies of Sodom. But Abraham, Gabriel, and Raphael refused to eat, saying that such food was an abomination before God. Abraham asked that some unleavened bread be prepared for him.

Lot's wife was mortified before her slaves. Bechirah and Tsirah felt shamed before their husbands.

Outside Lot's house a crowd had gathered. They threw stones at the windows, demanding that Abraham and his companions be brought out so they could make sport and torture them according to the customs of Sodom. With great difficulty Lot persuaded the rabble to leave.

It was very late when Lot and his family went to bed, but Abraham and his companions did not retire. Lot, who could not sleep, overheard Abraham pleading with his God:

"Wilt Thou destroy the just with the wicked? If there

be fifty just men in the city, wilt Thou also destroy and not spare the place for the fifty just that are therein? That be far from Thee to do after this manner . . . Shall not the judge of all the earth do right?

"What if there be five less than fifty just persons?

"What if there be forty found there?

"What if there be thirty found there?

"What if there be twenty found there?

"What if ten shall be found there?"

Lot's wife, too, had awakened. "The old man is certainly not in his right mind," she said to Lot. "If you do not get rid of him tomorrow, I will leave you, and the court will make you turn over your entire fortune to me. You will have to pay me a thousand shekels a week or go to jail."

"I implore you to be quiet," Lot pleaded. "Is it my fault that I have a silly old uncle?"

"It is certainly not my fault," Lot's wife hissed. "Nor is it the fault of our daughters and sons-in-law. They won't be able to show their faces in the street. Even so, they call us 'the Hebrews.' Whenever there is a disagreement, they yell, 'Dirty Hebrews,' and tell us to go back to Haran."

Finally Lot and his wife dozed off. The night was hot. A burning wind rose from the desert and blew fine hot sand through the cracks of the shutters. Jackals wailed in the distance.

At dawn, when Lot got out of bed and looked out the window, he grew afraid. The sky was unusually red. The air was heavy and smelled of scorch and sulphur. The rising sun was the color of blood.

Lot said to his wife, "Who knows, perhaps my Uncle

Abraham is right and a catastrophe is about to befall us. Sometimes the insane have a sixth sense."

"What should we do?"

"Let us get out of the city," urged Lot. "That can't hurt. We'll accompany the old fool a short distance and then turn back."

His wife disagreed. "If the neighbors see us leave, they'll think we've taken the old man's threats about the destruction of the city seriously. They'll accuse us of believing in Abraham's God, and if the elders hear about it, they'll make us leave for good."

"We'll say we're going on a picnic," Lot said. "Let's take a hamper of food and wine along."

Lot's wife and daughters were finally persuaded, but Lot's sons-in-law wanted nothing to do with the picnic. They whispered to each other that it was high time to get rid of their father-in-law and his family.

After much squabbling and haggling, Lot loaded a hamper of pork and a keg of wine on a donkey. Lot's wife did not lock the house because in Sodom a lock was of little value; lock-breaking was even studied by children in school. But the thieves' admiration for Lot would prevent them from robbing their beloved judge.

Now the sun had disappeared. The sky was overcast with yellowish clouds. The air became heavier and the smell of ashes and sulphur stronger. Flocks of crows flew about, croaking. Vultures appeared. The camels and donkeys brayed. The oxen bellowed. Dogs barked. Cats meowed. The earth burned the soles of people's feet. The animals stampeded from the city. Even the rats and mice departed from Sodom in droves.

The people of Sodom hurried to prostrate themselves

before their clay, stone, silver, and gold idols in the temples. They promised sacrifices of cattle and human beings to placate what they believed was the wrath of their gods.

Abraham and his companions, Lot and his family, had scarcely left the city, on the road toward Zoar, when a raging fire descended from the sky and turned Sodom into a furnace of smoke and flame. Abraham called to Lot and his family, "Don't look back! Run with all your might!"

"My house, my furniture! My clothes! My rugs! My furs, my jewelry!" wailed Lot's wife. She looked back, perhaps debating whether to return, and in that very instant became a pillar of salt.

"Woe, woe, see what has happened to our mother," Lot's daughters screamed. Lot tried to take his wife by the arm, and when he saw that she did not move, he put his hand to his mouth in fright. It tasted of salt. "Salt! My wife has turned into salt!" he wailed.

Abraham, however, urged them on, and only after they had covered a good distance did he permit them to stop and look back. What had been a teeming city only a short while before was now a mountain of smoldering ashes.

"Lot," Abraham said, "know you that my companions Gabriel and Raphael are angels. Now that you see the truth, repent and turn to God."

"What truth? I believe neither in God nor in angels," Lot said.

"But you see what has happened to Sodom," Abraham insisted.

"The volcano erupted. It has nothing to do with your God and His angels."

Turning to the angels, Abraham said, "He will remain as he is until he dies. Let us go on our way."

"Uncle Abraham," Lot said, "will you first give me part of my inheritance? You will soon die and I have no money left."

"I cannot give you part of your inheritance," Abraham answered, "because my wife, Sarah, is to give birth to a son. Thus have the angels promised. Is that not so, Gabriel and Raphael?"

"Yes, it is true. Sarah, thy wife, shall bear thee a son."

"Are you saying that in her old age Sarah will give birth to a son?" Lot asked in astonishment and began to laugh. His daughters laughed with him.

"Why do you laugh, Lot?" Gabriel said. "Is there anything the Lord cannot do?"

"Nonsense, superstition," Lot said. "Tell your fairy tales to the fools of Canaan, not to me. I'm too clever to believe such idiocy."

Abraham and the angels continued on their way, leaving Lot and his daughters behind.

"Father, what are we to do now?" Lot's daughters asked.

"I have lost my wife, and you have no more husbands," Lot replied, "but we do have a keg of wine." They uncorked the wine keg and were soon completely drunk.

After a while they found a cave, where they settled down and lived like savages. Except for defending criminals, there was nothing Lot knew how to do. His pampered daughters, who had learned little except how to eat, drink, and give orders to slaves and servants, and how to mock the poor, the beaten, and the sick, now lived in filth and sin.

The evil city of Sodom was never rebuilt. It remained a desert where not even wild animals ventured.

In time Lot again settled in some corrupt city and again became the champion of murderers, thieves, and swindlers. He never heard from Abraham again, but he no longer cared, because he learned from wandering peddlers that the angels had spoken the truth; there would be no inheritance for him.

Abraham did not again visit his faithless nephew, Lot, and Lot's sinful daughters. Sarah bore Abraham a son just as the angels had predicted.

He was called Isaac. He, in turn, sired Jacob, from whom stem the Twelve Tribes of Israel.

Translated by the author and Elizabeth Shub

Rabbi Leib &
the Witch Cunegunde

Rabbi Leib, the son of Sarah, and the witch Cunegunde were both miracle workers. The difference between them was that Rabbi Leib performed his wonders with the aid of divine power and Cunegunde used the power of the Devil. Cunegunde had a son, the famous brigand Bolvan, who robbed merchants on the roads. He had collected a fortune in stolen goods, which he hoarded in a cave. Although Bolvan did the actual hijacking, it was Cunegunde who made all the plans. By her witchcraft she was able to make invisible the entrance to the cave where their loot was kept, so that the police could never find it. At sixty, Cunegunde still had pitch-black hair and a smooth, fresh skin. It was said that she possessed a potion that kept her looking young.

For years Rabbi Leib and Cunegunde waged silent warfare. Whenever Rabbi Leib gave a merchant an amulet to guard him against evil, Bolvan could neither rob nor harm him. This resulted in many losses for the brigand. Cunegunde tried to outwit Rabbi Leib, but his prayers usually proved stronger than her witchcraft.

Rabbi Leib was so often the winner that finally Cunegunde could not help admiring him. And from admiration to love is but one step. However, Cunegunde could only love as a witch does. Here is the letter she wrote to Rabbi Leib:

You, Leib, are the strongest man on earth and I, Cunegunde, am the strongest woman. If we got married, we could rule the world. We could rob the greatest banks, empty the richest mints, and the mightiest rulers would tremble before us.

And Rabbi Leib's reply:

I don't want to rob banks or empty mints. I want to serve God and not the Devil. I'd rather live with a snake than with you.

When Cunegunde received Rabbi Leib's letter, her love for him became mixed with hatred. She vowed she would force him to marry her and then revenge herself on him. She wrote to him again.

You can't escape. You will fall into my clutches. You will marry me whether you like it or not, and you will have the same bitter end as my five husbands before you.

It was known that Cunegunde, five times a widow, had in each case destroyed her husband.

Rabbi Leib and Cunegunde both lived in the same huge forest. She had a luxurious underground house with a secret entrance through the hollow of a tree. He owned a small hut by a stream in which he immersed himself each morning before prayers. He liked to pray among the trees. From time to time, he went to the village nearby to purchase food. Rabbi Leib ate neither meat nor fish, nor anything else that came from a living creature. He bought his scant provisions and always laid in a large supply of seeds for the birds of the forest. Every day hundreds of them came to feed in the clearing in front of his hut. As he prayed, the birds sang and twittered and their voices lifted his spirit and strengthened his faith.

Suddenly strange things began to happen and Rabbi Leib recognized them as the work of Cunegunde. Venomous snakes appeared near his hut and attacked the birds. At night the howling of wild dogs disturbed him in his studies. One dawn as he bathed in the stream, a strange little beast not unlike a hedgehog bit into his leg with its sharp teeth. Rabbi Leib uttered a holy incantation and the beast let go. But the marks of its teeth remained behind.

Rabbi Leib bought loaves of bread fresh from the oven in the village, but when he arrived home the bread was moldy. Worms, mice, and rats invaded his hut. Rabbi Leib kept some fowl which he never slaughtered; he loved the sound of roosters crowing and chickens cackling. One night a weasel stole into his yard and killed them all.

The water of his stream, which had always been crystal clear, suddenly became muddy and began to smell.

One evening when Rabbi Leib went into the forest to pray, he noticed a man, covered with soot like a chimney sweep, on the roof of his hut. The man carried a broom as long as a sapling and a coil of thick rope. He had the wild eyes of a beast and pointed white teeth. Rabbi Leib called out to him:

Creature of darkness lurking here,
to the wastes of Sodom disappear.

For a moment the demon hesitated. Then he called back: "I will not move until you listen to what I have to say."

"Who are you? What do you want?"

"My name is Hurmizah. I am the devoted servant of my mistress, Cunegunde. She sent me to tell you that she is pining away for love of you. If you do not consent to marry her, she will avenge herself on all your friends and family. She has not the power to harm you, but she can do as she pleases with the others. However, if you agree to become her husband, she will give you half her treasures, bags full of gold, diamonds, and other precious things. She will also build you a palace on Mt. Seir, near Asmodeus's own castle, and have you appointed one of his seven councilors. A thousand he-demons and she-demons will do your bidding. Instead of immersing yourself in your muddy little stream, you will bathe in a pool of balsam. Naamah herself will dance for you, together with her maids. You will drink five-thousand-year-old wine from the cellars of Malkizedek." Hurmizah would have continued but Rabbi Leib intoned a holy name that he used only in cases of utmost need and Cunegunde's messenger was forced to leave. As he spread out a pair of batlike wings, he called, "Leib, think it over. I'll be back tomorrow. In the end Cunegunde's witchcraft will conquer your incantations."

He flew off, leaving behind him the smell of pitch, sulphur, and devil's dung.

That night Rabbi Leib could not sleep. He lit a candle, but the wind blew it out. From his chimney came the sound of whistling and laughter. Although he knew that Cunegunde could not harm him, he worried about his friends and relatives and about his beloved birds. He had to get rid of the witch once and for all. But how?

The following night when the demon chimney sweep appeared again on Rabbi Leib's roof, the rabbi said to him, "Hurmizah, last night I could not sleep a wink and I thought everything over. I came to the conclusion that Cunegunde is right. She and I together would be the mightiest pair in the world. Fly to your mistress and tell her that I am prepared to marry her."

When Hurmizah heard these words, he said, "It's a good thing you've come to your senses, my lord. My mistress Cunegunde planned to destroy your house, burn down the forest, dry up the stream, and that just as a start. Nobody is mightier or more beautiful. Together you will rule over man and beast." Hurmizah departed at once to carry the good news to Cunegunde.

Cunegunde wasted no time. She dressed in her best clothes, placed a diamond tiara on her head, and adorned herself with many precious bracelets and anklets. She mounted a broom with silver whisks and flew to Rabbi Leib's hut. Behind her came her retinue: creatures with pointed noses, twisted horns, long tails, and ears reaching down to their shoulders. A giant with a nose like a ram's horn carried a fat midget as round as a pot on his back. As they traveled along, they screamed, laughed, hooted, blasphemed.

Rabbi Leib, dressed in a white robe, stepped out of his hut to greet the bridal party. The entire company landed before him. Cunegunde said, "Leib, I forgive all the injustices you committed against me. You are about to become my husband, and I, your wife. As soon as we are married, the forces of good will lose their power, and you and I, with the help of Satan, will be the lords of heaven and earth."

"Cunegunde," Rabbi Leib replied, "I tried to resist your charms, but I could not. Do with me as you wish."

"My children, put up the wedding canopy," Cunegunde ordered.

Four goblins at once brought forth a black canopy. Instead of four posts, it was supported by four snakes. From somewhere the sound of caterwauling music started up. Hurmizah gave away the bride. Another giant devil played best man to Rabbi Leib. The wedding ceremony began at dawn, just before the sun rose. Cunegunde laughed to herself. She had already figured out how to destroy Rabbi Leib. But first she had to learn his holy incantations so as to deprive him of divine power. Gloatingly she thought to herself, With all your wisdom, Leib, you're just a fool.

One of the devils took out a black wedding ring and handed it to Rabbi Leib, who was to place it on Cunegunde's first finger. If he had done so, they would actually have become man and wife and he would have been a slave of the netherworld forever. But instead of putting the ring on her finger, Rabbi Leib said, "Cunegunde, my dear, before you become my wife, I want to give you a present."

"What kind of present?"

"A golden locket that will endow you with powers in both the upper and the nether world. Allow me to hang it around your lovely neck."

Cunegunde smiled smugly and said, "Very well, Leib. Hang your locket around my neck." And she lowered her head to help him. That was all Rabbi Leib needed. The locket held a charm blessed by the saintly Rabbi Michael of Zlotchev. Rabbi Leib placed the locket around Cunegunde's neck. Cunegunde turned to Hurmizah to show off the precious gift and to gloat over Rabbi Leib's faith in her. But suddenly she let out a terrifying scream. The locket was burning into her flesh like a fire of hell. She tried to tear it from her neck, but her hands were powerless.

Rabbi Leib had again managed to outwit the witch Cunegunde.

When the devils and hobgoblins saw that their mistress was powerless, they fled in fear. The evil ones are cowards at heart. Cunegunde remained alone. She fell on her knees and begged Rabbi Leib to remove the locket, promising him all the treasures in her possession. But Rabbi Leib had learned that there can be no compassion for the creatures of the netherworld. He knew what had happened in olden times to Joseph della Reina, the famous saint, who had captured Satan and bound him in chains. Satan had begged for some snuff and when Rabbi Joseph took pity and gave it to him, Satan turned the snuff into a fire that melted his chains and enabled him to escape.

"Cunegunde, although I now have the power to destroy you, I have decided not to kill you but to send you to a place from which you will never be able to return." Then he incanted:

Cunegunde, Keteff's daughter,
to the land of Admah fly
and remain there till you die.

Admah was one of the towns destroyed in biblical times together with Sodom and Gomorrah.

In vain Cunegunde wept, implored, and made all kinds of promises. A strong wind swept her up in the air and carried her away as swiftly as an arrow flies from a bow. The locket fell from her neck and she lost her power for all time. She lived out her life in the wasteland of Admah, not far from the place where Lot's wife had been turned into a pillar of salt.

Without the protection of his mother, Cunegunde's son, Bolvan, became an ordinary thief. The police soon found the hidden cave where his loot was stored and arrested him. All the gold, precious stones, and stolen goods were returned to their rightful owners, or to their heirs. Bolvan, bound in chains, died in prison while still waiting for his trial.

From then on, Rabbi Leib lived in peace. The stream in which he immersed himself each morning was again crystal clear and the birds gathered in front of his hut to be fed. He supported the poor, cured the sick, and helped those who were possessed by evil spirits.

As long as he lived, the black host stayed away from the forest. It was only after his death that they dared to return to try their old tricks. Soon after, a new saint appeared, the famous miracle worker Reb Baruch, and the ancient war between good and evil started all over again.

Translated by the author and Elizabeth Shub

The Parakeet
Named Dreidel

It happened about ten years ago in Brooklyn, New York. All day long a heavy snow was falling. Toward evening the sky cleared and a few stars appeared. A frost set in. It was the eighth day of Hanukkah, and my silver Hanukkah lamp stood on the windowsill with all candles burning. It was mirrored in the windowpane, and I imagined another lamp outside.

My wife, Esther, was frying potato pancakes. I sat with my son, David, at a table and played dreidel with him. Suddenly David cried out, "Papa, look!" And he pointed to the window.

I looked up and saw something that seemed unbelievable. Outside on the windowsill stood a yellow-green bird watching the candles. In a moment I understood what had happened. A parakeet had escaped from its home somewhere, had flown out into the cold street and landed on my windowsill, perhaps attracted by the light.

A parakeet is native to a warm climate, and it cannot stand the cold and frost for very long. I immediately took steps to save the bird from freezing. First I carried away the Hanukkah lamp so that the bird would not burn itself when entering. Then I opened the window and with a quick wave of my hand shooed the parakeet inside. The whole thing took only a few seconds.

In the beginning the frightened bird flew from wall to wall. It hit itself against the ceiling and for a while hung from a crystal prism on the chandelier. David tried to calm it: "Don't be afraid, little bird, we are your friends." Presently the bird flew toward David and landed on his head, as though it had been trained and was accustomed to people. David began to dance and laugh with joy. My wife, in the kitchen, heard the noise and came out to see what had happened. When she saw the bird on David's head, she asked, "Where did you get a bird all of a sudden?"

"Mama, it just came to our window."

"To the window in the middle of the winter?"

"Papa saved its life."

The bird was not afraid of us. David lifted his hand to his forehead and the bird settled on his finger. Esther placed a saucer of millet and a dish of water on the table, and the parakeet ate and drank. It saw the dreidel and began to push it with its beak. David exclaimed, "Look, the bird plays dreidel."

David soon began to talk about buying a cage for the bird and also about giving it a name, but Esther and I reminded him that the bird was not ours. We would try to find the owners, who probably missed their pet and were worried about what had happened to it in the icy weather. David said, "Meanwhile, let's call it Dreidel."

That night Dreidel slept on a picture frame and woke us in the morning with its singing. The bird stood on the frame, its plumage brilliant in the purple light of the rising sun, shaking as in prayer, whistling, twittering, and talking all at the same time. The parakeet must have belonged to a house where Yiddish was spoken, because we heard it say *"Zeldele, geh schlofen"* (Zeldele, go to sleep), and these simple words uttered by the tiny creature filled us with wonder and delight.

The next day I posted a notice in the elevators of the neighborhood houses. It said that we had found a Yiddish-speaking parakeet. When a few days passed and no one called, I advertised in the newspaper for which I wrote, but a week went by and no one claimed the bird. Only then did Dreidel become ours. We bought a large cage with all the fittings and toys that a bird might want, but because Hanukkah is a festival of freedom, we resolved never to lock the cage. Dreidel was free to fly around the house whenever he pleased. (The man at the pet shop had told us that the bird was a male.)

Nine years passed and Dreidel remained with us. We became more attached to him from day to day. In our house Dreidel learned scores of Yiddish, English, and Hebrew words. David taught him to sing a Hanukkah song, and there was always a wooden dreidel in the cage for him to play with. When I wrote on my Yiddish typewriter, Dreidel would cling to the index finger of either my right or my left hand, jumping acrobatically with every letter I wrote. Esther often joked that Dreidel was helping me write and that he was entitled to half my earnings.

Our son, David, grew up and entered college. One winter night he went to a Hanukkah party. He told us that he would be home late, and Esther and I went to bed early. We had just fallen asleep when the telephone rang. It was David. As a rule he is a quiet and composed young man. This time he spoke so excitedly that we could barely understand what he was saying. It seemed that David had told the story of our parakeet to his fellow students at the party, and a girl named Zelda Rosen had exclaimed, "I am this Zeldele! We lost our parakeet nine years ago." Zelda and her parents lived not far from us, but they had never seen the notice in the newspaper or the ones posted in elevators. Zelda was now a student and a friend of David's. She had never visited us before, although our son often spoke about her to his mother.

We slept little that night. The next day Zelda and her parents came to see their long-lost pet. Zelda was a beautiful and gifted girl. David often took her to the theater and to museums. Not only did the Rosens recognize their bird, but the bird seemed to recognize his former owners. The Rosens used to call him Tsip-Tsip, and when the parakeet heard them say "Tsip-Tsip," he became flustered and started to fly from one member of the family to the other, screeching and flapping his wings. Both Zelda and her mother cried when they saw their beloved bird alive. The father stared silently. Then he said, "We have never forgotten our Tsip-Tsip."

I was ready to return the parakeet to his original owners, but Esther and David argued that they could never part with Dreidel. It was also not necessary, because that day David and Zelda decided to get married after their graduation from college. So Dreidel is still with us, always eager to learn new words and new games. When David and Zelda marry, they will take Dreidel to their new home. Zelda has often said, "Dreidel was our matchmaker."

On Hanukkah he always gets a gift—a mirror, a ladder, a bathtub, a swing, or a jingle bell. He has even developed a taste for potato pancakes, as befits a parakeet named Dreidel.

Lemel & Tzipa

This story was told me by my mother, and I'm retelling it here word for word, as closely as possible.

Once there was a well-to-do countryman named Tobias, and he and his wife, Leah, had a daughter, Tzipa, who was a fool the likes of which you couldn't find in the entire region. When Tzipa grew up, marriage brokers began to propose matches for her, but as soon as a prospective groom came to look her over and she began to spout her nonsense, he would flee from her. It appeared that Tzipa would be left an old maid.

The husband and wife went to ask advice of a rabbi, who told them, "Marriages are made in heaven. Since Tzipa is a fool, heaven will surely provide a foolish groom for her. Just ask around about a youth who's a bigger fool than your daughter, and when the two fools marry, they'll be happy together."

The parents were pleased by this advice. They went to

a matchmaker and told him to find the biggest fool in the Lublin province for their daughter. They promised the matchmaker double the fee usually paid for arranging a match. The matchmaker knew that no city contained so many fools as Chelm, so that was where he headed.

He came to a house and saw a youth sitting in front of it and crying. The matchmaker asked, "Young fellow, why are you crying?"

And the youth said, "My mother baked a whole dish of blintzes for Shevuoth. When she went out to buy sour cream for the blintzes, she warned me, 'Lemel, don't eat the blintzes until Shevuoth.' I promised her that I wouldn't, but the moment she left the house I got a great urge for a blintz and I ate one, and after the first I got the urge for another, and a third, and a fourth, and before you know it, I finished the whole dish of blintzes. I was so busy eating blintzes I didn't see the cat watching me. Now I'm very much afraid that when Mother comes back the cat will tell her what I've done and Mother will pinch me and call me what she calls me anyhow—fool, oaf, dummy, ninny, simp, clod, donkey."

This Lemel is made for Tzipa, the matchmaker thought.

Aloud he said, "I know how to speak the cat language. I'll tell the cat to say nothing, and when I give a cat an order he listens, for I am the King of the Cats."

Hearing these words, Lemel commenced to dance with joy. The matchmaker began to utter fabricated words to the cat—whatever came to his lips: "Petche-metche-ketche-letche."

Then he asked, "Lemel, do you want a bride?"

"Certainly!"

"I have just the bride for you—no one like her in the whole world. Tzipa is her name."

"Does she have red cheeks?" Lemel asked. "I like a girl with red cheeks and long braids."

"She has everything you want."

Lemel began to dance anew and clap his hands. At that moment his mother came in with the pot of sour cream. When she saw her son dancing, she asked, "Lemel, what's the big celebration about?"

And Lemel replied, "I ate up all the blintzes and I was afraid the cat would tell, but this man ordered the cat not to talk."

"Dummox! Dolt!" the mother screamed. "What will I do with you? What girl would want to marry such a dunderhead?"

"Mama, I have a bride already!" Lemel exclaimed. "Her name is Tzipa and she has long cheeks and red braids."

A few days later Lemel and Tzipa drew up their articles of engagement. They could not write their names and Lemel signed with three dots and Tzipa with three dashes. Lemel got a dowry of two hundred gulden. Since Lemel didn't understand about money and didn't know the difference between one banknote and another, Tzipa's father wrapped the five-gulden notes in white paper and the ten-gulden notes in blue paper. Lemel also got a silver watch, but since he couldn't read figures, when he wanted to know the time he stopped a person in the street and asked, "What time is it?" At the same time he added, "I can't see because I've lost my glasses." This was what his mother had told him to use as an excuse.

When the day of the wedding came, Tzipa began to weep bitterly.

Her mother asked, "Tzipa, why are you crying?"

And Tzipa replied, "I'm ashamed to marry a stranger."

The mother said, "I married a stranger, too. After the wedding, the husband and wife become close and are no longer strangers."

But Tzipa countered, "You, Mama, married Papa, but I have to marry a complete stranger."

The mother said, "Tzipa, you're a big fool but your groom is a fool, too, and together you'll be, God willing, two happy fools."

After lengthy discussions, Tzipa allowed herself to be escorted to the wedding canopy.

Some time after the wedding, Tzipa's father said to his son-in-law, "Lemel, your father is a merchant, I'm a merchant, and I want you to be a merchant, too. I've given you a dowry. Use it to go into business."

"What's a merchant?" Lemel asked, and his father-in-law said, "A merchant is someone who buys cheap and sells dear. That's how he makes a profit. Take the dowry, go to Lublin, and if you spot a bargain there, buy it as cheaply as possible, then come back here and sell it at a high price."

Lemel did as his father-in-law ordered. Tzipa gave him a chicken wrapped in cabbage leaves for the road. In the wagon, Lemel got hungry and wanted to eat the chicken, but it was raw. Tzipa's mother had told her to give her husband a chicken, but since she didn't say anything about cooking it, Tzipa had given Lemel a raw chicken.

Lemel stopped at an inn. He was very hungry. They

asked him what he wanted to eat and he said, "Give me everything you have and I'll eat until I'm full."

Said and done. First they gave him a glass of wine, then another; then an appetizer of tripe with calf's foot. Lemel ate this with lots of bread and horseradish. Then they served him a bowl of noodle soup. After Lemel had finished one bowl of soup, he asked for another. Then they served Lemel a huge portion of meat with groats, cabbage, potatoes, and carrots. Lemel finished everything and was still hungry. Then they served him a compote of prunes, apples, pears, and raisins. Lemel gulped it all down and yet his hunger was still not sated. Finally, they served him tea with sponge cake and honey cake. Lemel drank the tea and ate the cake, but somehow the hunger still gnawed at him. The innkeeper said, "I hope that by now you are full."

But Lemel replied, "No, I'm still hungry."

The innkeeper took a cookie out of the cabinet and said, "Try this."

Lemel ate the cookie and immediately felt sated. He said, "Now I'm full. Had I known that you can get full from a cookie, I needn't have ordered all those other dishes."

The innkeeper promptly saw that he was dealing with a dolt. He himself was a swindler and he said, "Now it's too late. But if you ever come here again, I'll give you such a cookie right off the bat and you won't have to order the other dishes. Now, be so good as to pay for the meal."

Lemel took from his purse the banknotes rolled in white paper and those rolled in blue paper and he said, "One paper contains the five-gulden bills and the other the ten-gulden bills, but I don't remember which is which."

The innkeeper unrolled the two stacks, and as befits a swindler, he told Lemel that a ten-gulden was a five-gulden bill. He also swindled Lemel with the change.

In Lublin, Lemel went from store to store seeking bargains, but somehow there were no bargains to be found. Lying in bed at night, Lemel began to think about the miraculous cookie which made you instantly full. "If I knew how to bake such cookies I'd be rich," Lemel said to himself. "There isn't enough food in Chelm, the people are hungry, and everyone would welcome such cookies."

He himself had felt sated for nearly twenty hours after eating this cookie.

The next day Lemel headed home and he stopped at the same inn. He ordered the miraculous cookie, but the innkeeper said, "I just now served the last of them to a guest. But I can sell you the recipe. Believe me, when you bake these cookies in Chelm you'll sell them for a big profit and you'll become as rich as Rothschild."

"What does this recipe cost?"

The innkeeper named a high price, but Lemel decided that by baking such cookies he could get back all the money he would pay, with a huge profit besides. So he bought the recipe. Having already seen that Lemel couldn't read, write, or even determine the value of a coin, the innkeeper composed the following recipe:

Take three quarts of duck's milk, five pounds of flour ground from iron, two pounds of cheese made from snow, one pound of fat from a flintstone, a half pound of feath-

ers *from a red crow, and a quarter pound of juice squeezed from copper. Throw it all in a pot made of wax and let it cook three days and three nights over the fire of a potato tree. After three days, knead a dough out of the mixture, cut out the cookies with a knife made of butter, and bake them in an oven made of ice till they turn red, brown, and yellow. Then dig a pit, throw in the whole mess, and put up a board with a sign over it reading:* WHEN YOU SEND A FOOL TO MARKET, THE MERCHANTS REJOICE.

After Lemel finished paying for the meal and the recipe, he barely had enough left for the fare home. But he was pleased with the bargain he had made.

When he came home and told Tzipa about the miraculous cookie, she began to clap her hands and dance. But the joy didn't last long. When Lemel's father-in-law came home and read the recipe, he became furious and screamed, "Lemel, you've been swindled!"

Tzipa promptly began to cry. Tzipa's mother cried along with her.

After a while, Lemel said, "All my troubles stem from the fact that I can't read. I must learn to read, and the quicker the better."

"Yes, my son," Tzipa's father said. "A merchant must be able to read and write."

Since there were no teachers in the village, Lemel resolved to go to Lublin to learn to read. Again, the father-in-law gave him money for the fare and to pay for the lessons. In Lublin, Lemel went to Lewartow Street to seek out a teacher. He walked past a store displaying eyeglasses in the window. He looked inside and saw a customer put on a pair of glasses and glance into a book while the proprietor asked, "Now can you read?"

"Yes, now I can read well," the customer said.

Lemel thought to himself, Since putting on glasses enables you to read, what do I need with a teacher?

Lemel had no urge to study. He yearned to go home to Tzipa.

He went into the store and said to the proprietor, "Give me a pair of glasses so that I can read."

The proprietor asked what strength glasses he had worn before and Lemel said, "I don't know anything about it. Let me test them."

The proprietor handed him a pair of glasses and opened a book before him.

Lemel looked into the book and said, "I can't read."

"I'll give you stronger glasses," the proprietor said.

Lemel tested the second pair and said, "I still can't read."

The proprietor offered him many different glasses to try, but Lemel kept giving the same answer—he still couldn't read.

After a while, the proprietor said, "Forgive me, but maybe you can't read at all?"

"If I could read, I wouldn't have come to you in the first place," Lemel said.

"In that case, you must first go to a teacher and learn to read. You can't learn to read from putting on a pair of glasses," the storekeeper said.

Lemel grew depressed by the answer. He had been prepared to put on the glasses and go back home. After a while Lemel decided that he couldn't go on without

Tzipa. He missed her terribly. He went to seek out a teacher not so much to learn how to read as to have the teacher write a letter home for him. He soon found one. When Lemel asked how long it would take for him to learn to read, the teacher said, "It could take a year, but not less than a half year."

Lemel grew very sad. He said to the teacher, "Could you write a letter for me? I want to send a letter to my Tzipa."

"Yes, I could write a letter for you. Tell me what to write."

Lemel began to dictate:

Dear Tzipa,
I'm already in Lublin. I thought that if you put on glasses you could read, but the proprietor of the store said that glasses don't help. The teacher says it would take a half year or a whole year to teach me to read and that I would have to stay here in Lublin the whole time. Dear Tzipele, I love you so much that when I'm away from you one day I must die of longing. If I am without you for a half year, I'll have to die maybe a hundred times or even more. Therefore, I've decided to come home, if my father-in-law, your father, will agree. I hope to find some kind of work for which you don't have to read or write.

Longingly,
Your Lemel

When Tzipa received this letter and her father read it to her, she burst into tears and dictated a letter to Lemel which read as follows:

Dear Lemel,
When you don't see me for a day you must die, but when I don't see you for a minute, I go crazy. Yes, my dear Lemel, come back. I don't need a writer but a good husband and, later, a houseful of children—six boys and six girls. Father will find some kind of work for you. Don't wait but come straight home, because if you come back dead and find me crazy, it wouldn't be so good for either of us.

Your devoted Tzipa

When the teacher read Tzipa's letter to Lemel he burst out crying. That very same day he started for home. Before getting into the wagon in Lublin, he went to the market to buy a present for Tzipa. He went into a mirror store with the intention of buying her a mirror. At the same time he told the storekeeper everything that had happened to him—how he had been swindled with the cookie and how he had been unable to learn to read with the glasses.

The storekeeper was a prankster and dishonest as well. He said, "Such people as you, Lemel, and your wife, Tzipa, should be many. I have a potion which, when you drink it, will make you become double, triple, quadruple. How would you like there to be ten Lemels and ten Tzipas who would all love each other? One Lemel and one Tzipa could stay home all day, another set could go to market to buy goods, a third set could take a walk, a fourth set could eat blintzes with sour cream, and the fifth set could go to Lublin and learn to read and write."

"How is this possible?" Lemel asked.

"Drink the potion and you'll see for yourself."

The storekeeper gave Lemel a glass of plain water and told him to drink merely one drop of it. Then he led Lemel into a room where two mirrors hung facing each other, one of which was tilted slightly to the side. When Lemel came into the room he saw not one Lemel in the mirror but a whole row of Lemels. He walked over to the other mirror and there were many Lemels there, too.

The storekeeper stood by the door and said, "Well, did I deceive you?"

"Oh, I can't believe my own eyes!" Lemel exclaimed. "How much is this potion?"

"It's very expensive," the storekeeper said, "but for you, I'll make it cheap. Give me all the money you have except for your fare home. You've snagged a terrific bargain."

Lemel paid on the spot and the storekeeper gave him a big bottle filled with water. He told him, "You and your Tzipa need drink only one drop a day. This bottle will last you for years. If it gets used up, you can always come back to Lublin and I'll refill it for you for free. Wait, I'll give you a written guarantee."

The storekeeper took out a sheet of paper and wrote on it: "God loves fools. That's why He made so many of them."

When Lemel came home and his father-in-law saw the bottle of water and read the note, he realized that Lemel had been swindled again.

But when Lemel saw Tzipa his joy was so intense he forgot all his troubles. He kissed and hugged her and cried, "I don't need many Tzipas. One Tzipa is enough for me, even if I should live to be a thousand!"

"And I don't need many Lemels. One Lemel is enough

for me, even if I should live to be a million!" Tzipa exclaimed.

Yes, Lemel and Tzipa were both fools, but they possessed more love than all the sages. After a while, Lemel bought a horse and wagon and became a coachman. For this he didn't have to know how to read or write. He drove passengers to and from Chelm and everyone liked him for his punctuality, his friendliness, and for the love he showed his horse. Tzipa began to have children and bore Lemel six boys and six girls. The boys took after Tzipa and the girls after Lemel, but they were all good-natured fools and they all found mates in Chelm. Lemel and Tzipa lived happily to a ripe old age, long enough to enjoy a whole tribe of grandchildren, great-grandchildren, and great-great-grandchildren.

Translated by Joseph Singer

The Day I Got Lost

A CHAPTER FROM THE AUTOBIOGRAPHY

OF PROFESSOR SHLEMIEL

It is easy to recognize me. See a man in the street wearing a too long coat, too large shoes, a crumpled hat with a wide brim, spectacles with one lens missing, and carrying an umbrella though the sun is shining, and that man will be me, Professor Shlemiel. There are other unmistakable clues to my identity. My pockets are always bulging with newspapers, magazines, and just papers. I carry an overstuffed briefcase, and I'm forever making mistakes. I've been living in New York City for over forty years, yet whenever I want to go uptown, I find myself walking downtown, and when I want to go east, I go west. I'm always late and I never recognize anybody.

I'm always misplacing things. A hundred times a day I ask myself, Where is my pen? Where is my money?

Where is my handkerchief? Where is my address book? I am what is known as an absentminded professor.

For many years I have been teaching philosophy in the same university, and I still have difficulty in locating my classrooms. Elevators play strange tricks on me. I want to go to the top floor and I land in the basement. Hardly a day passes when an elevator door doesn't close on me. Elevator doors are my worst enemies.

In addition to my constant blundering and losing things, I'm forgetful. I enter a coffee shop, hang up my coat, and leave without it. By the time I remember to go back for it, I've forgotten where I've been. I lose hats, books, umbrellas, rubbers, and above all manuscripts. Sometimes I even forget my own address. One evening I took a taxi because I was in a hurry to get home. The taxi driver said, "Where to?" And I could not remember where I lived.

"Home!" I said.

"Where is home?" he asked in astonishment.

"I don't remember," I replied.

"What is your name?"

"Professor Shlemiel."

"Professor," the driver said, "I'll get you to a telephone booth. Look in the telephone book and you'll find your address."

He drove me to the nearest drugstore with a telephone booth in it, but he refused to wait. I was about to enter the store when I realized I had left my briefcase behind. I ran after the taxi, shouting, "My briefcase, my brief-case!" But the taxi was already out of earshot.

In the drugstore, I found a telephone book, but when I

looked under S, I saw to my horror that though there were a number of Shlemiels listed, I was not among them. At that moment I recalled that several months before, Mrs. Shlemiel had decided that we should have an unlisted telephone number. The reason was that my students thought nothing of calling me in the middle of the night and waking me up. It also happened quite frequently that someone wanted to call another Shlemiel and got me by mistake. That was all very well—but how was I going to get home?

I usually had some letters addressed to me in my breast pocket. But just that day I had decided to clean out my pockets. It was my birthday and my wife had invited friends in for the evening. She had baked a huge cake and decorated it with birthday candles. I could see my friends sitting in our living room, waiting to wish me a happy birthday. And here I stood in some drugstore, for the life of me not able to remember where I lived.

Then I recalled the telephone number of a friend of mine, Dr. Motherhead, and I decided to call him for help. I dialed and a young girl's voice answered.

"Is Dr. Motherhead at home?"

"No," she replied.

"Is his wife at home?"

"They're both out," the girl said.

"Perhaps you can tell me where they can be reached?" I said.

"I'm only the babysitter, but I think they went to a party at Professor Shlemiel's. Would you like to leave a message?" she said. "Who shall I say called, please?"

"Professor Shlemiel," I said.

"They left for your house about an hour ago," the girl said.

"Can you tell me where they went?" I asked.

"I've just told you," she said. "They went to your house."

"But where do I live?"

"You must be kidding!" the girl said, and hung up.

I tried to call a number of friends (those whose telephone numbers I happened to think of), but wherever I called, I got the same reply: "They've gone to a party at Professor Shlemiel's."

As I stood in the street wondering what to do, it began to rain. "Where's my umbrella?" I said to myself. And I knew the answer at once. I'd left it—somewhere. I got under a nearby canopy. It was now raining cats and dogs. It lightninged and thundered. All day it had been sunny and warm, but now that I was lost and my umbrella was lost, it had to storm. And it looked as if it would go on for the rest of the night.

To distract myself, I began to ponder the ancient philosophical problem. A mother chicken lays an egg, I thought to myself, and when it hatches, there is a chicken. That's how it has always been. Every chicken comes from an egg and every egg comes from a chicken. But was there a chicken first? Or an egg first? No philosopher has ever been able to solve this eternal question. Just the same, there must be an answer. Perhaps I, Shlemiel, am destined to stumble on it.

It continued to pour buckets. My feet were getting wet and I was chilled. I began to sneeze and I wanted to wipe my nose, but my handkerchief, too, was gone.

At that moment I saw a big black dog. He was standing in the rain getting soaked and looking at me with sad eyes. I knew immediately what the trouble was. The dog was lost. He, too, had forgotten his address. I felt a great love for that innocent animal. I called to him and he came running to me. I talked to him as if he were human. "Fellow, we're in the same boat," I said. "I'm a man shlemiel and you're a dog shlemiel. Perhaps it's also your birthday, and there's a party for you, too. And here you stand shivering and forsaken in the rain, while your loving master is searching for you everywhere. You're probably just as hungry as I am."

I patted the dog on his wet head and he wagged his tail. "Whatever happens to me will happen to you," I said. "I'll keep you with me until we both find our homes. If we don't find your master, you'll stay with me. Give me your paw," I said. The dog lifted his right paw. There was no question that he understood.

A taxi drove by and splattered us both. Suddenly it stopped and I heard someone shouting, "Shlemiel! Shlemiel!" I looked up and saw the taxi door open, and the head of a friend of mine appeared. "Shlemiel," he called. "What are you doing here? Who are you waiting for?"

"Where are you going?" I asked.

"To your house, of course. I'm sorry I'm late, but I was detained. Anyhow, better late than never. But why aren't you at home? And whose dog is that?"

"Only God could have sent you!" I exclaimed. "What a night! I've forgotten my address, I've left my briefcase in a taxi, I've lost my umbrella, and I don't know where my rubbers are."

"Shlemiel," my friend said, "if there was ever an absentminded professor, you're it!"

When I rang the bell of my apartment, my wife opened the door. "Shlemiel!" she shrieked. "Everybody is waiting for you. Where have you been? Where is your briefcase? Your umbrella? Your rubbers? And who is this dog?"

Our friends surrounded me. "Where have you been?" they cried. "We were so worried. We thought surely something had happened to you!"

"Who is this dog?" my wife kept repeating.

"I don't know," I said finally. "I found him in the street. Let's just call him Bow Wow for the time being."

"Bow Wow, indeed!" my wife scolded. "You know our cat hates dogs. And what about the parakeets? He'll scare them to death."

"He's a quiet dog," I said. "He'll make friends with the cat. I'm sure he loves parakeets. I could not leave him shivering in the rain. He's a good soul."

The moment I said this the dog let out a bloodcurdling howl. The cat ran into the room. When she saw the dog, she arched her back and spat at him, ready to scratch out his eyes. The parakeets in their cage began flapping their wings and screeching. Everybody started talking at once. There was pandemonium.

Would you like to know how it all ended?

Bow Wow still lives with us. He and the cat are great friends. The parakeets have learned to ride on his back as if he were a horse. As for my wife, she loves Bow Wow even more than I do. Whenever I take the dog out, she says, "Now, don't forget your address, both of you."

I never did find my briefcase, or my umbrella, or my rubbers. Like many philosophers before me, I've given up trying to solve the riddle of which came first, the chicken or the egg. Instead, I've started writing a book called *The Memoirs of Shlemiel*. If I don't forget the manuscript in a taxi, or a restaurant, or on a bench in the park, you may read them someday. In the meantime, here is a sample chapter.

Translated by the author and Elizabeth Shub

Menashe & Rachel

The poorhouse in Lublin had a special room for children—orphans, sick ones, and cripples. Menashe and Rachel were brought up there. Both of them were orphans and blind. Rachel was born blind and Menashe became blind from smallpox when he was three years old. Every day a tutor came to teach the children prayers, as well as a chapter of the five books of Moses. The older ones also learned passages of the Talmud. Menashe was now barely nine years old, but already he was known as a prodigy. He knew twenty chapters of the Holy Book by heart. Rachel, who was eight years old, could recite "I Thank Thee" in the morning, the Shema before going to sleep, make benedictions over food, and she also remembered a few supplications in Yiddish.

On Hanukkah the tutor blessed the Hanukkah lights for the children, and every child got Hanukkah money and a dreidel from the poorhouse warden. Rich women brought them pancakes sprinkled with sugar and cinnamon.

Some of the charity women maintained that the two blind children should not spend too much time together. First of all, Menashe was already a half-grown boy and a scholar, and there was no sense in his playing around with a little girl. Second, it's better for blind children to associate with seeing ones, who can help them find their way in the eternal darkness in which they live. But Menashe and Rachel were so very deeply attached to each other that no one could keep them apart.

Menashe was not only good at studying the Torah but also talented with his hands. All the other children got tin dreidels for Hanukkah, but Menashe carved two wooden ones for Rachel and himself. When Menashe was telling stories, even the grownups came to listen. Not only Rachel, but all the children in the poorhouse were eager to hear his stories. Some his mother had told him when she was still alive. Others he invented. He was unusually deft. In the summer he went with the other children to the river and did handstands and somersaults in the water. In the winter when a lot of snow fell, Menashe, together with other children, built a snowman with two coals for eyes.

Menashe had black hair. His eyes used to be black, too, but now they had whitish cataracts. Rachel was known as a beauty. She had golden hair and eyes as blue as cornflowers. Those who knew her could not believe that such shining eyes could be blind.

The love between Menashe and Rachel was spoken of not only in the poorhouse but in the whole neighborhood. Both children said openly that when they grew up they would marry. Some of the inmates in the poorhouse called them bride and groom. There were some do-gooders who believed the two children should be parted by force, but Rachel said that if she was taken away from Menashe she would drown herself in a well. Menashe warned that he would bite the hand that tried to separate him from Rachel. The poorhouse warden went to ask the advice of the Lublin rabbi, and the rabbi said that the children should be left in peace.

One Hanukkah evening the children got their Hanukkah money and ate the tasty pancakes; then they sat down and played dreidel. It was the sixth night of Hanukkah. Six lights burned in the brass lamp in the window. Until tonight Menashe and Rachel had played together with the other children. But tonight Menashe said to Rachel, "Rachel, I have no desire to play."

"Neither have I," Rachel answered. "But what shall we do?"

"Let's sit down near the Hanukkah lamp and just be together."

Menashe led Rachel to the Hanukkah lamp. They followed the sweet smell of the oil in which the wicks were burning. They sat down on a bench. For a while both of them were silently enjoying each other's company as well as the warmth that radiated from the little flames. Then Rachel said, "Menashe, tell me a story."

"Again? I have told you all my stories already."

"Make up a new one," Rachel said.

"If I tell you all my stories now, what will I do when we marry and become husband and wife? I must save some stories for our future."

"Don't worry. By then you will have many new stories."

"Do you know what?" Menashe proposed. "You tell me a story this time."

"I have no story," Rachel said.

"How do you know that you don't have any? Just say whatever comes to your mind. This is what I do. When I'm asked to tell a story I begin to talk, not knowing what will come out. But somehow a story crops up by itself."

"With me nothing will crop up."

"Try."

"You will laugh at me."

"No, Rachel, I won't laugh."

It grew quiet. One could hear the wood burning in the clay stove. Rachel seemed to hesitate. She wet her lips with the tip of her tongue. Then she began, "Once there was a boy and a girl—"

"Aha."

"He was called Menashe and she Rachel."

"Yes."

"Everyone thought that Menashe and Rachel were blind, but they saw. I know for sure that Rachel saw."

"What did she see?" Menashe asked in astonishment.

"Other children see from the outside, but Rachel saw from the inside. Because of this people called her blind. It wasn't true. When people sleep, their eyes are closed, but in their dreams they can see boys, girls, horses, trees, goats, birds. So it was with Rachel. She saw everything deep in her head, many beautiful things."

"Could she see colors?" Menashe asked.

"Yes, green, blue, yellow, and other colors, I don't know what to call them. Sometimes they jumped around and formed little figures, dolls, flowers. Once, she saw an angel with six wings. He flew up high and the sky opened its golden doors for him."

"Could she see the Hanukkah lights?" Menashe asked.

"Not the ones from the outside, but those in her head. Don't you see anything, Menashe?"

"I, too, see things inside me," Menashe said after a long pause. "I see my father and my mother and also my grandparents. I never told you this, but I remember things from the time I could still see."

"What do you remember?" Rachel asked.

"Oh, I was sick and the room was full of sunshine. A doctor came, a tall man in a high hat. He told Mother to pull down the curtain because he thought I was sick with the measles and it is not good when there is too much light in the room if you have measles."

"Why didn't you tell me this before?" Rachel asked.

"I thought you wouldn't understand."

"Menashe, I understand everything. Sometimes when I lie in bed at night and cannot fall asleep, I see faces and animals and children dancing in a circle. I see mountains, fields, rivers, gardens, and the moon shining over them."

"How does the moon look?"

"Like a face with eyes and a nose and a mouth."

"True. I remember the moon," Menashe said. "Sometimes at night when I lie awake I see many, many things and I don't know whether they are real or I'm only imagining. Once, I saw a giant so tall his head reached the clouds. He had huge horns and a nose as big as the trunk of an elephant. He walked in the sea but the water only reached to his knees. I tried to tell the warden what I saw and he said I was lying. But I was telling the truth."

For some time both children were silent. Then Menashe said, "Rachel, as long as we are small we should never tell these secrets to anybody. People wouldn't believe us. They might think we were making them up. But when we grow up we will tell. It is written in the Bible: 'For the Lord seeth not as man seeth; for man looketh on the outward appearance but the Lord looketh on the heart.' "

"Who said this?"

"The prophet Samuel."

"Oh, Menashe, I wish we could grow up quickly and become husband and wife," Rachel said. "We will have children that see both from the outside and from the inside. You will kindle Hanukkah lights and I will fry pancakes. You will carve dreidels for our children to play with, and when they go to bed we will tell them stories. Later, when they fall asleep, they will dream about these stories."

"We will dream also," Menashe said. "I about you and you about me."

"Oh, I dream about you all the time. I see you in my dreams so clearly—your white skin, chiseled nose, black hair, beautiful eyes."

"I see you, too—a golden girl."

Again there was a silence. Then Rachel said, "I'd like to ask you something, but I am ashamed to say it."

"What is it?"

"Give me a kiss."

"Are you crazy? It's not allowed. Besides, when a boy kisses a girl they call him a sissy."

"No one will see."

"God sees," Menashe said.

"You said before that God looks into the heart. In my heart we are already grown up and I am your wife."

"The other children are going to laugh at us."

"They are busy with the dreidels. Kiss me! Just once."

Menashe took Rachel's hand and kissed her quickly. His heart was beating like a little hammer. She kissed him back and both of their faces were hot. After a while Menashe said, "It cannot be such a terrible sin, because it is written in the Book of Genesis that Jacob loved Rachel and he kissed her when they met. Your name is Rachel, too."

The poorhouse warden came over. "Children, why are you sitting alone?"

"Menashe has just told me a story," Rachel answered.

"It's not true, she told me a story," Menashe said.

"Was it a nice story?" the warden asked.

"The most beautiful story in the whole world," Rachel said.

"What was it about?" the warden asked, and Menashe said, "About an island far away in the ocean full of lions, leopards, monkeys, as well as eagles and pheasants with golden feathers and silver beaks. There were many trees on the island—fig trees, date trees, pomegranate trees, and a stream with fresh water. There was a boy and a girl there who saved themselves from a shipwreck by clinging to a log. They were like Adam and Eve in Paradise, but there was no serpent and—"

"The children are fighting over the dreidel. Let me see what's going on," the warden said. "You can tell me the rest of the story tomorrow." He rushed to the table.

"Oh, you made up a new story," Rachel said. "What happened next?"

"They loved one another and got married," Menashe said.

"Alone on the island forever?" Rachel asked.

"Why alone?" Menashe said. "They had many children, six boys and six girls. Besides, one day a sailboat landed there and the whole family was rescued and taken to the Land of Israel."

Shlemiel the Businessman

Shlemiel, who lived in Chelm, was not always a
stay-at-home and there was a time when his wife did not
sell vegetables in the marketplace. Mrs. Shlemiel's father
was a man of means, and when his daughter married
Shlemiel, he gave her a dowry.

Shortly after the wedding, Shlemiel decided to use the
dowry to go into business. He had heard that in Lublin
goats could be bought cheaply and he went there to buy
one. He wanted a milk goat so that he could make cheese
to sell. The goat dealer offered him a goat whose large
udders were filled with milk. Shlemiel paid him the five
gulden he asked for the goat, tied a string around its
neck, and led it back toward Chelm.

On the way home, Shlemiel stopped in the village of
Piask, known for its thieves and swindlers, although
Shlemiel was not aware of this. He went into an inn to
eat and left the goat tethered to a tree in the courtyard.

He ordered some sweet brandy, an appetizer of chopped liver with onions, a plate of chicken soup with noodles, and, as befits a successful businessman, some tea and honey cake for dessert. Before long he began to feel the effects of the brandy. He boasted to the innkeeper about the wonderful animal he had picked up in Lublin. "What a bargain I got," he announced. "A young, healthy goat, and what a great milker she promises to be."

The innkeeper, who happened to be a typical Piask swindler, owned an old billy goat that was blind in one eye and had a long white beard and a broken horn. Only the fact that it was so emaciated saved it from the butcher. After listening to Shlemiel praise his new goat, the innkeeper went into the courtyard and replaced Shlemiel's young animal with his old one. Shlemiel was so preoccupied with his business plans that he hardly looked at the goat when he untied it and so didn't notice that he was leading back to Chelm a different goat from the one he had bought.

Since it was Shlemiel's first business venture, the entire family was waiting impatiently to see the animal he was bringing back from the big city. They were all gathered in Shlemiel's house—his father-in-law, his brothers- and sisters-in-law, as well as friends and neighbors. When Shlemiel finally arrived, they ran out to the yard to greet him. Even before he opened the gate, he began to extol the virtues of his purchase—the goat's strength, its full udders.

When the old billy goat followed Shlemiel through the gate, there was consternation. His father-in-law clutched at his beard, dumbfounded. His mother-in-law spread her arms in a gesture of bewilderment. The young men laughed and the young women giggled. His father-in-law was the first one to speak up: "Is this what you call a young goat? It's a half-dead billy."

At first Shlemiel protested violently, but then for the first time he took a good look at the animal he had brought home. When he saw the old billy goat, he beat his head with his fists. He was convinced that the goat dealer had cheated him, although he could not figure out when he could have managed to do so. Shlemiel was so furious that after a sleepless night he set out for Lublin to return the goat and give the dealer a piece of his mind.

On the way he again stopped in Piask, at the same inn. He told the innkeeper that he had been swindled in Lublin and that he was on his way to get the right goat or his money back. If the merchant did not give him satisfaction, he intended to call the police. The innkeeper had more than once been in trouble with the authorities. He realized that an investigation might lead to him and that was the last thing he wanted.

As Shlemiel poured out his complaints against the Lublin goat dealer, the innkeeper clicked his tongue in sympathy and said, "It's well known that the merchants of Lublin are cheaters. Be watchful or you will be swindled a second time." Soon thereafter, as Shlemiel was busy eating his lunch, the innkeeper went out into the courtyard and again exchanged the goats. When Shlemiel was ready to leave, he was so preoccupied with imagining what he would say to the dealer that he again paid little attention to the animal he was leading.

Shlemiel arrived at the goat dealer's and began to threaten and upbraid him. The astonished dealer pointed out that the goat Shlemiel was returning was indeed young and had milk-filled udders. Shlemiel took one look at the goat and was left speechless. When at last he found his tongue, he exclaimed, "All I can say is that I must have been seeing things." He apologized profusely, took the goat, and again started back to Chelm. When he reached Piask, he as usual stopped at the inn for some refreshment. He ordered chicken and dumplings and, to celebrate the fact that he had made a good bargain after all, some sweet brandy. The innkeeper, born thief that he was, couldn't resist swindling such an easy victim. Offering Shlemiel a second brandy on the house, he went out into the yard and again exchanged the goats.

When Shlemiel left the inn, night was falling. By this time he was a bit tipsy and hardly glanced at the goat as he untied it and started for home.

When Shlemiel returned to Chelm for the second time leading an old billy goat instead of a young female, there was pandemonium. Word spread quickly and the whole town went wild. The matter was immediately brought before the elders, who deliberated seven days and seven nights and came to the conclusion that when a nanny goat is take from Lublin to Chelm it turns into a billy goat on the way. They therefore proclaimed a law prohibiting the import of goats from Lublin by any resident of Chelm. The old goat soon died and Shlemiel had lost one-third of his wife's dowry.

Shlemiel, having failed in his business dealings with Lublin, decided to try his luck in Lemberg. He had no sooner arrived in that city and settled himself in his room at the inn than the street on which it was located was filled with the screams of people and the continuous loud blast of a trumpet. Shlemiel had slept little on his way to Lemberg and had gone to bed on his arrival. He called for a servant to ask what the commotion was all about and was told that a house across the road was on fire and that the fire wagons had arrived. Shlemiel might have gone out to look at the fire, but he was exhausted from his long journey. After being assured that there was no danger to the inn and that the fire was being extinguished, he dozed off.

On awakening, he went to the lobby and asked one of the guests how the fire had started and how long it had taken to put it out. "Was it done merely by blowing a trumpet?" he wanted to know.

The man Shlemiel addressed happened to be one of Lemberg's most cunning thieves and Shlemiel's question immediately gave him an idea. "Yes," he replied. "Here in Lemberg we have a trumpet that extinguishes fires. It has only to be blown and the fire goes out."

Shlemiel could hardly express his amazement. He had heard of the many wonders of Lemberg, but never of a fire-fighting trumpet. It immediately occurred to him what a great source of profit such a trumpet could be in a town like Chelm, where all the houses were made of wood and most of the roofs of straw.

"How much does such a trumpet cost?" Shlemiel inquired.

"Two hundred gulden," the man replied.

Two hundred gulden was a large sum of money. It amounted to almost the entire remainder of Mrs.

Shlemiel's dowry. But when Shlemiel thought it over, he came to the conclusion that such a trumpet was more than worth the money. In Chelm there were many fires each year, especially in summertime. Houses and entire streets burned down. Although there were several firemen in Chelm, their equipment consisted of a single wagon drawn by an ancient nag. By the time the wagon arrived with its one barrel of water, everything had usually burned down. Shlemiel hadn't the slightest doubt that the owner of a fire-fighting trumpet could make a fortune. He told the man that he would like to buy such a trumpet and the other was more than willing to supply one. It was not long before he delivered a huge brass trumpet and a written guarantee that when blown it would extinguish all fires.

Shlemiel was overjoyed. This time he was sure he was on his way to becoming a rich man.

Back in Chelm, Shlemiel displayed to his family and neighbors the amazing instrument he had brought back from Lemberg. The word spread quickly and soon the people of Chelm were divided: some believed in the trumpet's powers and others maintained that Shlemiel had again been swindled. The matter would most certainly have come before the elders, but it was summertime and they were not in session.

Shlemiel's father-in-law was one of those with no faith in the trumpet. "It's another billy goat," he said. Shlemiel was so eager to demonstrate what the trumpet could do that he decided to set his father-in-law's house on fire, intending, of course, to blow out the fire with the trumpet before any real damage was done.

His father-in-law's house was old and dry and it was soon enveloped in flames. Shlemiel blew his trumpet until he could blow no more, but alas, the house continued to burn. The family was able to escape, but all their possessions were lost.

Despite the season, an emergency session of the elders was called immediately. The elders pondered the event for seven days and seven nights, and came to the conclusion that a trumpet able to extinguish fires in Lemberg lost its power, for some unknown reason, in Chelm. Gronam Ox proposed a law prohibiting the import of fire-fighting trumpets from Lemberg to Chelm. It was unanimously passed and duly recorded by Feivel Thickwit.

Shlemiel had lost his wife's dowry and had burned down his father-in-law's house; nevertheless, he refused to give up the idea of going into business. Having failed in Lublin and Lemberg, Shlemiel decided to do business with some local product in Chelm itself.

Chelm produced a sweet brandy that was Shlemiel's favorite drink. He decided to buy a keg of it and sell it in the market for three groschen a glass. He had figured out that if he could sell the whole kegful each day, he would make three-gulden profit a day. This time Mrs. Shlemiel made up her mind to help her husband. Shlemiel had no money left to pay the vintner, but his wife pawned a pin and they bought the brandy.

The following day they set up a small stand in the marketplace, placed the keg and a few glasses on it, and began hawking their drink to passersby: "Sweet brandy, a refreshing and invigorating drink for all, three groschen a glass."

Sweet brandy was a popular drink in Chelm, but three groschen a glass was too high a price. Only one customer bought a glass, quite early in the day, and he paid for it with a three-groschen coin. When an hour had passed and there were no more buyers, Shlemiel began to lose heart. He became so restless that he needed a drink. He held the three-groschen coin in his hand and said to his wife, "In what way is my money inferior to another man's? Here is three groschen and sell me a drink."

Mrs. Shlemiel thought the matter over and said, "You are right, Shlemiel. Your coin is as good as anyone else's." And she gave him a glass of brandy. Shlemiel drank it up and licked his lips. Most delicious! After a while Mrs. Shlemiel got thirsty, too. And she said to Shlemiel, "In what way is my three-groschen piece worse than another's? Here is my money and let me have a drink."

To make a long story short, Shlemiel and Mrs. Shlemiel continued drinking and passing the coin between them all day long. When evening came, the best part of the keg's contents was consumed and all they had to show for the day's work was a single three-groschen coin.

Shlemiel and his wife tried in vain to figure out where they had made a mistake this time; no matter how they puzzled over the problem, they could not find the solution. They had sold almost an entire keg of sweet brandy for cash, but the cash was not to be seen. Shlemiel believed that not even the elders of Chelm could explain what had happened to the money he and his wife had paid to each other.

This ended Shlemiel's attempts to go into business, and it was from that time on that Mrs. Shlemiel began to sell vegetables in the market. As for Shlemiel, he stayed at home and when the children were born took care of them. He also fed the chickens Mrs. Shlemiel kept under the stove.

Shlemiel's father-in-law was so disgusted with his son-in-law that he moved to Lublin. It was the first time in the history of Chelm that one of its citizens left the village for good. Nevertheless, Mrs. Shlemiel, though she chided him, continued to admire her husband. Shlemiel would often say to her, "If the Lublin nanny goat had not turned into a billy goat, and if the trumpet had been able to extinguish fires in Chelm, I would now be the richest man in town."

To which Mrs. Shlemiel would reply, "You may be poor, Shlemiel, but you are certainly wise. Wisdom such as yours is rare even in Chelm."

Translated by the author and Elizabeth Shub

Joseph & Koza

It happened long, long ago in the land which is now Poland. The country was covered with thick forests and swamps and the people were divided into many tribes that waged bloody battles among themselves. They fought with bows and arrows, swords and spears, because in those days they had neither rifles nor guns.

The roads were dangerous. Highwaymen lay in wait for merchants to rob and murder them. Often, travelers were attacked by wolves, bears, boars, and other wild beasts. And there were the many warlocks and witches who had sworn allegiance to Baba Yaga the Terrible and other evil powers. No one in all of Poland could read or write. The people worshipped idols of stone, clay, and wood, to whom they sacrificed not only animals but human beings as well.

The most powerful tribe in Poland inhabited Mazovia, a huge tract of land near the river Vistula. Mazovia was ruled by a chieftain called Wilk, who had a wife named Wilkova. Wilk was a tall man with a ruddy face and flaxen hair. He had a mustache whose tips reached down to his shoulders. Other chieftains in the land possessed crowns made of gold, silver, and precious stones, but Wilk's crown was a hollow gourd with notches cut in its rim to hold beeswax candles. The candles were lit when Wilk wore the crown.

Wilk kept a witch and stargazer called Zla, and the chieftain never made a move without consulting her. It was said that Zla could perform miracles. She rode in a carriage drawn by wolves and used a living snake as a whip.

Once each year it was the custom of the Mazovians to sacrifice their most beautiful maiden to the river Vistula. The people gathered at the river's shore. They drank wine, beer, mead, killed and roasted pigs, sang and danced all day long. Late in the day, when the sun was about to sink below the horizon, they brought forth the maiden. She was carried to a high cliff overlooking the river and thrown in. The Mazovians believed that this sacrifice would pacify the evil spirits of the Vistula.

It was the witch Zla who each year chose the most beautiful maiden of the land. First she read the stars for signs and then she consulted with the Devil. No one ever questioned Zla's choice.

Wilk had seven sons but only one daughter, Koza. Koza had golden hair and blue eyes, and the chieftain and his wife loved her above all else. When Koza was seventeen, and the time had come for her to marry, many kings' sons came to Mazovia to woo her. They competed in feats of prowess to see who would win her hand. One young suitor tore a wolf in half with his bare hands. Another strangled an ox. A third tore up a tree by the roots. Finally the young men fought each other with swords. They were as cruel to one another as they had been to the animals.

Koza was forced to witness these wild tournaments, but none of the young princes pleased her. She was kind-hearted by nature and hated bloodshed.

Every year on the first night of the month of Kwiecien (our April, more or less), the witch Zla studied the stars to determine who was the prettiest girl in Mazovia. That spring as she searched the heavens on the appointed night, she suddenly moaned out loud. It was Koza whom the stars had revealed to her.

When Wilk heard that he must sacrifice his daughter, he was grief-stricken. His wife fainted away. But Koza tried to comfort her parents. She said to her father, "If by giving my life to the Vistula, I can satisfy the evil spirits and serve our people, I will gladly do so."

The sacrificial ceremony always took place at the beginning of summer, on the first day of the month of Lipiec, or July. During the ninety days of waiting, the chosen maiden lived in a large tent erected in an apple orchard not far from the riverbank. The highborn young ladies of Mazovia came to keep Koza company. They sang and danced for her, wove wreaths of flowers, and brought her gifts to sweeten the long vigil.

One day a wanderer appeared at the gate of Wilk's palace. He was tall, had a black beard, long black hair, and black eyes. He carried a pouch on his back and a large scroll under his arm. The Mazovians had never before seen a scroll and they looked at it in amazement. The stranger told the guards that he had come to see Chieftain Wilk.

"Who are you? Where do you come from?" he was asked.

"From Jerusalem."

The guards informed Wilk, who sent for the stranger.

"What is your name?" Wilk asked.

"Joseph."

"Joseph? I've never heard of such a name. Who are you? And what do you want?"

Joseph replied, "I'm a Jew and I come from the city of Jerusalem. I am a goldsmith by profession. I make bracelets, brooches, and rings. I am on my way from Cracow, where I made a crown with golden horns for the king. I spent over a year in his palace, and there I learned to speak your language."

"What are you carrying under your arm?" Wilk asked.

"A scroll."

"What is a scroll?"

"This one bears God's commandments."

"Which god's commandments? Is he made of bone? Wood? Stone? Copper?"

"My God cannot be made by human hands," Joseph replied. "He has always lived. He is the creator of the earth, the sky, the sea, of all livings things, men and animals. Many, many ages ago, He revealed Himself to Moses on Mt. Sinai and gave him His commandments."

Wilk did not know what to make of all this. Finally he said to Joseph, "I would order a crown like the one you made for the King of Cracow, but this year is a time of mourning for me. Return next year and I will have you make a crown for me."

"Why are you in mourning?" Joseph asked.

"In sixty days my daughter Koza is to be sacrificed to the Vistula."

"The God of Israel has forbidden human sacrifice!" Joseph protested.

"How can that be?" Wilk asked. "If we fail to present the river with our most beautiful maiden, the evil powers will see that we get neither rain nor sunshine, and so our fields will give no harvest. If we do not bring this sacrifice to the Vistula, the river will overflow. It will be cold in the summertime and our crops will perish."

"Nonsense!" Joseph exclaimed. "It is God who makes the crops grow. God does not demand that a young maiden be drowned. It is a sin!"

Wilk pondered Joseph's words, and then he said, "It is true that I am the ruler of my people, but I know little about such matters. The wisest person in my country is the witch Zla. I will order my servants to provide you with food and a tent to sleep in, and tomorrow you will speak to Zla. But remember, she reads the stars and serves Baba Yaga and other powers of evil. Should you anger her, she can destroy you or turn you into a hedgehog, a rat, or a frog. We all fear her, because the Devil and the abyss are the sources of her strength."

"I do not fear her," Joseph replied. "The word of God is stronger than all witches and devils."

When Wilk's headmen and councilors learned about Joseph and what he had said, there was fear and confusion among them. Some insisted that the stranger was a messenger of doom and should be executed at once. Others thought that his words should be put to the test. After long arguing, it was decided that a debate should be held between Joseph and Zla in the presence of the entire court, presided over by Chieftain Wilk himself. Joseph immediately consented. At first Zla insisted that it was beneath her dignity to debate with an unknown intruder. But Wilk ordered her to appear.

The debate was fierce and lasted from morning till night. Zla denied the existence of one god and pointed out how vengeful the spirits of the Vistula were, particularly Topiel, whose palace was at the bottom of the river. She claimed that the maidens sacrificed to the Vistula did not really die but became the wives and concubines of Topiel. They danced, sang, and played music to keep him entertained. As proof of Topiel's power, she related how, at the winter and summer solstices, Baba Yaga herself visited the king of the river. She came flying to the Vistula in a huge mortar, holding a pestle the size of a pine tree in one hand and, in the other, a giant broom with which she swept away the light of the world. Who could dare rebel against such power?

Zla warned that unless Koza was given to the river on the first day of the month of Lipiec, there would be a storm, floods, thunder and lightning such as never before. Hailstones as large as rocks would destroy the crops. And should any grain survive the storm, it would be consumed by locusts, worms, and field mice.

Joseph unrolled the scroll he had brought with him. He explained what it said in the language of the land.

"God created the world in six days. God does not demand human sacrifices. He instructs man not to kill, steal, or bear false witness, but to honor his father and mother, and to be just and help those in need." Turning to Zla, he said, "No matter how strong the devils are, it is God who rules the world, not they. And the maidens you throw into the Vistula—they drown and rot. No devil can keep them alive under the water. The Vistula is not deep. Look carefully and you will see their bones."

The sun was moving toward the west, but the debate continued. Wilk's followers were divided into two camps. The older ones sided with Zla; the younger ones were with Joseph. When Joseph saw that his arguments could not convince them all, he said, "My lords, I can prove to you that the truth is on my side."

"How can you prove it?" asked Chieftain Wilk.

"The grain is harvested in the month of Sierpien. Wait until the end of Sierpien before you sacrifice the maiden. If the plagues Zla has prophesied occur, you will throw Koza into the Vistula and I myself will accept death at your hands because I misled you. But should these catastrophes not take place, you will have proof that I am right and that the words I read to you are the words of the true God."

Upon hearing this, Zla flew into a rage and began threatening Mazovia with even greater misfortunes. But Wilk lifted his scepter, which was made of amber, and announced: "It will be as Joseph has said. The sacrifice of Koza is postponed until the end of Sierpien. Until that time, Joseph is to be imprisoned in the dungeon."

It was the law that once the chieftain lifted his scepter

and spoke, nothing further must be said. All were silent. Only Zla could not contain her anger, and she screamed, "By the end of the month of Sierpien, Mazovia will be a desert!"

The Princess Koza and her ladies-in-waiting had not been present at the debate, but they soon learned what had taken place. Koza was prepared to give her life, but nevertheless, deep in her heart, she was afraid. She wanted neither to die nor to become one of Topiel's many wives and live in his underwater palace. When Joseph's words were repeated to her, she was filled with gratitude and love for him. She prayed to the gods of Mazovia that what he had said be true. Her ladies prayed with her.

Meanwhile, the days were mild and sunny. The sky was blue. It rained several times, but there was no flood. Each time clouds gathered, Zla insisted that the storm was beginning, but the rain always stopped and the sky became clear again.

The month of Sierpien, our August, approached and the grain fields of Mazovia grew dense, golden, and ripe. The peasants had already begun to harvest the fields. They followed their usual rituals to ensure a good crop. Each village had its wooden rooster, decorated with green stalks of wheat and rye and tender twigs from fruit trees. The peasant girls, dancing around the rooster, sprayed water on it through a sieve. The Mazovians believed that in addition to Baba Yaga there were many lesser *babas*, as well as little imps called *dziads*, who lived in the furrows of the fields and who could do terrible damage unless they were exorcised through incantations and special ceremonies.

Although the time Joseph had set was almost at an end, Zla did not give up. She continued to prophesy that before Sierpien was out, the Vistula would overflow. She warned that day would become dark as night and that from the forest would come *babuks* riding vipers. They would destroy the sheaves of grain, the peasants' huts, the haystacks, and the granaries. Topiel himself, his face red, his beard white, with the wings of an eagle and the feet of a bear, would emerge from the Vistula. He would strangle children and kill the cattle. The river would spread itself over all the land.

On the twentieth day of Sierpien, Koza asked to be taken to her father. She begged him for permission to visit Joseph in his dungeon. Wilk agreed and sent two of her ladies with her. When Koza was shown into Joseph's cell, she found him sitting and writing on parchment with a quill. Koza had never seen a quill, ink, or parchment. She fell on her knees before him, and both ladies knelt beside her. "Joseph," she said, "you are the greatest god of all." She began to weep and kiss his sandals.

Joseph made her rise. "I am not a god. There are no gods. One God creates us all," he said.

"Do you have a wife?" Koza asked.

"No, Koza, I am not married."

"Then I wish to be your wife."

"As it is destined, so will it be," Joseph replied.

He took three golden bracelets from his pack. One of them was set with a jeweled Star of David. He placed it on Koza's wrist and presented each of her companions with one of the remaining bracelets.

Since Joseph was convinced that Koza would not be

drowned, that there would be no reason for Wilk to be in mourning, he had spent his time in prison making a golden crown for Mazovia's ruler. The Mazovians had no alphabet of their own, so Joseph had engraved the crown with Wilk's name in Hebrew letters, as well as the figure of a wolf, because Wilk means wolf.

Excitement grew in Mazovia as the end of Sierpien approached. Those who no longer believed in Zla—mostly the young—sang, danced, and were confident of Joseph's final victory. The harvest, an especially plentiful one, had been gathered by now. The women began to grind the grain into flour. As always after harvest time, the evenings were devoted to games and festivity. Riddles were asked, stories were told. It was the custom that the girl who had harvested the last furrow became a *baba*. She blackened her face with soot, braided thistles into her hair, and carried a large witch's hoop. One of the boys impersonated a rooster. He attached wings to his shoulders, put a comb on his head, and tied spurs to his heels. He crowed and flapped, and made believe he was about to attack the girl *baba*, while she cackled like a hen and plucked feathers from his fake wings. Later the harvesters and threshers built a huge bonfire on which they roasted sides of pork and chestnuts. They drank mead and beer. The nights were as dark as the days were bright, and falling stars were frequently seen. The frogs croaked with human voices. Despite Zla's prophecy that any day the evil spirits of the Vistula would emerge to bring havoc, the young people went bathing in the river at night.

The older people who still believed in Zla warned that

Sierpien was not yet over. They were certain the catastrophe would come. Many of them left their valley homes and camped on the hilltops to save themselves from the deluge. Others pointed out that it was not yet too late to choose another fair maiden to throw to the Vistula.

Zla continued to shower her curses on Joseph. She foretold that on the last day of Sierpien the sun would be extinguished, the moon would fall out of the sky, the trees would wither, and everything alive would perish. The waters of the Vistula would turn yellow and hot as boiling sulphur, and cover the entire earth.

The last day of Sierpien was the most beautiful of all. Not a single cloud marred the blue sky. The birds sang endlessly. The air was sweet as honey. Yet, until night fell, Zla was sure the flood would come. When the golden sun set behind the Vistula, she tore her hair, wailed, screamed, and whirled about in frenzy, but the world did not come to an end. Throughout Mazovia the news spread of Joseph's victory and of his coming marriage to Koza. Zla was so humiliated that she hid in a deep cave.

Now that Joseph had been proven right, his freedom was restored and Wilk was prepared to give him his daughter in marriage. But there were many obstacles. Some of the older courtiers and their wives remained on the side of Zla, and the witch sent word from her cave that Joseph was a warlock who would bring a curse on the land. In addition, Joseph followed strange customs that the people of Mazovia could not understand. He refused to eat pork. When he prayed, he wrapped himself in a shawl striped black and white and trimmed with fringes, and turned his face toward the east. At the entrance to his hut he had fastened a piece of parchment that he called a mezuzah. On the Sabbath he neither kindled a fire nor did his goldsmith's work. He also refused to bow before the idols of Mazovia—and he did not like to hunt. Chieftain Wilk soon came to realize that if Joseph remained among them, there would be a rebellion in Mazovia.

Wilk now tried to persuade his daughter that the stranger was not the right husband for her. But Koza, who had always obeyed her father, suddenly became stubborn. She fell at his feet and said, "I will never love anyone but Joseph. If I cannot be his wife, I will throw myself in the Vistula and the river will have its sacrifice."

"But Joseph cannot remain in Mazovia," Wilk said. "Because of him, the people are divided. If he stays, all will suffer."

"Then I will go with him to Jerusalem," said Koza.

Wilk called his councilors together to seek their advice. Most of them were of the opinion that a young woman's love must be respected. Others argued that it would be an insult to the chieftain's honor if he gave his daughter in marriage to a stranger who refused to worship the gods of Mazovia. Zla, who did not give up easily, sent a message to the council room announcing that the stars were against the match. However, faith in the stars and Zla's prophecies was no longer strong. The men whose daughters had been sacrificed to the Vistula now accused Zla of being a murderess who had sent to their deaths the most beautiful girls of Mazovia.

When Zla learned that Wilk had agreed to the marriage of Joseph and Koza despite her threats and warnings, she decided to make one final effort to interfere. There were magic powers that could be used only once. If she failed, her power would be destroyed forever. First she fasted three days and three nights, then she lit seven candles made of human fat. When this was done, she shaved off her elflocks and clipped her long, claw-like nails, kneaded these into a lump of dough, and burned it before an image of Baba Yaga, all the while invoking the evil powers.

On the fourth night she made her way to a thick forest, and using the most potent incantations and spells, she summoned Baba Yaga and her retinue of devils.

The night was hot and dark. Suddenly a wind arose and a scarlet light appeared. Baba Yaga arrived in her mortar, carrying her pestle in one hand and her tree broom in the other. Her face was like pitch, but her nose was red, turned up, with broad, flaring nostrils. Her eyes burned like live coals. Instead of hair, thistles grew out of her skull, and though she was a woman, she had a beard like a man. Her companions rode on brooms, canes, and shovels. Even Topiel, King of the Vistula, came—foaming with rage. The beasts of the forest, frightened by these apparitions, howled and screeched and hid themselves in ditches and tree hollows.

Zla bowed seven times to Baba Yaga. "Mighty Baba! As you already know, a man has come from the faraway city of Jerusalem and his name is Joseph. With cunning words, he has conquered the heart of Chieftain Wilk and won the love of Koza. Because of him, there was no sacrifice to the Vistula this year. Now he is about to marry Koza. If their marriage takes place, it will mean that we who worship you have lost our right to rule over human fate. I implore you, therefore, not to let this wedding take place."

"There will be no wedding!" Baba Yaga cried in a voice as hoarse as a saw. "I'll sweep it away with my broom and crush it with my pestle."

"There will be no wedding!" Topiel roared. "I will drown it with my waters."

"There will be no wedding!" chorused all the goblins, hobgoblins, sprites, and imps, each in his own shrill voice.

That night Zla went to bed assured that the evil spirits would emerge victorious, after all. It might have been impossible for them to destroy the crops and bring a flood, but surely they could stop a marriage. But Zla did not know that Joseph possessed the sacred powers of a soothsayer and could see what was happening long distances away. He knew that Zla had summoned the evil forces. He also knew how to overcome them. He prayed to God, and his prayer was heard. On the day of the wedding, Baba Yaga, Topiel, and all the evil creatures were suddenly overcome by a deep sleep. Zla tried desperately to summon them, but they did not wake up.

Since the wedding ceremony could not be performed in the temple of the idols, it took place in the palace garden. Koza's parents and her ladies-in-waiting were the only guests. Joseph placed a golden ring on her first finger and intoned the words of the marriage vow himself.

The following day, Joseph and Koza mounted two magnificent stallions, given to them by Wilk, and started on their long journey to the Holy Land. Although the gift of the horses was a very generous one, it did not compare with the crown Joseph had made for Wilk.

It was very difficult for Wilk and Wilkova to part with their only daughter. Koza, too, suffered at leaving her parents. But so it has always been—a wife must go with her husband, especially one who has saved her life. A huge throng accompanied them to the very edge of Mazovia. Trumpets were blown, drums and bells played; at night, torches were lit.

If one left one's country in those days, there was no way to send messages back. One was never heard from again. But somehow the Mazovians learned that Joseph and Koza were living happily in Jerusalem. Joseph's fame as a goldsmith spread far and wide. Koza bore him sons and daughters, who were brought up in the faith that there is only one God.

In Mazovia, from that time on, human sacrifice was forbidden. And later, when Mazovia and the surrounding tribal lands were united into one kingdom, called Poland, the Poles became Christians. Human sacrifice was then abolished throughout the country.

Zla had long since died; and Baba Yaga, Topiel, and all their evil band were heard about mainly in stories that grandmothers told their grandchildren as they churned butter or wove flax. But for many centuries it was the custom on the first day of summer for the girls of Mazovia to assemble on the shores of the Vistula. They would throw a straw dummy into the river in memory of the maidens sacrificed to Topiel. While the straw girl was bobbing up and down in the current, drifting toward the open sea, they would sing, dance, and celebrate Joseph's rescue of the beautiful Koza.

Translated by the author and Elizabeth Shub

A Hanukkah Evening
in My Parents' House

All year round my father, a rabbi in Warsaw, did not allow his children to play any games. Even when I wanted to play cat's cradle with my younger brother, Moshe, Father would say, "Why lose time on such nonsense? Better to recite psalms."

Often when I got two pennies from my father and I told him that I wanted to buy chocolate, ice cream, or colored pencils he would say, "You would do a lot better to find a poor man and give your pennies to him, because charity is a great deed."

But on Hanukkah, after Father lit the Hanukkah candles, he allowed us to play dreidel for half an hour. I remember one such night especially. It was the eighth night and in our Hanukkah lamp eight wicks were burning. Outside, a heavy snow had fallen. Even though our stove was hot, frost trees were forming on the windowpanes. My brother Joshua, who was eleven years older than I, already a grownup, was saying to my sister, Hindele, "Do you see the snow? Each flake is a hexagon; it has six sides with fancy little designs and decorations— every one a perfect jewel and slightly different from all the others."

My brother Joshua read scientific books. He also painted landscapes—peasants' huts, fields, forests, animals, sometimes a sunset. He was tall and blond. Father wanted him to become a rabbi, but Joshua's ambition was to be an artist. My sister, Hindele, was even older than Joshua and already engaged to be married. She had dark hair and blue eyes. The idea that Hindele was going to be the wife of some strange young man and even going to change her surname seemed to me so peculiar that I refused to think about it.

When Father heard what Joshua had said about the snow, he promptly said, "It's all the work of God Almighty, who bestows beauty on everything He creates."

"Why must each flake of snow be so beautiful, since people step on it or it turns to water?" Hindele asked.

"Everything comes easily to nature," Joshua answered. "The crystals arrange themselves in certain patterns. Take the frost trees—every winter they are the same. They actually look like fig trees and date trees."

"Such trees don't grow here in Poland but in the Holy Land," Father added. "When the Messiah comes, all God-fearing people will return to the Land of Israel. There will be the resurrection of the dead. The Holy Temple will be rebuilt. The world will be as full of wisdom as the sea of water."

The door opened and Mother came in from the kitchen.

She was frying the Hanukkah pancakes. Her lean face was flushed. For a while she stood there and listened. Although Mother was the daughter of a rabbi herself, she always pleaded with Father to be lenient and not to preach to us all the time as she felt he did. I heard her say, "Let the children have some fun. Who is winning?"

"It's little Moshe's lucky day," Hindele said. "He's cleaned us all out, the darling."

"Don't forget to give a few pennies to the poor," Father said to him. "In olden times one had to give tithe to the priests, but now the tithe should be given to the needy."

Mother nodded, smiled, and returned to the kitchen, and we continued our game. The tin dreidel, which I had bought before Hanukkah, had four Hebrew letters engraved on its sides: *nun*, *gimel*, *he*, and *shin*. According to Father, these letters were the initials of words which meant: a great miracle happened there—an allusion to the war between the Maccabees and the Greeks in 170 B.C. and the victory of the Maccabees. It is for this victory and the purification of the Holy Temple in Jerusalem from idols that Hanukkah is celebrated. But for us children *gimel* meant winning, *nun* losing, *he* half winning, and *shin* another chance for the player. Moshe and I took the game seriously, but Joshua and Hindele played only to keep us company. They always let us, the younger ones, win.

As for me, I was interested both in the game and in the conversation of the adults. As if he read my mind, I heard Joshua ask, "Why did God work miracles in ancient times, and why doesn't He work miracles in our times?"

Father pulled at his red beard. His eyes expressed indignation.

"What are you saying, my son? God works miracles in all generations even though we are not always aware of them. Hanukkah especially is a feast of miracles. My grandmother Hindele—you, my daughter, are named after her—told me the following story: In the village of Tishewitz there was a child named Zaddock. He was a prodigy. When he was three years old, he could already read the Bible. At five he studied the Talmud. He was very goodhearted both to human beings and to animals. There was a mouse where his family lived and every day little Zaddock used to put a piece of cheese at the hole in the wall where the creature was hiding. At night he put a saucer of milk there. One day—it happened to be the third day of Hanukkah—little Zaddock overheard a neighbor tell of a sick tailor in the village who was so poor that he could not afford to buy wood to heat his hut. Little Zaddock had heard that in the forest near the village there were a lot of fallen branches to be picked up for nothing, and he decided to gather as much wood as he could carry and bring it to the sick man. The child was so eager to help that he immediately set out for the forest without telling his mother where he was going.

"It was already late in the day when he left the house, and by the time he reached the forest it was dark. Little Zaddock had lost his way and he would surely have died from the cold, when suddenly he saw in the darkness three Hanukkah lights. For a while they lingered before his eyes, and then they began to move slowly. Little Zaddock went after them, and they brought him back to the village, to the hut where the sick man lived with his family. When the lights reached the door of the sick man's hut, they fell, turning into gold coins. The sick man was able to buy bread for his family and himself, fuel to heat the oven, as well as oil for the Hanukkah lights. It wasn't long before he got well and was again able to earn a living."

"Daddy, what happened to Zaddock when he grew up?" I asked.

"He became a famous rabbi," Father said. "He was known as the saintly Rabbi Zaddock."

It became so quiet that I could hear the spluttering of the Hanukkah candles and the chirping of our house cricket. Mother came in from the kitchen with two full plates of pancakes. They smelled delicious.

"Why is it so quiet—is the game over?" she asked.

My brother Moshe, who had seemed to be half asleep when Father told his story, suddenly opened his big blue eyes wide and said, "Daddy, I want to give the money I won to a sick tailor."

"You were preaching to them, huh?" Mother asked half reproachfully.

"I didn't preach, I told them a story," Father said. "I want them to know that what God could do two thousand years ago He can also do in our time."

Tsirtsur & Peziza

In a dark space between the stove and the wall, where the housewife stored her brooms, mops, and baking paddles, there lived an orphan imp called Peziza. She had only one friend in the world, Tsirtsur, a cricket. He, too, made his home behind the stove in a crevice between two bricks. An imp doesn't have to eat at all, but how Tsirtsur managed to survive is a riddle. Perhaps just the smell of fresh bread baking, a speck of flour that a house breeze swept back there, a drop of moisture in the air were enough for him. In any case, Tsirtsur never complained to Peziza about the lack of food. He dozed all day long. When evening came, he was wide awake and began chirping stories that often continued through the night.

Peziza had never known her father, Lantuch the imp. Her mother, Pashtida, who came from a wealthy family, had fallen in love with Lantuch. She had often told Peziza about the world that existed beyond the stove and about their relatives, the devils, gnomes, and hobgoblins, each with his own tricks and deviltries. Even so, if one has spent one's entire life behind a stove, one knows little of what is going on in the world, and Peziza had a strong curiosity, a trait no doubt inherited from her parents. While Tsirtsur chirped out his endless tales, Peziza dreamed of impish adventures.

Sometimes Peziza would ask Tsirtsur to tell her how it was outside and he would reply, "My mother said there's only trouble. Cold winds blow, cruel creatures devour one another."

"Nevertheless," Peziza would say thoughtfully, "I'd like to have a look myself at what the devils out there are doing."

And that is exactly what Fate had in mind.

One day there was a loud pounding and hammering. The stove shook, bricks fell. Peziza flew up and down in fright. The houseowners had decided to rebuild the stove. The racket continued all day long and both creatures huddled together until evening. When a piece of wall fell away, Tsirtsur cried, "If we don't get out of here, we'll be killed." There was a break which reached to the outside. They crept through it and found themselves in the back yard of the house. They stood on grass among shrubs and trees. It was the first time Peziza and Tsirtsur had breathed fresh air.

How beautiful the outside was! A huge sky, a moon, stars. Dew was forming. There was the whirring of myriads of crickets. They sounded just like Tsirtsur.

"I will dig myself a hole," Tsirtsur said, "because when the sun rises I must not stay in the open."

"My mother, too, warned me against the sun," Peziza agreed. "But a hole in the earth is not a proper hiding place for me. There is a hollow in that tree. I will spend the day there."

"The most important thing is that we don't lose each other," Tsirtsur declared. "I'll dig my hole near the roots of your tree."

Tsirtsur immediately began digging. He spoke to Peziza as he worked. "As long as it is summer, the outdoors is not so dangerous. But winter is a bitter time for crickets. It gets cold and something called snow covers the ground. Few crickets survive in such weather."

"Do you mind if I take a look around while you're busy?" Peziza asked.

"You may get lost."

"I won't fly far. I'll recognize this tree. It is taller than the others."

Tsirtsur urged Peziza not to wander away. But curious Peziza was not yet ready to settle down in her hollow. Her desire to see all the new things around her was too strong. She flew off and came to rest on a roof. I never knew I could fly so well, she thought. Suddenly she heard someone calling to her. She looked in the direction of the voice and saw an imp perched on a weather vane. Although the only other imp Peziza had ever seen was her mother, she knew at once that this imp was a young man. He had two pairs of wings and his horns were transparent. "What is your name?" he asked.

Peziza was so surprised that for a moment she remained speechless. Then she said, "Peziza."

"Peziza? My name is Paziz."

"Is that true or are you joking?"

"Why should I joke? That is my name. Maybe we're related. Let's fly."

Paziz jumped down from the weather vane and somersaulted over the roof to Peziza. He took off and she flew after him, amazed that she was not afraid. The night was full of shadowy creatures: imps, shades, goblins. One danced on a chimney, another slid down a drainpipe, a third whirled around using a weather vane as a carousel, a fourth clambered up a lamppost. Paziz flew so quickly that it made Peziza dizzy, but she managed to keep up with him. They passed over fields, forests, rivers, lakes, hamlets, and towns. As they flew along, Paziz entertained Peziza with stories of ruined castles, broken windmills, and forsaken houses. How large the world was! How strange the night! How endless the roads! Peziza could have flown on forever, but she knew that when the cock crows and the sun rises, an imp must hide. She also missed Tsirtsur.

"Where are we?" she asked. "I hope I will recognize my tree."

"There is no lack of trees here," Paziz remarked.

"Yes, but my friend Tsirtsur the cricket is waiting for me."

"What kind of a friendship is that? An imp and a cricket?"

"We've always been together. I could never live without him," Peziza replied.

"Very well, then. I will bring you back to where we started from."

They had been flying swiftly, but homeward bound

they traveled even more quickly than before. In her dreams Peziza had never imagined an imp as clever and brave as Paziz was. He had not spent his life, as she had, in a dark space between a stove and a wall. Each day he found a different resting place. At night he wandered wherever he pleased. He made many friends.

At last the roof where Paziz and Peziza had met came into view and Peziza recognized her tree nearby. To her amazement, when they landed she saw that Tsirtsur was not alone. There was another cricket with him. Tsirtsur, too, had found a friend, and the new cricket was helping him dig his home.

"Where have you been?" Tsirtsur called when he saw Peziza. "I was afraid you were lost."

"I never would have found my way back had it not been for Paziz," she replied, and introduced the imp to Tsirtsur.

Tsirtsur cricked politely: "As you see, I too have found a friend. Her name is Grillida."

Fate always has surprises up its sleeve. When Peziza and Tsirtsur were forced to leave their home behind the stove, they were sure their end was near. But the powers that be had their own plans. Instead of misfortune, Peziza found Paziz and Tsirtsur, Grillida. The couples soon became so attached to each other that they were inseparable and before long were married according to the customs of imps and crickets.

As long as summer lasted, they all enjoyed the outdoors. Paziz and Peziza spent their nights flying about and traveled as far as the big city of Lublin. Tsirtsur and Grillida amused themselves by telling each other stories.

When day came, the crickets rested in the nest they had dug and the imps slept in their tree hollow.

Little by little the nights began to get cool. A mist rose from the river. The frogs croaked less frequently. One seldom heard the whirring of crickets. Tsirtsur and Grillida kept close together for warmth. Sometimes it rained, lightninged, and thundered at night. Paziz and Peziza did not suffer from the cold, but they, too, had their troubles. First, they felt sorry for their friends, the crickets. Second, the tree in which they lived stood not far from the synagogue and every day they were disturbed by the blowing of a ram's horn. It is known that imps are afraid of the sound of a ram's horn. Whenever Peziza heard the horn's blast, she began to tremble and cry.

One evening Peziza noticed that the chimney leading to the stove behind which she and Tsirtsur used to live had smoke coming out of it. It had been rebuilt and was again in use. All four friends took counsel and decided to try to get behind the stove for the winter. Peziza and Paziz would have no difficulty getting there. They could fly into the house through an open window or through the chimney when the stove was cold. But for Tsirtsur and Grillida it would be a long and difficult journey. However, with the imps helping the crickets along, they all made their way to the old space between the stove and the wall.

The days became shorter, the nights longer. Outdoors it rained and snowed. The frosts came, but behind the stove it was dark, warm, and smelled of bread, cakes, and Sabbath pudding. The owners often toasted noodles and baked apples. In the kitchen, the housewife and her daughters plucked chickens and told stories about ghosts, hobgoblins, and imps. After having spent so much time listening to the people of the house, Peziza and Tsirtsur had learned to understand the language of humans. They had long since discovered that like crickets and imps, humans, too, dream of love and happiness.

Tsirtsur and Grillida never again left their nest, but Paziz and Peziza would often go out through the chimney to air their wings and revel in the adventures of the netherworld. Each time they returned they brought back new stories for the stay-at-homes. Some were gay and mischievous, others devilish and frightening, but all delighted the crickets and gave Tsirtsur much to chirp about with Grillida in the long winter nights.

Translated by the author and Elizabeth Shub

Naftali the Storyteller & His Horse, Sus

I

The father, Zelig, and the mother, Bryna, both complained that their son, Naftali, loved stories too much. He could never go to sleep unless his mother first told him a story. At times she had to tell him two or three stories before he would close his eyes. He always demanded: "Mama, more, more! ..."

Fortunately, Bryna had heard many stories from her mother and grandmother. Zelig himself, a coachman, had many things to tell—about spirits who posed as passengers and imps who stole into stables at night and wove braids into the horses' tails and elflocks into their manes. The nicest story was about when Zelig had still been a young coachman.

One summer night Zelig was coming home from Lublin with an empty wagon. It just so happened that he hadn't picked up any passengers from Lublin to his hometown, Janów. He drove along a road that ran through a forest. There was a full moon. It cast silvery nets over the pine branches and strings of pearls over the bark of the tree trunks. Night birds cried. From time to time a wolf's howl was heard. In those days the Polish woods still swarmed with bears, wolves, foxes, martens, and many other wild beasts. That night Zelig was despondent. When his wagon was empty of passengers, his wallet was empty of money, and there wouldn't be enough for Bryna to prepare for the Sabbath.

Suddenly Zelig saw lying in the road a sack that appeared to be full of flour or ground sugar. Zelig stopped his horse and got down to take a look. A sack of flour or sugar would come in handy in a household.

Zelig untied the sack, opened it, took a lick, and decided that it was ground sugar. He lifted the sack, which was unusually heavy. Zelig was accustomed to carrying his passengers' baggage and he wondered why a sack of sugar should feel so heavy.

It seems I didn't have enough to eat at the inn, Zelig thought. And when you don't eat enough, you lose your strength.

He loaded the sack into the wagon. It was so heavy that he nearly strained himself.

He sat down on the driver's box and pulled on the reins, but the horse didn't move.

Zelig tugged harder and cried out, "*Wyszta!*" which in Polish means "Giddap!"

But even though the horse pulled with all his might, the wagon still wouldn't move forward.

What's going on here, Zelig wondered. Can the sack be so heavy that the horse cannot pull it?

This made no sense, for the horse had often drawn a wagonful of passengers along with their baggage.

"There is something here that's not as it should be," Zelig said to himself. He got down again, untied the sack, and took another lick. God in heaven, the sack was full of salt, not sugar!

Zelig stood there dumbfounded. How could he have made such a mistake? He licked again, and again, and it was salt.

"Well, it's one of those nights!" Zelig mumbled to himself.

He decided to heave the sack off the wagon, since it was clear that evil spirits were toying with him. But by now the sack had become as heavy as if it were filled with lead. The horse turned his head backward and stared, as if curious as to what was going on.

Suddenly Zelig heard laughter coming from inside the sack. Soon afterward the sack crumbled and out popped a creature with the eyes of a calf, the horns of a goat, and the wings of a bat. The creature said in a human voice, "You didn't lick sugar or salt but an imp's tail."

And with these words the imp burst into wild laughter and flew away.

Dozens of times Zelig the coachman told this same story to Naftali but Naftali never grew tired of hearing it. He could picture it all—the forest, the night, the silver moon, the curious eye of the horse, and the imp. Naftali asked all kinds of questions: Did the imp have a beard? Did it have feet? How did its tail look? Where did it fly off to?

Zelig couldn't answer all the questions. He had been

too frightened at the time to notice the details. But to the last question Zelig replied, "He probably flew to beyond the Dark Regions, where people don't go and cattle don't stray, where the sky is copper, the earth iron, and where the evil forces live under roofs of petrified toadstools and in tunnels abandoned by moles."

2

Like all the children in town, Naftali rose early to go to cheder. He studied more diligently than the other children. Why? Because Naftali was eager to learn to read. He had seen older boys reading storybooks and he had been envious of them. How happy was one who could read a story from a book!

At six, Naftali was already able to read a book in Yiddish, and from then on he read every storybook he could get his hands on. Twice a year a bookseller named Reb Zebulun visited Janów, and among the other books in the sack he carried over his shoulder were some storybooks. They cost two groschen a copy, and although Naftali got only two groschen a week allowance from his father, he saved up enough to buy a number of storybooks each season. He also read the stories in his mother's Yiddish Pentateuch and in her books of morals.

When Naftali grew older, his father began to teach him how to handle horses. It was the custom in those days for a son to take over his father's livelihood. Naftali loved horses very much but he wasn't anxious to become a coachman driving passengers from Janów to Lublin and from Lublin to Janów. He wanted to become a bookseller with a sackful of storybooks.

His mother said to him, "What's so good about being a bookseller? From toting the sack day in day out, your back becomes bent, and from all the walking, your legs swell."

Naftali knew that his mother was right and he thought a lot about what he would do when he grew up. Suddenly he came up with a plan that seemed to him both wise and simple. He would get himself a horse and wagon, and instead of carrying the books on his back, he would carry them in the wagon.

His father, Zelig, said, "A bookseller doesn't make enough to support himself, his family, and a horse besides."

"For me it will be enough."

One time when Reb Zebulun the bookseller came to town, Naftali had a talk with him. He asked him where he got the storybooks and who wrote them. The bookseller told him that in Lublin there was a printer who printed these books, and in Warsaw and Vilna there were writers who wrote them. Reb Zebulun said that he could sell many more storybooks, but he lacked the strength to walk to all the towns and villages, and it didn't pay him to do so.

Reb Zebulun said, "I'm liable to come to a town where there are only two or three children who want to read storybooks. It doesn't pay me to walk there for the few groschen I might earn nor does it pay me to keep a horse or hire a wagon."

"What do these children do without storybooks?" Naftali asked. And Reb Zebulun replied, "They have to make do. Storybooks aren't bread. You can live without them."

"I couldn't live without them," Naftali said.

During this conversation Naftali also asked where the writers got all these stories and Reb Zebulun said, "First of all, many unusual things happen in the world. A day doesn't go by without some rare event happening. Besides, there are writers who make up such stories."

"They make them up?" Naftali asked in amazement. "If that is so, then they are liars."

"They are not liars," Reb Zebulun replied. "The human brain really can't make up a thing. At times I read a story that seems to me completely unbelievable, but I come to some place and I hear that such a thing actually happened. The brain is created by God, and human thoughts and fantasies are also God's works. Even dreams come from God. If a thing doesn't happen today, it might easily happen tomorrow. If not in one country, then in another. There are endless worlds and what doesn't happen on earth can happen in another world. Whoever has eyes that see and ears that hear absorbs enough stories to last a lifetime and to tell to his children and grandchildren."

That's what old Reb Zebulun said, and Naftali listened to his words agape.

Finally, Naftali said, "When I grow up, I'll travel to all the cities, towns, and villages, and I'll sell storybooks everywhere, whether it pays me or not."

Naftali had decided on something else, too—to become a writer of storybooks. He knew full well that for this you had to study, and with all his heart he determined to learn. He also began to listen more closely to what people said, to what stories they told, and to how they told them. Each person had his or her own manner of speaking. Reb Zebulun told Naftali, "When a day passes, it is no longer there. What remains of it? Nothing more than a story. If stories weren't told or books weren't written, man would live like the beasts, only for the day."

Reb Zebulun said, "Today we live, but by tomorrow today will be a story. The whole world, all human life, is one long story."

3

Ten years went by. Naftali was now a young man. He grew up tall, slim, fair-skinned, with black hair and blue eyes. He had learned a lot at the studyhouse and in the yeshiva and he was also an expert horseman. Zelig's mare had borne a colt and Naftali pastured and raised it. He called him Sus. Sus was a playful colt. In the summer he liked to roll in the grass. He whinnied like the tinkling sound of a bell. Sometimes, when Naftali washed and curried him and tickled his neck, Sus burst out in a sound that resembled laughter. Naftali rode him bareback like a Cossack. When Naftali passed the marketplace astride Sus, the town girls ran to the windows to look out.

After a while Naftali built himself a wagon. He ordered the wheels from Leib the blacksmith. Naftali loaded the wagon with all the storybooks he had collected during the years and he rode with his horse and his goods to the nearby towns. Naftali bought a whip, but he swore solemnly to himself that he would never use it. Sus didn't need to be whipped or even to have the whip waved at him. He pulled the light wagonful of books eagerly and easily. Naftali seldom sat on the box but walked alongside his horse and told him stories. Sus cocked his ears when Naftali spoke to him and Naftali was sure that Sus understood him. At times, when Naftali asked Sus whether he had liked a story, Sus whinnied, stomped his foot on the ground, or licked Naftali's ear with his tongue as if he meant to say, "Yes, I understand . . ."

Reb Zebulun had told him that animals live only for the day, but Naftali was convinced that animals have a memory, too. Sus often remembered the road better than he, Naftali, did. Naftali had heard the story of a dog whose masters had lost him on a distant journey and months after they had come home without their beloved pet, he showed up. The dog crossed half of Poland to come back to his owners. Naftali had heard a similar story about a cat. The fact that pigeons fly back to their coops from very far away was known throughout the world. In those days, they were often used to deliver letters. Some people said this was memory, others called it instinct. But what did it matter what it was called? Animals didn't live for the day only.

Naftali rode from town to town; he often stopped in villages and sold his storybooks. The children everywhere loved Naftali and his horse, Sus. They brought all kinds of good things from home for Sus—potato peels, turnips, and pieces of sugar—and each time Sus got something to eat he waved his tail and shook his head, which meant "Thank you."

Not all the children were able to study and learn to read, and Naftali would gather a number of young children, seat them in the wagon, and tell them a story, sometimes a real one and sometimes a made-up one.

Wherever he went, Naftali heard all kinds of tales—of demons, hobgoblins, windmills, giants, dwarfs, kings, princes, and princesses. He would tell a story nicely, with all the details, and the children never grew tired of listening to him. Even grownups came to listen. Often the grownups invited Naftali home for a meal or a place to sleep. They also liked to feed Sus.

When a person does his work not only for money but out of love, he brings out the love in others. When a child couldn't afford a book, Naftali gave it to him free. Soon Naftali became well known throughout the region. Eventually, he came to Lublin.

In Lublin, Naftali heard many astonishing stories. He met a giant seven feet tall who traveled with a circus and a troupe of midgets. At the circus Naftali saw horses who danced to music, as well as dancing bears. One trickster swallowed a knife and spat it out again, another did a somersault on a high wire, a third flew in the air from one trapeze to another. A girl stood on a horse's back while it raced round and round the circus ring. Naftali struck up an easy friendship with the circus people and he listened to their many interesting stories. They told of fakirs in India who could walk barefoot over burning coals. Others let themselves be buried alive, and after they were dug out several days later, they were healthy and well. Naftali heard astounding stories about sorcerers and miracle workers who could read minds and predict the future. He met an old man who had walked from Lublin to the Land of Israel, then back again. The old man told

Naftali about cabalists who lived in caves behind Jerusalem, fasted from one Sabbath to the next, and learned the secrets of God, the angels, the seraphim, the cherubim, and the holy beasts.

The world was full of wonders and Naftali had the urge to write them down and spread them far and wide over all the cities, towns, and villages.

In Lublin, Naftali went to the bookstores and bought storybooks, but he soon saw that there weren't enough storybooks to be had. The storekeepers said that it didn't pay the printers to print them since they brought in so little money. But could everything be measured by money? There were children and even grownups everywhere who yearned to hear stories and Naftali decided to tell all that he had heard. He himself hungered for stories and could never get enough of them.

4

More years passed. Naftali's parents were no longer living. Many girls had fallen in love with Naftali and wanted to marry him, but he knew that from telling stories and selling storybooks he could not support a family. Besides, he had become used to wandering. How many stories could he hear or tell living in one town? He therefore decided to stay on the road. Horses normally live some twenty-odd years, but Sus was one of those rare horses who live a long time. However, no one lives forever. At forty Sus began to show signs of old age. He seldom galloped now, nor were his eyes as good as they once were. Naftali was already gray himself and the children called him Grandpa.

One time Naftali was told that on the road between Lublin and Warsaw lay an estate where all booksellers came, since the owner was very fond of reading and hearing stories. Naftali asked the way and he was given directions to get there. One spring day he came to the estate. Everything that had been said turned out to be true. The owner of the estate, Reb Falik, gave him a warm welcome and bought many books from him. The children in the nearby town had already heard about Naftali the storyteller and they snatched up all the storybooks he had brought with him. Reb Falik had many horses grazing and when they saw Sus they accepted him as one of their own. Sus promptly began to chew the grass where many yellow flowers grew and Naftali told Reb Falik one story after another. The weather was warm, birds sang, twittered, and trilled, each in its own voice.

The estate contained a tract of forest where old oaks grew. Some of the oaks were so thick they had to be hundreds of years old. Naftali was particularly taken by one oak standing in the center of a meadow. It was the thickest oak Naftali had ever seen in his life. Its roots were spread over a wide area and you could tell that they ran deep. The crown of the oak spread far and wide, and it cast a huge shadow. When Naftali saw this giant oak, which had to be older than all the oaks in the region, it occurred to him: "What a shame an oak hasn't a mouth to tell stories with!"

This oak had lived through many generations. It may have gone back to the times when idol worshippers still lived in Poland. It surely knew the time when the Jews had come to Poland from the German states where they had been persecuted and the Polish king Kazimierz I had opened the gates of the land to them. Naftali suddenly realized that he was tired of wandering. He now envied the oak for standing so long in one place, deeply rooted in God's earth. For the first time in his life Naftali got the urge to settle down in one place. He also thought of his horse. Sus was undoubtedly tired of trekking over the roads. It would do him good to get some rest in the few years left him.

Just as Naftali stood there thinking these thoughts, the owner of the estate, Reb Falik, came along in a buggy. He stopped the buggy near Naftali and said, "I see you're completely lost in thought. Tell me what you're thinking."

At first Naftali wanted to tell Reb Falik that many kinds of foolish notions ran through the human mind and that not all of them could be described. But after a while he thought, Why not tell him the truth?

Reb Falik seemed a kindhearted man. He had a silver-white beard and eyes that expressed the wisdom and goodness that sometimes come with age. Naftali said, "If you have the patience, I'll tell you."

"Yes, I have the patience. Take a seat in the buggy. I'm going for a drive and I want to hear what a man who is famous for his storytelling thinks about."

Naftali sat down in the buggy. The horses hitched to the buggy walked slowly and Naftali told Reb Falik the story of his life, as well as what his thoughts were when he saw the giant oak. He told him everything, kept nothing back.

When Naftali finished, Reb Falik said, "My dear Naftali, I can easily fulfill all your wishes and fantasies. I am, as you know, an old man. My wife died some time

ago. My children live in the big cities. I love to hear
stories and I also have lots of stories to tell. If you like,
I'll let you build a house in the shade of the oak and
you can stay there as long as I live and as long as you
live. I'll have a stable built for your horse near the house
and you'll both live out your lives in peace. Yes, you are
right. You cannot wander forever. There comes a time
when every person wants to settle in one place and drink
in all the charms that the place has to offer."

When Naftali heard these words, a great joy came over
him. He thanked Reb Falik again and again, but Reb
Falik said, "You need not thank me so much. I have many
peasants and servants here, but I don't have a single person I can talk to. We'll be friends and we'll tell each
other lots of stories. What's life, after all? The future isn't
here yet and you cannot foresee what it will bring. The
present is only a moment and the past is one long story.
Those who don't tell stories and don't hear stories live
only for that moment, and that isn't enough."

5

Reb Falik's promise wasn't merely words. The
very next day he ordered his people to build a house for
Naftali the storyteller. There was no shortage of lumber
or of craftsmen on the estate. When Naftali saw the plans
for the house, he grew disturbed. He needed only a small
house for himself and a stable for Sus. But the plans called
for a big house with many rooms. Naftali asked Reb
Falik why such a big house was being built for him, and
Reb Falik replied, "You will need it."

"What for?" Naftali asked.

Gradually, the secret came out. During his lifetime Reb Falik had accumulated many books, so many that he couldn't find room for them in his own big house and many books had to be stored in the cellar and in the attic. Besides, in his talks with Reb Falik, Naftali had said that he had many of his own stories and stories told him by others written down on paper and that he had collected a chestful of manuscripts, but he hadn't been able to have these stories printed, for the printers in Lublin and in the other big cities demanded a lot of money to print them and the number of buyers of storybooks in Poland wasn't large enough to cover such expenses.

Alongside Naftali's house, Reb Falik had a print shop built. He ordered crates of type from Lublin (in those days there was no such thing as a typesetting machine) as well as a hand press. From now on Naftali would have the opportunity to set and print his own storybooks. When he learned what Reb Falik was doing for him, Naftali couldn't believe his ears. He said, "Of all the stories I have ever heard or told, for me this will be by far the nicest."

That very summer everything was ready—the house, the library, the print shop. Winter came early. Right after Succoth the rains began, followed by snow. In winter there is little to do on an estate. The peasants sat in their huts and warmed themselves by their stoves or they went to the tavern. Reb Falik and Naftali spent lots of time together. Reb Falik himself was a treasure trove of stories. He had met many famous squires. In his time he had visited the fairs in Danzig, Leipzig, and Amsterdam. He had even made a trip to the Holy Land and had seen the Western Wall, the Cave of Machpelah, and Rachel's Tomb. Reb Falik told many tales and Naftali wrote them down.

Sus's stable was too big for one horse. Reb Falik had a number of old horses on his estate that could no longer work so Sus wasn't alone. At times, when Naftali came into the stable to visit his beloved Sus, he saw him bowing his head against the horse on his left or his right, and it seemed to Naftali that Sus was listening to stories told him by the other horses or silently telling his own horsy story. It's true that horses cannot speak, but God's creatures can make themselves understood without words.

That winter Naftali wrote many stories—his own and those he heard from Reb Falik. He set them in type and printed them on his hand press. At times, when the sun shone over the silvery snow, Naftali hitched Sus and another horse to a sleigh and made a trip through the nearby towns to sell his storybooks or give them away to those who couldn't afford to buy them. Sometimes Reb Falik went along with him. They slept at inns and spent time with merchants, landowners, and Hasidim on their way to visit their rabbis' courts. Each one had a story to tell and Naftali either wrote them down or fixed them in his memory.

The winter passed and Naftali couldn't remember how. On Passover, Reb Falik's sons, daughters, and grandchildren came to celebrate the holiday at the estate, and again Naftali heard wondrous tales of Warsaw, Cracow, and even of Berlin, Paris, and London. The kings waged wars, but scientists made all kinds of discoveries and inventions. Astronomers discovered stars, planets, comets. Archaeologists dug out ruins of ancient cities. Chemists found new elements. In all the countries, tracks were being laid for railroad trains. Museums, libraries, and theaters were being built. Historians uncovered writings from generations past. The writers in every land described the life and the people among whom they dwelled. Mankind could not and would not forget its past. The history of the world grew ever richer in detail.

That spring something happened that Naftali had been expecting and, therefore, dreading. Sus became sick and stopped grazing. The sun shone outside, and Naftali led Sus out to pasture, where the fresh green grass and many flowers sprouted. Sus sat down in the sunshine, looked at the grass and the flowers, but no longer grazed. A stillness shone out from his eyes, the tranquillity of a creature that has lived out its years and is ready to end its story on earth.

One afternoon, when Naftali went out to check on his beloved Sus, he saw that Sus was dead. Naftali couldn't hold back his tears. Sus had been a part of his life.

Naftali dug a grave for Sus not far from the old oak where Sus had died, and he buried him there. As a marker over the grave, he thrust into the ground the whip that he had never used. Its handle was made of oak.

Oddly enough, several weeks later Naftali noticed that the whip had turned into a sapling. The handle had put down roots into the earth where Sus lay and it began to sprout leaves. A tree grew over Sus, a new oak which drew sustenance from Sus's body. In time young branches grew out of the tree and birds sang upon them and built their nests there. Naftali could hardly bring himself to believe that this old dried-out stick had possessed enough life within it to grow and blossom. Naftali considered it a miracle. When the tree grew thicker, Naftali carved Sus's name into the bark along with the dates of his birth and death.

Yes, individual creatures die, but this doesn't end the story of the world. The whole earth, all the stars, all the planets, all the comets represent within them one divine history, one source of life, one endless and wondrous story that only God knows in its entirety.

A few years afterward, Reb Falik died, and years later, Naftali the storyteller died. By then he was famous for his storybooks not only throughout Poland but in other countries as well. Before his death Naftali asked that he be buried beneath the young oak that had grown over Sus's grave and whose branches touched the old oak. On Naftali's tombstone were carved these words from the Scriptures:

LOVELY AND PLEASANT IN THEIR LIVES,

AND IN THEIR DEATH

THEY ARE NOT DIVIDED

Translated by Joseph Singer

Hershele & Hanukkah

Three lights burned in old Reb Berish's menorah. It was so quiet in the studyhouse one could hear the wick in the ceiling lamp sucking kerosene. Reb Berish was saying:

"Children, when one lives as long as I do, one sees many things and has many stories to tell. What I am going to tell you now happened in the village of Gorshkow.

"Gorshkow is small even today. But when I was a boy the marketplace was the entire village. They used to joke, 'Whenever a peasant comes with his cart to Gorshkow, the head of the horse is at one end of the village and the rear wheels of the cart at the other end.' Fields and forests surrounded Gorshkow on all sides. A man by the name of Isaac Seldes who lived there managed a huge estate owned by a Polish squire. The squire, a count, spent all his time abroad and came to Poland only when his money was exhausted. He borrowed more money from Reb Isaac Seldes on mortgage and gradually his whole estate became Isaac's property. Officially, it still belonged to the squire because a Jew was not allowed to own land in the part of Poland which belonged to Russia.

"Reb Isaac managed the property with skill. The squire used to flog the peasants when they did something wrong or if the mood struck him. But Reb Isaac spoke to the peasants as if they were his equals and they were loyal to him. When there was a wedding among them or when a woman gave birth, he attended the celebration. When a peasant fell sick, Reb Isaac's wife, Kreindl, rolled up her sleeves and applied cups or leeches or rubbed the patient with turpentine. Reb Isaac Seldes owned a britska with two horses, and he rode alongside the fields and advised the peasants when to plow, what to sow, or what vegetables to plant. He had a special dairy house on the estate for churning butter and making cheese. He had a large stable of cows, hundreds of chickens that laid eggs, as well as beehives and a water mill.

"He had everything except children. It caused Reb Isaac and his wife grief. The medications that the doctors of Lublin prescribed for Kreindl never did any good.

"Even though they were only two people, Reb Isaac and his wife lived in a large house that had once belonged to the present squire's grandfather. But what use is a big house for just a husband and a wife? However, they both had poor relatives whose children came to live on the estate. Reb Isaac hired a teacher to instruct the boys in the Bible and the Talmud. Kreindl taught the girls sewing, knitting, and needlepoint. They stitched biblical scenes onto canvas with colored thread, like the story of Abraham attempting to sacrifice his only son on an altar and the angel preventing him from doing so, or Jacob meeting Rachel at the well and rolling the stone away so she could water the sheep.

"Hanukkah was always a gay occasion in Reb Isaac's house. After blessing the candles, he gave Hanukkah money to all the children and they all played dreidel. Kreindl and her maids fried potato pancakes in the kitchen and they were served with jam and tea. Often poor people turned up at the estate, and whoever came hungry, in tattered clothes and bare feet, left with a full belly, warm clothing, and proper footwear.

"One Hanukkah evening when the children were playing dreidel and Reb Isaac was playing chess with the teacher, who was not only a Talmud scholar but also well versed in mathematics and language, Reb Isaac heard a scratching at the door. A deep snow had fallen outside. If guests visited the estate in the winter, they came during the day, not in the evening. Reb Isaac opened the door himself, and to his amazement, on the other side of the threshold stood a fawn, still without antlers. Normally, an animal keeps away from human beings, but this fawn seemed hungry, cold, and emaciated. Perhaps it had lost its mother. For a while Reb Isaac stared in wonder. Then he took the young animal by its throat and brought it into the house. When the children saw the fawn, they forgot about the dreidel and the Hanukkah gifts. They were all thrilled with the charming animal. When she

saw the fawn, Kreindl almost dropped the tray of pancakes she was holding. Reb Isaac wanted to give a pancake
to the fawn, but Kreindl called out, 'Don't do it. It's too
young. It needs milk, not pancakes.' The maids came in
and one of them went to bring a bowl of milk. The fawn
drank all of it and lifted up its head as if to say, 'I want
more.' This little creature brought much joy to everybody in the house. All agreed that the fawn should not be
let out again in the woods, which teemed with wolves,
foxes, martens, and even bears. A servant brought in some
hay and made a bed for the fawn in one of the rooms.
Soon, it fell asleep.

"Reb Isaac thought that soon the children would return to their games, but all they could talk about was the
fawn, and Reb Isaac and Kreindl had to give them a
solemn promise to keep it safe in the house until after
Passover.

"Now that the children had extracted this promise, a
new debate began—what name to give the fawn? Almost everyone wanted to call it Hershele, which is the
Yiddish word for fawn, but for some strange reason
Kreindl said, 'You are not going to give this name to
the animal.'

" 'Why not?' the children and even the grownups asked
in astonishment.

" 'I have a reason.'

"When Kreindl said no, it remained no. The children
had to come up with another name, and then Kreindl
said, 'Children, I have it.'

" 'What is it?' the children asked in unison. And
Kreindl said, 'Hanukkah.'

"No one had ever heard of an animal called Hanukkah, but they liked it. Only now did the children start to eat the pancakes, and they washed them down with tea with lemon and jam. Then they began to play dreidel again and they did not finish the games until midnight.

"Late at night, when Reb Isaac and Kreindl went to bed, Reb Isaac asked Kreindl, 'Why didn't you like the name Hershele for the fawn?' and Kreindl replied, 'That is a secret.'

" 'A secret from me?' Isaac asked. 'Since we married you've never had any secrets from me.'

"And Kreindl answered, 'This time I cannot tell you.'

" 'When will you tell me?' Isaac asked, and Kreindl said, 'The secret will reveal itself.'

"Reb Isaac had never heard his wife speak in riddles but it was not in his nature to insist or to probe.

"Now, dear children, I am going to tell you the secret even before Kreindl told it to her husband," old Reb Berish said.

"A few weeks earlier an old man came to the estate with a sack on his back and a cane in his hand. He had a white beard and white sidelocks. When Kreindl gave him food to eat he took a large volume out of his sack, and while he ate, he read it. Kreindl had never seen a beggar behave like a rabbi and a scholar. She asked him, 'Why do you carry books on your back? Aren't they heavy?' And the old man replied, 'The Torah is never heavy.' His words impressed Kreindl, so she began to talk to him and she told him how grieved she was at not having children. Suddenly she heard herself say, 'I see that you are a holy man. Please, pray to God for me and give me your blessing. I promise you that if your blessing is answered in heaven, I will give you a sack full of silver guldens when you return and you will never need to beg for alms.'

" 'I promise you that in about a year's time you will have a child.'

" 'Please, holy man,' Kreindl said. 'Give me a token or a sign that your promise will come true.' And the old man said, 'Some time before your child is conceived an animal will enter your house. When the child is born, call it by the name of this animal. Please remember my words.'

"Before the old man left, Kreindl wanted to give him clothes and food, but he said, 'God will provide all this for me. I don't need to prepare it in advance. Besides, my sack is filled with sacred books and there is no place for anything else.' He lifted his hands over Kreindl's head and blessed her. Then he left as quietly as he had come. Kreindl pondered the words of this strange old man for many weeks. Reb Isaac happened not to be at home when he came and Kreindl did not tell her husband about his visit. She had received many wishes and benedictions from gypsies, fortune-tellers, and wanderers, and she did not want to arouse hopes in Isaac that might never materialize.

"That night when the fawn came into the house Kreindl understood that this was the animal the beggar had mentioned. Since a fawn is called Hershele in Yiddish, she would give birth to a male child and call him Hershele. Kreindl's words that the secret would reveal itself soon came true. She became pregnant and Reb Isaac understood that the coming of the fawn was an omen of this hoped-for event. He said, 'When our child is born, if it is a male we will call it Hershele,' and Kreindl answered, 'As you wish, my beloved, so it will be.'

"Winter had passed, spring had come. Hanukkah had been growing in the cold winter months and he sprouted antlers. Everyone could see that the animal was no longer happy indoors. His beautiful eyes expressed a yearning to go back to the forest. One morning Kreindl gave Hanukkah a tasty meal of hay mixed with chopped potatoes and carrots and then opened the gate to the fields and forests. Hanukkah gave his mistress a look that said 'Thank you,' and he ran to the green pastures and the woods.

"Kreindl predicted that in the winter Hanukkah would turn up again, but Reb Isaac said such things cannot be foretold. 'Hanukkah has grown up and an adult deer can find its own food even in the winter.'

"Not long after, Kreindl gave birth to a healthy little boy with dark hair and brown eyes, and there was great joy in the house. The happy father and mother had prepared a special repast for the poor on the day of the circumcision ceremony. Reb Isaac and Kreindl both hoped that the old beggar might hear about it and come to the feast. But he never came. However, other poor people heard about it and they came. A large table was placed on the lawn and the needy men and women were served challah, gefilte fish, chicken, fruit, as well as wine and honey cake. Some of the younger crowd danced a scissor dance, a good-morning dance, an angry dance, a kazatske. Before they left, all the poor got gifts of money, food, and clothes.

"The summer drew to a close and it became cool again. After the Succoth holiday the rains, the snowfall, and the frosts began. The feast of Hanukkah approached, and although everyone wondered what had happened to the fawn in the cold weather, nobody spoke about it, so as not to worry Kreindl. This winter was even more severe than the former one. The whole estate was buried in snow. On the first night of Hanukkah, Kreindl and the maids were busy frying pancakes. After Reb Isaac blessed the first light and gave coins to the children, they sat down to play dreidel. The baby, Hershele, slept in his cradle. The children of the house had prepared a gift for him—a fawn made of sugar, and on its belly was the inscription *Hanukkah*. When it was given to Hershele, he immediately began to suck on it. But the fawn didn't come that night. Reb Isaac comforted Kreindl by quoting the Gemara: 'Miracles don't happen every day.'

"Kreindl shook her head. 'I hope to God that Hanukkah is not hungry and cold.'

"On the second night of Hanukkah, while all the children were playing dreidel, Reb Isaac was about to checkmate the teacher, and Kreindl, along with the maids, was preparing to clean the table, they heard a scratching on the door. Kreindl ran to open it and cried out with joy. At the door stood Hanukkah, already a half-grown deer, his body silvery with frost. He had not forgotten his benefactors. He had come to stay for the winter. Hershele woke up from the noise, and when he was shown the animal, he stretched out his little hand toward him. Hanukkah licked the hand with his tongue, as if he knew that Hershele was his namesake.

"From then on, the deer came to the estate every year and always about the time of Hanukkah. He had become a big stag with large antlers. Hershele grew, too, although not as fast. The third winter the deer brought a doe with him. It seemed that he had fought for his mate with another stag because a part of his antler was broken. Hanukkah and his mate were taken in. There was much discussion among the children what to name Hanukkah's wife. This time the teacher made a proposal. She was named Zot Hanukkah. This is how the section of the Bible that is read on the Sabbath of Hanukkah begins. The word 'zot,' which means 'this,' indicates the feminine gender. This name pleased everyone."

Reb Berish paused for a long while. The lights in the brass lamp were still burning. The children felt that the little flames were also listening to the story. Then a boy asked, "Did the old beggar ever come back?"

"No, I never heard that he did, but you can be sure that this man was not just an ordinary beggar."

"What was he?" another boy asked.

"The prophet Elijah," Reb Berish said. "It is known that Elijah is the angel of good tidings. He never comes in the image of an angel. People would go blind if they looked into the dazzling light of an angel. He always comes disguised as a poor man. Even the Messiah, according to the Talmud, will come in the disguise of a poor man, riding on a donkey."

Old Reb Berish closed his eyes and it was hard to know whether he was dozing or contemplating the coming of the Messiah. He opened them again and said, "Now you can go home and play dreidel."

"Will you tell us another story tomorrow?" another boy asked, and old Reb Berish replied, "With God's help. I have lived long and I have more stories to tell than you have hair in your sidelocks."

When Shlemiel Went
to Warsaw

Though Shlemiel was a lazybones and a sleepy-head and hated to move, he always daydreamed of taking a trip. He had heard many stories about faraway countries, huge deserts, deep oceans, and high mountains, and often discussed with Mrs. Shlemiel his great wish to go on a long journey. Mrs. Shlemiel would reply, "Long journeys are not for a Shlemiel. You better stay home and mind the children while I go to market to sell my vegetables." Yet Shlemiel could not bring himself to give up his dream of seeing the world and its wonders.

A recent visitor to Chelm had told Shlemiel marvelous things about the city of Warsaw. How beautiful the streets were, how high the buildings and luxurious the stores. Shlemiel decided once and for all that he must see this great city for himself. He knew that one had to prepare for a journey. But what was there for him to take? He had nothing but the old clothes he wore. One morning, after Mrs. Shlemiel left for the market, he told the older boys to stay home from cheder and mind the younger children. Then he took a few slices of bread, an onion, and a clove of garlic, put them in a kerchief, tied it into a bundle, and started for Warsaw on foot.

There was a street in Chelm called Warsaw Street and Shlemiel believed that it led directly to Warsaw. While still in the village, he was stopped by several neighbors who asked him where he was going. Shlemiel told them that he was on his way to Warsaw.

"What will you do in Warsaw?" they asked him.

Shlemiel replied, "What do I do in Chelm? Nothing."

He soon reached the outskirts of town. He walked slowly because the soles of his boots were worn through. Soon the houses and stores gave way to pastures and fields. He passed a peasant driving an ox-drawn plow. After several hours of walking, Shlemiel grew tired. He was so weary that he wasn't even hungry. He lay down on the grass near the roadside for a nap, but before he fell asleep he thought, When I wake up, I may not remember which is the way to Warsaw and which leads back to Chelm. After pondering a moment, he removed his boots and set them down beside him with the toes pointing toward Warsaw and the heels toward Chelm. He soon fell asleep and dreamed that he was a baker baking onion rolls with poppy seeds. Customers came to buy them and Shlemiel said, "These onion rolls are not for sale."

"Then why do you bake them?"

"They are for my wife, for my children, and for me."

Later he dreamed that he was the King of Chelm.

Once a year, instead of taxes, each citizen brought him a pot of strawberry jam. Shlemiel sat on a golden throne and nearby sat Mrs. Shlemiel, the queen, and his children, the princes and princesses. They were all eating onion rolls and spooning up big portions of strawberry jam. A carriage arrived and took the royal family to Warsaw, America, and to the river Sambation, which spurts out stones the week long and rests on the Sabbath.

Near the road, a short distance from where Shlemiel slept, was a smithy. The blacksmith happened to come out just in time to see Shlemiel carefully placing his boots at his side with the toes facing in the direction of Warsaw. The blacksmith was a prankster, and as soon as Shlemiel was sound asleep he tiptoed over and turned the boots around. When Shlemiel awoke, he felt rested but hungry. He got out a slice of bread, rubbed it with garlic, and took a bite of onion. Then he pulled his boots on and continued on his way.

He walked along and everything looked strangely familiar. He recognized houses that he had seen before. It seemed to him that he knew the people he met. Could it be that he had already reached another town, Shlemiel wondered. And why was it so similar to Chelm? He stopped a passerby and asked the name of the town. "Chelm," the man replied.

Shlemiel was astonished. How was this possible? He had walked away from Chelm. How could he have arrived back there? He began to rub his forehead and soon found the answer to the riddle. There were two Chelms and he had reached the second one.

Still, it seemed very odd that the streets, the houses,

the people were so similar to those in the Chelm he had left behind. Shlemiel puzzled over this fact until he suddenly remembered something he had learned in cheder: "The earth is the same everywhere." And so why shouldn't the second Chelm be exactly like the first one? This discovery gave Shlemiel great satisfaction. He wondered if there was a street here like his street and a house on it like the one he lived in. And indeed, he soon arrived at an identical street and house. Evening had fallen. He opened the door and to his amazement saw a second Mrs. Shlemiel with children just like his. Everything was exactly the same as in his own household. Even the cat seemed the same. Mrs. Shlemiel at once began to scold him.

"Shlemiel, where did you go? You left the house alone. And what have you there in that bundle?"

The children all ran to him and cried, "Papa, where have you been?"

Shlemiel paused a moment and then he said, "Mrs. Shlemiel, I'm not your husband. Children, I'm not your papa."

"Have you lost your mind?" Mrs. Shlemiel screamed.

"I am Shlemiel of Chelm One and this is Chelm Two."

Mrs. Shlemiel clapped her hands so hard that the chickens sleeping under the stove awoke in fright and flew out all over the room.

"Children, your father has gone crazy," she wailed. She immediately sent one of the boys for Gimpel the healer. All the neighbors came crowding in. Shlemiel stood in the middle of the room and proclaimed, "It's true, you all look like the people in my town, but you are not the same. I came from Chelm One and you live in Chelm Two."

"Shlemiel, what's the matter with you?" someone cried. "You're in your own house, with your own wife and children, your own neighbors and friends."

"No, you don't understand. I come from Chelm One. I was on my way to Warsaw, and between Chelm One and Warsaw there is a Chelm Two. And that is where I am."

"What are you talking about. We all know you and you know all of us. Don't you recognize your chickens?"

"No, I'm not in my town," Shlemiel insisted. "But," he continued, "Chelm Two does have the same people and the same houses as Chelm One, and that is why you are mistaken. Tomorrow I will continue on to Warsaw."

"In that case, where is my husband?" Mrs. Shlemiel inquired in a rage, and she proceeded to berate Shlemiel with all the curses she could think of.

"How should I know where your husband is?" Shlemiel replied.

Some of the neighbors could not help laughing; others pitied the family. Gimpel the healer announced that he knew of no remedy for such an illness. After some time, everybody went home.

Mrs. Shlemiel had cooked noodles and beans that evening, a dish that Shlemiel liked especially. She said to him, "You may be mad, but even a madman has to eat."

"Why should you feed a stranger?" Shlemiel asked.

"As a matter of fact, an ox like you should eat straw, not noodles and beans. Sit down and be quiet. Maybe some food and rest will bring you back to your senses."

"Mrs. Shlemiel, you're a good woman. My wife

wouldn't feed a stranger. It would seem that there is some small difference between the two Chelms."

The noodles and beans smelled so good that Shlemiel needed no further coaxing. He sat down, and as he ate he spoke to the children:

"My dear children, I live in a house that looks exactly like this one. I have a wife and she is as like your mother as two peas are like each other. My children resemble you as drops of water resemble one another."

The younger children laughed; the older ones began to cry. Mrs. Shlemiel said, "As if being a Shlemiel wasn't enough, he had to go crazy in addition. What am I going to do now? I won't be able to leave the children with him when I go to market. Who knows what a madman may do?" She clasped her head in her hands and cried out, "God in heaven, What have I done to deserve this?"

Nevertheless, she made up a fresh bed for Shlemiel; and even though he had napped during the day, near the smithy, the moment his head touched the pillow he fell fast asleep and was soon snoring loudly. He again dreamed that he was the King of Chelm and that his wife, the queen, had fried for him a huge panful of blintzes. Some were filled with cheese, others with blueberries or cherries, and all were sprinkled with sugar and cinnamon and were drowning in sour cream. Shlemiel ate twenty blintzes all at once and hid the remainder in his crown for later.

In the morning, when Shlemiel awoke, the house was filled with townspeople. Mrs. Shlemiel stood in their midst, her eyes red with weeping. Shlemiel was about to scold his wife for letting so many strangers into the house, but then he remembered that he himself was a stranger here. At home he would have gotten up, washed, and dressed. Now in front of all these people he was at a loss as to what to do. As always when he was embarrassed, he began to scratch his head and pull at his beard. Finally, overcoming his bashfulness, he decided to get up. He threw off the covers and put his bare feet on the floor. "Don't let him run away," Mrs. Shlemiel screamed. "He'll disappear and I'll be a deserted wife, without a Shlemiel."

At this point Baruch the baker interrupted. "Let's take him to the elders. They'll know what to do."

"That's right! Let's take him to the elders," everybody agreed.

Although Shlemiel insisted that since he lived in Chelm One, the local elders had no power over him, several of the strong young men helped him into his pants, his boots, his coat and cap and escorted him to the house of Gronam Ox. The elders, who had already heard of the matter, had gathered early in the morning to consider what was to be done.

As the crowd came in, one of the elders, Dopey Lekisch, was saying, "Maybe there really are two Chelms."

"If there are two, then why can't there be three, four, or even a hundred Chelms?" Sender Donkey interrupted.

"And even if there are a hundred Chelms, must there be a Shlemiel in each one of them?" argued Shmendrick Numskull.

Gronam Ox, the head elder, listened to all the arguments but was not yet prepared to express an opinion. However, his wrinkled, bulging forehead indicated that he was deep in thought. It was Gronam Ox who questioned Shlemiel. Shlemiel related everything that had happened to him, and when he finished, Gronam asked, "Do you recognize me?"

"Surely. You are wise Gronam Ox."

"And in your Chelm is there also a Gronam Ox?"

"Yes, there is a Gronam Ox and he looks exactly like you."

"Isn't it possible that you turned around and came back to Chelm?" Gronam inquired.

"Why should I turn around? I'm not a windmill," Shlemiel replied.

"In that case, you are not this Mrs. Shlemiel's husband."

"No, I'm not."

"Then Mrs. Shlemiel's husband, the real Shlemiel, must have left the day you came."

"It would seem so."

"Then he'll probably come back."

"Probably."

"In that case, you must wait until he returns. Then we'll know who is who."

"Dear elders, my Shlemiel has come back," screamed Mrs. Shlemiel. "I don't need two Shlemiels. One is more than enough."

"Whoever he is, he may not live in your house until everything is made clear," Gronam insisted.

"Where shall I live?" Shlemiel asked.

"In the poorhouse."

"What will I do in the poorhouse?"

"What do you do at home?"

"Good God, who will take care of my children when I go to market?" moaned Mrs. Shlemiel. "Besides, I want a husband. Even a Shlemiel is better than no husband at all."

"Are we to blame that your husband left you and went to Warsaw?" Gronam asked. "Wait until he comes home."

Mrs. Shlemiel wept bitterly and the children cried, too. Shlemiel said, "How strange. My own wife always scolded me. My children talked back to me. And here a strange woman and strange children want me to live with them. It looks to me as if Chelm Two is actually better than Chelm One."

"Just a moment. I think I have an idea," interrupted Gronam.

"What is your idea?" Zeinvel Ninny inquired.

"Since we decided to send Shlemiel to the poorhouse, the town will have to hire someone to take care of Mrs. Shlemiel's children so she can go to market. Why not hire Shlemiel for that? It's true, he is not Mrs. Shlemiel's husband or the children's father. But he is so much like the real Shlemiel that the children will feel at home with him."

"What a wonderful idea!" cried Feivel Thickwit.

"Only King Solomon could have thought of such a wise solution," agreed Treitel Fool.

"Such a clever way out of this dilemma could only have been thought of in our Chelm," chimed in Shmendrick Numskull.

"How much do you want to be paid to take care of Mrs. Shlemiel's children?" asked Gronam.

For a moment Shlemiel stood there completely bewildered. Then he said, "Three groschen a day."

"Idiot, moron, ass?" screamed Mrs. Shlemiel. "What are three groschen nowadays? You shouldn't do it for less than six a day." She ran over to Shlemiel and pinched him on the arm. Shlemiel winced and cried out, "She pinches just like my wife."

The elders held a consultation among themselves. The town budget was very limited. Finally Gronam announced: "Three groschen may be too little, but six groschen a day is definitely too much, especially for a stranger. We will compromise and pay you five groschen a day. Shlemiel, do you accept?"

"Yes, but how long am I to keep this job?"

"Until the real Shlemiel comes home."

Gronam's decision was soon known throughout Chelm, and the town admired his great wisdom and that of all the elders of Chelm.

At first, Shlemiel tried to keep the five groschen that the town paid him for himself. "If I'm not your husband, I don't have to support you," he told Mrs. Shlemiel.

"In that case, since I'm not your wife, I don't have to cook for you, darn your socks, or patch your clothes."

And so, of course, Shlemiel turned over his pay to her. It was the first time that Mrs. Shlemiel had ever gotten any money for the household from Shlemiel. Now when she was in a good mood, she would say to him, "What a pity you didn't decide to go to Warsaw ten years ago."

"Don't you ever miss your husband?" Shlemiel would ask.

"And what about you? Don't you miss your wife?" Mrs. Shlemiel would ask.

And both would admit that they were quite happy with matters as they stood.

Years passed and no Shlemiel returned to Chelm. The elders had many explanations for this. Zeinvel Ninny believed that Shlemiel had crossed the black mountains and had been eaten alive by the cannibals who live there. Dopey Lekisch thought that Shlemiel most probably had come to the Castle of Asmodeus, where he had been forced to marry a demon princess. Shmendrick Numskull came to the conclusion that Shlemiel had reached the edge of the world and had fallen off. There were many other theories; for example, that the real Shlemiel had lost his memory and had simply forgotten that he was Shlemiel. Such things do happen.

Gronam did not like to impose his theories on other people; however, he was convinced that Shlemiel had gone to the other Chelm, where he had had exactly the same experience as the Shlemiel in this Chelm. He had been hired by the local community and was taking care of the other Mrs. Shlemiel's children for a wage of five groschen a day.

As for Shlemiel himself, he no longer knew what to think. The children were growing up and soon would be able to take care of themselves. Sometimes Shlemiel would sit and ponder: Where is the other Shlemiel? When will he come home? What is my real wife doing? Is she waiting for me, or has she got herself another

Shlemiel? These were questions that he could not answer.

Every now and then Shlemiel would still get the desire to go traveling, but he could not bring himself to start out. What was the point of going on a trip if it led no-where? Often, as he sat alone puzzling over the strange ways of the world, he would become more and more confused and begin humming to himself:

> *Those who leave Chelm*
> *end up in Chelm.*
> *Those who remain in Chelm*
> *are certainly in Chelm.*
> *All roads lead to Chelm.*
> *All the world is one big Chelm.*

Translated by the author and Elizabeth Shub

Elijah the Slave

In ancient times, in a distant land, there was a large city where many rich men lived. It had magnificent palaces, broad avenues, parks, and gardens.

In their midst was a tiny street of broken-down houses. They had narrow windows and doorways, and their roofs leaked. In the humblest of these, there lived a holy man. Tobias was his name, and his wife was called Peninah. They had five children, three sons and two daughters.

Tobias was a scribe who copied the sacred scrolls. In this way he was able to earn a meager living.

But suddenly he was taken ill and lost the use of his right hand. Soon there was no bread in the house. The larder was so empty that even the mice ran away. There was nothing for the cat to catch. The boys could not go to school because they had no shoes. Tobias's clothes were in rags and tatters.

When the neighbors saw the family's need, they tried

to help. But Tobias refused their offers, saying, "There is a God and He will help us."

One day Tobias's wife said to him, "If God intends to help us, it better be soon. But whatever He might do, for you to just sit at home doesn't improve matters. You must go out into the city. Even while waiting for a miracle, it's good to do something. Man must begin and God will help him."

"How can I show my face among people when I have no clothes to wear?"

"Wait, my husband, and I will take care of that."

Peninah went to a neighbor and borrowed a coat, a hat, and shoes. She helped Tobias dress, and truly he looked like a new man. "Now, go," Peninah said, "and luck be with you." When he left, she told the children to pray that their father would not come home with empty hands.

As Tobias approached the center of the city, a stranger stopped him. He was tall and had a white beard. He wore a long coat and carried a staff. "Peace be with you, Tobias," he said, and held out his hand. Tobias, forgetting he could not move his right hand, clasped the stranger's with it. He was baffled by this miraculous recovery.

"Who do I have the honor of greeting?" Tobias asked.

"My name is Elijah and I am your slave."

"My slave?" Tobias said in astonishment.

"Yes, your slave, sent from heaven. Take me to the marketplace and sell me to the highest bidder."

"If you come from heaven, I am *your* slave," Tobias answered. "How can a slave sell his master?"

"Do as I say," Elijah replied.

Since Elijah was a messenger from God, Tobias had no choice but to obey.

In the marketplace, many rich merchants gathered around Tobias and Elijah. Never before had a slave who looked so noble and wise been offered for sale.

The richest and most forward of the merchants addressed him. "What can you do, slave?"

"Anything you wish," Elijah said.

"Can you build a palace?"

"The most magnificent you have ever seen."

"Even more splendid than the king's?"

"More splendid—and bigger."

"Why should we believe you?" asked one of the merchants.

Elijah took a sack of wooden blocks from his pocket and with them built a miniature palace. He did it with such speed and the palace's beauty was so unusual that the merchants were dazzled.

"Can you build a real palace like this one?" the richest merchant asked.

"A better one," said Elijah.

The merchants, sensing that this slave had supernatural powers, began the bidding at once. "Ten thousand gulden," one shouted.

"Fifty thousand," called another.

"One hundred thousand," offered a third.

The highest price—800,000 gulden—was finally offered by the richest merchant, and he paid the money to Tobias.

Turning to Elijah, the merchant said, "If the real palace

is as beautiful as you promise, I will make you a free man."

"Very well," Elijah replied. And to Tobias he said, "Go home and rejoice with your wife and children. Your days of poverty are over."

After giving praise to God and thanking Elijah for his goodness, Tobias returned home.

The joy of his wife and children was great.

As always, Tobias gave a tenth part of his money to the poor; and even though he was now a rich man, he decided to go back to his beloved work as a scribe.

Night came and Elijah spoke to God: "I sold myself as a slave to save your servant Tobias. I pray you now to help me build the palace."

Immediately a band of angels descended from heaven. They worked all night long. When the sun rose, the palace was finished.

The rich merchant came and gazed in awe. Never had an edifice of such splendor been seen by human eyes.

"Here is your palace," Elijah said. "Keep your word and give me my freedom."

"You are free, my lord," replied the merchant, and he bowed low before God's messenger.

The angels laughed.

God looked down from his seventh heaven and smiled.

The angels spread their wings and, together with Elijah, flew upward into the sky.

Translated by the author and Elizabeth Shub

The Power of Light

During World War II, after the Nazis had bombed and bombed the Warsaw ghetto, a boy and a girl were hiding in one of the ruins—David, fourteen years old, and Rebecca, thirteen.

It was winter and bitter cold outside. For weeks Rebecca had not left the dark, partially collapsed cellar that was their hiding place, but every few days David would go out to search for food. All the stores had been destroyed in the bombing, and David sometimes found stale bread, cans of food, or whatever else had been buried. Making his way through the ruins was dangerous. Sometimes bricks and mortar would fall down, and he could easily lose his way. But if he and Rebecca did not want to die from hunger, he had to take the risk.

That day was one of the coldest. Rebecca sat on the ground wrapped in all the garments she possessed; still, she could not get warm. David had left many hours before, and Rebecca listened in the darkness for the sound of his return, knowing that if he did not come back nothing remained to her but death.

Suddenly she heard heavy breathing and the sound of a bundle being dropped. David had made his way home. Rebecca could not help but cry "David!"

"Rebecca!"

In the darkness they embraced and kissed. Then David said, "Rebecca, I found a treasure."

"What kind of treasure?"

"Cheese, potatoes, dried mushrooms, and a package of candy—and I have another surprise for you."

"What surprise?"

"Later."

Both were too hungry for a long talk. Ravenously they ate the frozen potatoes, the mushrooms, and part of the cheese. They each had one piece of candy. Then Rebecca asked, "What is it now, day or night?"

"I think night has fallen," David replied. He had a wristwatch and kept track of day and night and also of the days of the week and the month. After a while Rebecca asked again, "What is the surprise?"

"Rebecca, today is the first day of Hanukkah, and I found a candle and some matches."

"Hanukkah tonight?"

"Yes."

"Oh, my God!"

"I am going to bless the Hanukkah candle," David said.

He lit a match and there was light. Rebecca and David stared at their hiding place—bricks, pipes, and the uneven ground. He lighted the candle. Rebecca blinked her eyes. For the first time in weeks she really saw David. His hair was matted and his face streaked with dirt, but his eyes shone with joy. In spite of the starvation and persecution David had grown taller, and he seemed older than his age and manly. Young as they both were, they had decided to marry if they could manage to escape from war-ridden Warsaw. As a token of their engagement, David had given Rebecca a shiny groschen he found in his pocket on the day when the building where both of them lived was bombed.

Now David pronounced the benediction over the Hanukkah candle, and Rebecca said, "Amen." They had both lost their families, and they had good reason to be angry with God for sending them so many afflictions, but the light of the candle brought peace into their souls. That glimmer of light, surrounded by so many shadows, seemed to say without words: Evil has not yet taken complete dominion. A spark of hope is still left.

For some time David and Rebecca had thought about escaping from Warsaw. But how? The ghetto was watched by the Nazis day and night. Each step was dangerous. Rebecca kept delaying their departure. It would be easier in the summer, she often said, but David knew that in their predicament they had little chance of lasting until then. Somewhere in the forest there were young men and women called partisans who fought the Nazi invaders. David wanted to reach them. Now, by the light of the Hanukkah candle, Rebecca suddenly felt renewed courage. She said, "David, let's leave."

"When?"

"When you think it's the right time," she answered.

"The right time is now," David said. "I have a plan."

For a long time David explained the details of his plan to Rebecca. It was more than risky. The Nazis had enclosed the ghetto with barbed wire and posted guards armed with machine guns on the surrounding roofs. At night searchlights lit up all possible exits from the destroyed ghetto. But in his wanderings through the ruins, David had found an opening to a sewer which he thought might lead to the other side. David told Rebecca that their chances of remaining alive were slim. They could drown in the dirty water or freeze to death. Also, the sewers were full of hungry rats. But Rebecca agreed to take the risk; to remain in the cellar for the winter would mean certain death.

When the Hanukkah light began to sputter and flicker before going out, David and Rebecca gathered their few belongings. She packed the remaining food in a kerchief, and David took his matches and a piece of lead pipe for a weapon.

In moments of great danger people become unusually courageous. David and Rebecca were soon on their way through the ruins. They came to passages so narrow they had to crawl on hands and knees. But the food they had eaten, and the joy the Hanukkah candle had awakened in them, gave them the courage to continue. After some time David found the entrance to the sewer. Luckily the sewage had frozen, and it seemed that the rats had left because of the extreme cold. From time to time David and Rebecca stopped to rest and to listen. After a while they crawled on, slowly and carefully. Suddenly they stopped in their tracks. From above they could hear the clanging of a trolley car. They had reached the other side of the ghetto. All they needed now was to find a way to get out of the sewer and to leave the city as quickly as possible.

Many miracles seemed to happen that Hanukkah night. Because the Nazis were afraid of enemy planes, they had ordered a complete blackout. Because of the bitter cold, there were fewer Gestapo guards. David and Rebecca managed to leave the sewer and steal out of the city without being caught. At dawn they reached a forest where they were able to rest and have a bite to eat.

Even though the partisans were not very far from Warsaw, it took David and Rebecca a week to reach them. They walked at night and hid during the days—sometimes in granaries and sometimes in barns. Some peasants stealthily helped the partisans and those who were running away from the Nazis. From time to time David and Rebecca got a piece of bread, a few potatoes, a radish, or whatever the peasants could spare. In one village they encountered a Jewish partisan who had come to get food for his group. He belonged to the Haganah, an organization that sent men from Israel to rescue Jewish refugees from the Nazis in occupied Poland. This young man brought David and Rebecca to the other partisans who roamed the forest. It was the last day of Hanukkah, and that evening the partisans lit eight candles. Some of them played dreidel on the stump of an oak tree while others kept watch.

From the day David and Rebecca met the partisans, their life became like a tale in a storybook. They joined more and more refugees who all had but one desire—to settle in the Land of Israel. They did not always travel by train or bus. They walked. They slept in stables, in burned-out houses, and wherever they could hide from the enemy. To reach their destination, they had to cross Czechoslovakia, Hungary, and Yugoslavia. Somewhere at the seashore in Yugoslavia, in the middle of the night, a small boat manned by a Haganah crew waited for them, and all the refugees with their meager belongings were packed into it. This all happened silently and in great secrecy, because the Nazis occupied Yugoslavia.

But their dangers were far from over. Even though it was spring, the sea was stormy and the boat was too small for such a long trip. Nazi planes spied the boat and tried without success to sink it with bombs. They also feared the Nazi submarines which were lurking in the depths. There was nothing the refugees could do besides pray to God, and this time God seemed to hear their prayers, because they managed to land safely.

The Jews of Israel greeted them with a love that made them forget their suffering. They were the first refugees who had reached the Holy Land, and they were offered all the help and comfort that could be given. Rebecca and David found relatives in Israel who accepted them with open arms, and although they had become quite emaciated, they were basically healthy and recovered quickly. After some rest they were sent to a special school where foreigners were taught modern Hebrew. Both David and Rebecca were diligent students. After finishing high school, David was able to enter the academy of engineering in Haifa, and Rebecca, who excelled in languages and literature, studied in Tel

Aviv—but they always met on weekends. When Rebecca was eighteen, she and David were married. They found a small house with a garden in Ramat Gan, a suburb of Tel Aviv.

I know all this because David and Rebecca told me their story on a Hanukkah evening in their house in Ramat Gan about eight years later. The Hanukkah candles were burning, and Rebecca was frying potato pancakes served with applesauce for all of us. David and I were playing dreidel with their little son, Menahem Eliezer, named after both of his grandfathers. David told me that this large wooden dreidel was the same one the partisans had played with on that Hanukkah evening in the forest in Poland. Rebecca said to me, "If it had not been for that little candle David brought to our hiding place, we wouldn't be sitting here today. That glimmer of light awakened in us a hope and strength we didn't know we possessed. We'll give the dreidel to Menahem Eliezer when he is old enough to understand what we went through and how miraculously we were saved."

Growing Up

I

The whole night I kept dreaming. What I dreamed, I couldn't recall later, but they must have been fantastic dreams full of youthful valor, for I awoke feeling strong and cheerful. Everything was pleasurable—washing with the cold water at the sink, putting on the gabardine and fringed garment, even praying from the new prayer book with the large type. At the age of eleven I already understood the meaning of the Hebrew words—"How goodly are thy tents, Jacob, thy tabernacles, O Israel. As for me, in the abundance of thy loving kindness will I come into thy house."

In my fantasy I envisioned the city of Jerusalem and the Holy Temple. The Messiah had come and the Resurrection had taken place. I donned the robes of a priest about to offer a sacrifice. I saw the altar, the table with the shewbread, the ark, the cherubim—all in gold. And beyond stretched Mt. Zion and the mighty city of Jerusalem, with its walls, gates, and flat-roofed houses. King David again occupied his royal throne, and his son Solomon learned the language of lions, tigers, eagles, and the woodcock. The light of the sun was seven times brighter than ever. A day was as long as a year. Everything that had ever been existed once again. All my ancestors, going back to Adam and Eve, had risen from their graves. There was no more death or injustice, only happiness and divine revelation.

At the same time I knew full well that all this was just in my head. Actually, I was in Warsaw, my father was a poor neighborhood rabbi, the Land of Israel belonged to the Turks, the Temple lay in ruins. David, Solomon, Bathsheba, and the Queen of Sheba were all dead. My friend was not a prince of the Kingdom of Israel but Black Feivel, whose father was a porter in Janash's bazaar and whose mother sold crockery in the marketplace. Until just a few weeks ago I had attended cheder on Twarda Street, but I had stopped going because my father couldn't afford the two rubles a month tuition.

I rushed through my prayers and breakfast. For weeks Feivel and I had been formulating a secret, outlandish plan. This was the day I was to become a writer and Feivel a printer. I would soon publish my first book—all of sixteen pages long. Its price would be two kopeks. Feivel and I had figured it all out with precision. There were at least fifty thousand boys and girls in Warsaw who liked to read storybooks. If every boy and girl bought my book, we would take in a hundred thousand kopeks, or a thousand rubles. With this sum we could buy our own printing shop and publish additional books.

We would accumulate so much money that we would be able to take a ship to the Land of Israel.

This trip was vital not only for us but for all the Jews in the world. Someone had told me that in Jerusalem there was a cave where cabalists sat seeking a hidden name of God that would bring the Messiah. This name had come in a dream to me, Isaac, son of Pinhos Menahem. An angel with six wings had shown himself to me and uttered the name, which consisted of twenty-four letters. The angel had warned me not to utter this name in any other city except Jerusalem. If my lips let it slip in Warsaw, the sky would turn red and the whole world would be consumed by fire.

For a while I had kept this secret to myself, but one day I blurted it out to Feivel. It happened while we were walking on Senators Street to see the courtyard of the Warsaw firemen, its huge fire bell and the tower with the circular balcony where a fireman walked round and round on the lookout for fires. This tower was so tall that the fireman, a fully grown man, looked like a toy from below. When the sunlight struck his brass helmet, it glowed as if it were on fire.

The situation was this—sometime before, Black Feivel had found a silver forty-kopek piece and had confided to me his delight over this windfall. Feivel was a year older than I, but he listened to me as if I were his senior. He loved to hear my stories. Not a day went by that I didn't make up some tale about kings, demons, savages, giants, dwarfs, treasures, villains. I had boasted to him that I was versed in the cabala. Feivel's faith in me was like that of a Hasid in his rabbi. I had told him that I was possessed by the spirit of Joseph della Reina, a saint who centuries before had captured Satan and put him in chains. Had Satan remained so confined, Rabbi Joseph could have brought the Messiah at that time, but he had taken pity on Satan, who had cried and bemoaned his fate and pleaded with Rabbi Joseph for something to eat or drink, or at least for a pinch of snuff. When Rabbi Joseph gave him the snuff, Satan broke into hellish laughter and two sparks shot from his nostrils. Right after that, the chains crumpled from his body and he flew away along with ten thousand demons to Mt. Sair near Sodom, where the dark powers hold sway.

I told Feivel that Rabbi Joseph's soul had entered my body and that I was destined to carry out what he had commenced.

2

The practical plan was this: Black Feivel had found an incredible bargain for a gulden—a case of rubber type, a pad for ink, and a kind of composing stick into which to set the rubber type to form words. There was even a brush with which to pull proofs. Feivel would serve as the typesetter and printer, and I would be the author. Until we launched ourselves on a grander scale, I would get the paper from Father's notebooks, into which he wrote his interpretations of the Talmud. All we lacked was a place to do our work. But after an intense search, Feivel found what he was after—a Hasidic studyhouse that stood empty all day. It was used only in the mornings and evenings for services. I knew full well that what we were doing was fraught with danger. The beadle or someone else was liable to drop in and catch us at it. Nor would it be easy to go around selling these books, but Feivel and I had grown so enthused about the writing, the publishing, and the big profits that we had become bedazzled by it all. Feivel had already set my name as well as the title page of my first book, *Into the Wild Forest*.

This was to be the story of a boy, Haiml, whose mother had died and whose father had been remarried to a wicked woman. The stepmother caused the boy so much grief that he ran away from home and went to live in the woods. He found a hollow in a big tree, a thousand-year-old oak, and he settled there. He lived on berries, mushrooms, and the other foodstuffs found in a forest. Everything would have been fine, but one night Haiml heard the soft moaning of a girl. It soon turned out that this hollow was the entrance to an underground cave where a monster by the name of Mordush lived. This monster had kidnapped a girl, Rebecca, the daughter of a wealthy man, and was trying to force her to become his wife. But Rebecca was engaged already to a young man named Ben Zion, a rabbi's son, and she didn't want to trade him for an old villain who had only one eye in the middle of his forehead and who ate human flesh. Mordush even tried to make a cannibal out of her, but Rebecca swore that she would sooner starve to death than eat the flesh of a human being who had just recently lived, hoped, and loved . . .

I was supposed to plan out this story to its end this very night. Ben Zion had to rescue Rebecca and take revenge upon Mordush, and Haiml also had to receive some sort of reward for uncovering the crime. But somehow my creative juices dried up at this point and I couldn't continue the thread of the story. In the process of writing I had grown so attached to Rebecca that I desired her for myself. Actually, in this story, Haiml (who was really myself) was only eleven years old and Rebecca was sixteen, and this would hardly have been a suitable match, but what prevented me from adding a few years to Haiml? I had to find some way to dispose of Ben Zion. Should he die of longing? Should he become a hermit? Should he forget Rebecca and marry the daughter of some magnate? I had just launched my writing career and already I had fallen into a literary dilemma.

When I went down later to meet Feivel, I envied the boys playing tag, hide-and-seek, cops-and-robbers, and nuts, who didn't have to worry about plots and stories. I had prematurely assumed the duties of a writer and publisher, a printer already awaited my efforts, and I knew somehow that I would bear this burden as long as I lived . . .

3

The plan to publish a book had fallen through. First of all, Feivel had lost several of the rubber characters. Second, I couldn't find the right paper in my father's desk drawer. Third, each time we went to the studyhouse we encountered several youths swaying over open volumes. Fourth, I hadn't found a way of getting rid of Ben Zion and the whole story would have to be rewritten. Feivel said it couldn't be otherwise but that Satan had gotten wind of our plan and had arranged it that I couldn't go to Jerusalem and bring the Messiah.

We roved the streets of Warsaw with the impetus of those against whom all the evils have combined to conspire. My velvet cap was pushed back onto my nape, my red earlocks were drenched with sweat, the wide fringed garment peeped out from my unbuttoned gabardine. Despite my youth, my parents dressed me in rabbinical fashion. They wanted me to become a rabbi. Each time I passed a mirror I grew frightened at my own appearance. My hair was as red as fire, my face and neck an unusual white. A frenzied eagerness shone from my blue eyes. I was fully aware that I was too young to probe into the cabala. I had often heard my father say that those who tried to study the cabala before thirty went crazy or slid into heresy. At times it seemed to me that I *was* actually crazy. Wild notions flashed through my brain, fantasies that I could not bridle. Now I was an emperor and now a sorcerer; now I donned a cap that rendered me invisible, and now I flew to the moon and brought back treasures of gold and diamonds and a potion that rendered me wiser than King Solomon and stronger than Samson. Instead of bringing the Messiah, in my imagination I became the Messiah himself. I blew the ram's horn so that its blast resounded around the world. I mounted a cloud and flew to Jerusalem, followed by hordes of angels ready to do my bidding.

Feivel was taller than I. His earlocks were so black they appeared blue. His eyes were just as black and his skin as swarthy as a gypsy's. Feivel's gabardine had perhaps a hundred rents in it revealing the lining beneath.

His toes stuck out of his boots. Feivel was not only taller but much stronger than I. He always carried a heavy stick torn from a bush, ready to protect me. If some boy called me names, like shlemiel, shmagega, and the like, Feivel would chase after him and beat him. Feivel was both my disciple and my bodyguard. He never grew tired of hearing my outlandish words and weird stories. At times, when I flew into a temper, I abused him and I even gave him a shove or a slap, but he never struck back. At the same time he waged a silent war with me—the rebelliousness of a slave against his master seethed within him . . .

I could talk while we walked, but when Feivel wanted to say something he had to stop. Before he could get anything out he first blinked his eyes a few times. Even as he praised me, he implied that I fabricated things that made no sense whatsoever. He would say, "Since you say it, it's probably so . . ." And his gypsy-like eyes flashed with mockery.

Our plan to publish a book had gone awry, but I had a dozen other plans that day: we would establish a yeshiva for the secret study of the cabala. I would be the rabbi and he, Feivel, would be my beadle. I would become a heretic, and while I rode horseback on the Sabbath he, Feivel, would follow behind and listen to my wisdom. I would seal a covenant with Satan while he would bring the daughter of the Grand Vizier to me in my palace.

"What would you do with her?" Feivel asked me.

"Fly with her to the Mountains of Darkness."

"Oh, the things you say!"

"I fear no one . . ."

We crossed the Praga Bridge and our feet brought us of their own volition to the Terespol railroad station. I was drawn to trains. We went out on the platform. A train was about to depart for somewhere deep in Russia. The black locomotive belched smoke, hissed steam, and gushed hot water like some other-world beast. Its mighty driving wheel dripped oil. A hugh gendarme—tall and broad, his face red and pockmarked, his deep chest hung with medals—paced to and fro issuing orders in Russian.

I said, "This train is going to Siberia."

"Where is Siberia?" Feivel asked.

"In the cold regions. The people there eat bear meat. For six months—the whole winter—it's night."

"When is it the Sabbath?" Feivel asked.

"There are no Jews there. It's never the Sabbath . . ."

"What's beyond Siberia?" Feivel asked.

"That's the end of the world. Giants live there who have three eyes in the center of their bellies."

"What do they eat?"

"Each other . . ."

4

In the evening I came home tired and sweaty. I hadn't eaten any lunch. My boots were dusty. My mother angrily brought me a mirror to show me how grimy my face was. She asked me again and again where I had been all day, but I couldn't tell her. In the living room, the ceiling lamp was lit. We had a guest from Bilgoray, a man who traveled around collecting subscriptions for the author of a holy book. His name was Wolf Bear, but he looked like a goat with his narrow white beard and red-rimmed eyes. When he spoke, he moved his gums like a goat chewing its cud. He wore a patched gabardine and a soiled shirt with a wrinkled collar. He had eaten supper at our house and he conversed in a bleating voice. My older brother, Joshua, also sat at the table, as did my sister, Hindele. Mother gave me what was left over from both the meals I had missed—potatoes with rice, dumplings with soup, a roast chicken liver, and a slice of bread.

I was so hungry that I bolted down whole mouthfuls of food, while at the same time I pricked up my ears to hear Wolf Bear's words. I heard him say, "You become depressed when you travel around, but you get to see the world. Every town presents a different face. The people of Zelechow are just as vicious as in the days when they drove out Rabbi Levi Yitzchok in an ox wagon. In other places they gave me the few gulden without any questions, but in Zelechow they wanted to know who the author was and demanded to see the manuscript. They sat me down and began to argue with me just as if I were the author. They also found errors in the text. The women there all use too much salt and pepper. They serve you a tiny morsel of meat and a lot of mustard. They eat rice pudding with horseradish. Everything there is done with sharpness. I go to a cobbler and ask if he can put half-soles on my boots, so what does he say? 'Why half-soles? Why not full soles? And why do you have to mention your boots? Where else would I put the soles, on your skullcap?' His eyes were as piercing as a hedgehog's. They're all like that there, even the rabbi. You'll laugh, but in no other town do so many thorns grow as in Zelechow.

"How far is Zichlin from Zelechow? Not far. But the people there are as soft as silk. I come to the rabbi and show him the manuscript and he says, 'Thank God, holy books are still being written in this world. Jews don't forget the Torah.' In Zichlin the rabbi's wife herself made up a bed for me. They put honey on the table every day of the week. In Zelechow it's hard to arrange a match. All the girls become old maids. The young men go off to America and are never heard from again. I spent eight days in Zichlin and there was a wedding held each day. What's the sense behind this, eh? On the other hand, why did Sodom become Sodom? One leprous sheep infects the whole flock. It starts with one vicious person and it spreads to all. How did Warsaw become Warsaw? First they built one house, then another, and gradually a city emerged. Everything grows. Even stones grow."

"Stones don't grow, Reb Wolf Bear," my brother, Joshua, interjected.

"No? Well, so be it. There is a town in Volhynia called Maciejow where the sand is so deep that, when you fall into it, you can't get out. You sink down slowly. They say that if you put your ear to the sand, you can hear the cries of those trapped below. How can this be? How long can a person live underground, unless it's a doorway to Gehenna? On the road, I met a man from the Land of Israel. He spoke Hebrew. Aramaic, too. He has seen the whole world. At first he said that he didn't know any Yiddish, but as we got to talking I saw that he did know it. He had visited Shushan, the old capital of Persia. He had been to Mt. Ararat and seen Noah's ark. It rests on the tip of the mountain and eagles soar above it. You try to reach it because it seems so close, but when you get to the top, there is no ark. And that's how it is with all things. Illusion or who knows what. In what connection do I say this, eh? Yes, now I remember. The man was riding in the desert and he came to a place that was the gateway to Gehenna. You could hear the cries of the sinners. The earth is hollow there. There are caves underneath and cities and who knows what else."

"The earth isn't hollow," my brother, Joshua, said.

"Why not? Everything is possible. If you sit in one spot you think it's the same all over, but when you travel, you get to see all kinds of wonders. I've been to Wieliczka. They dig for salt there. There is enough salt for the whole world. They made houses out of salt, beds, even a wardrobe. In Czestochowa again, a statue of the Virgin Mary stands on a mountain. She is completely of gold and her eyes are diamonds. One time a man stole one of the eyes and replaced it with a glass one. He was caught in the act and sentenced to hard labor."

"Yes, I know, Macuch," I piped up.

"Eh? How do you know?" Reb Wolf Bear asked me.

"It was in the paper," I replied.

"Oh so? In olden times children knew nothing. Today they know everything. In Lublin there was a wonder child, a Yenuka, and at the age of three he sprouted a beard. At five he gave a sermon in the synagogue and scholars came to debate with him. He was married at seven. When he reached nine, his beard turned as white as snow. He died at ten, an old man."

"Did you see this Yenuka with your own eyes?" Joshua asked.

"See him? No. But the whole world knows about it."

My father arched the brows over his blue eyes and his red beard glowed like gold. "Joshua, don't contradict!"

"It isn't true," Joshua said. He turned pale and his blue eyes reflected scorn.

"Have you been everywhere and do you know the truth?" Father asked. "The world is full of wonders. We only know what goes on down here. Only God the Almighty knows what happens in the other spheres."

I didn't know the reason myself, but an urge to cry came over me. I barely contained my tears. I went to my parents' bedroom and lay down on the bed in the dark. I suddenly realized—without knowing how myself—that I was too young to write a book. My brother, Joshua, often mentioned the word "literature." He told Mother that each nation creates its own literature. That which Reb Wolf Bear now related at the table has to be literature, I thought. But how can a beggar from a small village create literature?

It was all one great mystery. I wasn't asleep yet, but my brain had already begun to weave a dream. Each time I tried to grasp it, its threads dissolved. I lay in bed, and at the same time I rode that train to Siberia. I heard the clacking of the wheels, the whistle of the locomotive. I heard my mother open the door and mumble, "Dozed off, the poor boy."

A few minutes later, I really fell asleep. The fantastic dreams started, the wild adventures. All the fantasies of the day turned into nocturnal visions. That night I dreamed that I was Rabbi Joseph della Reina. I uttered God's name and the daughter of the Grand Vizier came flying to me. She looked like a neighbor's daughter,

Estherel, who lived in our house on the third floor. In the dream, I asked Estherel, "What shall we do?"

And she replied, "I'll become your bride."

I awoke frightened, drenched in sweat. I had often heard my brother and my sister talk of love. Suddenly it became clear to me that I loved Estherel. I had heard that novels were written about love and it occurred to me to name the girl in my book Estherel and that I could become Ben Zion, who saved her from the cannibal and married her. I decided that when I grew up I would write not just a storybook but a whole novel about Estherel and myself.

Translated by Joseph Singer

The Lantuch

In the summers, my Aunt Yentl liked to tell stories on the Sabbath after the main meal, when my Uncle Joseph lay down for a nap. My aunt would take a seat on the bench in front of the house, and the cat, Dvosha, would join her. On the Sabbaths the cat would be given the remnants of the Sabbath meal—scraps of meat and fish. Dvosha would plant herself at my aunt's feet; she liked to hear my aunt tell stories. From the way she cocked her ears and narrowed her eyes, green as gooseberries, it was apparent she understood what my aunt was saying.

For the Sabbath, my aunt wore a dress sewn with arabesques and a bonnet with glass beads, festooned with green, red, and blue ribbons. Presently, my mother came out, and two of our female neighbors, Riva and Sheindel. I was the last to emerge and I took a seat on a footstool. Besides the fact that I liked to listen to my Aunt Yentl's stories, sooner or later I would get from her the Sabbath fruit—an apple, a pear, plums. Sometimes she would give me a Sabbath cookie baked with cinnamon and raisins. She always said the same thing when she gave it to me, "It'll give you the strength to study."

This time the conversation centered on a house demon or a sprite called a lantuch. Aunt Yentl liked to talk about spirits, demons, and hobgoblins, and I heard her say, "A lantuch? Yes, there is such a spirit as a lantuch. These days people don't believe in such things, but in my time they knew that everything can't be explained away with reason. The world is full of secrets. A lantuch is an imp, but he's not malicious. He causes no harm. On the contrary, he tries to help the members of the household all he can. He is like a part of the family. Usually he is invisible, but it sometimes happens that you can see him. Where do they live? Sometimes in a cellar, sometimes in a woodshed, sometimes behind the stove along with the cricket. Lantuchs love crickets. They bring them food and they understand their language."

"Aunt Yentl, when I grow up I'll learn the language of crickets," I piped up.

Aunt Yentl smiled with every wrinkle in her face. "My child, this isn't a language that can be learned. Only King Solomon knew the language of beasts. He could talk with the lions, the bears, the wolves, and with all the birds, too. But let's get back to the lantuch. There was a lantuch at my parents' house. In the summers he lived in the woodshed, and in the winters behind the stove. We didn't see him, but sometimes we heard him. One time when my sister Keila sneezed, he said, 'God bless you!' We all heard it. The lantuch loved us all, but he loved my sister Keila most of all. When Keila married and went to live in Lublin with her in-laws—I was only a girl of eight then —the lantuch came to her on her last night home to say goodbye. In the middle of the night Keila heard a rustle and the door opened by itself.

"The lantuch came up to Keila's bed and said in rhyme:

> *Wash basin,*
> *soak basin,*
> *meat cleaver,*
> *kugel-eater,*
> *I'll fret*
> *And you won't forget.*

"Keila became so frightened that she lost her tongue. He kissed her forehead, and soon after he left. For a long time Keila lay there in a daze, then she lit a candle. Keila was very fond of almond cake. When my mother, may she rest in peace, baked almond cake for Simchas Torah or Purim, Keila would nibble half of it. Anyway, she lit the candle and on her blanket lay an almond cake still warm from the oven. She started to cry and we all came running in to her. I saw the almond cake with my own eyes. Where the lantuch got it from, I haven't the slightest idea. Maybe some housewife happened to bake almond cakes and he pinched one, or maybe they know how to bake them themselves. Keila didn't eat the cake, but she put it away some place, and it grew hard as a stone.

"In our town of Janów there was a teacher who had a sick wife and an only daughter who had been blind from birth. All of a sudden the teacher died and the two women were left all alone and helpless. There was talk in town of putting the two women in the poorhouse, but who wants to go to a poorhouse? The paupers there lay on straw pallets right on the bare floor and the food wasn't good either. When the attendant came to take the mother and daughter to the poorhouse, they both began to lament: 'Rather than rot away in the poorhouse we'd sooner die!'

"You can't force anyone to go to the poorhouse. The attendant thought, The husband probably left them a few gulden, and so long as they still have some bread, they'll put on airs. When they get hungry enough, they'll thank God there is such a place as the poorhouse.

"Days went by and weeks, and the mother and daughter still didn't give in. The town grew curious—what were they up to? The mother was bedridden and the daughter blind. There are blind people who can get around, but the teacher's daughter—Tzirel was her name —never strayed beyond her own courtyard. I can see her now: reddish hair, a glowing face, trim limbs. Her eyes were blue and appeared healthy but she couldn't see a thing. People began to wonder if maybe the mother and daughter had more money than had been assumed, but that couldn't be. First of all, the teacher had been poor, and second, neither the mother nor the daughter ever left the house. Neither of them was ever seen in any store. Then where did they get the food, even if they did have the money?

"My dear people, there was a lantuch in their house, and when he saw that the breadwinner was gone and the women had been left penniless and without a stitch to their backs, he assumed the burden himself. You're laughing? It's nothing to laugh at. He brought them everything they needed—bread, sugar, herring. He did it all at night. One time a youth walked by their house in the middle of the night and he heard wood being chopped in the yard. He grew suspicious. Who would be chopping wood in the middle of the night? He opened the gate to the courtyard and saw an ax swinging and chips flying, but there was no one there. It was the lantuch chopping wood for the winter. The next day, when the youth revealed what he had seen, people laughed at him. 'You probably dreamed it,' they said. But it was true.

"A few weeks later, a shipping agent came back from Lublin, also in the middle of the night. He walked past a well and he saw the rope descending into the water and a pailful of water coming up. But there was no one around. He promptly realized that this was the work of *that* band —the creatures of the night. But the shipping agent— Meir David was his name—was a strong person and not easily frightened. He took hold of his ritual fringes, quietly recited 'Hear, O Israel,' and stopped to see what would happen next. After the unseen one had drawn one pail of water, he drew a second, and then the two pails began to be borne along as if an invisible water carrier was carrying them on a yoke. Meir David followed the pails of water to where the widow and her blind daughter lived. The next day the shipping agent went to the rabbi and told him what his eyes had seen. This Meir

David was an honest man and not one to make up things. A fuss erupted in town. The rabbi summoned the widow and her daughter to him, but the widow was too sick to walk. She couldn't talk either. Soon after, she died.

"The blind daughter said to the rabbi, 'Someone provides for us, but who it is I do not know. It must be an angel from heaven.'

"No, it wasn't any angel but the lantuch. After the mother died, the daughter sold the house and went to live with relatives in Galicia."

"The lantuch didn't go along?" our neighbor Riva asked.

"Who knows? As a rule, they don't stir from the house," Aunt Yentl said.

"Do they live forever?" Sheindel asked.

"No one lives forever," Aunt Yentl replied.

It grew silent. I looked at the cat; she had fallen asleep.

Aunt Yentl glanced at me. "I'll get you the Sabbath fruit now. If a young man wants to study the Torah, he must keep up his strength."

And she brought me a Sabbath cookie and three plums.

Translated by Joseph Singer

Utzel &
His Daughter, Poverty

Once there was a man named Utzel. He was very
poor and even more lazy. Whenever anyone wanted to
give him a job to do, his answer was always the same:
"Not today."

"Why not today?" he was asked. And he always replied, "Why not tomorrow?"

Utzel lived in a cottage that had been built by his
great-grandfather. The thatched roof needed mending,
and although the holes let the rain in, they did not let the
smoke from the stove out. Toadstools grew on the
crooked walls and the floor had rotted away. There had
been a time when mice lived there, but now there
weren't any because there was nothing for them to eat.
Utzel's wife had starved to death, but before she died she
had given birth to a baby girl. The name Utzel gave his
daughter was very fitting. He called her Poverty.

Utzel loved to sleep and each night he went to bed

with the chickens. In the morning he would complain that he was tired from so much sleeping and so he went to sleep again. When he was not sleeping, he lay on his broken-down cot, yawning and complaining. He would say to his daughter, "Other people are lucky. They have money without working. I am cursed."

Utzel was a small man, but as his daughter, Poverty, grew, she spread out in all directions. She was tall, broad, and heavy. At fifteen she had to lower her head to get through the doorway. Her feet were the size of a man's and puffy with fat. The villagers maintained that the lazier Utzel got, the more Poverty grew.

Utzel loved nobody, was jealous of everybody. He even spoke with envy of cats, dogs, rabbits, and all creatures who didn't have to work for a living. Yes, Utzel hated everybody and everything, but he adored his daughter. He daydreamed that a rich young man would fall in love with her, marry her, and provide for his wife and his father-in-law. But not a young man in the village showed the slightest interest in Poverty. When her father reproached the girl for not making friends and not going out with young men, Poverty would say, "How can I go out in rags and bare feet?"

One day Utzel learned that a certain charitable society in the village loaned poor people money, which they could pay back in small sums over a long period. Lazy as he was, he made a great effort—got up, dressed, and went to the office of the society. "I would like to borrow five gulden," he said to the official in charge.

"What do you intend to do with the money?" he was asked. "We lend money only for useful purposes."

"I want to have a pair of shoes made for my daughter," Utzel explained. "If Poverty has shoes, she will go out with the young people of the village and some wealthy young man will surely fall in love with her. When they get married, I will be able to pay back the five gulden."

The official thought it over. The chances of anyone falling in love with Poverty were very small. Utzel, however, looked so miserable that the official decided to give him the loan. He asked Utzel to sign a promissory note and gave him five gulden.

Utzel had tried to order a pair of shoes for his daughter a few months before. Sandler the shoemaker had gone so far as to take Poverty's measurements, but the shoemaker had wanted his money in advance. From the charitable society Utzel went directly to the shoemaker and asked whether he still had Poverty's measurements.

"And supposing I do?" Sandler replied. "My price is five gulden and I still want my money in advance."

Utzel took out the five gulden and handed them to Sandler. The shoemaker opened a drawer and after some searching brought out the order for Poverty's shoes. He promised to deliver the new shoes in a week, on Friday.

Utzel, who wanted to surprise his daughter, did not tell her about the shoes. The following Friday, as he lay on his cot yawning and complaining, there was a knock on the door and Sandler came in carrying the new shoes. When Poverty saw the shoemaker with a pair of shiny new shoes in his hand, she cried out in joy. The shoemaker handed her the shoes and told her to try them on. But, alas, she could not get them on her puffy feet. In the months since the measurements had been taken, Pov-

457

erty's feet had become even larger than they were before. Now the girl cried out in grief.

Utzel looked on in consternation. "How is it possible?" he asked. "I thought her feet stopped growing long ago."

For a while Sandler, too, stood there puzzled. Then he inquired, "Tell me, Utzel, where did you get the five gulden?" Utzel explained that he had borrowed the money from the charitable loan society and had given them a promissory note in return.

"So now you have a debt," exclaimed Sandler. "That makes you even poorer than you were a few months ago. Then you had nothing, but today you have five gulden less than nothing. And since you have grown poorer, Poverty has grown bigger, and naturally her feet have grown with her. That is why the shoes don't fit. It is all clear to me now."

"What are we going to do?" Utzel asked in despair.

"There is only one way out for you," Sandler said. "Go to work. From borrowing one gets poorer and from work one gets richer. When you and your daughter work, she will have shoes that fit."

The idea of working did not appeal to either of them, but it was even worse to have new shoes and go around barefoot. Utzel and Poverty both decided that immediately after the Sabbath they would look for work.

Utzel got a job as a water carrier. Poverty became a maid. For the first time in their lives, they worked diligently. They were kept so busy that they did not even think of the new shoes, until one Sabbath morning Poverty decided she'd try them on again. Lo and behold, her feet slipped easily into them. The new shoes fit.

Utzel & His Daughter, Poverty

At last Utzel and Poverty understood that all a man possesses he gains through work, and not by lying in bed and being idle. Even animals were industrious. Bees make honey, spiders spin webs, birds build nests, moles dig holes in the earth, squirrels store food for the winter. Before long Utzel got a better job. He rebuilt his house and bought some furniture. Poverty lost more weight. She had new clothes made and dressed prettily like the other girls of the village. Her looks improved, too, and a young man began to court her. His name was Mahir and he was the son of a wealthy merchant. Utzel's dream of a rich son-in-law came true, but by then he no longer needed to be taken care of.

Love for his daughter had saved Utzel. In his later years he became so respected he was elected a warden of that same charitable loan society from which he had borrowed five gulden.

On the wall of his office there hung the string with which Sandler had once measured Poverty's feet, and above it the framed motto: *Whatever you can do today, don't put off till tomorrow.*

Translated by the author and Elizabeth Shub

The Squire

Five Hanukkah lights burned in the Hanukkah lamp in the Trisker Hasidic studyhouse, as well as the large candle called the beadle. In the oven, potatoes were roasting and their smell tickled everyone's nostrils. Old Reb Berish sneezed and the boys around him wished him good health.

He wiped his nose with a large handkerchief and said, "Some people think that in olden times miracles were more frequent than today. That is not true. The truth is that miracles were rare in all times. If too many miracles occurred, people would rely on them too much. Free choice would cease. The Powers on High want men to do things, make an effort, not to be lazy. But there are cases where only a miracle can save a man.

"Something like this happened when I was a boy here in Bilgoray about eighty years ago—and perhaps even a little longer. Our village was much smaller than it is today. Where Zamość Street is now there was still forest. Lublin Street was only an alley. Where we are sitting now there was a pasture for cows. There lived then in Bilgoray a wealthy young man by the name of Falik, a talmudic scholar. He was the owner of a dry-goods store. He had other businesses as well. His wife, Sarah, came from Lublin, from a fine family. Suddenly the couple's good luck changed. Whether it was a punishment for some transgression or just a decree from heaven, I don't know. First, the store burned down. There was no fire insurance in those years. Then Sarah became ill. There was no doctor or druggist in Bilgoray. There were only three remedies for people to apply—leeches, cups, and bleeding. If these three didn't help, nothing more could be done. Sarah died and left three orphans, a boy by the name of Mannes and two younger girls, Pessele and Etele.

"Not long after Sarah's death, Falik himself became mortally sick. He grew pale and emaciated, and after a while he became bedridden and it seemed he would never recover. Lippe the healer recommended chicken broth, barley soup, and goat milk. Nothing changed. First of all, Falik lost his appetite, and second, he was left without any income. Nowadays people are selfish, they don't care about others, but in former times people helped one another when in need. They tried to send bread to Falik, and meat, butter, and cheese, but he refused to accept charity. The community leader came to him and offered him help secretly, so that no one would know, but Falik said, 'I would know.'

"It happened the first night of Hanukkah. As always

there was a great deal of snow, frost, blizzards. Things had reached such a stage in Falik's house that finally there was not even a loaf of bread. In better times Falik had possessed a number of silver objects—candlesticks, a spice box, a Passover plate—but Mannes, the oldest child, had sold them all. There was one precious article still in the house, an antique Hanukkah lamp made by some ancient silversmith. There lived a usurer in town who would pay a pittance for the most costly objects. Mannes wanted to sell him the Hanukkah lamp, too, but Falik said to his son, 'Wait until after Hanukkah.' There were a few pennies left in the house, but instead of buying bread Mannes bought oil and wicks for the Hanukkah lights. The girls complained that they were hungry, and Mannes said to them, 'Let's imagine that it is Yom Kippur.' I know this story, because Mannes told it to me years later.

"Since Falik could not leave his bed anymore, Mannes brought the lamp to his father on the first night of Hanukkah and Falik made the proper benedictions and lit the first light. He also hummed the song 'Rock of Ages,' and kissed his children. Then Mannes took the Hanukkah lamp to the living room and put it on the windowsill, according to the law. The children sat at the table hungry, without having eaten supper. It was cold in the house. Only a year before, Falik had given his children Hanukkah money to play dreidel and Sarah had fried pancakes for the family. Now everything was bathed in gloom. The children looked at each other with eyes that seemed to ask, 'From whence cometh my help?'

"Suddenly someone knocked at the door. 'Who could

this be?' Mannes asked himself. 'Probably someone with a gift.' His father had warned him again and again not to accept any gifts. Mannes decided not to open the door this time, so as to avoid arguing with the good people. But the knocking at the door did not stop. After a while Mannes went to the door, ready to say, 'Father told me not to accept anything.' When he opened it he saw a squire—tall, broad-shouldered, in a long fur coat with tails down to his ankles and a fur hat sprinkled with snow. Mannes became so frightened that he lost his tongue. It almost never happened that a squire came into a Jewish house, especially in the evening. In my day, when a squire visited a village, he came in a carriage harnessed to eight horses, and his valets rode in front to clear a way for him. Often they blew trumpets to announce that the great lord was coming. Bilgoray still belonged to Count Zamojski, who was as rich and mighty as a king. To Mannes the squire said, 'I passed by in my sleigh and I saw a little light in a lamp the likes of which I had never seen in all my life—with goblets, flowers, a lion, a deer, a leopard, an eagle, all beautifully done. Why did you kindle only one light if there are eight holders? Is this some Jewish holiday? And where are your parents?' Mannes knew Polish and how to speak to an important man. He said, 'Come in, your excellency. It is for us a great honor.'

"The squire entered the living room and for a long while he stared at the Hanukkah lamp. He began to question Mannes, and the boy told him the story of Hanukkah—how the Jews fought the Greeks in ancient times in the Land of Israel. He also told him of the miracle that had happened with the oil for lighting the menorah in the temple: how after the war there was barely enough oil left to light the menorah for one day, but a miracle happened and the oil was sufficient for eight days. Then the squire saw a dreidel on the table and asked, 'What is this?'

"Although the children had no money with which to play, they had put a dreidel there just to remember former times. Mannes explained to the squire that Hanukkah is the only holiday when children are allowed to play games. He told him the rules of dreidel. The squire asked, 'Could I play with you? My driver will wait with the sleigh. It's cold outside, but my horses are covered with blankets and the driver has a fur jacket.'

" 'Your excellency,' Mannes said, 'my father is sick. We have no mother and we don't have a penny to our name.' The squire said, 'I intend to offer you a thousand gulden for your magnificent lamp, but I don't have the whole sum with me, so I will give you five hundred gulden in advance and with this money you can play.' As he said this, he took a large bag of gold coins from his coat and threw it on the table. The children were so astounded that they forgot their hunger. The game began and the greatest unbeliever could have seen that the whole event was a wonder from heaven. The children kept winning and the squire kept losing. In one hour the squire lost all his gold and the children won every coin. Then the squire cried out, 'Lost is lost. My driver and my horses must be cold. Good night, happy Hanukkah, and don't worry about your father. With God's help he will soon recover.'

"Only after the squire had left did the children realize what had happened to them. Not only had they gotten five hundred gulden as an advance on the lamp, but the squire had lost additional money. Half the table was covered with coins. The girls, Pessele and Etele, burst out crying. Mannes ran outside to see if the squire, the sleigh, the horses and driver were still there, but they had all vanished without leaving any tracks in the snow. Usually horses harnessed to a sleigh have bells on their necks and one can hear the jingling from far away, but the night was quiet. I will make it short. The moment the squire left, Falik opened his eyes. He had gone to sleep near to death and he woke up a healthy man. Nothing but a miracle could have saved him, and so the miracle occurred."

"Who was the squire? The prophet Elijah?" the boys asked.

"Who knows? He certainly was not a Polish squire."

"Did he ever come to get the lamp?"

"Not as long as I was in Bilgoray," the old man replied.

"If he had been the prophet Elijah, he would have kept his promise," one of the boys remarked.

Old Reb Berish did not answer immediately. He pulled his beard and pondered. Then he said, "They have a lot of time in heaven. He might have come to their children's children or to their grandchildren. I married and moved to another village. As far as I know, the Hanukkah lamp remained with Falik and his children as long as they lived. Some rabbi said that when God works a miracle, He often does it in such a way that it should appear natural. There were some unbelievers in Bilgoray and they said that it was a real squire, a rich spendthrift who was in a mood to squander his money. Those who deny God always try to explain all wonders as normal events or as coincidences—I'm afraid the potatoes are already burning," he added.

Old Reb Berish opened the door of the oven and with his bare fingers began to pull out half-burned potatoes from the glowing coals.

Ole & Trufa

A STORY OF TWO LEAVES

The forest was large and thickly overgrown with all kinds of leaf-bearing trees. It was in the month of November. Usually it's cold this time of year and it even happens that it snows, but this November was relatively warm. The nights were cool and windy, but as soon as the sun came out in the mornings, it turned warm. You might have thought it was summer except that the whole forest was strewn with fallen leaves—some yellow as saffron, some red as wine, some the color of gold, and some of mixed color. The leaves had been torn down by the rain, by the wind, some by day, some at night, and they now formed a deep carpet over the forest floor. Although their juices had run dry, the leaves still exuded a pleasant aroma. The sun shone down on them through the living branches, and worms and flies which had somehow survived the autumn storms crawled over them. The space beneath the leaves provided hiding places for crickets, field mice, and many other creatures who sought protection in the earth. The birds that don't migrate to warmer climates in the winter but stay behind perched on the bare tree limbs. Among them were sparrows—tiny birds, but endowed with much courage and the experience accumulated through thousands of generations. They hopped, twittered, and searched for the food the forest offered this time of year. Many, many insects and worms had perished in recent weeks, but no one mourned their loss. God's creatures know that death is merely a phase of life. With the coming of spring, the forest would again fill with grasses, green leaves, blossoms, and flowers. The migrating birds would return from far-off lands and locate their abandoned nests. Even if the wind or the rain had disturbed a nest, it could be easily repaired.

On the tip of a tree which had lost all its other leaves, two still remained. One leaf was named Ole and the other, Trufa. Ole and Trufa both hung from one twig. Since they were at the very tip of the tree they received lots of sunlight. For some reason unknown to Ole or Trufa, they had survived all the rains, all the cold nights and winds, and still clung to the tip of the twig. Who knows the reason one leaf falls and another remains? But Ole and Trufa believed the answer lay in the great love they bore each other. Ole was slightly bigger than Trufa and a few days older, but Trufa was prettier and more delicate. One leaf can do little for another when the wind blows, the rain pours, or the hail begins to fall. It even happens in summer that a leaf is torn loose—come autumn and winter nothing can be done. Still, Ole encouraged Trufa at every opportunity. During the worst storms, when the thunder clapped, the lightning flashed, and the wind tore off not only leaves but even whole branches, Ole pleaded with Trufa, "Hang on, Trufa! Hang on with all your might!"

At times during cold and stormy nights, Trufa would complain, "My time has come, Ole, but you hang on!"

"What for?" Ole asked. "Without you, my life is senseless. If you fall, I'll fall with you."

"No, Ole, don't do it! So long as a leaf can stay up it mustn't let go . . ."

"It all depends if you stay with me," Ole replied. "By day I look at you and admire your beauty. At night I sense your fragrance. Be the only leaf on a tree? No, never!"

"Ole, your words are so sweet but they're not true," Trufa said. "You know very well that I'm no longer pretty. Look how wrinkled I am! All my juices have dried out and I'm ashamed before the birds. They look at me with such pity. At times it seems to me they're laughing at how shriveled I've become. I've lost everything, but one thing is still left me—my love for you."

"Isn't that enough? Of all our powers love is the highest, the finest," Ole said. "So long as we love each other we remain here, and no wind, rain, or storm can destroy us. I'll tell you something, Trufa—I never loved you as much as I love you now."

"Why, Ole? Why? I'm all yellow."

"Who says green is pretty and yellow is not? All colors are equally handsome."

And just as Ole spoke these words, that which Trufa

had feared all these months happened—a wind came up and tore Ole loose from the twig. Trufa began to tremble and flutter until it seemed that she, too, would soon be torn away, but she held fast. She saw Ole fall and sway in the air, and she called to him in leafy language, "Ole! Come back! Ole! Ole!"

But before she could even finish Ole vanished from sight. He blended in with the other leaves on the ground and Trufa was left all alone on the tree.

So long as it was still day, Trufa managed somehow to endure her grief. But when it grew dark and cold and a piercing rain began to fall, she sank into despair. Somehow she felt that the blame for all the leafy misfortunes lay with the tree, the trunk with all its mighty limbs. Leaves fell but the trunk stood tall, thick, and firmly rooted in the ground. No wind, rain, or hail could upset it. What did it matter to a tree which probably lived forever what became of a leaf? To Trufa, the trunk was a kind of God. It covered itself with leaves for a few months, then it shook them off. It nourished them with its sap for as long as it pleased, then it let them die of thirst. Trufa pleaded with the tree to give her back her Ole and to make it summer again, but the tree didn't heed, or refused to heed, her prayers . . .

Trufa didn't think a night could be so long as this one —so dark, so frosty. She spoke to Ole and hoped for an answer, but Ole was silent and gave no sign of his presence.

Trufa said to the tree, "Since you've taken Ole from me, take me, too."

But the tree didn't acknowledge even this prayer.

After a while, Trufa dozed off. This wasn't sleep but a strange languor. Trufa awoke and to her amazement found that she was no longer hanging on the tree. The wind had blown her down while she was asleep. This was different from the way she used to feel when she awoke on the tree with the sunrise. All her fears and anxieties had now vanished. The awakening also brought with it an awareness she had never felt before. She knew now that she wasn't just a leaf that depended on every whim of the wind, but that she was a part of the universe. She no longer was small or weak or transient, but a part of eternity. Through some mysterious force, Trufa understood the miracle of her molecules, atoms, protons, and electrons—the enormous energy she represented and the divine plan of which she was a part. Next to her lay Ole and they greeted each other with a love they hadn't been aware of before. This wasn't a love that depended on chance or caprice, but a love as mighty and eternal as the universe itself. That which they had feared all the days and nights between April and November turned out to be not death but redemption. A breeze came and lifted Ole and Trufa in the air, and they soared with the bliss known only by those who have freed themselves and have joined with eternity.

Translated by Joseph Singer

Dalfunka, Where the Rich Live Forever

It happened in Chelm, a city of fools. Where else could it have happened? On a winter morning in the community house Gronam Ox, the wisest man of Chelm, and his five sages, Dopey Lekisch, Zeinvel Ninny, Treitel Fool, Sender Donkey, and Shmendrick Numskull sat at a long table. All six looked tired and had red eyes from lack of sleep. For seven days and nights they had been thinking about a problem which they could not solve. The treasury of the city of Chelm was empty. For many weeks Gronam Ox and his sages had not received their salaries.

Even though it was not Hanukkah, Shlemiel the beadle sat at the other end of the table playing dreidel by himself. Suddenly the door opened and Zalman Typpish entered. He was the richest man in Chelm. He had a long white beard. When they saw Zalman Typpish, Gronam and the sages looked up in surprise. Zalman Typpish never paid a visit to the community house because they levied high taxes on him.

"Good morning, Gronam Ox. Good morning, sages," Zalman Typpish greeted them solemnly.

"A good morning to you, Zalman Typpish," all of them answered in accord. "What made you pay such an early visit?"

"I came to ask your advice," Zalman Typpish said. "If it is good I will pay the treasury two thousand gold pieces."

"What sort of advice?" Gronam Ox asked.

"You all know I have just turned eighty. You also know that no man lives forever. But I, Zalman Typpish, wish to live forever. I would like forever to eat blintzes with sour cream, drink tea with jam, coffee with chicory, forever smoke my long pipe. To make it short, I want to live forever."

"Live forever!" exclaimed Gronam Ox and his five sages. "How is this possible?"

"This is the reason I came to you," Zalman said. "If you will tell me how to live forever, you will get what I just promised." Saying these words, Zalman Typpish took out a bag filled with gold coins and poured them on the table.

When Gronam and his sages saw the pile of gold, they began to murmur. Zalman Typpish was known as a miser. Gronam Ox immediately put his index finger on his forehead in order to think hard. The other sages did the same thing. After long thought, Gronam Ox said, "You know well that Chelm is the wisest city in the world and I, Gronam Ox, am the wisest man in Chelm, which means that I am the wisest man in the universe. But just the same, I cannot give you the kind of advice you desire. No man can live forever. Even I, Gronam Ox, won't live forever."

"Even Methuselah did not live forever," Dopey Lekisch chimed in.

"Even King Solomon did not live forever," Zeinvel Ninny added.

"Even our rabbi is not going to live forever," Treitel Fool pronounced.

"Even a lion does not live forever," Sender Donkey remarked.

"Even an elephant does not live forever," Shmendrick Numskull said.

"All this is true, but I, Zalman Typpish, decided that I must live forever. If you won't advise me how to do it, you won't get a penny."

Gronam Ox was about to say that he was sorry, but at that moment Shlemiel the beadle stuck out his tongue and placed his thumb on the tip of his nose as a sign that he wanted to speak.

"What do you want to say, Shlemiel?" Gronam Ox asked.

"I found a way," Shlemiel said.

"You found a way?" Gronam Ox asked in astonishment.

"Yes, my lord. The thing is like this. Last week I had nothing to do all day long and I started to look over the records of our Chelm suburbs. Among others I glanced through the records of our suburb Dalfunka."

"Dalfunka, where all the paupers and beggars of Chelm live?" Gronam Ox asked.

"Yes, Dalfunka," Shlemiel said. "As you know, we have in our books the names of all those who are born and died in the last three hundred years. When I went through the list of all who died in Dalfunka, I realized that no rich man ever died there. This means that the rich in Dalfunka live forever. My advice, therefore, is that Zalman Typpish should buy a house in Dalfunka, settle there, and never die. As simple as that."

Gronam Ox opened his mouth and stared agape. "Shlemiel, you gave the right advice. But how is this possible? Are you cleverer than I am?"

"No one is cleverer than you, Gronam Ox," the five sages sang out in chorus.

"My only explanation is that since you have been sitting so many years near us, a part of our wisdom spilled over on you," said Gronam Ox.

"True," the five sages agreed.

Dopey Lekisch added, "Even a horse would become wise if it stayed with us so long."

"Zalman, you got good advice. Now give us the two thousand gold coins," Gronam Ox suggested.

"Before I give you so much money, I must be sure that the advice is right," Zalman Typpish answered. "I will give you an advance of ten gold coins now, and after I have moved to Dalfunka and have lived forever, I will pay the balance."

"We cannot wait that long," Gronam Ox protested. "We need the payment right now."

"Either take the ten gold coins or you will receive nothing," Zalman Typpish insisted.

For a long while Gronam Ox and his sages haggled

with Zalman Typpish, but as always Zalman Typpish prevailed. He gave Gronam Ox the ten gold coins and left.

For five years Zalman Typpish lived in Dalfunka, ate blintzes with sour cream, drank tea with jam, coffee with chicory, smoked his long pipe, and did not die. Gronam Ox often asked for the balance, but Zalman Typpish always had the same answer: "First let me live forever and then I will pay." It seemed that Zalman Typpish was right in not paying beforehand, because one day in the sixth year he became sick and died.

When Gronam Ox heard the bad news he immediately called for the sages and they pondered seven days and seven nights why Zalman Typpish had died. Again Shlemiel found the explanation. For five years Zalman did no business because one could not earn any money in Dalfunka. Instead, he spent a fortune on such luxuries as sour cream, coffee, tobacco, chickory. He most probably became poor and so he died like all the other poor people. "To live forever in Dalfunka one must be as rich as Rothschild," Shlemiel said.

Gronam Ox and the five sages again admired Shlemiel's sharp mind. Gronam Ox promptly dispatched letters to the Rothschilds inviting them to come speedily to Dalfunka and begin to live forever. But months passed and the Rothschilds did not arrive. This time Gronam Ox discovered the reason himself. He said, "The rich are so stingy that they would rather die cheaply in London, Paris, and Vienna than live forever in Dalfunka at a higher cost."

"So what should we do now?" the sages asked.

"We must get rich ourselves."

"How?" the sages asked.

"Of course, by levying taxes on the paupers of Chelm," Gronam Ox replied.

Shlemiel made the usual sign that he wanted to speak. He wanted to say that, according to his latest figures, even the Rothschilds were not rich enough to live forever in Dalfunka, but Gronam Ox said, "Shlemiel, everything is crystal clear. We don't need your advice anymore. Keep quiet."

"Be silent," Dopey Lekisch chimed in.

"You are only a beadle, not a sage," Zeinvel Ninny shouted.

"Not even half a sage," Treitel Fool screamed.

"And you will never live forever," Sender Donkey hollered.

"Not even a half of forever," Shmendrick Numskull yelled.

Since he was forbidden to talk and he had nothing else to do, Shlemiel took out his dreidel and began to play by himself. While the dreidel spun, Shlemiel was muttering, "If it falls to the right, I lose, and if it falls to the left, you win."

Topiel & Tekla

I

The village of Wislowka lay on the very edge of the Vistula. It had belonged to a Squire Warlicki, who committed suicide when he heard that the tsar would free the serfs. Actually, Wislowka had never brought any income. It had been madness to settle peasants on soil that was almost entirely sand. Even in years of plenty the crops grew sparse and meager. The peasants all became fishermen. Since there was no shipbuilder in the area to build proper boats, the men of Wislowka went fishing on rafts made of rotten logs and in boats resembling troughs and washtubs. Thus, Topiel, the spirit of the river, got his victims each year. Besides the fishermen who drowned in times of storms, it often happened that men and women would drown themselves for lack of food, out of sickness or unrequited love. This was referred to in Wislowka as "going on the Vistula." The peasants had a saying: "Topiel called in his victim."

For some reason no one had drowned in the past two years, which everyone considered a bad omen, because it meant that Topiel was angry, not having gotten the sacrifice due to him. In the third year there came a famine the likes of which the eldest couldn't remember. The winter seed froze and the summer seed dried out. Not a drop of rain fell all summer, and in the month of Sierpien (August) the men assembled in the tavern and after lengthy debates agreed that a child would have to be sacrificed to Topiel. The decision was kept from the women, who were softhearted and had a habit of divulging secrets. Besides, the Russians who ruled Poland had forbidden such things.

There was a peasant in Wislowka by the name of Maciek Kowadlo, whose daughter Tekla, aged sixteen, was pregnant with a child whose father, a tramp, had run away and was never heard from again. Maciek and his wife, Zocha, were the parents of six girls, there was no bread in the house, and Maciek agreed to offer his first grandchild as the sacrifice to Topiel. For this, Maciek would be presented by the peasant community with a young hog to raise until Christmas. The villagers would supply Maciek with enough potato peels, turnips, and cabbage heads to fatten the porker. On the day before Christmas Maciek would slaughter the hog, which would provide him with enough ham and bacon for the whole year. The child would be offered to Topiel as soon as it was born, which, according to Maciek and Zocha's reckonings, would occur during the month of Listopad (November) or, at the very latest, the month of Styczen (January).

The peasants deceived themselves about keeping the matter a secret. All the villagers quickly learned of the decision, even the magistrate. When Tekla heard what would be demanded of her, her mouth twisted as if she was about to cry, but she didn't shed a tear. All her tears dried up within her. Maciek had warned his daughter to keep away from this vagabond by the name of Stefan. But Tekla felt sorry for him. He spoke like a city man and told her he was studying for the priesthood. He promised that she would become his housekeeper and gave her a box of matches for a present, which was a rarity in the village because the peasants made fires by rubbing two sticks together.

Tekla was small for her age. She had watery blue eyes set too far apart, high cheekbones, a snub nose, a round forehead, hair white as flax, and lots of freckles. Because she had grown up during years of famine, she was frail. Her younger sisters were gay and talkative, but Tekla was a silent one. She liked to listen to the stories old women told as they spun flax: tales of demons, evil spirits, werewolves, wizards, witches, and wild beasts. For some reason unknown to herself, she foresaw that she would die young. She even confessed this to the priest, Pawel Domb, who told her, "Everything is in God's hands."

The others in the family never discussed their dreams. But Tekla remembered her dreams and probed them for interpretation. One dream was repeated often—she was sick, cupping glasses were being applied to her as well as leeches, and the undertaker came to measure her for a coffin. Years before, Maciek had owned a goat, and when

Tekla grazed the animal in the pasture she fantasized all kinds of things: that the gypsies abducted her and sold her to cannibals, who cooked her in a pot and ate her like a goose; that she got lost in the forest and a she-wolf raised her and taught her the lupine language; that a robber with one eye in the middle of his forehead caught her in a sack and forced her to bear a monster. The peasant women in Wislowka said that Stefan might have been a devil in disguise. Before Tekla even found out that she would have to give up her child to Topiel, an old crone warned her that she might give birth to a child with fangs and horns and that it was dangerous to nurse such a creature since it could bite off a nipple.

The hog was still small when Maciek brought him home, but grew fatter from day to day. The women of the village kept bringing him garbage and leftovers. The hog had no name and was simply called Wieprz, the Polish word for a male pig. Wieprz could eat from morning to night. He loved to wallow in the mud, and as he did he grunted with pleasure. A childish joy shone out of his little eyes. He is happy, Tekla thought. He doesn't know what awaits him.

Tekla's spirit lagged from day to day. She had allowed herself to be deceived by a tramp, and her father had sold his grandson for a pig. She grew even more silent. She could no longer love her father, her mother, her sisters. She compared herself to the hog the community had chosen for a sacrifice. She no longer went to church on Sundays and no one urged her to go. In the evenings her sisters talked, laughed, and braided one another's hair, but Tekla just sat in a corner and didn't hear their chatter. A bed was made up for her on a bench, but Tekla could no longer stand the house and went to sleep in the hay in the attic. Her belly kept getting higher. The child within her jerked and pushed. In the nights the wind barked and wailed like a pack of wolves.

2

How fast the time flew! Only yesterday, it seemed to Tekla, it was autumn and gossamers floated in the air. Now the rains came along with the cold. The Vistula spilled over its banks and threatened to inundate the village. Since Maciek had no pigsty, the animal was kept inside the hut. He grew so fat that his thin legs could barely support him, and he sat and lay more than he stood. At times his eyes—the color of hazelnuts—reflected a porcine sadness. Does the beast know its end is near, Tekla wondered. She was by nature inclined to ponder things: How high is the sky? How deep is the earth? Why do people live and die? What are dreams? Why are some babies born male and others female? And why are the days in Wislowka so dreary?

Everyone in the house allegedly loved the hog. The girls kissed him and played with him, but soon he would be butchered. Maciek had already honed his ax in anticipation, and Zocha had prepared the vat where the animal's skin would be scorched. She even spoke about the pork cutlets they would fry on the holidays. The neighbors proposed that Zocha lend them some bacon for Christmas which they would repay later. "How can this be?" Tekla asked herself. "How does merciful God allow such wrongs to happen?" On Sundays the priest, Pawel Domb, often preached from the pulpit that God was love and that He had sent down His only begotten son to redeem the world. But why had this son to be crucified? Tekla wanted to ask someone about this, but whom might she ask?

Before the holiday a lot of snow fell, which lent hope that the drought would not be repeated the following year. The Vistula grew ever wilder. In other years by this time the river was covered with ice and one could cross it on sleds, but this year the water was too stormy to freeze over. News came that whole communities had been flooded, bridges had collapsed, and men had drowned. There were witnesses who had seen tables, chairs, noodle boards, and cribs driven by the turbulent current. Tekla was well aware of the reason why Topiel was mad. He foamed with rage at the delay in delivering to him his sacrifice. Tekla once heard the old women say that Topiel had a palace in the depths of the Vistula where he reigned like a king, and that he had many wives and concubines. He had crystal horns, a silver beard, and a fish tail. In the summer he enticed his victims with song, and the naiads helped him lure young lads and maidens. In the winter he roared like a lion. "Is Topiel a man-eater?" Tekla asked herself. But at least he didn't eat his own wives, who sang in chorus with him.

A weird notion flashed through Tekla's mind—maybe she should become one of Topiel's wives and thus bring up her child together with him. She daydreamed of how she would throw herself into the river and Topiel would seize her in his mighty arms and carry her off to his castle. He would sit her down on his lap, kiss her, fondle her, and call her his most beloved Rusalka. She would kneel before him, kiss his feet, and he would promise not to devour her baby, but to bring it up as a son.

The closer it came to Christmas, the more indulgent Zocha and the girls grew toward the hog. They kept on bringing him tidbits and made believe they were angry with Maciek, who would do away with Wieprz.

Zocha grumbled, "Oh, men are so heartless! How can you kill our lovely Wieprz? You glutton!"

The girls, too, complained: "Why kill him? Let him live a while longer. He is still so young."

But Maciek replied, "You'll eat his flesh and you'll lick your fingers."

On the morning of Wieprz's killing, Tekla didn't get out of bed at all. It was too cold now to sleep in the attic, and she lay on a straw pallet near the stove. Her belly was as hard as a drum, her face yellow and bloated. A few feet away Wieprz snored. Maciek, who usually moved slowly and spoke quietly, suddenly grew loud and angry. He tied a rope around Wieprz and dragged him out into the yard. Wieprz erupted into frantic shrieks. Soon Tekla heard a ghastly scream. It seemed to Tekla that Wieprz yelled, "Murderers! Help! Save me! . . ."

Tekla covered herself with the mat and stuffed her ears with her fingers so as not to hear the screams. She was filled with rage toward her father, her mother, her sisters. "I don't want to live in this false world anymore!" a voice within her cried. "I'll go on the Vistula . . ."

It suddenly became clear to her that she had foreseen this end a long time ago, possibly from childhood.

3

The church in Wislowka was small, but when its bell tolled, even the deaf could hear. It called the people of Wislowka to Christmas Eve Mass, but Tekla told her mother that she couldn't go to God's house because she had cramps. The family left her at home. On the stove sat a huge pot containing chunks of Wieprz. A tiny oil lamp glimmered. Shadows danced over the walls and low ceiling.

"I must do it this very minute!" Tekla told herself. She possessed a holiday dress, but now it would be too narrow for her loins, so she put on her everyday skirt, a sheepskin, and a pair of rag shoes with soles of oak bark. Outside, the moon wasn't shining, but the sky teemed with stars. Tekla stood a moment, staring up at the sky. What were stars? Why did they flicker so?

From the church came the sound of singing. Poor as the people of Wislowka were, they had cooked and baked for the holiday, and the smells of meat and fat cakes were carried in the air. The few young men left behind in the village were supposed to disguise themselves in masks with beards, take long staffs in hand, and go from hut to hut singing carols, but Tekla could no longer listen to the songs. She had an urge to say goodbye to someone, but to whom? She headed for the Vistula. The wind slapped her face and the cold pierced her sheepskin. Soon she reached the river. It wasn't completely frozen, but icy floes rushed downstream. The sky swayed on the waves. Tekla's hair tried to tear loose from

488

her skull. She wanted to recite the Lord's Prayer but couldn't remember the words. Suddenly she saw Wieprz. What's Wieprz doing here, she wondered. The hog stood looking up at her with his hazel eyes and raised his snout as if to speak. What happened, did he run away from the hut, Tekla wondered. Oh, this will make a commotion in the village.

She leaned down as if about to pet him, and at that moment she remembered that he was dead. At once Wieprz turned into emptiness and Tekla's breath caught in grief. Nothing was left of Wieprz's body except bones and bristles, but his spirit lived and had come to say goodbye to her. "Goodbye to you, Wieprz," Tekla murmured, and a great love came over her for the tortured creature who, rather than take revenge, showed attachment for the daughter of his murderer.

It was too cold to wait and brood. Tekla walked into the turbulent water. She came to a deep spot and threw herself facedown to Topiel, the King of the Vistula, who emerged from the depths, embraced her in his icy arms, and sunk with her to his glittering castle.

4

Maciek swore that his daughter had drowned herself—he had found one of her rag shoes on the bank—but the people of Wislowka insisted that Maciek had spirited Tekla away somewhere in order to save his grandchild. The peasants burst into Maciek's hut and took away all the meat and tripe that remained of Wieprz. The women even carried off the pot of soup simmering on the stove.

That Christmas no one sang carols in Wislowka. It was clear that Maciek and Zocha had lied, for instead of Topiel's rage being assuaged, it became wilder. He thundered into the gale and laughed a mad laughter. He tore the straw roof off the huts and sent them flying over the village like some otherworldly birds. Topiel was heard to hurl curses of cholera, of lightning, of the fires of hell, and of Baba Yaga, who would come riding astride a mortar and pestle and with her long broom sweep away the light of the world.

Topiel's curses immediately came true. In the middle of the night cries were heard. A spark escaped the chimney of a hut and set the thatched roof on fire. Soon the hut blazed up like a paper lantern. Neighbors watching the flames saw a fiery hobgoblin and three she-devils in the flames. Before morning the storm toppled the chapel with the statue of God's mother, an omen that Satan reigned over the village. The dogs barked all night, and several of them howled so violently that they dropped dead. The dawn broke dark and dismal. A thick fog mixed with smoke and soot hovered over Wislowka. The few roosters still living seemed to forget to crow.

From then on one misfortune followed another. Someone had apparently told the Russians that the peasants in Wislowka had sacrificed a pregnant woman and her unborn child to Topiel, for in the morning when the priest, Pawel Domb, sighing and coughing, preached that the Devil had chosen the day of Christ's birth to snare the faithful, the Russians came and arrested Maciek and his wife, along with some other householders. The prisoners were shackled in chains. True, the tsar had freed the Polish serfs, but the officials still bore a grudge against the former slaves and only sought to frame charges against them. They were sent to Siberia without a trial.

The following summer the crops around Wislowka were scantier than ever. The ears of rye were half empty and those kernels still left were thrashed by hail and wind. Swarms of locusts fell over the fields. They must have been disguised imps, because one heard them chatter in human tongue. In the famine the peasants abandoned their huts and roamed to wherever their feet carried them. Their daughters went into service in the cities. The old people perished of hunger and sickness.

It seemed that Topiel desired the whole of Wislowka for himself. He strewed dunes of sand over the village so deep that in time they covered the roofs and only the chimneys thrust out. The last inhabitants swore that in the night their huts crawled toward the river like snakes. The huts had twisted so that where before there had been a door now there was a window. In the nearby hamlets the peasants said that Topiel came out at night onto the dunes and danced in a whirl with Tekla—she in a shawl of pearls over her naked body, with a child in her arms, and he with a beard of foam-sparkling curls, and a crown of ice.

Translated by Joseph Singer

Hanukkah
in the Poorhouse

Outside there was snow and frost, but in the poor-house it was warm. Those who were mortally ill or para-lyzed lay in beds. The others were sitting around a large Hanukkah lamp with eight burning wicks. Goodhearted citizens had sent pancakes sprinkled with sugar and cinnamon to the inmates. They conversed about olden times, unusual frost, packs of wolves invading the vil-lages during the icy nights, as well as encounters with demons, imps, and sprites. Among the paupers sat an old man, a stranger who had arrived only two days before. He was tall, straight, and had a milk-white beard. He didn't look older than seventy, but when the warden of the poorhouse asked him his age, he pondered a while, counted on his fingers, and said, "On Passover I will be ninety-two."

"No evil eye should befall you," the others called out in unison.

"When you live, you get older not younger," the old man said.

One could hear from his pronunciation that he was not from Poland but from Russia. For an hour or so he listened to the stories which the other people told, while looking intensely at the Hanukkah lights. The conversation turned to the harsh decrees against the Jews and the old man said, "What do you people in Poland know about harsh decrees? In comparison to Russia, Poland is Paradise."

"Are you from Russia?" someone asked him.

"Yes, from Vitebsk."

"What are you doing here?" another one asked.

"When you wander, you come to all kinds of places," the old man replied.

"You seem to speak in riddles," an old woman said.

"My life was one great riddle."

The warden of the poorhouse, who stood nearby, said, "I can see that this man has a story to tell."

"If you have the patience to listen," the old man said.

"Here we *must* have patience," the warden replied.

"It is a story about Hanukkah," said the old man. "Come closer, because I like to talk, not shout."

They all moved their stools closer and the old man began.

"First let me tell you my name. It is Jacob, but my parents called me Yankele. The Russians turned Yankele into Yasha. I mention the Russians because I am one of those who are called the captured ones. When I was a child Tsar Nicholas I, an enemy of the Jews, decreed that Jewish boys should be captured and brought up to be soldiers. The decree was aimed at Russian Jews, not at Polish ones. It created turmoil. The child catchers would barge into a house or into a cheder, where the boys studied, catch a boy as if he were some animal, and send him away deep into Russia, sometimes as far as Siberia. He was not drafted immediately. First he was given to a peasant in a village where he would grow up, and then, when he was of age, he was taken into the army. He had to learn Russian and forget his Jewishness. Often he was forced to convert to the Greek Orthodox faith. The peasant made him work on the Sabbath and eat pork. Many boys died from the bad treatment and from yearning for their parents.

"Since the law stipulated that no one who was married could be drafted for military service, the Jews often married little boys to little girls to save the youngsters from being captured. The married little boy continued to go to cheder. The little girl put on a matron's bonnet, but she remained a child. It often happened that the young wife went out in the street to play with pebbles or to make mud cakes. Sometimes she would take off her bonnet and put her toys in it.

"What happened to me was of a different nature. The young girl whom I was about to marry was the daughter of a neighbor. Her name was Reizel. When we were children of four or five, we played together. I was supposed to be her husband and she my wife. I made believe that I went to the synagogue and she prepared supper for me, a shard with sand or mud. I loved Reizel and we promised ourselves that when we grew up we really would become husband and wife. She was fair, with red hair and blue eyes. Some years later, when my parents brought me the good tidings that Reizel was to marry me, I became mad with joy. We would have married immediately; however, Reizel's mother insisted on preparing a trousseau for the eight-year-old bride, even though she would grow out of it in no time.

"Three days before our wedding, two Cossacks broke into our house in the middle of the night, tore me from my bed, and forced me to follow them. My mother fainted. My father tried to save me, but they slapped him so hard he lost two teeth. It was on the second night of Hanukkah. The next day the captured boys were led into the synagogue to take an oath that they would serve the tsar faithfully. Half the townspeople gathered before the synagogue. Men and women were crying, and in the crowd I saw Reizel. In all misery I managed to call out, 'Reizel, I will come back to you.' And she called back, 'Yankele, I will wait for you.'

"If I wanted to tell you what I went through, I could write a book of a thousand pages. They drove me somewhere deep into Russia. The trip lasted many weeks. They took me to a hamlet and put me in the custody of a peasant by the name of Ivan. Ivan had a wife and six children, and the whole family tried to make a Russian out of me. They all slept in one large bed. In the winter they put their pigs in their hut. The place was swarming with roaches. I knew only a few Russian words. My fringed garment was taken away and my sidelocks were cut off. I had no choice but to eat unkosher food. In the first days I spat out the pig meat, but how long can a boy fast? For hundreds of miles around there was not a single

Jew. They could force my body to do all kinds of things, but they could not make my soul forsake the faith of my fathers. I remembered a few prayers and benedictions by heart and kept on repeating them. I often spoke to myself when nobody was around so as not to forget the Yiddish language. In the summer Ivan sent me to pasture his goats. In later years I took care of his cows and horse. I would sit in the grass and talk to my parents, to my sister Leah, and to my brother Chaim, both younger than I, and also to Reizel. Though I was far away from them, I imagined that they heard me and answered me.

"Since I was captured on Hanukkah, I decided to celebrate this feast even if it cost me my life. I had no Jewish calendar, but I recalled that Hanukkah comes about the time of Christmas—a little earlier or later. I would wake up and go outside in the middle of the night. Not far from the granary grew an old oak. Lightning had burned a large hole in its trunk. I crept inside, lit some kindling wood, and made the benediction. If the peasant had caught me, he would have beaten me. But he slept like a bear.

"Years passed and I became a soldier. There was no old oak tree near the barracks, and you would be whipped for leaving the bunk bed and going outside without permission. But on some winter nights they sent me to guard an ammunition warehouse, and I always found an opportunity to light a candle and recite a prayer. Once, a Jewish soldier came to our barracks and brought with him a small prayer book. My joy at seeing the old familiar Hebrew letters cannot be described. I hid somewhere and recited all the prayers, those of the weekdays, the Sabbath, and the holidays. That soldier had already served out his term, and before he went home, he left me the prayer book as a gift. It was the greatest treasure of my life. I still carry it in my sack.

"Twenty-two years had passed since I was captured. The soldiers were supposed to have the right to send letters to their parents once a month, but since I wrote mine in Yiddish, they were never delivered, and I never received anything from them.

"One winter night, when it was my turn to stand watch at the warehouse, I lit two candles, and since there was no wind, I stuck them into the snow. According to my calculation it was Hanukkah. A soldier who stands watch is not allowed to sit down, and certainly not to fall asleep, but it was the middle of the night and nobody was there, so I squatted on the threshold of the warehouse to observe the two little flames burning brightly. I was tired after a difficult day of service and my eyelids closed. Soon I fell asleep. I was committing three sins against the tsar at once. Suddenly I felt someone shaking my shoulder. I opened my eyes and saw my enemy, a vicious corporal by the name of Kapustin—tall, with broad shoulders, a curled mustache, and a thick red nose with purple veins from drinking. Usually he slept the whole night, but that night some demon made him come outside. When I saw that rascal by the light of the still-burning Hanukkah candles, I knew that this was my end. I would be court-martialed and sent to Siberia. I jumped up, grabbed my gun, and hit him over the head. He fell down and I started running. I ran until sunrise. I didn't know where my feet were carrying me. I had entered a thick forest and it seemed to have no end.

"For three days I ate nothing, and drank only melted snow. Then I came to a hamlet. In all these years I had saved some fifteen rubles from the few kopeks that a soldier receives as pay. I carried it in a little pouch on my chest. I bought myself a cotton-lined jacket, a pair of pants, and a cap. My soldier's uniform and the gun I threw into a stream. After weeks of wandering on foot, I came to railroad tracks. A freight train carrying logs and moving slowly was heading south. It had almost a hundred cars. I jumped on one of them. When the train approached a station, I jumped off in order not to be seen by the stationmaster. I could tell from the signs along the way that we were heading toward St. Petersburg, then the capital of Russia. At some stations the train stood for many hours, and I went into the town or village and begged for a slice of bread. The Russians had robbed me of my best years and I had the right to take some food from them. And so I arrived in Petersburg.

"There I found rich Jews, and when I told them of my predicament, they let me rest a few weeks and provided me with warm clothes and the fare to return to my home-town, Vitebsk. I had grown a beard and no one would have recognized me. Still, to come home to my family using my real name was dangerous because I would be arrested as a deserter.

The train arrived in Vitebsk at dawn. The winter was about to end. The smell of spring was in the air. A few stations before Vitebsk, Jewish passengers entered my car, and from their talk I learned that it was Purim. I remembered that on this holiday it was the custom for poor young men to put on masks and to disguise themselves as the silly King Ahasuerus, the righteous Mordecai, the cruel Haman, or his vicious wife, Zeresh. Toward evening they went from house to house singing songs and performing scenes from the Book of Esther, and the people gave them a few groschen. I remained at the railroad station until late in the morning, and then I went into town and bought myself a mask of Haman with a high red triangular hat made of paper, as well as a paper sword. I was afraid that I might be recognized by some townspeople after all, and I did not want to shock my old parents with my sudden appearance. Since I was tired, I went to the poorhouse. The poorhouse warden asked me where I came from and I gave him the name of some faraway city. The poor and the sick had gotten chicken soup and challah from wealthy citizens. I ate a delicious meal—even a slice of cake—washed down by a glass of tea.

"After sunset I put on the mask of the wicked Haman, hung my paper sword at my side, and walked toward our old house. I opened the door and saw my parents. My father's beard had turned white over the years. My mother's face was shrunken. My brother, Chaim, and my sister, Leah, were not there. They must have gotten married and moved away.

"From my boyhood I remembered a song which the disguised Haman used to sing and I began to chant the words:

> *I am wicked Haman, the hero great,*
> *And Zeresh is my spiteful mate,*
> *On the king's horse ride I will,*
> *And all the Jews shall I kill.*

"I tried to continue, but a lump stuck in my throat and I could not utter another word. I heard my mother say, 'Here is Haman. Why didn't you bring Zeresh the shrew with you?' I made an effort to sing with a hoarse voice, and my father remarked, 'A great voice he has not, but he will get his two groschen anyhow.'

" 'Do you know what, Haman,' my mother said, 'take off your mask, sit down at the table, and eat the Purim repast with us.'

"I glanced at the table. Two thick candles were lit in silver candlesticks as in my young days. Everything looked familiar to me—the embroidered tablecloth, the carafe of wine. I had forgotten in cold Russia that oranges existed. But on the table there were some oranges, as well as mandelbread, a tray of sweet and sour fish, a double-braided challah, and a dish of poppy cakes. After some hesitation I took off my mask and sat down at the table. My mother looked at me and said, 'You must be from another town. Where do you come from?'

"I named a faraway city. 'What are you doing here in Vitebsk?' my father asked. 'Oh, I wander all over the world,' I answered. 'You still look like a young man. What is the purpose of becoming a wanderer at your age?' my father asked me. 'Don't ask him so many questions,' my mother said. 'Let him eat in peace. Go wash your hands.'

"I washed my hands with water from the copper pitcher of olden days, and my mother handed me a towel and a knife to cut the challah. The handle was made of mother-of-pearl and embossed with the words 'Holy Sabbath.' Then she brought me a plate of kreplach filled with mincemeat. I asked my parents if they had children and my mother began to talk about my brother, Chaim, and my sister, Leah. Both lived in other towns with their families. My parents didn't mention my name, but I could see my mother's upper lip trembling. Then she burst out crying, and my father reproached her, 'You are crying again? Today is a holiday.' 'I won't cry anymore,' my mother apologized. My father handed her his handkerchief and said to me, 'We had another son and he got lost like a stone in water.'

"In cheder I had studied the Book of Genesis and the story of Joseph and his brothers. I wanted to cry out to my parents, 'I am your son.' But I was afraid that the surprise would cause my frail mother to faint. My father also looked exhausted. Gradually he began to tell me what happened on that Hanukkah night when the Cossacks captured his son Yankele. I asked, 'What happened to his bride-to-be?' and my father said, 'For years she refused to marry, hoping that our Yankele would return. Finally her parents persuaded her to get engaged again. She was about to be married when she caught typhoid fever and died.'

" 'She died from yearning for our Yankele,' my mother interjected. 'The day the murderous Cossacks captured him she began to pine away. She died with Yankele's name on her lips.'

"My mother again burst out crying, and my father said, 'Enough. According to the law, we should praise God for our misfortunes as well as for our good fortunes.'

"That night I gradually revealed to my parents who I was. First I told my father, and then he prepared my mother for the good news. After all the sobbing and kissing and embraces were over, we began to speak about my future. I could not stay at home under my real name. The police would have found out about me and arrested me. We decided that I could stay and live in the house only as a relative from some distant place. My parents were to introduce me as a nephew—a widower without children who came to live in their house after the loss of his wife. In a sense it was true. I had always thought of Reizel as my wife. I knew even then that I could never marry another woman. I assumed the name of Leibele instead of Yankele.

"And so it was. When the matchmakers heard that I was without a wife, they became busy with marriage propositions. However, I told them all that I loved my wife too much to exchange her for another woman. My parents were old and weak and they needed my care. For almost six years I remained at home. After four years my father died. My mother lived another two years, and then she also died and was buried beside him. A few times my brother and sister came to visit. Of course they learned who I really was, but they kept it a secret. These were the happiest years of my adult life. Every night when I went to sleep in a bed at home instead of a bunk bed in the barracks and every day when I went to pray in the synagogue, I thanked God for being rescued from the hands of the tyrants.

"After my parents' deaths I had no reason to remain in Vitebsk. I was thinking of learning a trade and settling down somewhere, but it made no sense to stay in one place all by myself. I began to wander from town to town. Wherever I went I stopped at the poorhouse and helped the poor and the sick. All my possessions are in this sack. As I told you, I still carry the prayer book that the soldier gave me some sixty-odd years ago, as well as my parents' Hanukkah lamp. Sometimes when I am on the road and feel especially downhearted, I hide in a forest and light Hanukkah candles, even though it is not Hanukkah.

"At night, the moment I close my eyes, Reizel is with me. She is young and she wears the white silk bridal gown her parents had prepared for her trousseau. She pours oil into a magnificent Hanukkah lamp and I light the candles with a long torch. Sometimes the whole sky turns into an otherworldly Hanukkah lamp, with the stars as its lights. I told my dreams to a rabbi and he said, 'Love comes from the soul and souls radiate light.' I know that when my times comes, Reizel's soul will wait for me in heaven. Well, it's time to go to sleep. Good night, a happy Hanukkah."

Shrewd Todie
& Lyzer the Miser

In a village somewhere in the Ukraine there lived a poor man called Todie. Todie had a wife, Sheindel, and seven children, but he could never earn enough to feed them properly. He tried many trades, failing in all of them. It was said of Todie that if he decided to deal in candles the sun would never set. He was nicknamed Shrewd Todie because whenever he managed to make some money, it was always by trickery.

This winter was an especially cold one. The snowfall was heavy and Todie had no money to buy wood for the stove. His seven children stayed in bed all day to keep warm. When the frost burns outside, hunger is stronger than ever, but Sheindel's larder was empty. She reproached Todie bitterly, wailing, "If you can't feed your wife and children, I will go to the rabbi and get a divorce."

"And what will you do with it, eat it?" Todie retorted.

In the same village there lived a rich man called Lyzer.

Because of his stinginess he was known as Lyzer the miser. He permitted his wife to bake bread only once in four weeks because he had discovered that fresh bread is eaten up more quickly than stale.

Todie had more than once gone to Lyzer for a loan of a few gulden, but Lyzer had always replied, "I sleep better when the money lies in my strongbox rather than in your pocket."

Lyzer had a goat, but he never fed her. The goat had learned to visit the houses of the neighbors, who pitied her and gave her potato peelings. Sometimes, when there were not enough peelings, she would gnaw on the old straw of the thatched roofs. She also had a liking for tree bark. Nevertheless, each year the goat gave birth to a kid. Lyzer milked her but, miser that he was, did not drink the milk himself. Instead, he sold it to others.

Todie decided that he would take revenge on Lyzer and at the same time make some much-needed money for himself.

One day, as Lyzer was sitting on a box eating borscht and dry bread (he used his chairs only on holidays so that the upholstery would not wear out), the door opened and Todie came in.

"Reb Lyzer," he said, "I would like to ask you a favor. My oldest daughter, Basha, is already fifteen and she's about to become engaged. A young man is coming from Janev to look her over. My cutlery is tin, and my wife is ashamed to ask the young man to eat soup with a tin spoon. Would you lend me one of your silver spoons? I give you my holy word that I will return it to you to-morrow."

Lyzer knew that Todie would not dare to break a holy oath and he lent him the spoon.

No young man came to see Basha that evening. As usual, the girl walked around barefoot and in rags, and the silver spoon lay hidden under Todie's shirt. In the early years of his marriage Todie had possessed a set of silver tableware himself. He had, however, long since sold it all, with the exception of three silver teaspoons that were used only on Passover.

The following day, as Lyzer, his feet bare (in order to save his shoes), sat on his box eating borscht and dry bread, Todie returned.

"Here is the spoon I borrowed yesterday," he said, placing it on the table together with one of his own teaspoons.

"What is the teaspoon for?" Lyzer asked.

And Todie said, "Your tablespoon gave birth to a teaspoon. It is her child. Since I am an honest man, I'm returning both mother and child to you."

Lyzer looked at Todie in astonishment. He had never heard of a silver spoon giving birth to another. Nevertheless, his greed overcame his doubt and he happily accepted both spoons. Such an unexpected piece of good fortune! He was overjoyed that he had loaned Todie the spoon.

A few days later, as Lyzer (without his coat, to save it) was again sitting on his box eating borscht with dry bread, the door opened and Todie appeared.

"The young man from Janev did not please Basha, because he had donkey ears, but this evening another young man is coming to look her over. Sheindel is cook-

ing soup for him, but she's ashamed to serve him with a
tin spoon. Would you lend me . . ."

Even before Todie could finish the sentence, Lyzer
interrupted. "You want to borrow a silver spoon? Take it
with pleasure."

The following day Todie once more returned the spoon
and with it one of his own silver teaspoons. He again
explained that during the night the large spoon had given
birth to a small one and in all good conscience he was
bringing back the mother and the newborn baby. As for
the young man who had come to look Basha over, she
hadn't liked him either, because his nose was so long that
it reached to his chin. Needless to say that Lyzer the
miser was overjoyed.

Exactly the same thing happened a third time. Todie
related that this time his daughter had rejected her suitor
because he stammered. He also reported that Lyzer's silver spoon had again given birth to a baby spoon.

"Does it ever happen that a spoon has twins?" Lyzer
inquired.

Todie thought it over for a moment. "Why not? I've
even heard of a case where a spoon had triplets."

Almost a week passed by and Todie did not go to see
Lyzer. But on Friday morning, as Lyzer (in his under-
drawers, to save his pants) sat on his box eating borscht
and dry bread, Todie came in and said, "Good day to
you, Reb Lyzer."

"A good morning and many more to you," Lyzer replied in his friendliest manner. "What good fortune
brings you here? Did you perhaps come to borrow a silver spoon? If so, help yourself."

"Today I have a very special favor to ask. This evening

a young man from the big city of Lublin is coming to look Basha over. He is the son of a rich man, and I'm told he is clever and handsome as well. Not only do I need a silver spoon, but since he will remain with us over the Sabbath, I need a pair of silver candlesticks, because mine are brass and my wife is ashamed to place them on the Sabbath table. Would you lend me your candlesticks? Immediately after the Sabbath, I will return them to you."

Silver candlesticks are of great value and Lyzer the miser hesitated, but only for a moment.

Remembering his good fortune with the spoons, he said, "I have eight silver candlesticks in my house. Take them all. I know you will return them to me just as you say. And if it should happen that any of them give birth, I have no doubt that you will be as honest as you have been in the past."

"Certainly," Todie said. "Let's hope for the best."

The silver spoon, Todie hid beneath his shirt as usual. But taking the candlesticks, he went directly to a merchant, sold them for a considerable sum, and brought the money to Sheindel. When Sheindel saw so much money, she demanded to know where he had gotten such a treasure.

"When I went out, a cow flew over our roof and dropped a dozen silver eggs," Todie replied. "I sold them and here is the money."

"I have never heard of a cow flying over a roof and laying silver eggs," Sheindel said doubtingly.

"There is always a first time," Todie answered. "If you don't want the money, give it back to me."

"There'll be no talk about giving it back," Sheindel

said. She knew that her husband was full of cunning and tricks—but when the children are hungry and the larder is empty, it is better not to ask too many questions. Sheindel went to the marketplace and bought meat, fish, white flour, and even some nuts and raisins for a pudding. And since a lot of money still remained, she bought shoes and clothes for the children.

It was a very gay Sabbath in Todie's house. The boys sang and the girls danced. When the children asked their father where he had gotten the money, he replied, "It is forbidden to mention money during the Sabbath."

Sunday, as Lyzer (barefoot and almost naked, to save his clothes) sat on his box finishing up a dry crust of bread with borscht, Todie arrived and, handing him his silver spoon, said, "It's too bad. This time your spoon did not give birth to a baby."

"What about the candlesticks?" Lyzer inquired anxiously.

Todie sighed deeply. "The candlesticks died."

Lyzer got up from his box so hastily that he overturned his plate of borscht.

"You fool! How can candlesticks die?" he screamed.

"If spoons can give birth, candlesticks can die."

Lyzer raised a great hue and cry and had Todie called before the rabbi. When the rabbi heard both sides of the story, he burst out laughing. "It serves you right," he said to Lyzer. "If you hadn't chosen to believe that spoons give birth, now you would not be forced to believe that your candlesticks died."

"But it's all nonsense," Lyzer objected.

"Did you not expect the candlesticks to give birth to

other candlesticks?" the rabbi said admonishingly. "If you accept nonsense when it brings you profit, you must also accept nonsense when it brings you loss." And he dismissed the case.

The following day, when Lyzer the miser's wife brought him his borscht and dry bread, Lyzer said to her, "I will eat only the bread. Borscht is too expensive a food, even without sour cream."

The story of the silver spoons that gave birth and the candlesticks that died spread quickly through the town. All the people enjoyed Todie's victory and Lyzer the miser's defeat. The shoemaker's and tailor's apprentices, as was their custom whenever there was an important happening, made up a song about it:

> *Lyzer, put your grief aside.*
> *What if your candlesticks have died?*
> *You're the richest man on earth*
> *with silver spoons that can give birth*
> *and silver eggs as living proof*
> *of flying cows above your roof.*
> *Don't sit there eating crusts of bread—*
> *To silver grandsons look ahead.*

However, time passed and Lyzer's silver spoons never gave birth again.

Translated by the author and Elizabeth Shub

The Fearsome Inn

It was as if the snow treasures of heaven had been opened. The snow fell day and night, sometimes straight down and sometimes slanting. Now and then it swirled in the air like a dog chasing its tail. All the roads were covered. The branches of the trees, glazed with ice, resembled the arms of crystal candelabra. In the middle of a field stood what was left of a scarecrow. It shook in the wind, flapping its rags and laughing madly.

On a hill overgrown with thistles, by a windmill with a broken vane and a smithy whose forge had long been cold, stood the inn that belonged to Doboshova the witch. She was the widow of Dobosh, the famous highwayman. For forty years Dobosh had preyed on the roads of Poland, robbing merchants on the way to Warsaw, Cracow, Danzig, Leipzig, and had amassed a huge fortune. When he was finally caught and hanged, Doboshova married Lapitut, her present husband, who was half man, half devil. They settled in the inn and kept themselves busy plying their witchcraft on travelers who stumbled their way.

Doboshova held captive three girls who were her servants. One was called Reitze, one Leitze, and the third Neitze. Reitze had black hair and black eyes; Leitze, blond hair and blue eyes; and Neitze, red hair and green eyes. The girls slaved all day long. At night they slept in the hayloft with the rats and field mice. Many times they tried to escape, but Doboshova and Lapitut had cast a spell on the road so that it led nowhere. Each time a girl tried to run away, she wandered around in circles and returned to the inn completely exhausted. When this happened, Doboshova soaked a reed whip in slops to make it supple. Lapitut gave the girl thirty-nine lashes.

In the summertime wayfarers seldom came to the inn. But in the winter, when blizzards wiped out the roads, travelers often lost their way, and victims were plentiful. This particular morning three young men had strayed to the inn. One was called Herschel. He was on his way on foot to the yeshiva of Lublin and had taken a wrong turn in the storm. The second, Velvel, had been traveling by sleigh to the city of Lemberg to buy merchandise for his father's store. He had fallen asleep and had slipped off the sleigh. The howling wind had prevented the coachmen from hearing him call. Velvel wandered about looking for shelter and finally found himself at Doboshova's inn. The third, Leibel, was returning home from a faraway city where he had been studying the cabala, the ancient Hebrew books that reveal the mysteries of heaven and earth. As a parting gift, his master had given him a piece of chalk, saying, "If you draw a line around man or beast with this piece of chalk, it will imprison them in a circle. Not only will they be unable to escape, but no one will be able to get into the magic ring." But the chalk was of no help in a snowstorm, and Leibel, too, arrived at the inn.

When Doboshova and Lapitut saw the three young guests, they were overjoyed. Doboshova looked like any other innkeeper. But like all witches she had an elflock, which she kept well hidden under a cap. Lapitut had a stumpy horn on his forehead. However, he carefully combed his matted hair down to cover it. The three young men were wet through and frozen. Doboshova led them to the stove so their clothes could dry out and gave orders to the girls to prepare the oven for baking.

"You must be hungry," she said to the young men. "Be kind enough to wait just a bit. I always serve my guests hot rolls fresh from the oven." To Lapitut she said, "Go to the well and fetch water for the barrel so that our visitors can wash their hands and make the benediction before their meal."

The three girls, Reitze, Leitze, and Neitze, knew what was in store for the young men, but they dared not give even a word of warning. First of all, if Lapitut was to catch them, he would whip them to death. Secondly, they knew only too well that all roads led back to the inn.

Everybody went to work at once. Reitze added wood to the oven. Leitze put flour in a bowl and mixed some dough. Neitze kneaded it and shaped it into rolls. Doboshova herself sprinkled the rolls with something that resembled caraway seed. Actually, it was an herb, the very smell of which, when baked, gave nightmares to those Doboshova wanted to ensnare. When the rolls were baked and about to be removed from the oven, Doboshova said to the young men, "You'll find three dippers and three towels by the barrel. Go and wash your hands. The moment you are ready, the rolls will be taken out, and they will be hot and crisp. You can smell them now."

"You are a good housekeeper," Herschel said.

"I wish I could find a wife like you," added Velvel.

"It brings good luck to treat wayfarers well," stated Leibel, the cabala student.

Each took hold of a dipper and bent over the barrel. In that very instant the spicy smell of the herb-covered rolls took effect. All three young men suddenly felt dizzy and began to dream.

Herschel dreamed that he was a slave in a strange land. He had become a trainer of wild beasts. His master, a prince, had ordered him to teach a huge lion, called Arieh, the most dangerous of tricks. Herschel was to make the lion keep its jaws open while he placed his head in the beast's mouth. Then the animal was to close its jaw just enough so as not to harm Herschel and release him on command. At last the trick was learned, and the day came when Herschel was to perform for the first time before the prince and his court. Herschel was in the lion's cage making one last test before the performance. He placed his head in the lion's mouth, patted him on the neck, and after a minute called, "Arieh, enough!" But Arieh did not loosen his jaws. Herschel patted him again and coaxed, "Arieh, enough! Open your mouth!"

But the lion did not move. Instead, he began to roar so terrifyingly that Herschel felt his blood freezing in his veins. The roaring continued, louder and louder, until Herschel could hardly breathe. "God save me," he prayed.

This was Herschel's nightmare.

Velvel also dreamed he was in a strange land. He knew no one. He looked for work but couldn't find any. Finally, he had to beg to eat. One late afternoon he found himself on a street with many buildings. He walked through a gate into a courtyard. He turned to leave, but it had become dark, and he couldn't find his way. He called out, but no one heard him. Groping along a wall, he found an opening. He entered it, hoping it would bring him back to the street. Instead, a stairway led him downward. It got darker and darker. Suddenly he came to a large room. In the glow of the single oil lamp he saw bricks of solid gold, barrels filled with coins. He had stumbled into the vault of the king's mint.

Velvel knew that if he was discovered he would be taken for a thief. He searched the room for the opening through which he had come. He soon found it, but at that moment two workmen appeared and began to close it up with bricks. He crouched in a corner so they would not see him, yet he knew that he had to get out before their work was finished or he would remain without bread and water, perhaps even without air to breathe.

Did he dare ask the workmen to let him out? They would believe that he was there to steal the gold. They would summon the guards. He would be put in chains and thrown into a dungeon. They might torture him.

517

Finally, he decided that it would be better to appeal to the mercy of the workmen than to be buried alive with the king's treasure. Just as he stepped from his corner, the last brick moved into place and the lamp flickered out. "Wait!" he shouted with all his might, but it was too late.

This was Velvel's nightmare.

Leibel dreamed that he was in a desert. He was hungry and thirsty. After long searching, all he found was a dried-out stream, in the middle of which lay snakes, crocodiles, and lizards. They looked as hungry and parched as he. Their mouths were wide open, showing their pointed teeth. The trunk of a tree lay across the bed of the stream. On the other side, Leibel saw a grove of date palms surrounding what looked like a shimmering pool. Leibel realized that one false step could land him among the monsters. But his thirst was so great that he was prepared to take the risk. He stepped onto the tree trunk and spread out his arms to help him keep his balance as he made his way across.

He had reached the middle of the stream when he saw coming toward him a woman whom he recognized immediately as a witch. Her head was covered with elf-locks, and she had the webbed feet of a goose. Even though she did not resemble her, somehow she reminded him of Doboshova.

Leibel stopped in his tracks. To fall into the hands of such a creature was even worse than being devoured by crocodiles. He turned carefully back to retrace his steps, only to see a male devil coming toward him. A short horn, which spun like a top, protruded from his forehead.

Even though he did not resemble him, somehow he reminded Leibel of Lapitut.

"O Holy Powers, what shall I do now?" cried Leibel in terror.

This was Leibel's nightmare.

At the same moment, all three—Herschel, Velvel, and Leibel—awoke. Their nightmares, which had seemed so long, in reality had lasted only a few seconds. All three still stood bent over the barrel as they heard Doboshova saying, "Well, why don't you wash your hands, my dear lads? The girls are taking the rolls out of the oven."

Dazed, all three washed their hands and wiped them. At last they were seated at the table. Herschel and Velvel were about to recite the benediction for bread and begin eating. Had they done this, they would have been lost, because in addition to the diabolic seeds, Doboshova had put a potion into the dough that deprived human beings of all will. But all at once Leibel cried out, "Wait!"

"What's the matter?" asked Herschel.

"Why?" added Velvel.

"Eat, young men," Doboshova urged in a wheedling tone.

"What is this?" Lapitut grumbled.

"While getting the water, I lost my ring in the barrel," Leibel explained quickly. "It was a family heirloom that goes all the way back to King Solomon. It was given to him by the Queen of Sheba. It can show the way to buried riches, locate sunken ships and caravans covered by the sands of the desert. It can also heal the sick and make the old young. I beg of you, help me find my ring."

Despite the many treasures that they already had, the greed of Doboshova and Lapitut could not be satisfied.

Even more important, they had a great desire to be young again. When they heard what the ring could do, they both ran to the barrel and stuck their hands into the water to search for it.

Leibel jumped up, rushed over to Doboshova and Lapitut, and quickly drew a circle around them with his chalk.

When the two could find no ring in the barrel, they straightened up, ready to return to the table, but they could not step beyond the magic line surrounding them.

"What's going on here?" growled Lapitut.

"What's this circle?" screamed Doboshova.

Reitze, Leitze, and Neitze stood openmouthed.

Herschel and Velvel sat without saying a word, as if they had lost their tongues in astonishment.

This is what had happened.

Just as Leibel was about to say the benediction, he had glanced at Doboshova, and it had suddenly struck him that she resembled the witch he had seen in his nightmare. He cast a quick look at Lapitut and recognized the devil in his dream. Leibel, who had studied the cabala and knew something about the tricks of the evil host, realized that there was something wrong here and that he must act immediately. He made up the story about the ring to prevent the other boys from eating.

Held within the magic boundary, Doboshova and Lapitut were captives for the first time in their lives. As soon as Leitze, Reitze, and Neitze were convinced that Doboshova and Lapitut had lost their power, they told the young men about all they had suffered under the wicked couple's spell.

All three had parents, sisters, and brothers who had

surely searched for them, but since the road to the inn was bewitched, their relatives had been unable to find them.

As the girls related how they had been tricked away from their homes, Doboshova shouted and waved her fists. She threatened to turn them all into hedgehogs, rats, and skunks. Lapitut shouted that he would whip them to death. But Leibel assured the girls that they no longer had anything to fear. To prevent any devils from coming to the aid of their kin, Leibel made a chalk line along the inside of the entire house and around all the doors and windows. He also circled the oven and the fireplace to make sure that no evil spirit could get in through the chimney.

It soon became clear that all these precautions were needed. No sooner did Doboshova and Lapitut discover they were trapped than they began to call on the dark forces of the forest to come to their rescue. In no time demons, devils, imps, sprites, and other impure spirits began to arrive. Some appeared as snakes with wings, others as huge bats, and still others looked like rams, weasels, and toads. Had Leibel not protected the house with his magic chalk, they would have swarmed in. Instead, they hovered around the windows screeching and threatening those inside.

"There's no reason to fear them," Leibel again reassured the young people. "They can do us no harm. It's time to prepare some food so that we can eat."

Reitze, Leitze, and Neitze set about making fresh dough without potions and magic caraway seeds. They baked rolls, pretzels, and cookies and made a delicious meal. Reitze was the best baker, Leitze excelled in roasting, and Neitze could fry the crispest food. The good smells filled the house. Doboshova and Lapitut became exceedingly hungry and begged for food. But Leibel said, "We won't give you a bite unless you sign a pledge in your blood that you will leave the inn and return to the Lower Regions."

This Doboshova and Lapitut refused to do. Devils and witches can easily break a promise, but once they have signed in blood, they must keep their word or lose their powers forever.

When the evil pair realized that they were getting nowhere with threats, they tried flattery. They called Leibel a master of the cabala. They complimented Herschel and Velvel, and even had something nice to say about the girls. They promised all kinds of gifts. Reitze, Leitze, and Neitze were to get beautiful dresses, precious jewelry, and silk underclothing embroidered in gold. Lapitut swore he would teach the young men never-heard-of magic tricks.

"We want neither your gifts nor your teachings," Leibel replied.

For hours Doboshova and Lapitut alternated between curses and coaxing. The devils outside continued their racket, pressing against the windows. Inside, the young people knew that they were safe, protected by the magic chalk.

The winter day passed quickly. Night brought new terrors and temptations. The evil ones laughed and cried, imitated the sounds of trumpets and horns, bleated and hopped about, blasphemed and boasted of their ungodly powers. Some of the creatures of darkness decided to tempt the young people by disguising themselves as beautiful girls, handsome noblemen. The night suddenly became day. The snow outside turned into a sunlit, flower-filled meadow, through which a blue stream flowed. A devil called Topiel, who specialized in luring humans into the water so that they would drown, sang one of his most entrancing melodies to get the young people out of the house. But Leibel would not let any of them succumb, explaining that it was all a delusion.

When the black band saw that no one was coming out, they brought back the night. Three black cats with eyes like green fire appeared in a window. Their meowing was like the ringing of bells. After a while the cats, too, vanished. Instead, a whirling wind shook the roof and whistled in the chimney. There was a howling of wolves and a growling of bears. The outdoors turned fiery red as if reflecting a great conflagration. It began to thunder and lightning, and the inn swayed as in an earthquake. The young people could not help being afraid, but they trusted Leibel and ate their supper while the demons raged.

"No matter how strong the Devil is," Leibel said, "God is stronger."

Immediately after supper, the three girls undressed and went to sleep in the same large bed so that they would be less frightened. They put blindfolds on their eyes and cotton in their ears so as not to see the terrifying sights and not to hear the mocking voices of the fiends. Herschel and Velvel made themselves a bed on the top of the large brick oven. They were so exhausted that they soon fell into a deep sleep. Leibel stayed awake to keep watch. He knew that Doboshova and Lapitut could not hold out much longer. He had a parchment scroll and a sharp quill pen in readiness. One by one the monsters outside tired and departed, each for his own lair. Doboshova and Lapitut were left alone.

Leibel overheard Doboshova whispering to Lapitut: "We can't escape. We'll have to sign."

"I wish I'd never known you," Lapitut snarled in reply.

"If you won't sign now," Leibel called out, "I will go to bed, and you'll have to stand on your feet until morning."

"Oh, I cannot stand another minute," Doboshova moaned.

"I'm dying of hunger," Lapitut wailed. "I can't do without a smoke of mandrake root. If only you'd hand me my pipe."

"Sign the oath, and you will have all you need."

The pair had no choice. They each pricked a wrist with the point of the quill and signed their oath in blood.

I, the witch Doboshova, and I, the devil Lapitut, swear by Satan, Lilith, and by all the impure powers to leave this inn, never to return, neither we nor our children, grandchildren, and great-grandchildren to the tenth generation. We leave all our possessions to our guests Herschel, Velvel, and Leibel, and to our onetime servants, Reitze, Leitze, and Neitze. Furthermore, the treasure of the late highwayman Dobosh, hidden in the hollow of the old oak in the yard, is from now on also to belong to the aforementioned parties. Furthermore, we remove all spells,

---

charms, witchcraft, evil signs, and curses from the inn and its surroundings, and command that everything return to the state it was in before we came. Signed: *Lapitut, the son of Briri, the son of Shabriri, the son of Karteigus, and so on back to my ancestor Satan. Doboshova, the daughter of Naamah, the daughter of Igrath, the daughter of Machlath, and so on back to my grandmother Lilith the First.*

The haggling had continued for so long that the sky was beginning to gray with the light of dawn. The young people had awakened. They watched as Leibel erased a small section of the circle around Doboshova and Lapitut and another bit under a window. Then, opening the window, he called in Aramaic, "*Pik*, out."

Doboshova and Lapitut turned into shadows and vanished. Off they went to the desert of deserts, to the wastes of the netherworld, behind the Mountains of Darkness, where there is neither day nor night and dusk is eternal.

The girls were so happy they began to cry for joy.

"Why cry?" Leibel said. "Your troubles are over. The road is open and each of us can return home."

But neither the boys nor the girls made a move to go. The truth is that the inn, which only a few minutes before had looked so gloomy, was now cozy and pleasant. The snow shimmered in the sunlight. Ice spears hung from the roof, reflecting the colors of the rainbow. From the nearby woods came the sound of winter birds chirping and trilling. The smell of pine filled the air.

After breakfast, Leibel led the young people outside

to a huge oak tree that was hundreds of years old. There was a great hollow in its trunk. At the back of the hollow they discovered chests full of gold and precious stones. The jewels lit up the darkness. When the girls saw the treasure, they began to scream with delight. But even with so many riches to take home, not one of them thought of leaving.

The reason was that the greatest magic of all had begun to do its work among them.

Of course, all three girls were filled with admiration and love for Leibel. Had he not driven away Doboshova and Lapitut and the other devils? However, they all knew that Leibel could marry only one of them, and Herschel and Velvel, too, were charming fellows. But who should marry whom?

Again they decided to trust to Leibel's wisdom. And Leibel said, "Let each of us write down on a slip of paper the name of the one we love best and the one we love next best. Then we will study our choices, and we will know what to do."

It turned out that each girl's first choice remained Leibel, but when it came to second choice, Reitze chose Herschel and Leitze chose Velvel, but Neitze's second choice was the same as her first. It so happened that Herschel's first choice was Reitze and Velvel's Leitze. As for Leibel, he, too, had made only one choice: Neitze. When the slips were read out, it was quite clear who should marry whom.

At first the girls thought the weddings should be postponed so that they could invite their parents and friends. But all three boys were eager to get married, and Leibel said, "We can arrange the wedding ceremonies right now and later make a big celebration and invite everyone."

Since they had Dobosh's treasure, there was no lack of wedding rings. The girls found a large embroidered shawl that with the aid of four sticks made a perfect bridal canopy. As there were six young people, four of them could hold up the canopy while a pair stood beneath it for the ceremony. The first pair was Herschel and Reitze. They were the oldest. Herschel, the bridegroom, placed the wedding band on Reitze's finger and recited, "With this ring thou art consecrated to me according to the law of Moses and Israel." Bride and bridegroom both sipped wine from the same goblet and the rest called out, "*Mazel tov.*" Then in turn the other two couples stood beneath the canopy. And so they were married, according to the strictest law of the Talmud.

The brides had found beautiful dresses in Doboshova's cupboards, and even though the clothes were long out of fashion, they looked splendid in them. Reitze and Leitze were a little envious of Neitze, because she had been chosen by Leibel, but they wished her luck with all their hearts just the same. And although Leibel had studied the cabala and was generally better educated than the others, Herschel and Velvel were both taller and better-looking. Besides, Herschel, the yeshiva student, was a scholar in his own way. As for Velvel, he was an excellent businessman and clever in practical matters. None of the girls had made a bad bargain.

For the time being, all the couples remained at the inn. They sent word to their relatives and friends to tell them they were safe and to invite them to a great wedding celebration. Because some of the guests had to come from distant places, the celebration was postponed until spring.

Now that the inn was no longer spellbound, its entire surroundings had changed. Doboshova and Lapitut had thrown a curse on all the land for miles around. Suddenly streams, hills, and valleys appeared where there had been nothing but flat wasteland. Rabbits, deer, wild ducks, geese, pheasants, and other animals abounded where before there had been no living creatures. Winter passed. Spring came. The sky was blue and clear. The earth was richly covered with grass, flowers, and shrubbery. Trees that had seemed dead bore leaves and blossoms.

Word had spread about the inn that, like a mirage, had for years appeared only to those unlucky enough to go astray.

On the thirty-third day after the first day of Passover, the celebration took place. In addition to the guests. people came from all over the country to admire the changed inn and the three happy couples. Wedding jesters and musicians arrived from nearby towns to take part in the festivities. Magicians outdid each other to entertain the crowd with their tricks. After many entreaties, Leibel agreed to show his guests how the magic chalk that had saved the young people worked. He fetched the liveliest rooster from the barn, stood him on a table, and drew a circle around him. No matter how strongly the rooster flapped his wings, he could not fly off the table until Leibel wiped away the chalk to free him. Everybody was amazed.

They sang, danced, and made merry for seven days and seven nights. The moon was full and threw a silver light over the entire landscape. Even though there was not room enough in the inn for so many people and many of the guests slept outdoors, no evil intruder dared to disturb or frighten anyone.

After the last guest had left, it was time for Herschel and Velvel to go home with their wives, as had been decided. Leibel and Neitze had made up their minds to remain in the inn. "Because," Leibel said, "people often go astray, especially in the winter, and there should be someone to give them food and shelter." Leibel and Neitze were determined never to take any money from their guests, since Dobosh's treasure had made them rich.

The couples said goodbye to each other, and Leibel returned to his studies of the holy cabala, the wisdom of which can never be learned in full.

As the years went by, Herschel completed his education and became the head of a yeshiva. He used his money to help poor students.

Velvel became a great merchant and was renowned as a man of charity. All three couples lived happily and had many children and grandchildren. It became a custom each year for the couples and their children to gather at the inn and celebrate the day they had been set free.

Since Leibel's ring with the power to make the old young had never existed, Doboshova and Lapitut lived their allotted years and died. However, other devils have taken their place. These still live somewhere far in the desert, in the underground city of Asmodeus, their king. It is said that Asmodeus has a beard that reaches to the ground and two huge horns on his head. He sits on a throne held up by four snakes instead of legs. He has many wives, but his favorite is still Lilith, who dances for him each night to the caterwauling of a devil's band.

In time the once fearsome inn became known as the greatest academy of the cabala. It is believed that the ancient cabalists could, with the power of holy words, create pigeons, sap wine from a wall, and take seven-league steps.

In his old age Leibel was no longer called merely Leibel, but the saintly Reb Leib. His beard became white as silver. He could cure the sick with a touch, know what was happening in faraway cities, and foresee the future. Neitze, even though she was busy with her grandchildren—most of whom had red hair and green eyes—helped her husband and copied his writings with a quill pen.

The inn was a haven for all travelers who lost their way. It was said that no candles or oil lamps were needed there at night, because angels, seraphim, and cherubs descended at dark and lit the inn with heavenly light.

Translated by the author and Elizabeth Shub

The Cat Who Thought She Was a Dog & the Dog Who Thought He Was a Cat

Once there was a poor peasant, Jan Skiba by name. He lived with his wife and three daughters in a one-room hut with a straw roof, far from the village. The house had a bed, a bench bed, and a stove, but no mirror. A mirror was a luxury for a poor peasant. And why would a peasant need a mirror? Peasants aren't curious about their appearance.

But this peasant did have a dog and a cat in his hut. The dog was named Burek and the cat Kot. They had both been born within the same week. As little food as the peasant had for himself and his family, he still wouldn't let his dog and cat go hungry. Since the dog had never seen another dog and the cat had never seen another cat and they saw only each other, the dog thought he was a cat and the cat thought she was a dog. True, they were far from being alike by nature. The dog barked and the cat meowed. The dog chased rabbits and the cat lurked after mice. But must all creatures be exactly like their own kind? The peasant's children weren't exactly alike either. Burek and Kot lived on good terms, often ate from the same dish, and tried to mimic each other. When Burek barked, Kot tried to bark along, and when Kot meowed, Burek tried to meow, too. Kot occasionally chased rabbits and Burek made an effort to catch a mouse.

The peddlers who bought groats, chickens, eggs, honey, calves, and whatever was available from the peasants in the village never came to Jan Skiba's poor hut. They knew that Jan was so poor he had nothing to sell. But one day a peddler happened to stray there. When he came inside and began to lay out his wares, Jan Skiba's wife and daughters were bedazzled by all the pretty doodads. From his sack the peddler drew yellow beads, false pearls, tin earrings, rings, brooches, colored kerchiefs, garters, and other such trinkets. But what enthralled the women of the house most was a mirror set in a wooden frame. They asked the peddler its price and he said a half gulden, which was a lot of money for poor peasants. After a while, Jan Skiba's wife, Marianna, made a proposition to the peddler. She would pay him five groschen a month for the mirror. The peddler hesitated a moment. The mirror took up too much space in his sack and there was always the danger it might break. He therefore decided to go along, took the first payment of five groschen from Marianna, and left the mirror with the family. He visited the region often and he knew the Skibas to be honest people. He would gradually get his money back and a profit besides.

The mirror created a commotion in the hut. Until then Marianna and the children had seldom seen themselves. Before they had the mirror, they had only seen their reflections in the barrel of water that stood by the door. Now they could see themselves clearly and they began to find defects in their faces, defects they had never noticed before. Marianna was pretty but she had a tooth missing in front and she felt that this made her ugly. One daughter discovered that her nose was too snub and too broad; a second that her chin was too narrow and too long; a third that her face was sprinkled with freckles. Jan Skiba, too, caught a glimpse of himself in the mirror and grew displeased by his thick lips and his teeth, which protruded like a buck's. That day, the women of the house became so absorbed in the mirror they didn't cook supper, didn't make up the bed, and neglected all the other household tasks. Marianna had heard of a dentist in the big city who could replace a missing tooth, but such things were expensive. The girls tried to console each other that they were pretty enough and that they would find suitors, but they no longer felt as jolly as before. They had been afflicted with the vanity of city girls. The one with the broad nose kept trying to pinch it together with her fingers to make it narrower; the one with the too long chin pushed it up with her fist to make it shorter; the one with the freckles wondered if there was a salve in the city that could remove freckles. But where would the money come from for the fare to the city? And what about the money to buy this salve? For the first time the Skiba family deeply felt its poverty and envied the rich.

But the human members of the household were not the

only ones affected. The dog and the cat also grew disturbed by the mirror. The hut was low and the mirror had been hung just above a bench. The first time the cat sprang up on the bench and saw her image in the mirror, she became terribly perplexed. She had never before seen such a creature. Kot's whiskers bristled; she began to meow at her reflection and raised a paw to it, but the other creature meowed back and raised her paw, too. Soon the dog jumped up on the bench, and when he saw the other dog he became wild with rage and shock. He barked at the other dog and showed him his teeth, but the other barked back and bared his fangs, too. So great was the distress of Burek and Kot that for the first time in their lives they turned on each other. Burek took a bite out of Kot's throat and Kot hissed and spat at him and clawed his muzzle. They both started to bleed, and the sight of blood aroused them so that they nearly killed or crippled each other. The members of the household barely managed to separate them. Because a dog is stronger than a cat, Burek had to be tied outside, and he howled all day and all night. In their anguish, both the dog and the cat stopped eating.

When Jan Skiba saw the disruption the mirror had created in his household, he decided a mirror wasn't what his family needed. "Why look at yourself," he said, "when you can see and admire the sky, the sun, the moon, the stars, and the earth, with all its forests, meadows, rivers, and plants?" He took the mirror down from the wall and put it away in the woodshed. When the peddler came for his monthly installment, Jan Skiba gave him back the mirror and, in its stead, bought kerchiefs and slippers for the women. After the mirror disappeared, Burek and Kot returned to normal. Again Burek thought he was a cat and Kot was sure she was a dog. Despite all the defects the girls had found in themselves, they made good marriages. The village priest heard what had happened at Jan Skiba's house and he said, "A glass mirror shows only the skin of the body. The real image of a person is in his willingness to help himself and his family and, as far as possible, all those he comes in contact with. This kind of mirror reveals the very soul of the person."

Translated by Joseph Singer

Menaseh's Dream

Menaseh was an orphan. He lived with his Uncle
Mendel, who was a poor glazier and couldn't even manage to feed and clothe his own children. Menaseh had
already completed his cheder studies and after the fall
holidays was to be apprenticed to a bookbinder.

Menaseh had always been a curious child. He had
begun to ask questions as soon as he could talk: How
high is the sky? How deep is the earth? What is beyond
the edge of the world? Why are people born? Why do
they die?

It was a hot and humid summer day. A golden haze
hovered over the village. The sun was as small as a moon
and yellow as brass. Dogs loped along with their tails
between their legs. Pigeons rested in the middle of the
marketplace. Goats sheltered themselves beneath the
eaves of the huts, chewing their cuds and shaking their
beards.

Menaseh quarreled with his Aunt Dvosha and left the house without eating lunch. He was about twelve, with a longish face, black eyes, sunken cheeks. He wore a torn jacket and was barefoot. His only possession was a tattered storybook which he had read scores of times. It was called *Alone in the Wild Forest*. The village in which he lived stood in a forest that surrounded it like a sash and was said to stretch as far as Lublin. It was blueberry time, and here and there one might also find wild strawberries. Menaseh made his way through pastures and wheat fields. He was hungry and he tore off a stalk of wheat to chew on the grain. In the meadows, cows were lying down, too hot even to whisk off the flies with their tails. Two horses stood, the head of one near the rump of the other, lost in their horse thoughts. In a field planted in buckwheat the boy was amazed to see a crow perched on the torn hat of a scarecrow.

Once Menaseh entered the forest, it was cooler. The pine trees stood straight as pillars and on their brownish bark hung golden necklaces, the light of the sun shining through the pine needles. The sounds of cuckoo and woodpecker were heard, and an unseen bird kept repeating the same eerie screech.

Menaseh stepped carefully over moss pillows. He crossed a shallow streamlet that purled joyfully over pebbles and stones. The forest was still, and yet full of voices and echoes.

He wandered deeper and deeper into the forest. As a rule, he left stone markers behind, but not today. He was lonely, his head ached, and his knees felt weak. Am I getting sick, he thought. Maybe I'm going to die. Then I will soon be with Daddy and Mama. When he came to a blueberry patch, he sat down, picked one berry after another, and popped them into his mouth. But they did not satisfy his hunger. Flowers with intoxicating odors grew among the blueberries. Without realizing it, Menaseh stretched full length on the forest floor. He fell asleep, but in his dream he continued walking.

The trees became even taller, the smells stronger, huge birds flew from branch to branch. The sun was setting. The forest grew thinner, and he soon came out on a plain with a broad view of the evening sky. Suddenly a castle appeared in the twilight. Menaseh had never seen such a beautiful structure. Its roof was of silver and from it rose a crystal tower. Its many tall windows were as high as the building itself. Menaseh went up to one of the windows and looked in. On the wall opposite him, he saw his own portrait hanging. He was dressed in luxurious clothes such as he had never owned. The huge room was empty.

Why is the castle empty, he wondered. And why is my portrait hanging on the wall? The boy in the picture seemed to be alive and waiting impatiently for someone to come. Then doors opened where there had been none before, and men and women came into the room. They were dressed in white satin and the women wore jewels and held holiday prayer books with gold-embossed covers. Menaseh gazed in astonishment. He recognized his father, his mother, his grandfathers and grandmothers, and other relatives. He wanted to rush over to them, hug and kiss them, but the window glass stood in his way. He began to cry. His paternal grandfather, Tobias the scribe, separated himself from the group and came to the window. The old man's beard was as white as his long coat. He looked both ancient and young. "Why are you crying?" he asked. Despite the glass that separated them, Menaseh heard him clearly.

"Are you my Grandfather Tobias?"

"Yes, my child. I am your grandfather."

"Who does this castle belong to?"

"To all of us."

"To me, too?"

"Of course, to the whole family."

"Grandpa, let me in," Menaseh called. "I want to speak to my father and mother."

His grandfather looked at him lovingly and said, "One day you will live with us here, but the time has not yet come."

"How long do I have to wait?"

"That is a secret. It will not be for many, many years."

"Grandpa, I don't want to wait so long. I'm hungry and thirsty and tired. Please let me in. I miss my father and mother and you and Grandma. I don't want to be an orphan."

"My dear child. We know everything. We think about you and we love you. We are all waiting for the time when we will be together, but you must be patient. You have a long journey to take before you come here to stay."

"Please, just let me in for a few minutes."

Grandfather Tobias left the window and took counsel with other members of the family. When he returned, he said, "You may come in, but only for a little while. We will show you around the castle and let you see some of our treasures, but then you must leave."

A door opened and Menaseh stepped inside. He was no sooner over the threshold than his hunger and weariness left him. He embraced his parents, and they kissed and hugged him. But they didn't utter a word. He felt strangely light. He floated along and his family floated with him. His grandfather opened door after door and each time Menaseh's astonishment grew.

One room was filled with racks of boys' clothing—pants, jackets, shirts, coats. Menaseh realized that these were the clothes he had worn as far back as he could remember. He also recognized his shoes, socks, caps, and nightshirts.

A second door opened and he saw all the toys he had ever owned: the tin soldiers his father had bought him; the jumping clown his mother had brought back from the fair at Lublin; the whistles and harmonicas; the teddy bear Grandfather had given him one Purim; and the wooden horse that was the gift of Grandmother Sprintze on his sixth birthday. The notebooks in which he had practiced writing, his pencils and Bible lay on a table. The Bible was open at the title page, with its familiar engraving of Moses holding the holy tablets and Aaron in his priestly robes, both framed by a border of six-winged angels. He noticed his name in the space allowed for it.

Menaseh could hardly overcome his wonder when a third door opened. This room was filled with soap bubbles. They did not burst as soap bubbles do, but floated serenely about, reflecting all the colors of the rainbow. Some of them mirrored castles, gardens, rivers, windmills, and many other sights. Menaseh knew that these were the bubbles he used to blow from his favorite bubble pipe. Now they seemed to have a life of their own.

A fourth door opened. Menaseh entered a room with no one in it; yet it was full of the sounds of happy talk, song, and laughter. Menaseh heard his own voice and the songs he used to sing when he lived at home with his parents. He also heard the voices of his former playmates, some of whom he had long since forgotten.

The fifth door led to a large hall. It was filled with the characters in the stories his parents had told him at bedtime and with the heroes and heroines of *Alone in the Wild Forest*. They were all there: David the warrior and the Ethiopian princess whom David saved from captivity; the highwayman Bandurek, who robbed the rich and fed the poor; Velikan the giant, who had one eye in the center of his forehead and who carried a fir tree as a staff in his right hand and a snake in his left; the midget Pitzeles, whose beard dragged on the ground and who was jester to the fearsome King Merodach; and the two-headed wizard Malkizedek, who by witchcraft spirited innocent girls into the desert of Sodom and Gomorrah.

Menaseh barely had time to take them all in when a sixth door opened. Here everything was changing constantly. The walls of the room turned like a carousel. Events flashed by. A golden horse became a blue butterfly; a rose as bright as the sun became a goblet out of which flew fiery grasshoppers, purple fauns, and silver bats. On a glittering throne with seven steps leading up to it sat King Solomon, who somehow resembled Menaseh. He wore a crown and at his feet knelt the Queen of Sheba. A peacock spread his tail and addressed

King Solomon in Hebrew. The priestly Levites played their lyres. Giants waved their swords in the air and Ethiopian slaves riding lions served goblets of wine and trays filled with pomegranates. For a moment Menaseh did not understand what it all meant. Then he realized that he was seeing his dreams.

Behind the seventh door, Menaseh glimpsed men and women, animals, and many things that were completely strange to him. The images were not as vivid as they had been in the other rooms. The figures were transparent and surrounded by mist. On the threshold stood a girl Menaseh's own age. She had long golden braids. Although Menaseh could not see her clearly, he liked her at once. For the first time he turned to his grandfather. "What is all this?" he asked. And his grandfather replied, "These are the people and events of your future."

"Where am I?" Menaseh asked.

"You are in a castle that has many names. We like to call it the place where nothing is lost. There are many more wonders here, but now it is time for you to leave."

Menaseh wanted to remain in this strange place forever, together with his parents and grandparents. He looked questioningly at his grandfather, who shook his head. Menaseh's parents seemed to want him both to remain and to leave as quickly as possible. They still did not speak, but signaled to him, and Menaseh understood that he was in grave danger. This must be a forbidden place. His parents silently bade him farewell and his face became wet and hot from their kisses. At that moment everything disappeared—the castle, his parents, his grandparents, the girl.

Menaseh shivered and awoke. It was night in the forest. Dew was falling. High above the crowns of the pine trees the full moon shone and the stars twinkled. Menaseh looked into the face of a girl who was bending over him. She was barefoot and wore a patched skirt; her long, braided hair shone golden in the moonlight. She was shaking him and saying, "Get up, get up. It is late and you can't remain here in the forest."

Menaseh sat up. "Who are you?"

"I was looking for berries and I found you here. I've been trying to wake you."

"What is your name?"

"Channeleh. We moved into the village last week."

She looked familiar, but he could not remember meeting her before. Suddenly he knew. She was the girl he had seen in the seventh room, before he woke up.

"You lay there like dead. I was frightened when I saw you. Were you dreaming? Your face was so pale and your lips were moving."

"Yes, I did have a dream."

"What about?"

"A castle."

"What kind of castle?"

Menaseh did not reply and the girl did not repeat her question. She stretched out her hand to him and helped him get up. Together they started toward home. The moon had never seemed so light or the stars so close. They walked with their shadows behind them. Myriads of crickets chirped. Frogs croaked with human voices.

Menaseh knew that his uncle would be angry at him for coming home late. His aunt would scold him for leaving without his lunch. But these things no longer mattered. In his dream he had visited a mysterious world. He had found a friend. Channeleh and he had already decided to go berry picking the next day.

Among the undergrowth and wild mushrooms, little people in red jackets, gold caps, and green boots emerged. They danced in a circle and sang a song which is heard only by those who know that everything lives and nothing in time is ever lost.

Translated by the author and Elizabeth Shub

Tashlik

Aaron the watchmaker did not live on our street, but when I climbed to the highest branch of the lime tree that grew in our garden, I could see his house clearly; it was the only one in the village that had a small lawn in front of it. The shutters of Aaron's house were painted green; flowerpots stood in the windows; there were sunflowers in the garden. Aaron and his family lived on the ground floor, that is, with the exception of his daughter, Feigele; she had a room in the attic. At night a lamp burned in Feigele's window long after the lights downstairs had been extinguished. Occasionally I caught a glimpse of her shadow passing across the curtain. Mottel, Feigele's younger brother, had built a dovecote on the roof and often stood on the top of the building chasing pigeons with a long stick. Leon, the older boy, who was studying at a polytechnic in Cracow, rode around the village on a horse when he came home on vacation. There was nothing that that emancipated family did not possess: they had a parrot, canaries, a dog. Aaron played the zither; his wife owned a piano—she came from Lublin and didn't wear a wig. Aaron the watchmaker, who was also both goldsmith and jeweler, was the only man in the village with a telephone in his house; he could speak directly to Zamość . . .

I was not a native of that hamlet. I had been brought up in Warsaw, but when the war came, my parents left the city and went to live with my grandfather the rabbi. There we were stuck in a village which was on no railroad and was surrounded by pine forests. My father was appointed assistant rabbi. I never stopped longing for Warsaw, its streets, its trolley cars, its illuminated show windows, and its tall balconied residences. Aaron the watchmaker and his family represented for me a fragment of the metropolis. Aaron had a library containing books written in several languages. In his store one could put on earphones and listen to the radio. He subscribed to two Warsaw newspapers, one in Polish and one in Yiddish, and was always hunting for a chess partner. Feigele had attended the Gymnasium in Lublin, boarding with an aunt while she was away from home, but now having received her diploma, she had returned to her parents.

Aaron the watchmaker had been a student of my grandfather's and had been considered a religious prodigy until he had been caught reading the Bible in German translation, a sure sign of heresy. Like Moses Mendelssohn, Aaron was a hunchback. Although he had not been officially excommunicated, it was almost as if he had been. He had a high forehead, a mangy-looking goatee, and large black eyes. There was something ancient and half forgotten in his gaze for which I knew no name and which made me think of Spinoza and Uriel Acosta. When he sat at the window of his store studying some mechanism through a watch glass, he seemed to be reading the wheels as a fortune-teller does his crystal. All day his sad smile enunciated over and over again, "Vanity of vanities." Feigele had inherited her father's eyes. She kept to herself, was always to be seen strolling alone, a tall, thin girl with a long, pale face and a thin nose and lips. She always carried two books under her arm, one thick and one thin. A strange gentleness emanated from her. By this time the fashionable girls cut their hair *au garçon*, but Feigele wore hers in a bun. She always took the road to the Russian cemetery. Once I saw her reading the inscriptions in the graveyard.

I was too shy to talk to her, wasn't even sure she knew who I was, since she had a way of looking over people's heads. But I knew that, like me, she was living in exile. She didn't seem to ever stop meditating, would pause to examine trees, and would reflectively stare down well shafts. I kept trying to meet her but couldn't think of a plan. Moreover, I was ashamed of my appearance, decked out as I was in a velvet cap, a long gabardine, and red earlocks. I knew that I must seem to her just another Hasidic boy. How could she guess that I was reading Knut Hamsun and Strindberg on the sly and studying Spinoza's *Ethics* in a Hebrew translation? In addition, I owned a work by Flammarion and was dabbling in the cabala. In the evening, when I perched on the highest branch of the lime tree, I gazed up at the moon and the stars like an astronomer. Feigele's window was also visible to me and just as inaccessible as the sky. I had already been matched with the daughter of a rabbi. Every day my father read me a lesson from the Shulhan Arukh on how to become a rabbi. The villagers watched me constantly to make sure that I committed no transgressions. My father complained that my frivolity jeopardized his livelihood. All I needed was to be caught talking to a girl, particularly Aaron the watchmaker's daughter.

But when I sat in my tree at night watching Feigele's window I knew indubitably that my longing for her must someday bring a response. I already believed in telepathy, clairvoyance, mesmerism. I would narrow my eyes until the light from Feigele's lamp became thin, fiery filaments. My psychic messages would speed across the blackness to her, for I was seeking to emulate Joseph della Reina, who by using the powers of Holy Names had brought the Grand Vizier's daughter in a trance to his bed. I called out to Feigele, trying to invade both her waking thoughts and her dreams. I wrapped a phantom net around her like some sorcerer from the *Arabian Nights*. My incantations must inevitably kindle love in her heart and make her desire me passionately. In return I would give her caresses such as no woman had ever received before...

I would adorn her with jewels dug from the moon. We would fly together to other planets and she would dwell a queen in supernal palaces. For reasons which I was unable to explain I became convinced that the beginning of our friendship would date from the reading of the tashlik prayer on Rosh Hashanah afternoon. This premonition was totally illogical. Probably an enlightened girl like Feigele would not even attend the ceremony. But the idea had entered into me like a dybbuk. I kept counting the days and hours until the holiday, formulated plans, conceived of the words I would say to her. Two or three times, perching among the leaves and branches, I noticed Feigele standing at the window looking out. I could not see her eyes but knew that she had heard my call and was searching for me in the darkness. It was the month of Elul and every day the ram's horn was blown in the studyhouse to drive away Satan. Spiderwebs drifted through the air; cold winds blew from the Arctic ice cap. So bright was the moon that night and day were nearly indistinguishable. Crows, awakened by the light, croaked. The grasshoppers were singing their final songs; shadows scampered across the fields surrounding the village. The river wound through the meadows like a silver snake.

It was Rosh Hashanah, and I put on the new gabardine and new shoes I had been given and brushed my sidelocks behind my ears. What more could a young Hasid do to look modern? In the late afternoon I started to loiter on Bridge Street, watching the townspeople file by on their way to the tashlik ceremony. The day was sunny, the sky as blue and transparent as it is in midsummer. Cool breezes mingled with the warmth exuded by the earth. First came the Hasidim, marching together as a group, all dressed in fur hats and satin coats. They hurried along as if they were rushing from their womenfolk and temptation. I had been raised among these people, but now I found their disheveled beards, their ill-fitting clothes, and their insistent clannishness odd. They ran from the Evil One like sheep from a wolf.

After the Hasidim came the ordinary Jews, and after them the women and girls. Most of the older women wore capes and gowns which dated from the time of King Sobieski; they had tiaras and bonnets with ribbons on their heads. Their jewelry consisted of gold head chains, long earrings so weighty they almost tore the lobes of their ears, and brooches inherited from grandmothers and great-grandmothers that vibrated as the women walked. My mother had on a gold silk dress and a pelerine decorated with rhinestones. But the younger women had studied the fashion magazines (which always showed up in the village a year or two after they had been issued) and were dressed in what they considered to be the latest style. Some of them wore narrow skirts that scarcely covered their knees and even bobbed their hair. The ladies' tailors stood to one side commenting on the dress of the women. They contrasted their handiwork with that of their competitors and ridiculed not only one another's designs but the clients who wore them. I kept looking in vain for Feigele. My sorcery had failed and I walked with downcast eyes among the stragglers. Some of the townspeople stood on the wooden bridge reciting the tashlik; others lined the riverbanks. Young women took out their handkerchiefs and shook out their sins. Boys playfully emptied their pockets to be sure that no transgression remained. The village wits made the traditional tashlik jokes: "Girls, shake as hard as you want, but a few sins will remain." "The fish will get fat feeding on so many errors."

I made no attempt to say the prayer but stood under a willow watching a huge red sun which was split in half by a wisp of cloud sinking in the west. Flocks of birds dipped toward the water, their wings one instant silver, the next leaden black. The color of the river turned from green to rose. I had lost everything that mattered here on earth, but still found comfort in the sky. Several of the smaller clouds seemed to be on fire and sailed across the heavens like ships with burning sails. I gaped at the sun as if I were seeing it for the first time. I had learned from Flammarion that this star was a million and a half times as large as the earth and had a temperature of six thousand degrees centigrade on its surface and hundreds of thousands in its interior. Everything came from it—light, warmth, the wood for the oven, and the food in the pot. Even life and suffering were impossible without it. But what was the sun? Where did it come from? Whence did it travel, moving in the Milky Way and also with the galaxy?

Suddenly I understood why the pagans had worshipped it as a god. I had a desire to kneel and bow down myself. Well, could one be certain that it lacked consciousness? *The Guide to the Perplexed* said that the heavenly bodies possess souls and are driven in their orbits by Ideas emitting a divine music as they circle. The music of the spheres now seemed to mingle with the twittering of the birds, the sounds of the coursing river, and the murmur of the praying multitude. Then a greenish-blue shimmer appeared on the horizon, the first star, a brilliant miniature sun. I knew that it had taken years for the rays from this fixed star to reach my eyes. But what were rays? I was seized by a sort of cosmic yearning. I wanted to cease existing and return to my sources, to be once again a part of the universe. I muttered a prayer to the sun: "Gather me to you. I am weary of being myself."

Suddenly I felt a tug at my sleeve. I turned and trembled. Feigele stood next to me. So great was my amazement that I forgot to marvel. She wore a black suit, a black beret, and a white collar. Her face lit by the setting sun shone with a Rosh Hashanah purity. "Excuse me," she said. "Can you locate the tashlik for me? I can't seem to find the place." Her smile seemed to be saying, "Well, this was the best pretext available." In her gaze there were both pride and humility. I, like Joseph della Reina, had summoned my beloved from the Grand Vizier's palace.

She held in her hand a prayer book which had covers stamped in gold. I took one cover of the book and she grasped the other. I started to turn the pages. On one side of the page was Hebrew and on the other Polish. I kept turning the leaves but couldn't find the prayer either. The crowd had already begun to disperse and heads kept turning in our direction. I started to thumb through the book more quickly. The tashlik prayer just could not have been omitted. But where was it? Feigele glanced at me in wonder and her eyes seemed to be saying, "Don't get yourself so wrought up. It's nothing but a strategem." The letters tumbled before my eyes; the prayer book trembled as though it were living. Inadvert ently Feigele's elbow and mine touched and we begged each other's pardon. The prayer seemed to have flown from the book. But I knew that it was there and that my eyes had been bewitched. I was just about to give up looking when I saw the word "tashlik" printed in big bold letters. "Here it is," I cried out, and my heart seemed to stop.

"What? Thank you."

"I haven't recited the tashlik myself," I said.

"Well, suppose we say it together."

"Can you read Hebrew script?"

"Of course."

"This prayer symbolizes the casting of one's sins into the ocean."

"Naturally."

We stood muttering the prayer together as the crowd slowly moved off. Boys threw mocking glances at us; women scowled; girls winked. I knew that this encounter was going to get me into a great deal of trouble at home. But for the moment I reveled in my triumph, a sorcerer whose charms and incantations had worked. The look of religious devotion on Feigele's face made her appear even gentler. The sun had already disappeared behind the trees, and in the distance the forest looked blue and like mountains. Suddenly I felt that I had experienced this moment before. Had it been in a dream or in a former life? The air was alive with sound: the croaking of birds, the buzzing of insects, a ringing as if from bells. The frogs began their evening conversation. A herd of cows passed nearby, their hooves pounding the ground. It was a miracle that the animals did not drive us into the river. No longer did the book tremble in our hands. I heard Feigele murmur:

"The Lord looketh from heaven. He beholdeth all the sons of men . . . He fashioneth all their hearts alike. He considereth all their works . . ."

Translated by the author and Cecil Hemley

Are Children the Ultimate Literary Critics?

Children are the best readers of genuine literature. Grownups are hypnotized by big names, exaggerated quotes, and high-pressure advertising. Critics who are more concerned with sociology than with literature have persuaded millions of readers that if a novel doesn't try to bring about a social revolution it is of no value. Hundreds of professors who write commentaries on writers try to convince their students that only writers who require elaborate commentaries and countless footnotes are the true creative geniuses of our time.

But children do not succumb to this kind of belief. They still like clarity, logic, and even such obsolete stuff as punctuation. Even more, the young reader demands a real story, with a beginning, a middle, and an end, the way stories have been told for thousands of years.

In our epoch, when storytelling has become a forgotten art and has been replaced by amateurish sociology and hackneyed psychology, the child is still the independent reader who relies on nothing but his own taste. Names and authorities mean nothing to him. Long after literature for adults has gone to pieces, books for children will constitute the last vestige of storytelling, logic, faith in the family, in God, and in real humanism.

When I sit down to write a story, I must first have a real topic or theme. One cannot write for children what some critics call "a slice of life." The truth is that the so-called slices of life are a bore even for adults.

I must also have a real desire or a passion to write the story. Sometimes I have a topic but somehow no compulsion to deal with it. I've written down hundreds of topics which I will never use because they don't really interest me.

Finally, I must have the conviction—or at least the illusion—that I am the only one who can write this particular story. It has to be my story. It has to express my individuality, my character, my way of looking at the world.

If these three conditions are present, I will write a story. This holds true when I write for children or for adults.

Some bad books lack these three conditions. They have no story to tell, there's no passion in them, and they have no real connection with the writer.

Because children like clarity and logic, you may wonder how I can write about the supernatural, which, by its very definition, is not clear and not logical. Logic and "realism," as a literary method, are two different things. One can be a very illogical realist and a highly logical mystic. Children are by nature inclined to mysticism. They believe in God, in the Devil, in good spirits and bad spirits, and in all kinds of magic. Yet they require true consistency in these stories. There is often great logic in religion and there is little logic in materialism. Those who maintain that the world created itself are often people without any respect for reason.

It is tragic that many writers who look down on stories of the supernatural are writing things for children which are nothing but sheer chaos. There are books for children where one sentence has nothing to do with another. Things happen arbitrarily and haphazardly, without any connection with the child's experience or ideas.

Not only does such writing not amuse a child, but it damages his way of thinking. Sometimes I have a feeling that the so-called avant-garde writers for children are trying to prepare the child for James Joyce's *Finnegans Wake* or other such puzzles which some of the professors love so much to explain. Instead of helping them think, such writing cripples the child's mind. Put it this way— the supernatural, yes; nonsense, no.

Folklore plays a most important role in children's literature. The tragedy of modern adult literature is that it has completely divorced itself from folklore. Many modern writers have lost their roots. They don't belong and they don't want to belong to any special group. They are afraid of being called clannish, nationalistic, or chauvinistic.

Actually there is no literature without roots. One cannot write good fiction just about a man generally. In literature, as in life, everything is specific. Every man has his actual and spiritual address. It is true that in certain fables the address is not necessary or even superfluous, but all literature is not fables. The more a writer is rooted in his environment, the more he is understood by all people; the more national he is, the more international he becomes.

When I began to write the stories of my collection *Zlateh the Goat*, I knew that these stories would be read not only by Jewish children but by Gentile ones as well. I described Jewish children, Jewish sages, Jewish fools, Jewish bridegrooms, Jewish brides. The events I related did not happen in no-man's-land but in the little towns and villages I knew well and where I was brought up. My saints were Jewish saints and the demons Jewish demons. And this book has been translated into many languages.

Many of today's books for children have no local color, no ethnic charm. The writers try so hard to be international—to produce merchandise which appeals to all—that they appeal to no one. (By the way, the Bible, especially the Book of Genesis, teems with stories for children—all of them short, clear, deeply rooted in their time and soil. This is the reason for their universal appeal.)

Without folklore and deep roots in a specific soil, literature must decline and wither away. This is true in all literature of all times. Luckily children's literature is even now more rooted in folklore than the literature for adults. And this alone makes children's literature so important in our generation.

Some writers sit down to write a book, not because

they love the story, but because they are in love with the message it might bring. There is no famine of messages in our time or in any other time. If all the messages disappeared and only the Ten Commandments remained, we would still have enough messages for the present and the future. Our trouble is not that we don't have enough messages but that we refuse to fulfill them and practice them.

The writer who writes a bad novel and whose message is peace and equality and other such virtues does us no great favor. We've heard all this before and will continue to hear about it in newspaper editorials, in sermons, even from diplomats of the most aggressive nations. There are multitudes of writers whose only claim to literature is that they are on the right side and that their messages are righteous.

Literature needs well-constructed and inventive stories, not stale messages, for every good story has a message that, even if it is not obvious, will be discovered by readers or critics sooner or later. I do not yet know the message of Tolstoy's *War and Peace*, but it was a great book just the same. A genuine story can have many interpretations, scores of messages, mountains of commentaries. Events never get stale; commentaries often are stale from the very beginning.

As a child, I was glad that I was told the same stories my father and grandfathers heard. The children of my time didn't read stories about little ducklings which fell into kettles of soup and emerged as clay frogs. We preferred the stories of Adam and Eve, the Flood, the people who built the Tower of Babel, the divine adventures of

Abraham, Isaac, Jacob, Joseph. We were taught never to rely completely on any authority. We tried to find motivation and consistency in God's laws and His commandments. A lot of the evil taking place today, I often feel, is the result of the rotten stuff this modern generation read in its school days.

Since I began to write for children I have spoken to many children, read stories to them (even though my accent is far from perfect), and answered hundreds of their questions. I am always amazed to see that when it comes to asking questions, children possess the same curiosity as adults: How do you get the idea for a book? Is it invented or taken from life? How long does it take you to write a book? Do you use stories that your mother and father told you?

No matter how young they are, children are deeply concerned with so-called eternal questions: Who created the world? Who made the earth, the sky, people, animals? Children cannot imagine the beginning or end of time and space. As a child I asked all the questions I later found discussed in the works of Plato, Aristotle, Spinoza, Leibnitz, Hume, Kant, and Schopenhauer. Children think about and ponder such matters as justice, the purpose of life, the why of suffering. They often find it difficult to make peace with the idea that animals are slaughtered so that man can eat them. They are bewildered and frightened by death. They cannot accept the fact that the strong should rule the weak.

Many grownups have made up their minds that there is no purpose in asking questions and that one should accept the facts as they are. But the child is often a philosopher and a seeker of God. This is one reason I always suggest they read the Bible. It does not answer all the questions, but it does deal with these questions. It tells us that there is a God who created heaven and earth. It condemns Cain's murder of Abel. It tells us that the wicked are punished and that the just, though they may suffer a lot, are rewarded and loved by the Almighty.

If I had my way, I would publish a history of philosophy for children, where I would convey the basic ideas of all philosophers in simple language. Children, who are highly serious people, would read this book with great interest. In our time, when the literature for adults is deteriorating, good books for children are the only hope, the only refuge. Many adults read and enjoy children's books. We write not only for children but also for their parents. They, too, are serious children.